PRAISE FOR JENN McKINLAY'S ROMANCES

"Jenn McKinlay writes sexy, funny romances that will leave you begging for more!"
—*New York Times* bestselling author Jill Shalvis

"Funny, charming, and heart-stoppingly romantic. Jenn McKinlay is a rising star."
—*New York Times* bestselling author Jaci Burton

"McKinlay delivers heartwarming humor at its finest."
—*New York Times* bestselling author Lori Wilde

"Clever writing, laugh-out-loud humor, and a sizzling romance. This one is a keeper."
—*USA Today* bestselling author Delores Fossen

"A beautifully written love letter to the romance genre from someone who understands just how important these books are to their readers."   —*Booklist* (starred review)

"Enchants from the very first page. . . . A sparkling gem of a book that is sure to lift your spirits!"
—RT Book Reviews (top pick)

"Funny and sweet. . . . A book to enjoy."   —*USA Today*

"A sweet, endearing, heartwarming read that is perfect for the holidays."   —Harlequin Junkie

Titles by Jenn McKinlay

Happily Ever After Romances

THE GOOD ONES
THE CHRISTMAS KEEPER

Bluff Point Romances

ABOUT A DOG
BARKING UP THE WRONG TREE
EVERY DOG HAS HIS DAY

Cupcake Bakery Mysteries

SPRINKLE WITH MURDER
BUTTERCREAM BUMP OFF
DEATH BY THE DOZEN
RED VELVET REVENGE
GOING, GOING, GANACHE
SUGAR AND ICED
DARK CHOCOLATE DEMISE
VANILLA BEANED
CARAMEL CRUSH
WEDDING CAKE CRUMBLE
DYING FOR DEVIL'S FOOD

Library Lover's Mysteries

BOOKS CAN BE DECEIVING
DUE OR DIE
BOOK, LINE, AND SINKER
READ IT AND WEEP
ON BORROWED TIME
A LIKELY STORY
BETTER LATE THAN NEVER
DEATH IN THE STACKS
HITTING THE BOOKS
WORD TO THE WISE

Hat Shop Mysteries

CLOCHE AND DAGGER
DEATH OF A MAD HATTER
AT THE DROP OF A HAT
COPY CAP MURDER
ASSAULT AND BERET

the
CHRISTMAS KEEPER

JENN McKINLAY

JOVE
New York

A JOVE BOOK
Published by Berkley
An imprint of Penguin Random House LLC
penguinrandomhouse.com

Copyright © 2019 by Jennifer McKinlay Orf
Excerpt from *Paris Is Always a Good Idea* by Jenn McKinlay
copyright © 2019 by Jennifer McKinlay Orf
Penguin Random House supports copyright. Copyright fuels creativity, encourages
diverse voices, promotes free speech, and creates a vibrant culture. Thank you for buying
an authorized edition of this book and for complying with copyright laws by not
reproducing, scanning, or distributing any part of it in any form without permission.
You are supporting writers and allowing Penguin Random House to continue to
publish books for every reader.

A JOVE BOOK, BERKLEY, and the BERKLEY & B colophon
are registered trademarks of Penguin Random House LLC.

ISBN: 9780451492456

First Edition: October 2019

Printed in the United States of America
1   3   5   7   9   10   8   6   4   2

Cover art: cowboy leading horse by David Aaron Troy/Getty Images
Cover design by Katie Anderson
Book design by George Towne

For my mom, Susan Norris McKinlay:
thank you for always making Christmas,
and every holiday, so magical.
Love you forever.

ACKNOWLEDGMENTS

This was such a fun book to write, and I had so many people help it come into being that I'm hoping I don't forget anyone. So here goes. I am very fortunate to have a plot group that gleefully helps me rewrite and revise my ideas until I've sufficiently tortured my characters. Hugs and high fives to Kate Carlisle and Paige Shelton! They are both brilliant authors, and I feel very lucky to call them my friends.

Also, I so appreciate the enthusiasm of my editor, associate editor, and agent—Kate Seaver, Sarah Blumenstock, and Christina Hogrebe—who cheer me along through the entire process, from the original idea all the way to the finished book. I swear I could not get there without the three of you. Special thanks to the team at Berkley, who are amazing at making all the stuff happen: Jessica Mangicaro, Fareeda Bullert, Tara O'Connor, Brittanie Black, Katie Anderson, and Stacy Anderson.

Special thanks to my friend author Beth Kendrick (who is also a doctor), whose brilliance helped me to understand how to write about head traumas accurately. Any mistakes are mine, all mine!

Lastly, to my fam—the Hub and the Hooligans—thank you so much for making every day a laughter-filled adventure. Truly, I am so blessed to have you three in my life. But also, thank you for Maktao, Shukuru, and Esampu. When I asked for an elephant for my birthday, well, you three certainly delivered, and I am now the foster mama of these babies at the David Sheldrick Wildlife Trust. Watching their shenanigans on Instagram has brought me great joy!

For anyone interested, there are amazing groups out there supporting wildlife, and I urge you to find an organization with a solid reputation that will allow you to foster an animal in need (Hub got to name a sea turtle for his birthday). There really is no greater feeling in the world than to know you're making a difference, even if it's just a little one.

Happy holidays and happy reading, everyone!

Chapter One

She had never believed in love. Maybe for others but not for her. But then he smiled at her and it was as if she'd found a piece of herself that she didn't know was missing. When he took her in his arms and held her close, she knew that for the first time in her life, she was home.

SAVANNAH Wilson closed the book and sighed. No one, but no one, wrote a love story that hit her in all the feels like Destiny Swann did. The woman plucked her heartstrings like a virtuoso playing a sonata.

"Savy, come on," Maisy Kelly said as she entered the room. She slapped Savannah's feet off the coffee table, grabbed her arm, and hauled her up to stand, which was no small feat given that Maisy was the short side of petite and Savannah was more Amazonian in height and build.

"I'm reading," Savannah said. She held up her book. "Isn't that sacred time? You own a bookstore; I would think you of all people would respect that."

Maisy glanced at the book. Then she crossed her hands

over her heart and said, "Oh, *Her One and Only*, that's one of my favorite Destiny Swann books. I totally get it, I do, but you're my sous-chef, and I need you in the kitchen. Besides, you shouldn't be hiding in the parlor when we have a house full of people coming for Thanksgiving dinner."

"I'm not hiding. I'm just not very good company right now," Savannah said. She tossed the book onto the coffee table.

"Work stuff?" Maisy asked. She tipped her head to the side and studied Savy through the black-framed rectangular glasses she always wore.

"Yes, but it's not about the bookstore. It's stuff about my old job in New York, and I don't want to talk about it," Savy said. "Thus, the book."

"Escapism 101?"

"I'm getting an A," she said. "Although, Swann does set the bar pretty high in the hero department. I mean what man could possibly live up to Tag McAllister? He's smart, kind, devoted to his grandmother, and completely swoon-worthy."

"Maisy, where do you want me to put my famous smashed potatoes with green chilies?" Joaquin Solis called from the doorway.

Maisy glanced at him and then turned toward Savannah with her eyebrows raised above the frames of her glasses as if to say, *Him.* Savannah shook her head. It made her long wavy red hair, which she'd twisted into a sloppy knot on the top of her head, unravel and fall down around her shoulders. She glanced at the man in the doorway.

He was watching her as if he could happily do so for the rest of the day, never mind the Crock-Pot of mashed potatoes he held in his hands. This little bit of domesticity only added to the package of hotness that was Joaquin Solis, but Savannah was immune to him. Mostly.

She could, in a completely objective way, acknowledge that he had a certain something, sort of like acknowledging that diamonds were sparkly and chocolate was yummy. It didn't mean she was going to partake of either and break her bank account or add some squish to her middle. She had greater willpower than that. Still, Joaquin, Quino to his friends, was the sort of man who made girls with good intentions do naughty things and not regret it one little bit.

Tall with broad shoulders, he sported a thick thatch of dark hair, chiseled features, and eyes so dark they appeared bottomless. Joaquin was the sort of man women noticed. If it wasn't his rugged good looks and honed physique, it was his wicked sense of humor and flirty ways that made ladies fan themselves when he walked by with a casual wink and his charmer's grin. It worked on every female who crossed his path, Savannah had noticed—every one except Savannah.

While she could admit that he was a fine specimen of a man, she had less than no interest in getting tangled up with Quino Solis. He was as entrenched in Fairdale as the old maple trees on the town green. Which was saying something, since their trunks were the size of small cars, as they'd been there since the founding fathers had declared Fairdale a town and planted them in an attempt to tame this wild patch of earth in the Smoky Mountains of North Carolina. Joaquin was like those trees—the roots ran deep.

He owned the Shadow Pine Stables on the outskirts of Fairdale, where he offered trail rides and riding lessons and worked with special-needs kids using equine therapy. He was never going to leave this town he loved, and Savannah had no intention of staying. Anything that happened between them was just flirting with heartbreak, most likely hers, and she'd had enough of that to last a lifetime.

She was leaving Fairdale as soon as she got her old job in Manhattan back and no ridonkulously hot stable boy was going to change her career trajectory. She was 100 percent immune to him—okay, more like 95 percent. But she figured if she stayed out of his gravitational pull, she'd be fine.

"You don't know what you're missing," Maisy said under her breath. She tossed her short dark curls and turned away, but not before Savannah retorted, "Neither do you. You're marrying his best friend but that does not mean you are an expert on all things Quino."

"I don't need to be," Maisy said. "He is legendary in Fairdale."

Savy rolled her eyes. Like she cared if Joaquin had dated every available woman in their quaint college town of seventy-five thousand.

"I'll take those, Quino," Maisy said. She scooped the Crock-Pot out of his hands and swept from the room, leaving Savannah and Joaquin alone. Subtle, Maisy was not.

Savannah would have cursed her friend, but Maisy had been doing this for months, pushing the two of them together, clearly hoping to start a romance between them that would prevent Savy from returning to New York. Not gonna happen.

An awkward silence filled the room. At least for Savannah it was awkward. Joaquin just shoved his hands in the back pockets of his jeans and studied her in a way that made her feel like he really saw her and that he liked what he saw. It was too much. He was too much.

She twisted her hair back up into its sloppy knot and he tipped his head to the side as he watched her. He seemed fascinated. It made Savy self-conscious, which never happened. Being taller than average with fiery red hair, freckles, and broad features, she was used to being overlooked as unfeminine, more handsome than pretty. She was fine with it as she liked getting by on her brains more than her looks, but Joaquin never overlooked her. She faced him, crossed her arms over her chest, and tried to stare him down. This was a mistake.

He looked amused as he met her gaze. As if she was issuing him a challenge and he was eager to accept it.

"Quit looking at me like that," he said. The twinkle in his eye let her know he was teasing but she stepped in it anyway.

"Like what?"

"You know."

"I assure you, I don't."

"Like you want me to kiss you," he said. His gaze moved to her mouth and then back up to her eyes. It made her heart beat a little faster. She ignored it.

"What?" she scoffed. "Did you fall off your horse and hit your head? I do *not* want you to kiss me."

"No?" he asked.

He was the picture of innocence. Meanwhile Savy could feel her face heat up, because in fact she had thought about him kissing her. Not right now, but the idea might have flashed through her mind once; okay, twice; all right, probably five or more times since she'd met him, but that was only because she hadn't been on a date in months and her hormones were wreaking havoc with her common sense.

"No." The word fired out of her like a bullet shot from a gun.

"Huh," he said. His gaze dropped back to her mouth. "My mistake."

"I'll say it is." She tried to sound indignant but the attempt was shaky at best.

She marched stiffly past him, not giving him a chance to back up as she brushed by his muscle-hardened shoulder. A quick glance up and her gaze met his. His dark eyes were amused but they were also full of desire.

It occurred to Savy that all she had to do was rise up on her toes, twine her arms about his neck, and kiss him and she could finally put to rest the curiosity she had about the feel of those full lips against hers. Would his kiss be soft or firm, gentle or rough? Would he hold her low and tight or high and loose? Would he bury his fingers in her hair while his mouth plundered hers, making it bruised from the impact of his kiss?

Her thoughts must have been reflected upon her face, because the teasing glint left his eyes and he let out an unsteady breath. His voice when he spoke dropped an entire octave and was little more than a growl when he said, "You really need to stop looking at me like that."

Savy felt a pull in her lower belly as strongly as if he had hooked a finger in her waistband and was drawing her in close. From the overheated look in his eyes, she knew he'd most definitely been thinking about kissing her. The attraction between them had its own sizzle and zip and she knew if she gave in to it, she was going to get burned. She quickly stepped away.

"I don't know what you're talking about," she said. She

made an exaggerated shrug. "I was just thinking about how badly my toilet needs a good scrubbing."

Joaquin blinked at her and then he tipped his head back and laughed. Full lips parting over white teeth in a deep masculine chuckle that made her want to laugh in return. Whatever he'd been expecting that clearly wasn't it.

Savy took some satisfaction there, but the grin he sent her was full of admiration with a nice dose of heat, making it nearly irresistible. She fought the urge to fan herself as she hurried to the kitchen to help Maisy with dinner, and maybe while there, she'd just crawl into the freezer until her body temperature went down.

"THE countdown has begun," Ryder Copeland said as he handed Quino a beer. They were standing outside Ryder's half-restored Victorian house in the chilly midday air because Ryder thought deep-frying a fourteen-pound turkey was the coolest thing ever.

"What are you counting down?" Quino asked. "How long until Maisy kicks your butt for drying out her bird?"

"Ha ha," Ryder said. He gestured to the bird that was sitting in a plastic tub on the wrought iron table beside them. "This poultry is going to be amazing. Just look at him."

"He looks like Deadweight Dougie," Quino said. "Same male-pattern baldness and beer gut."

Ryder looked at the bird, then he picked it up under the wings and made it dance across the container. "He's got about the same sense of rhythm, too."

Quino snorted. "Worst foreman ever."

"And how," Ryder agreed. "I wonder what ever happened to that guy." He put the bird down with a pat on its rump.

Ryder and Quino had become fast friends while working construction over a decade ago in Texas, under the dubious supervision of Deadweight Dougie, so named because he was usually drunk, and when he passed out he had to be rolled because he was deadweight and too heavy to pick up and carry. Dougie spent more time sleeping it off in the bed of his pickup truck than he did supervising his crew.

"No idea, but I'd bet dollars to donuts he's snoring on someone's couch today." Quino glanced at the stone patio that was covered in a heavy tarp to catch all of the oil splatter. "So what are we counting down, the time until kickoff?"

"Nope. The ticktock is for you," Ryder said. "I'm calling you out. You said in July that Savannah would be your wife by Christmas, we are one month out, and unless I am misinformed, you haven't even had a date with her."

Quino took a long pull on his beer. "Details."

"Yeah, kind of important details," Ryder said. He squinted at his friend. "She may be the first woman who has not succumbed to the Joaquin Solis magic."

Quino lifted one eyebrow. He knew Ryder was teasing him, and he was cool with that, but his friend was also speaking the truth. Quino had never felt the sting of rejection from a woman before. Savannah was the first woman in memory who seemed indifferent to him. She was a challenge, which he had to admit made her sexy as hell.

"That's how I know she's the one," he said.

"Or *not* the one," Ryder countered. "You've been playing it pretty chill with her, keeping your distance, working the banter angle without being a pain in her ass."

"Is that what she said?" Quino asked.

"No, that's what Maisy said she said."

"I love having spies." Quino grinned. "So, what's the intel? Think she's ready for me to go full-court press in the charm-and-disarm department?"

"Not unless you want to be dropped by a sharp knee to your junk," Ryder said. "Last I heard, Savannah was still planning to move back to Manhattan by the end of the year. She wants her old life back. She's a city girl through and through, and living here in the Smoky Mountains is not her bag."

Ryder checked the temperature on the oil in the deep fryer. Then he hefted up the naked bird and gently lowered it into the boiling oil. Quino felt for the bird. Whenever the subject of Savannah moving back to New York came up, he felt exactly like that, a dead bird hanging by a metal handle from his innards while being dipped in boiling oil. He clearly needed to step up his game. He pondered his options while the bird sizzled and Ryder talked about Maisy, football, and more Maisy. He came up with a whole lot of nothing.

"Why the face, bro?" Desiree asked as she stepped through the French doors and paused beside him. "You look like someone ate the last piece of pumpkin pie."

Quino glanced down at his sister. She was twenty-five but to him she would always be fifteen. That was the day he stepped up and became her guardian. It hadn't just been legalese so he could take care of her. Quino felt the need to protect his sister, the only member of his family to survive a horrible car crash, all the way down to his soul. He'd lay down his life for her without hesitation.

"Ryder's going to burn the bird," he said.

"I am not," Ryder protested. "You're such a doubter."

"Oh," Desi said. She tossed her long black hair over her shoulder and gave him the side-eye. "I thought you were frowning because Savannah is ignoring you."

"She is not ignoring me," he protested.

"Yes, she is," Desi said. Then she grinned at him and hit him with a one-two punch of deep dimples and twinkling eyes.

"Snot," he said. He tapped her nose with his finger the same way he had when she was a toddler and dragging her pink blanket behind her as she tried to follow him on all of his twelve-year-old-boy adventures.

Desi smacked his hand away. "Quit it. I'm a grown woman in case you haven't noticed."

"Sorry, you'll always be a kid to me," he said.

And she would. Not just because she'd been so stinking cute at that age but also because when it came to life skills and common sense that's about where Desi would always be. Her insides didn't match her outsides. The traumatic brain injury she had sustained in the accident that had killed their parents had left her with a diffuse axonal injury, the fallout of which had left her judgment impaired. She lived her life as trusting as a child, and Quino was on constant alert to keep her safe from people who would use that to take advantage of her.

Desi blew out a breath and it stirred the bangs that were cut in a blunt line across her forehead. She looked like their mother. The same round eyes with thick curly lashes, the same button for a nose, and a full mouth that was usually curved into a smile as if Desi found the world to be a happy, friendly place of which she was pleased to be a part. He never wanted that to change.

"One of these days, big brother," Desi said. She looked at him in exasperation as if she was about to put up more of a fuss, but then the door to the kitchen opened and Maisy popped her head out.

"How's the bird coming, honey?"

"He has a name now. We're calling him Deadweight Dougie, or Dougie for short," Ryder said.

"Um . . . okay, but why?" she asked. "Is naming the bird a Copeland family tradition or something?"

"Nah, he just reminds me and Quino of our first boss," he said. "He even looks like him in a bald and paunchy way."

"I'm not calling my turkey Dougie," Maisy said. "Perry, back me up here."

Ryder's teen daughter popped her head out beside Maisy's. "Yeah, naming the turkey is weird, and I say this as a teenager well versed in all things strange."

"She's got us there," Quino said. "How about we call him Dougie Fresh?"

"No." Savannah appeared beside the other two. "Focus, people. We're critical on timing if we want everything served hot. Corn bread and green beans are cooking while the sweet potato casserole and mashed potatoes are warming up. Get cracking!"

"Time for wine!" Maisy said. She disappeared into the house and Savannah followed with Perry and Desi right behind them.

Quino wistfully watched the redhead who'd been making him crazy for months vanish from sight. When the door closed with a decisive bang, he turned back around to find Ryder watching him.

"You got it bad, my friend."

Quino looked at him and said, "To quote your teenage daughter, 'Duh.'"

Ryder laughed and then turned away to tend his bird. Quino moved into position to help him hoist Dougie out of the fryer and onto a fresh platter on the table. When they pulled the bird from the oil, letting it drip for a bit, he had to acknowledge that his friend had done an amazing job. Dougie looked perfectly seared on the outside while the juices from inside ran clear when Ryder stabbed him with a fork. Quino had a feeling this was exactly how his poor heart was going to look if Savannah left Fairdale without giving the two of them a shot.

It was in that moment of turkey clarity that Quino decided he did not want to look or feel like Dougie. It was time to work his magic. The question was how. How did a guy get a gal—who seemed to be attracted to him but was doing her level best to keep it on lockdown—to take a chance?

Flowers? Nah, too cliché. Candy? Same. Plus, he needed to approach her in a way that made her want to spend time with him. She was a publicist. She had come to Fairdale to help Maisy open up her romance bookstore. He happened to know that she was trying to make Maisy's bookstore a massive success not only to help her friend but also to show the publisher from which she'd been let go that she still had game. That, in fact, hers was the best game in town.

Once she succeeded and a job offer came from the Big Apple, she'd be gone, baby, gone. There was no help for it—Quino was going to have to make his move, and soon.

Chapter Two

SAVANNAH took one more bite of turkey slathered in cranberry sauce before she was forced to put her fork down in surrender. She was wearing jeans and a soft heather-green cable-knit sweater and the urge to pop the top button on her pants was almost more than she could stand. She glanced around the table and noted everyone looked exactly as she felt. Stuffed. The table was sagging in the middle it was still so full of food, and this was after all six of them had already done their damage to the feast. Even King George, a gray tabby that technically belonged to the bookstore but was mostly Perry's, was sacked out on an empty chair. Probably because Perry had been sneaking him bites of turkey all evening. Did tryptophan work on cats? Looking at George's closed eyes, Savy figured it must.

The doorbell rang but no one moved. The post-turkey lethargy was that strong. The doorbell rang again.

"Are we expecting anyone?" Ryder asked.

"No." Maisy glanced at Savannah. "Rule of closeness."

"What?" Savannah protested. "How is that fair?"

"What's the rule of closeness?" Desi asked.

"The closest person to the door answers the door," Maisy said. "Rule of closeness."

"But this isn't even my house," Savannah protested.

Maisy shrugged.

"Fine." Savannah struggled to her feet and dropped her napkin onto her seat. "But someone else clears the table." She looked around the table at Quino, Desi, and Perry. They didn't look super motivated but that was not her problem. She left the dining room and cut through the front parlor to reach the front door.

She wondered if it was a salesperson but that would be crazy on Thanksgiving. Still, just to be safe, she glanced out the side window to see who was on the porch. She blinked. A man, a cowboy, stood on the front porch with a big autumn bouquet in one arm and a pink bakery box in the other. What?!

Savannah yanked the door open and said, "Hi."

"Hi there," the man drawled.

He looked uncertain when his gaze met hers. But it was his bright-blue eyes that immediately clued Savannah in to who he was. There were two pairs of eyes in the house that matched his exactly—Ryder's and Perry's. She had heard that Ryder had a younger brother. This had to be him.

"You must be a Copeland," she said. He was tall and dark haired, with broad shoulders and suntanned skin, just like Ryder.

"Yes, ma'am. I'm Sawyer," he said. His smile was wide and warm. "And you are?"

"Savannah Wilson, a friend of the family," she said. "Come on in."

She stepped back and he entered the house. Savannah led him back through the parlor to the dining room. Everyone was up and clearing the table, so she called over the noise, "Hey, look who's here!"

Ryder glanced up and then his jaw dropped as his eyes went wide. Perry, who had a stack of plates in hand, set them back on the table with a thump.

"Uncle Sawyer!" she cried.

She shot around the table at a run. Savannah just had

time to grab the bakery box out of Sawyer's hand before Perry tackled her uncle in a hug.

"Hey, kiddo," Sawyer said as he hugged her tight and kissed the top of her head. "Wait. Where are the pigtails and tutu you always wear and how the heck did you get so tall?"

Perry leaned back and laughed at him. "Uncle Sawyer, I'm a teenager now."

"No." He shook his head. "You're five, like, forever."

Perry laughed. "So, I shouldn't tell you I have a boyfriend?"

"That's a hard no, young lady," Sawyer said. He glanced up with laughing eyes and met his brother's gaze. "Hi, Ryder."

"Hey, Sawyer." Ryder looked dumbfounded, but Maisy was beside him and she took his hand in hers and dragged him around the table so that the two men were standing in front of each other.

"Hi, I'm Maisy," she said.

"Of course you are," Sawyer said. He held out the enormous bouquet of flowers to her. "I apologize for showing up without warning. I didn't really plan to be in North Carolina for the holiday, but the wind sort of blew me in this direction."

"Our house is your house," Maisy said. She stepped forward and gave him a hug. "You never need to warn us. Right, Ryder?"

Ryder stood staring at his brother as if he couldn't quite wrap his head around the fact that Sawyer was here. Maisy gave him a hard nudge to the side and Ryder snapped out of it.

"Absolutely," Ryder said. He opened his arms. "Come here, you dope."

The two brothers hugged, and Savannah didn't think she was imagining that Ryder seemed to hang on to his brother for an extra beat or two as if to prove to himself that Sawyer was real.

"Sawyer, these are our friends, Joaquin Solis and his sister, Desi Solis," Ryder introduced them and they said hello and shook hands. Then he turned to Savannah and said, "And this is Savannah Wilson."

Savannah moved the bakery box to her left hand and shook the hand he offered. His fingers were cold from being outside but his grip was solid, his hands calloused. She got the feeling that Sawyer was definitely a man's man. She also had a feeling he and Joaquin were going to get along like a house on fire.

"Are you hungry?" Maisy asked. "Can I fix you a plate? We've already eaten but there is plenty left."

"That'd be real nice," Sawyer said. "Thanks."

"I'll do it," Savannah said.

"Are you sure?" Maisy asked.

"Rule of closeness." Savannah hooked her thumb at the kitchen behind her and then winked.

Maisy laughed and joined Ryder and Sawyer when they sat back down at the table with Desi and Perry. Quino didn't sit but instead cleared the dishes that had already been stacked up, taking the plates to the kitchen.

Savannah heaped a large portion of everything onto a plate and heated it up, delivering it to the dining room. Sawyer beamed at her as he tucked in and she lingered to hear that he was in between jobs at the moment and figured it would be a good time to visit. Judging by the looks of joy on Ryder's and Perry's faces, they were certainly glad to have him here.

Savannah felt a pang in her chest. Grabbing two empty serving bowls, she decided to finish clearing the table, not wanting to dwell on family or the fact that her family hadn't given two hoots whether she came home for Thanksgiving or not.

Maisy had abandoned her chair and was sitting in Ryder's lap at the head of the table. A petite thing, she was small but mighty, as Ryder had discovered when she hired the handsome architect to help her renovate the Victorian house she'd inherited into the romance bookstore of her dreams. They were sickeningly in love, which made them Savannah's favorite couple in the whole wide world.

"Oh, Savy, Quino, you don't have to do that," Maisy protested. "You're our guests. I'll do it later."

"No, you visit," Savannah said. "Clearly, you all have some catching up to do. Besides, it's the least I can do since I didn't bring anything for dinner."

"But you brought pumpkin pie from the Pie in the Sky bakery," Ryder said. He tore his gaze away from his brother, who was eating like he hadn't had a home-cooked meal, well, ever. "Which, second to Dougie, is the most important contribution to the meal."

"Not my mashed potatoes?" Joaquin asked with mock offense from the kitchen door.

"You cannot compare a potato to a pumpkin," Ryder said.

"Well, when you put it like that." Joaquin pushed off the doorjamb and approached the table. He glanced at Savy with an easy smile. "Here, we can do this together."

"No, really," she said. "I've got this."

He ignored her and continued gathering the remaining dishes until he had a huge stack that he carted to the kitchen without even a bobble. Savy followed in his wake, feeling as if she'd just been outmaneuvered but she wasn't sure how. It was dish duty. No one wanted dish duty, right?

Savy put all of the extra food into plastic containers while Joaquin filled the sink. She watched him covertly to see if he knew what he was doing or if he was bluffing just to try and impress her. He put the pots and pans aside to hand-wash. Okay. He put the glasses in the top of the dishwasher and the plates in the bottom. He understood to leave a little space between the dishes so that they actually got clean. So, not a faker.

After Savy put the lid on the Jell-O salad and tucked it into the fridge, she grabbed a dish towel and took her place beside Quino at the sink. He had filled the basin with hot soapy water and was scrubbing baked-on sweet potato. She would have told him just to let it soak, but he'd taken off his striped dress shirt and she was distracted by the way his biceps bunched beneath the sleeves of his white T-shirt.

Savannah was an athlete. She enjoyed running and working out. She liked keeping her body strong. Partly, it was because she lived in the city and wanted to give herself a fighting chance if ever she was caught off guard by a mugger, but also because she liked the way exercise made her feel. It cleared her head and gave her an outlet for her frustration and anxiety.

Staring at Joaquin's bulging arms, however, made the celibate life she'd been living since arriving in Fairdale seem like an error in judgment. At first, she hadn't had the time or inclination to get involved with anyone, but looking at him standing just mere inches away from her, she could feel the attraction make her brain go fuzzy, and she had the sudden urge to lick his neck or bite his shoulder.

She resisted the impulse to poke his triceps with her pointer finger just to see if they were as hard as they looked. Barely. She forced her gaze to move over his shoulders, pecs, and abs. Even in the T-shirt, she could tell he was sporting a six-pack. *Lord-a-mercy*, as Maisy, a real Southern gal, was fond of saying. A woman had only so much willpower, and Joaquin Solis could tempt even the most virtuous of women, which she was not.

"You're doing it again," he said. He didn't look at her but kept scouring the pot in the sink, splashing sudsy water up onto his forearms, where the tiny bubbles clung to the fine hairs.

"Doing what?" Her voice came out breathy and she cleared her throat.

"Looking at me like that," he said.

"You're delusional."

"Really?" He rinsed the pot in clean water and turned toward her. He leaned close and Savy knew he was going to kiss her. Her fight-or-flight response completely shut down on her and she felt herself leaning toward him in return. He reached one arm around her and deposited the dripping pot onto the dish rack behind her. Oh.

When he leaned back and grabbed the next pot and dunked it into the sink, he was grinning as if he knew very well he could have kissed her and she would have let him.

Savy felt her face get hot with embarrassment. She snatched up the pot and began to dry it with a vigor that wasn't warranted. She didn't care. Anything to hide the fact that for a few moments, she'd been his for the taking. It was too mortifying for words.

"Quino, I have one more for you." Desi, carrying a forgotten relish tray, entered the kitchen. There were only three black olives left and she polished them off before handing the delicate crystal dish to her brother.

Savy noticed that the cut glass looked tiny in his large work-roughened hands. He put it on the counter and said, "Thanks, Des, do you mind doing dish recon and make sure nothing was left anywhere else in the house?"

"On it." Desi gave a mock salute.

She was a beautiful woman, with the same arching brows, dark eyes, and sculpted features as her brother, but where Quino had fine lines around his eyes and skin that was bronzed from the sun, Desi looked unmarked by the trials and tribulations of life. Savy knew Desi was only four years her junior but the younger woman had a well of optimism that radiated out of her like sunbeams, making her seem even younger than she was.

"Oh, and don't forget I'm driving into Asheville tomorrow to shop on Black Friday," Desi said. "I want to get a jump on the holiday bargains."

Joaquin glanced up from the sink. "Do you think that's a good idea, Des? I don't really like the idea of you alone in a town you're unfamiliar with."

"It's Asheville, I've been there a million times." Desi smiled at him. "I'll be fine."

"But there's going to be traffic and tons of people will be out shopping," he said.

"Yep, it's Black Friday—that's kind of the whole point."

"Why don't you wait until Sunday?" he asked. "I could go with you on Sunday."

"I don't need you to go with me, plus, all the good stuff will be gone by then."

He studied his sister for a moment and then finally nodded.

"Fine, but call me when you get there," he said. He turned

back to the sink. "Then call me when you leave Asheville, so I know when to expect you home. Make sure you leave early enough so you're not driving in the dark, and—Desi, what's wrong?" He dropped the pot and the sponge and hurried to her side.

Desi had a hand at her throat and her mouth was open. She looked as if she was gasping for breath. Savannah felt her heart race. Oh, God, was she choking?

"You're . . . suffocating . . . me," Desi gasped. Then she straightened up and laughed. "Quit worrying so much. I've got this."

"That was not funny," Quino said. He blew out a breath.

"It was a little funny," Desi countered. She held up her thumb and pointer finger. "Right, Savy?"

"Oh, no, I'm not getting in the middle of this." She held up her hands as if they were passing a hot potato and she was refusing to participate.

"I'll be fine." Desiree stepped forward and hugged her brother tight. She pressed herself into his side and grinned up at him. "How did I get so lucky to have such a wonderful older brother? I know I don't tell you often enough, but I really appreciate everything you do for me. I love you, Quino."

"I love you, too, squirt," he said. Then he kissed the top of his sister's head, and Savy felt all of her insides cry *Aw.*

Ridiculously good-looking, a charmer, and a caring older brother, Joaquin was proving much harder to ignore than she had thought. It had been a struggle over the past few months to resist him, but at least she'd been so busy throwing herself into the promotion of Maisy's newly opened bookstore that she hadn't really had a chance to appreciate the man he was, other than in a superficial, surface-good-looks sort of way. Now that she was seeing him with his sister, she found the stable boy had layers of attraction she hadn't even anticipated. Uh-oh.

Desi slipped out of the room and it was just the two of them again. Savy felt like she should say something but she was struggling not to say what she was thinking, which was, *Oh, my God, you're so hot*. She tried to keep it friendly but with no wiggle room for shenanigans.

"You two seem very close," she said. There, that was nice and neutral.

"We are. Desi is all the family I have, so I'm a little protective of her." He looked rueful. "She'd probably prefer it if I backed off, but she's—well, she's my baby sister."

"I think it's sweet," Savy said. "Every girl should have an older brother like you."

Joaquin glanced at her. "Do you have older brothers?"

"No, I'm the youngest of three sisters," she said. "And I'm younger by quite a lot, so we're not very close."

"Ah, you were a surprise," he said. There was a smile on his lips as if he thought being a surprise suited her. She hated to disabuse him of the notion but she'd come to terms with her status a long time ago.

"More like my father's last-ditch effort to have a boy," she said. "The disappointment upon my arrival was great, or so I've been told."

Joaquin frowned. His black brows met in the middle of his forehead in a dark line of unhappy. Savannah wanted to kick herself. She hadn't planned to share that much, or anything, really. It had to be the tryptophan from the turkey coursing through her system like truth serum. Sheesh, she sounded like a whiny brat. She tried to redirect.

"That being said, I had a very happy childhood," she lied.

"And that's a load of horseshit," he said.

Savannah blinked. "You don't know—"

"Yes, I do," he said. He sounded so confident, so supremely arrogant, that Savy felt compelled to take him down.

"No. You. Don't."

"Then why didn't you go home for the holiday?" he asked.

"Because tomorrow is the biggest retail day of the year, and I'm working," she said.

She didn't mention that her parents had told her not to bother since both of her sisters were coming home with their families and her parents' house in the Hamptons would be full to bursting. They didn't think they'd have room for Savannah. The hurt had cut deep but Savy was used to it.

"That's not the only reason." He shook his head.

"It's mostly the reason," she countered. "The truth is my sisters are both going home and my parents felt that the house would be overcrowded and they're not wrong. Between them my sisters have seven kids between the ages of two and ten. It was going to be a circus and one more person would have been one too many."

"How is that even possible? One person too many. That's ridiculous. You're amazing, and I'll bet they're all missing you like crazy." Joaquin's frown returned and this time a really deep WTF line appeared in between his eyebrows, too. He looked at her as if he couldn't imagine a scenario where she wasn't missed. Although Savy had come to terms with the reality of her existence years ago—therapy helped—it was still a balm to her soul to have him so indignant on her behalf.

"Thank you, but I'm fine," she said. "I grew up in a house of privilege if not affection, so I learned to get by on shopping sprees and spa days." When he didn't smile, she put her hand on his arm. "My life really wasn't that bad. I swear."

He glanced down at her hand on his arm and Savannah hastily let go, hoping it didn't look as awkward as it felt.

He shook his head as he studied her face. "As long as I live, I swear I will never understand some people. It's like they don't understand what a gift having a family is."

Savannah watched him as he turned back to the sink and scrubbed the pan as if it had done something to offend him. He attacked the grease and grit with a ferocity of repressed feeling that made her wonder about his story. She had learned from Maisy that his parents had been killed in a horrific car accident and that he had taken on the responsibility of raising Desi from that point on. No one talked about it, but she had caught on to the fact that Desi had some issues. She was twenty-five but still lived at home, had commuted to college instead of living there, and her days were spent working with the horses in their stable.

Savannah wanted to ask him about Desi but she couldn't figure out how to do it without being rude. It was none of her business, and if she wasn't going to get involved with him then she'd best let it go. She put away the pot she'd dried and reached for the next one.

"I think families are only a gift if you're lucky enough to have a good one," she said. "That's one of the reasons I decided a long time ago to never marry or have children."

Joaquin stood up straight and snapped his gaze to her face. "You don't want a family?"

"Nope," she said. "I don't think I have the skill set."

"Sure you do," he said.

She raised her eyebrows at him. "How could you possibly know if I would make a good wife or mother?" She used one hand to pull the turtleneck sweater, which suddenly felt too tight, away from her skin. "Even the thought of it makes me rashy."

She thought she'd score a laugh off him. But no. Instead, he looked at her with an intensity in those black eyes that made her hold her breath.

"You are so full of it," he said.

"Are you calling me out?" she asked. "Because it's very rude to contradict a woman, who at the ripe old age of twenty-nine knows who she is, what she wants, and what she doesn't."

"Fair enough. I can't speak to your abilities at mothering, having never seen you with a baby or a toddler or a child," he said. "But I know for a fact, you'd be an excellent wife, or life partner, if the word *wife* offends you."

Savannah propped a hand on her hip. She looked him up and down. He had some nerve.

"What could you possibly know about me that makes you think I'd be a good little wife?" she asked. Her voice crackled with challenge.

Joaquin dropped the pot into the sudsy water and grabbed another dish towel to dry his hands. Then he draped it on his shoulder and began to tick off reasons on his fingers.

"One, I never said 'good' or 'little,' I said 'excellent,' which is way better. Two, I know that Maisy was in trouble when she opened her business and you came down here to help her. That's selfless, which is a rare quality in anyone. Three, I've watched you with the customers in the shop— you go all in, trying to help. You care about them. They're strangers and you care. Four, I've seen you use your online wizardry skills to help anyone who asks—from me and my website for the stables to Roger at the local hardware store and his newsletter. Five, you are without question the hottest woman I've ever seen, and I'm pretty sure it would take me a lifetime to get enough of you."

Savannah blinked. She didn't know what to say. She knew what she needed to say, but the words wouldn't come. She cleared her throat. She pointed at him. She cleared her throat again. He looked smug, like he didn't think she could argue his points. That, right there, proved he did not know her at all.

"First off, *excellent* is subjective. What is one person's excellent is another person's waking nightmare, so that's out. Second, I only came to help Maisy because I was out of work and she's my friend. It was convenient. Third, helping customers in the bookstore is the whole point of working there. Fourth, of course I help people with their online presence and publicity questions. That's just good business because then they refer you to other people. And lastly, you—" She was doing so well with her rebuttal and then she had no words.

The man just called her the hottest woman he had ever seen, which was completely ludicrous—he was either a flatterer like no other or he really needed to have his eyes checked—but for some reason, she couldn't, or didn't want to, argue with him on that point.

"You were saying?" he asked. The grin he directed her way was positively wicked.

Chapter Three

"HEY, can I lend a hand in here?" Sawyer, carrying yet another plate, cruised into the room.

Savannah blinked at him. She had completely lost her train of thought under the hot dark gaze of the man beside her. "Huh?"

"No, we're good, thanks," Joaquin said.

He reached out and took the plate from Sawyer. Joaquin wasn't unfriendly but he wasn't particularly approachable, either. Savannah sensed a current of tension coming from him toward the other man, but wondered if she was imagining it.

"Okay," Sawyer said. He glanced at Savannah and added, "Thank you, that was delicious."

"You bet," she said. "There's more if you're hungry."

"Thanks, but I'm stuffed." He raised his hands in surrender and backed out of the kitchen with a smile so like Ryder's and Perry's that she was struck by the strength of the Copeland family genes.

Joaquin turned away and faced he sink. He began to

scrub the remaining plate and Savannah moved beside him to grab it when he was done.

She waited a moment and then said, "Okay, what gives?"

"About what?"

"You. Sawyer. The draft of Arctic air that blew through here when he stepped into the kitchen," she said.

"I don't know what you mean," he said. He wasn't making eye contact with her.

Savannah wondered if she should push him since it really wasn't any of her business, but really, when had that ever stopped her? "You, Joaquin Solis, are a horrible liar. Possibly the worst I've ever seen, and that's saying something since Maisy is my best friend and she can't fib for beans."

"What are you talking about? I could lie if I wanted to," he said. "I just choose not to."

"Except for a few seconds ago when you said you didn't know what I meant when you clearly knew exactly what I was talking about. So what is your deal with Sawyer anyway?"

Joaquin handed her the plate and she began to dry it, all the while keeping her gaze on him, waiting for his explanation.

"I don't have a problem with him," he said. "I've only met him a couple of times. I don't even know him."

"Try again."

"All right, maybe I have a small issue with the fact that he up and abandoned his brother when he needed him the most."

"Sawyer abandoned Ryder?" she asked.

"As far as I could tell, he did. I was attending college and working on a construction crew in Texas with Ryder when he hooked up with Whitney, Perry's mother," he said. "Suddenly, Whitney was pregnant, they got married, and Sawyer just bounced out of the picture and off onto his own life."

"Uh-huh," she said. "How old was he?"

"Same age as me at the time, nineteen," he said. "Ryder may be older by a couple of years, but he needed Sawyer and he wasn't there."

"Maybe Sawyer felt like Ryder didn't need him anymore because he had a wife and a kid," she said. "Maybe he felt like the big brother he'd always been close to had suddenly abandoned him, leaving him alone and adrift without a safety net or anyone to turn to when life got rough."

Joaquin leaned back and looked at her. Really looked at her. His voice when he spoke was soft and full of understanding. "Is that what happened to you with your older sisters, Red?"

"No," she snapped. "I'm just theorizing. And don't call me Red."

"Your older siblings left to start families of their own and you felt totally abandoned and replaced," he continued.

"Stop! No. We're not talking about me," she said. "I am merely pointing out that maybe there are two sides to the story and Sawyer felt a bit cut loose when his brother unexpectedly started a family of his own."

Quino considered her. Then he gave a slow nod. "I never thought of it like that."

"Because Ryder's your friend and Perry's your goddaughter, and you are very protective of those you care about," she said.

"Maybe," he agreed. "A little."

She didn't laugh in his face. She thought she should get points for her restraint, given that calling himself *a little protective* was the understatement of the decade. But any thought she had about laughing at him vanished as he leaned in close. He was four or five inches taller than her, which was weird because given her own unusual height most men were either shorter than her or the same height. She rarely had to look up at anyone.

She did it now and she wasn't sure she liked the feeling. It felt as if there was a power shift of which she was unaware and it wasn't in her favor. Joaquin must have sensed it, too, because he hunkered down so they were on the same level.

When his gaze met hers, he said, "For the record, you're a terrible liar, too."

"Ah," she gasped. "That's not true. I can spin a tall tale

with the best of them. I mean, look at this hair. I'm half Scots and half Irish, so I'm thrifty and full of malarkey. Honestly, you can't trust a word I say."

"Is that so?" he asked. "Does that mean that all those times you gave me the brush-off when I asked you out, you didn't mean it?"

"Uh . . ." Savy stared at him. She wasn't sure how to answer. The man had verbally outmaneuvered her. She could either admit that she had been telling the truth when talking about feeling abandoned or that she hadn't meant it when she rejected all of his offers to dinner, movies, and so on. Dilemma!

She tipped her head to the side and then cupped her ear. "Do you hear that? Is that Maisy calling me? Why, yes, I believe she is. Excuse me."

She tossed her dish towel onto the counter and scooted toward the door. She heard him chuckle behind her, but she didn't allow herself to look back even when she heard him call after her, "Coward."

Savy knew this was an argument she couldn't win. When it came to Joaquin Solis, she was a big, yellow-bellied, lily-livered, fainthearted fraidycat. The man was too attractive for his own good, and just like an endless bag of potato chips, if she tried even one, she was doomed.

She knew that man would get under her skin and then she'd be making all sorts of life decisions based on his hotness and not on the revenge that drove her to regain her reputation in the publishing world. There was nothing in life she wanted more than getting her cred back, and no cutie pie cowboy was going to distract her from her purpose. Period.

Several months before, Savannah had been unceremoniously kicked to the curb by her boss, Linda Briggs. At the time, no explanation of her firing had been given. Savannah didn't have an employee contract and was considered an at-will employee, meaning she could be fired at any time with no reason given.

It had taken some time, but Savannah had her friend and colleague Archer Vossen from human resources find out why Linda had fired her. Apparently, Linda had proof that Savannah had taken credit for Linda's publicity campaign for Billie Latham, an up-and-coming author the publisher was promoting heavily. Linda had computer files that she said were stolen from her own computer, and an e-mail exchange between Savannah and Billie where Savannah proposed several innovative publicity strategies.

The kick in the teeth was that the strategies and the e-mail exchange were real. Savannah had been busting her butt to get Billie's book to shine. What had been false was the lie that Savannah had taken Linda's work. Somehow Linda had managed to steal Savy's work and put it on her own computer with a time stamp that made it look like Linda had drafted the strategy before Savannah. It was utter bullshit and Savy had no idea how to fight it.

At the time, she hadn't been given a chance to defend herself as she didn't even know why she was being fired when security had arrived at her desk and watched her pack her stuff and then escorted her from the building. Linda had been conveniently away from the office. It had been the most confusing, humiliating moment of Savannah's life to date.

Savy had told Maisy that she'd been let go from her former position, but she hadn't shared the shaming that had been involved. She didn't like to talk about it. Word had gotten out in the industry and her reputation was in tatters. She had no defense, as Linda had spent months working behind her back to build a case against Savannah that she hadn't even suspected. Savy and Archer logged hours on the phone trying to figure out why Linda had done what she did. Archer theorized that Linda felt threatened by Savannah and had decided to get rid of her before management caught on and let Linda go and replaced her with Savannah. He promised to keep his ear to the ground and look for an opportunity to help Savannah. Archer felt that Linda would slip up. It was just a matter of time. This was cold comfort for Savannah.

When Maisy called Savy in a panic about the Victorian house she'd inherited from her great-aunt Eloise, Savy had come down from New York to help Maisy organize Auntie El's hoarder's trove of romance novels into one of the few romance bookstores in the country. Savy loved doing the publicity for a shop that celebrated books by women, for women, about women. Sure, there were some male authors who wrote romance, and the market stats said that 16 percent of the readership was male, but mostly, it was a chick thing, which was one of the things Savannah loved most about it.

Together she and Maisy had decided that the Happily Ever After Bookstore would celebrate *all* the things that brought women joy. Such as the color pink, working out to achieve a rocking bod, crafting, pursuing higher education, accumulating wealth, being the smartest person in the room, cupcakes, a love of science and math, glitter, hairdos, and video games. Okay, so maybe not all of those things were commonly known as *girly*, but Savannah believed that the two greatest gifts a woman could give herself were knowledge and strength, and she loved that Maisy felt the exact same way.

They were committed to making the bookstore a space that celebrated all women from all walks of life, living their best lives. Truly, the past few months had been some of the most fulfilling of Savy's publicist career, although she didn't tell Maisy this because she knew her friend would leverage it into a talk about why she should stay in Fairdale. This was not a conversation Savy was willing to have.

She had left New York under a cloud of disgrace in the publishing industry and until she gained her reputation back, she felt stuck and couldn't move forward until there was a resolution to what had happened with her old job. Everything she did felt like a lateral shift where she was just biding her time. She was determined that she would rise from the ashes and prove her detractors wrong, especially Linda Briggs, the cause of all her pain.

Even the thought of the woman made Savy want to punch something, really hard. Instead, she pictured the day that she would strut back into New York in her favorite power suit, wearing her spikiest heels, and launch a campaign to bring a heretofore unknown author out of the shadows to catapult onto the bestseller lists followed by guest spots on *Ellen*, *The View*, a fifty-city book tour, and a movie deal with Reese Witherspoon's production company. She simply would not, could not, rest until she achieved her comeback.

D ECK the halls with boughs of holly, Fa la la la la la la la la."

Savannah opened one eye and noted that her bedroom was still dark, which meant the sun wasn't up and it was still the darker side of dawn, so unless she had dreamed that someone was singing then the noise that had awoken her was actually someone singing.

"'Tis the season to be jolly, Fa la la la—"

That did it. Savannah shoved her covers aside, grabbed her robe, and jammed her feet into her slippers. She stormed out of her bedroom door and into her apartment. Up until a few months ago, she'd been sharing the small two-bedroom apartment atop the Happily Ever After Bookstore with Maisy, but Maisy had fallen in love with Ryder. In a gesture of his devotion, Ryder had bought the house literally right next door, giving Maisy the shortest commute to work ever but also leaving Savannah alone in the apartment. Most of the time, she didn't mind. In fact, she liked getting away from everyone after the end of a busy workday, but sometimes it was too quiet. This was not one of those times.

Savannah marched across the living room and yanked open her front door. She glanced over the staircase railing to the second-floor landing. The singing was definitely coming from there. She knew Maisy was hoping for a good holiday season and, yes, today was Black Friday, but did that mean they had to be up before the sun, singing Christmas tunes, no less?

It was a man's voice she heard so she assumed it must be Ryder. Poor bastard, he was so in love with Maisy, she probably had him convinced he wanted to decorate the store today. Savannah staggered toward the steps. She would relieve him of his duty and send him home. It was the least she could do.

Savannah was not a fan of Christmas. She didn't need a psychiatrist to tell her that it all stemmed from her childhood and her family's complete inability to do Christmas. Once launched, her sisters refused to come home. And who could blame them? Her father ignored the holiday, expecting his wife to do it all, and her mother tried to decorate the house, throw the expected parties, and be the hostess with the mostest, before succumbing to the lure of one too many martinis, which more times than not quickly went from taking the edge off her stress to leaving her in an embarrassing stupor.

The day usually peaked with stilted dinner conversation with extended family they never saw except at Christmas, where at some point her mother would pass out face-first in her yams, sending her father into one of his quiet rages where he disappeared into his study and didn't come out for days. Good times. Unfortunately, after so many years with holidays like that, Savannah had discovered that she had an aversion to the entire thing, and try as she might, she just couldn't enjoy the holiday festivities. When the calendar flipped to January first, she was always thrilled to know that she wouldn't have to deal with the holiday again for another 358 days.

She often wondered if she hadn't been brought up dreading the holiday, if she would have found it as annoying as she did. She didn't know for sure, but given that she considered it all off-putting—the music, the lights, the movies, the shopping, the cookies (no, wait, actually, the cookies were about the only thing she liked about the holidays)— she thought it was definitely her upbringing.

The forced family cheeriness, the dread of a dramatic episode, the hurt feelings—Savannah would spend weeks with a ball of anxiety in her stomach. This usually made her overindulge in everything, making it all worse because then she felt bloated, which her mother would feel compelled to comment on in a pretend bout of concern, which was really a passive-aggressive way of pointing out how big

Savannah was compared to her own petite self. Even thinking about it made Savannah's stomach cramp.

"Fa la la la—"

Savannah hit the stairs at a run.

"Stop!" she cried. "Stop. Stop. Stop."

She stepped out onto the second-floor landing to find all
the lights were on in the shop, and Joaquin was cheerfully
winding a silver tinsel garland around the railing of the
staircase toward the landing.

He glanced at her in surprise. Savy could only imagine
what she looked like. She was no doubt sporting a spectacular case of bedhead. She likely had dried-up drool on
her chin and eye crusties on a pale freckled face that was
makeup-less. *Oh, God.*

Naturally, being caught totally off guard by him, she
snapped, "What are you doing here?"

Joaquin looked from her to the garland and back.
"Seems kind of self-explanatory." Then he grinned and his
eyes moved over the mess that was Savy. "Did you just
wake up?"

"Not by choice," she said. "Someone's singing roused
me. What time is it, anyway?"

"Five," he said.

"In the morning?!" She was outraged. "Why are you
here this early?"

"Maisy asked us to start decorating extra early so the
place is ready before opening."

"Who is 'us'?"

Joaquin glanced over his shoulder and Savy followed his
gaze beyond the second-floor railing at the first floor below.
Jeri, the store bookkeeper, and Ryder, Perry, Sawyer, and
Maisy were bustling around, stringing lights and garlands
and other holiday-related decorations.

"Morning, Savy," Maisy called up to her. "Hope we
didn't wake you."

"Ugh." Savannah was not at full capacity yet.

"We have coffee," Ryder called. "Lots of coffee."

Savy would have told him where to stick it but . . . coffee.
She turned on her slipper and trudged away from Joaquin.

He immediately started singing again, which forced her back around. She pointed at him and snapped, "No singing before everyone has had their coffee. It's a rule."

"Okay, okay," he said. He held up his hands in surrender but the garland dangled from his big square hands, looking ridiculous. Her gaze narrowed. He looked happy. Then she got an eyeful of his sweater.

"What is *that*?" she asked.

He was wearing a green-and-red plaid sweater with a snowman embroidered on the front.

"It's my Christmas sweater," he said. "Like it? I have a closetful of them."

"Oh, man, you're one of those people, aren't you?" she asked. His sweater was giving her the dry heaves.

"One of what people?" he asked. He bent over to continue wrapping the tinsel around the wooden banister.

"Those people who love Christmas and everything that comes with it," she said. Her voice was full of disdain and she could feel her lip curl into the slightest sneer.

"Well, yeah," he said. He looked at her as if he couldn't imagine being any other way. "What's not to love?"

"Let me consult my list," she said.

He looked shocked. "You don't like the holidays?"

"Not even a little," she said.

"Ah!" He let out a high-pitched yelp and clutched the snowman on his chest as if he couldn't believe what he was hearing. Savy resisted the urge to laugh, mostly because she suspected that he was trying to make her laugh but also because she was pre-coffee and nothing was funny before caffeine.

She turned away from him, not wanting to pursue this conversation anymore. She didn't want to be judged for her lack of holiday spirit. As far as she was concerned the whole thing was a sham. It was a commercially driven gimme holiday and people were held hostage by a warm, fuzzy expectation of the holidays that rarely proved out. While the publicist in her understood the commercial demands of the day, the regular person in her loathed the whole manufactured extravaganza of shop, shop, shop, and shop some more. It just led to debt and disappointment and who needed that?

"There has to be something about the holidays that you like," he said. He abandoned his garland and fell into step beside her as she went down the stairs.

"Nope," she said.

"What about all the great holiday movies?" he persisted.

"Nope."

"The music?"

"Nuh-uh."

"The ballet," he said with a snap of his fingers. "There is not a woman alive who doesn't love *The Nutcracker*."

"As much as I love the title of that ballet right now"—Savy paused and gave him a pointed look in the crotch area before she continued—"no, I don't like that ballet. The king of the rats is terrifying. Who thought it was a great idea to scare little girls into thinking their toys would be killed off by giant rats? Blerg." She feigned a shiver and kept walking.

"He's the Mouse King, not a rat," Joaquin corrected her. "Who cares?"

On the first floor, they passed Maisy, who had taken a waterfall display rack and was stuffing it with Christmas romances from holiday heavy hitters Susan Mallery, Jill Shalvis, and Lisa Kleypas. Jeri was decorating the front counter with blinking lights, the sort that gave Savannah a headache.

She trudged into the kitchen with Joaquin right behind her. Clearly, he was not appreciating the boundary issues of a woman who hadn't had her java yet. Well, if she bit him, it was his own fault.

She beelined to the coffeepot, giddy to find it full, and grabbed a sunshine-yellow mug out of the cupboard. She filled it to the brim, leaving just enough room for a splash of milk. Quino watched her quietly.

"Presents," he said. "You have to like getting presents. Who doesn't like getting presents?"

She stared at him over the rim of her mug. "What am I? Five?"

"Oh, you're a hard one," he said. "How about the spirit of the holiday? You must appreciate that the holidays make everyone a little better, kinder, more thoughtful?"

"That hasn't been my experience," she said. "Rather, it seems to make them meaner, greedier, and more selfish."

Quino slid onto a stool at the counter and propped his chin in his hand as he studied her. "Who did you so wrong, Red?"

"Stop calling me Red," she said. She sipped her coffee. The aroma soothed her as the bitter heat moved from her tongue to her belly, uncoiling the knot of tension inside of her. "And for your information, no one did me wrong. I just think the holidays have gotten way out of hand. I mean, people lose their ever-loving minds trying to twist themselves in knots to have the *best holiday ever*. It's ridiculous. Like we haven't all been members of our own families for years and should know better."

Quino pushed a big pink bakery box at her. "Have a donut. It'll sweeten your disposition."

"I don't want—"

He flipped the lid and Savannah sighed. Donuts went so well with coffee. It would be a shame to deny such a perfect pairing. She scanned the selection from Big Bottom Donuts, searching for—aha! There it was. A coconut-encrusted donut. She snagged it and took a big bite. Then she washed it down with some coffee. Perfection.

She glanced at Joaquin as he perused the donuts. He looked good in the morning light—yes, even in that hideous sweater. His dark hair flopped over his forehead, deep dimples bracketed his mouth, and his black eyes sparked with amusement. She got the feeling he was one of those people who found joy in every day, not just the holiday. She envied him that.

She wasn't sure when she'd turned into such a cranky pants about the holidays but she had a feeling it was about the same time her dad informed her, at the age of four, that Santa was a lie and, no, she would not be getting any presents from him. At the time, Savannah had been convinced that her father told her that because she was naughty and Santa wasn't coming to her house because she was on the bad list. She'd thought he'd been trying to spare her. Every year, she'd been filled with shame to discover no presents from Santa. It was a few more years before she figured it out and, yet, the shame stayed. She shook the memory off.

"You were saying," he said.

"Nothing, it's just, who can stand to watch all of those Christmas movies? I mean, there's like a new one on every day from Thanksgiving until Christmas," she said. She took another bite of her donut. He said nothing. In fact, he looked away, staring at the wall as if avoiding her gaze.

Savannah sucked in a breath, taking a piece of coconut with it, which caused her to cough so hard her eyes watered. She put down her coffee. Joaquin, with a look of alarm, hopped off his seat and came around the counter to pat her on the back. It was a solid thump right between her shoulder blades, as if it might distract her from her new-found realization. No such luck.

Chapter Four

SHE held up her hand, picked up her mug, and took a long swallow. When her throat felt clear, she looked at him and said, "You watch all of those movies, don't you?"

"Me?" he asked. He gestured to himself even though they were the only two people in the room. "Well, you know, they're on, like, all month. It's impossible to avoid them."

Savannah arched an eyebrow and stared him down. "You like them."

"My sister, Desi—"

Savannah shook her head. Her mass of red curls flew about her face and she puffed out her lower lip to blow one hank of hair out of her eyes. "This is not about Desi."

"Fine, so I like Christmas movies," he said. He rolled his eyes. "Is that a crime?"

"Only if you cry," she said. She was kidding, but judging by the guilty look on his face, he did get emotional while watching. "Oh, wow, you do cry."

"No—maybe—okay, only at the really good ones that involve kids or dogs," he said. "You know, some of the writing is just brilliant."

Savannah stared at him over the rim of her mug. "I don't even know what to say to you right now. In my entire life, I have never met a man who loves Christmas. Usually, it's something to be avoided at all costs and shopping, if there is any to be done, is finessed late at night on Christmas Eve at the local pharmacy. Seriously, I once had a guy give me a sports sock stuffed with beef jerky, batteries, and the matching sock."

Joaquin made a face like he couldn't comprehend this breach of holiday etiquette. "Was he a student?"

"Lawyer."

"Oh, well, that explains it."

She laughed at his dry tone and then said, "Don't get me wrong. I think it's sweet that you enjoy the holiday, but it just proves my point about us."

"And what point was that?" he asked. He moved away from her to pour his own cup of coffee, and Savannah tried not to stare at how small the mug looked in his big hands. She had a brief vision of those hands on her skin and she felt her entire body get hot.

"That we are completely incompatible," she said. "I'm a city girl and you're a country boy, you're a morning person and I like to sleep late, you love holidays and I feel like I'm being tortured. Complete opposites."

He blew on his coffee and Savannah watched the steam drift away from his pursed lips. She was staring. She knew she shouldn't but her caffeine hadn't really kicked in yet, and he did have the most fascinating mouth. Full lips that looked as if they would be good at softly sliding up the side of her neck to nestle in the sweet spot right below her ear.

As if he knew the wayward path her thoughts had taken, Joaquin put his mug on the counter and leaned close. He was just inches away from her, studying her with those fathomless black eyes, when he said, "The only compatibility that matters, Red, is in the bedroom. And you and I both know we are way more than compatible there—we're positively combustible."

He said it with such confidence that she found herself believing him 100 percent. There was definitely some hard-core desire crackling between them—in fact, she couldn't remember a time when she'd been as attracted to a man as she was to him. The feeling lured her in and beguiled her with visions of late nights and rumpled sheets and sweaty sexcapades—

"Wait a second," she said. He was too close. The scent of him, a subtle cedar and bergamot, weakened her resistance to him as it made her want to move in closer and press up against him. She put her hand on his festive snowman chest and pushed him back a pace. Now she could think. Almost. "There is no way you could possibly know how it would be between us, given that we've never even kissed. Anything you say is strictly a hypothetical."

She picked up her mug and made her way to the door. Since everyone was here and she'd fortified herself with a donut and some coffee, she might as well go ahead and take her shower and prepare to face the day. She'd sent out notices to the local news outlets and on their social media that they were having a BOGO special today on all the used books. She expected that alone to bring in the Black Friday bargain hunters.

Joaquin was right behind her as she pushed through the swinging door back into the bookstore. A stepladder was in her path but when she went to duck around it, the tie on her bathrobe got snagged in the legs. She reached out to tug it loose but his hand was there first.

"Here," he said. He held out the cloth belt and Savy took it from him, ignoring the awareness of his fingers brushing against hers. It was electric and she tried to convince herself it was just static from the area rug below their feet. Yeah, that was it. She turned away, trying not to run, but he caught her hand in his.

"Hold up there, Red, we have a situation," he said.

She turned back around not because she wanted to, she told herself, but because it was the polite thing to do.

"Really?" she asked. "And what situation is that?"

"Mistletoe," he said. He pointed up.

Savy tipped her head back to study him. "Seriously? You're going to kiss me now?"

"I have to," he said. He was the picture of innocence,

which Savy did not believe for one second. "It's bad luck to refuse a kiss under the mistletoe. You don't want to risk that, do you?"

"You're making that up," she said.

"Nope." He shook his head. His black eyes sparkled as if he'd gotten her right where he wanted her. It shouldn't have been thrilling, but it was.

He reached out and took her coffee cup from her hand and put it on a bookcase. Then he took the ties of her bathrobe and used them to pull her inexorably closer. Savy felt her breathing get short in anticipation as if she were winding up the slow side of a roller coaster. Her hands were suddenly sweaty and she wasn't sure what to do with them. Joaquin was going to kiss her. Now!

She glanced around the shop but none of their friends were in the vicinity. In fact, judging by the muted sound of conversation coming from beyond the front door, she suspected they were all outside decorating the front of the shop. Great.

Joaquin didn't seem to care if their friends were around or not. In fact, he didn't seem put off by anything. But he should be. Savy did a quick inventory. She hadn't showered. Her hair was a rat's nest. She had no makeup on, and she was pretty sure she smelled like the leftover pepperoni pizza she had consumed as a midnight snack. In fact, she glanced down. Yep, there was a splat of sauce on her pajama top that she hadn't quite sponged clean. The man was crazy if he thought any kiss between them at this moment was going to be anything other than utterly underwhelming.

Wait! That was it. This was perfect. Joaquin had been sniffing around her for months, and Maisy had been doing her level best to throw them together. If Savy let him kiss her right now in this sloppy state it would absolutely squash anything he thought might be between them. Sure, it was likely going to be awkward and weird, but she could totally put up with that if it shut down this misguided attraction she had for the stable boy once and for all.

"All right," she said. "But I'm going to kiss you and not the other way around. I don't want to feel like I'm being mauled by a bear under this parasitic vegetation."

Joaquin let out a deep chuckle and let go of her sash. "Have it your way, Red."

Oh, the arrogance. He must really think he was something special, Savy thought. She took a deep breath and braced herself to put her mouth against his. There would be no parted lips or tongue here. This was going to be swift, a one and done, and then she was off to take her shower, possibly a cold one, but she could live with that.

She stepped close but he didn't. Hmm. She was going to have to go up on her toes to reach his mouth. Being a tall girl, this was a new sensation for Savy, especially when the man in question was not bending down to meet her halfway. In fact, if she went up on her toes, she was going to have to grab ahold of him to maintain her balance. She considered her options. She could grab his forearms or his upper arms, but that seemed weird. There was no help for it. She put her hands on his shoulders. He kept his hands at his sides, not budging an inch.

Savy considered the logistics. She was going to have to lean up against him and pull him down at least a little bit in order to kiss him. She wondered if she could get away with kissing him on the cheek. She glanced at his freshly shaved face and noted he had some spectacular cheekbones.

"No," he said.

"No what?"

"Unless you're family, mistletoe kisses are on the lips," he said. He gestured between them. "We are not family." His eyes crinkled in the corners in amusement. He was enjoying her conundrum. If they were in a Regency novel, he would without question be a rogue.

"I bet you're making that up, too," she said.

He winked at her and she bit her lip and shook her head. Fine. Enough games. She tried to pull him down to her level so she could plant a swift smooch on him, but he was as solid as a marble statue. She couldn't budge him, and it occurred to her that she was going to have to climb the big galoot like he was a tree if she hoped to have a chance at kissing him on the mouth.

As if sensing her dilemma, he asked, "Need a hand?"

That did it! If the boy was going to insist on playing with fire, Savannah was going to make sure he felt the burn. She shook her head, sending her curls spinning. She rolled up on her toes and slid her hands over his shoulders, pressing herself against him as she curled one hand around his neck and dug the other into his thick, inky black hair. She pulled him down while she rose up and then planted her mouth on his in a firm, lip-to-lip kiss that she hoped was seared into his brain for the rest of his natural-born days.

It was supposed to end there. She was supposed to let go, release his hair, uncurl her hand from around the back of his neck, let her hands slide down his shoulders as she lowered herself back to the floor. Small problem—she didn't do any of those things.

The shock when her mouth met his rendered her instantly stupid. Suddenly, she didn't know which way was up or down; all she knew was the feel of his soft sweater beneath her fingers, the hard, lean line of his body where her curves leaned against him, and his mouth. The firm press of his lips beneath hers. It wasn't enough.

Instinct overrode common sense and Savy parted her lips, wanting to get just the smallest taste of him. It was a drive, a need, a longing that couldn't be ignored. Joaquin responded by parting his lips, too. It encouraged Savy to deepen the kiss and she let her tongue run along his full lower lip in a taunt or an invitation, she wasn't sure.

The man beneath her fingers didn't move. Whether it was from good manners or shock, Savy didn't know and she didn't much care. She was too caught up in the scent of him and the taste of him to remember that this was supposed to be a nothing kiss, a throwaway embrace, an awkward interlude between two people who'd been circling each other for months, undecided about what exactly was between them. It wasn't that at all.

Instead, it was an exploration, a discovery, a moment in time when everything in the universe suddenly made sense because his mouth fit hers perfectly. His lips were firm and persuasive, opening beneath hers and inviting her in to explore the taste and texture of him, which made her knees buckle and her heart rate kick up into high gear. He didn't touch her in any other way—his hands stayed fisted at his sides—but his mouth made love to hers with small sips and soft kisses, willing a response from her that she couldn't suppress.

"More," she whispered with a shiver.

Joaquin pulled back just slightly and glanced at her. Any teasing from earlier had left his eyes and he looked at her with an intensity that should have fried her hair.

"Are you sure?" he asked.

She didn't overthink it. She nodded. He held her gaze, staring into her eyes as his hands left his sides and circled her waist, gently pulling her up high and tight. Savy found herself lifted off her feet and locked against him with his arm supporting her lower back while he dug into her thick mass of curls, holding her still while he kissed her with a thoroughness that left her gasping for breath even as she wanted more and more and more.

He lowered his lips to her throat and Savy let her head drop back. He moved his mouth in a soft sensual slide from her collarbone up the side of her neck to the sensitive spot below her ear. It was a good thing he was holding her or she was sure she would have slid down his body and dissolved into a shallow puddle of desire at his feet.

"Admit it," he said. His voice was a sexy growl in her ear. "This thing between us is crazy hot."

He slowly lowered her to her feet, pressing his forehead against hers while they both gasped for breath. His hands cruised up the curve of her spine and over her shoulders, moving to cup her face so that she was forced to meet his gaze. He looked like he wanted to devour her and didn't the thought of that give her the thrill of a lifetime? Savy knew instinctively that if she let this man into her life, he would ruin her. There was only one way out. She had to lie.

She pulled back, giving herself some space while holding his gaze. Then she tossed out a careless shrug. "Meh."

His eyes went wide. Then he blinked. Then his gaze lowered to her throat, where Savy knew he could see her pulse pounding triple time.

"Liar," he said. His grin was a slash of white and it curled up on one side as if in delight at the challenge she presented. Before she could track him, he'd lowered his head until his lips were right on that fluttery pulse point in the softest, sexiest kiss she'd ever received. Her heart thumped hard in her chest and she knew that he knew she was responding to him on the most elemental level.

Savy thought she might faint. Probably, her eyes would roll back into her head and she'd make some unintelligible grunt before she splatted right onto the floor. Except he was still holding her face as if she was something rare and precious and she was clutching his forearms as if they were a life raft in a choppy sea.

He pressed his mouth to hers one more time and she made a sound that resembled a groan of longing, possibly even a moan of desire. When he pulled back, she couldn't help but notice the satisfied look on his face. She'd given herself away with her response to him. Damn it.

She didn't want any complications when she left Fairdale to go back to New York, and a lovesick stable boy was definitely a complication. She had to get it together. She shook her head. Her curls went everywhere and she dug her hand into the mass and pushed it off her face.

"Fine," she said. "Are we good now?"

"Not quite," he said. He reached up and plucked one of the berries off the mistletoe. He held it out to her. "You're supposed to pick one every time there is a kiss under the mistletoe, and when the bough runs out of berries, there are no more kisses."

"How do you know this stuff?" she asked. She opened her hand and he dropped the hard berry into her palm.

He got a gentle look in his eyes. "My parents. My dad loved to catch my mom under the mistletoe. He used to string it up all over the house just so he'd have an excuse to kiss her. I used to be so embarrassed to catch them smooching, but now I'm glad I have that memory."

"Oh." She didn't know what to say to that. She didn't think she'd ever seen her parents kiss other than a perfunctory peck on the cheek, never mind any shenanigans under the mistletoe, which was a weed she was pretty sure her mother would never allow into her house. "Well, I'd better go get dressed. We'll be opening soon."

She grabbed her coffee cup from the bookcase and hurried for the stairs. For her own good she had to put some space between them. She'd let him kiss her and it had been amazing. What had she been thinking?

"Oh, and Red," he called.

She was three steps up the staircase. She thought about ignoring him but good manners wouldn't let her.

"Yes?" she asked. She glanced at him over her shoulder.

"Just so you know, by my count there are about thirty berries left." He pointed up at the mistletoe and then winked at her.

She felt her face go hot. She crushed the berry in her hand, knowing that things had just gotten way complicated.

S AVANNAH scraped her hair back into the most unattractive headband she could find. She didn't put on any makeup. She dressed in a baggy gray sweatshirt and brown cargo pants, which she actually loved because . . . pockets! Whoever in fashion had decided in this age of cell phones that women didn't need pockets in their clothing was a sadist. Then she pulled on a pair of white high-top Converse sneakers. It was quite the look, and if Joaquin was still in the shop, it should scare him into the next county, no question.

She hurried downstairs to join Maisy in their office on the first floor. While she herself wasn't much for decorating, Savannah figured the holiday bling was social media gold and she could take some pictures of the decorations and send out reminder posts to let their customers know that today was a happening sale day at the Happily Ever After Bookstore.

She scanned the area when she reached the first floor, but there was no sign of the stable boy. She assured herself that the twinge she felt was relief. Still, she took the long way around the bough of mistletoe that was hanging in the center of the lobby. She wondered if she should talk to Maisy about moving it, possibly outside. After all, if someone got kissed under the mistletoe who didn't want to be, it could be a cause for a lawsuit or some other nasty publicity, and who needed that?

She strode into their office space, expecting to find everyone there. It was just Maisy, who was sitting at her desk, working on her laptop. The sound of Christmas music was playing softly in the background and Savannah tried to block it out. It was no use. She figured she'd have to start wearing earbuds in the bookstore for the next month until the holiday madness was over.

She slid onto her chair at the desk across from Maisy's and her friend glanced up and then her eyes went wide. "Oh, honey, are you all right? Are you feeling under the weather?"

"What?" Savy asked. She shook her head. "No, why?"

"Um, no reason," Maisy said. She glanced back down at her desk and then back up. "I'm your friend, right?"

"My best friend," Savy said. She frowned. "Why, are you thinking of replacing me?"

"No, I just wanted to make sure that the foundation of BFF is firm before I inform you, in the most loving way I can, that you look like crap," Maisy said. "And not just bad, but like *left outside overnight in the rain and left for dead* bad."

"Gee, thanks," Savannah said.

"So, what gives?" Maisy asked. "I know you. You used to go to class after a full night of carousing, freshly showered and with full hair and makeup. You either have the bubonic plague or . . ."

"Or what?" Savy asked.

"I don't know," Maisy said. "That's the blank I'm waiting for you to fill in. So, what's with the slovenly attire, or is that what's trending in New York these days, because I have to say it's not a good look—even Chrissy Teigen could not pull this off."

"Can't a girl just dress down every now and again?"

"A girl? Sure. You? No. I'm surprised you haven't broken

out in a rash from the alarmingly high level of comfort you
must be feeling in those clothes."

"The bagginess of the sweatshirt is annoying," Savy con-
ceded. "But the pants have pockets. Me like the pockets."

She stood and jammed her hands into the side pockets,
modeling them for Maisy. Then she pulled the sweatshirt
off and was left in just a formfitting waffle-knit thermal
shirt and her cargo pants, which were actually flattering for
pants that sported so many pockets. Next she pulled off the
headband and her long red curls sprang free. Since Quino
wasn't here, she didn't feel the need to look so dowdy.

"That's more like it," Maisy said. "You had me worried
there."

"Sorry, I'm not myself today."

"Who are you, then?" a deep voice asked from the
doorway.

Savannah turned at the same time Maisy jumped from
her seat with a clap and yelled, "Santa!"

Savannah felt her jaw drop. Standing in the doorway
dressed from head to toe in red velvet with white faux fur
trim, sporting a fluffy white beard and shiny black boots,
was the jolly old elf himself.

One look at his twinkling eyes and Savannah felt a hot
flush creep into her cheeks. She knew this Santa, she knew
him very well, as she had in fact just been making out
with him.

Chapter Five

SHE thought about diving for her headband and her sweat-shirt but it was too late. Besides, who was she kidding? Joaquin had already seen her without makeup, in her bath-robe, and with hair that was flat on one side and exploding out of her skull on the other. Clearly, nothing put the man off.

"Joaquin, you look amazing!" Maisy cried. "How's your laugh? Can you do a good laugh?"

"Ho ho ho," he rolled out a deep guffaw.

"Perfect!" Maisy squealed. She clapped her hands. "Are you sure you don't mind? Ryder felt horrible that he had to go and couldn't do it."

"I'm sure he did," Savy muttered. Neither Joaquin nor Maisy acknowledged her.

"Are you kidding?" he asked. "I was born to play Santa Claus. Ho ho ho."

"This is so great!" Maisy grabbed his gloved hand and pulled him to the door. "I'm going to have you start on the porch, handing out candy canes."

"Sounds great," he said. "But wait. What if people want pictures and stuff? Wouldn't it be great for the bookstore's social media if you posted pictures of Santa with customers?"

"Ah," Maisy gasped. "You're right. We need a photographer."

They both looked at Savannah. She shook her head. "No."

"But the bookstore needs you," Maisy implored. "You know I'm terrible at photography. I cut off everyone's head. What kind of publicity would that be? A bunch of decapitated customers with Santa?"

Savy rolled her eyes. She would have argued, but the sad fact was, it was true. Maisy was horrible with pictures. "All right, I'll take a few pictures."

"You will?" Maisy raised her hands in the air in triumph. "Fabulous. Oh, and there's an elf costume in the bathroom for you to wear, you know, because Santa needs an elf. Great. See you outside."

"What? No! Hey!"

Maisy shoved Joaquin through the door and slammed it behind them, effectively ending the discussion.

"I am not dressing like an elf!" Savy yelled at the closed door. "I have dignity and a sense of decorum. A twenty-nine-year-old woman does not dress like an elf. Plus, I'm too tall."

She was talking to no one. They were already gone. She pulled her cell phone out of her pocket and checked the battery. The easiest way to take pictures was with her phone, then she could also live-stream Joaquin, as Santa, on their social media pages. Oh, jeez, maybe she did want to dress as an elf because she most definitely did not want anyone to recognize her when she was out there as Santa's little helper.

Good grief. What had her life become? She rose from her desk and strode to the staff bathroom in the corner. Hanging on the back of the door was a garment bag. She unzipped it with a wince. It was even worse than she feared. Green-and-white-striped tights, a green velvet dress with white faux fur trim, and a matching pointy hat. This wasn't even sexy-time elf attire; this was more like elf as a crossing guard. Maisy was going to owe her so huge for this.

Savannah slipped into the outfit and was surprised and delighted to find that the dress actually had pockets. So that was something, at least. She put her cell phone into the side pocket and glanced at her reflection in the mirror. It was not good.

The striped stockings were not flattering, and the length of the dress on her tall frame made it a minidress. She cinched the costume's wide black belt in a desperate attempt to show that she had a waistline but the Peter Pan collar still made her look like a doofus. To top it all off, her pointy hat had a jingle bell on the end of it and it rang with every step she took. Ridiculous.

The outfit didn't come with shoes, so she slipped on her high-top sneakers and stomped out of the bathroom and through the office. Whose idea was this Santa-and-elf thing? Shouldn't they have run it by her? When she'd signed on for this gig, it had not included dressing up in horrible costumes. Yeah, sure, they'd all dressed up as witches for Halloween, but they had been dead-sexy witches, which was a whole other thing. This outfit made her feel like she should be running away from the Abominable Snowman, her reindeer sidekick lighting the way with his nose.

She found Maisy and Santa on the front porch. He was leaning over the railing and waving at cars that drove by and calling, "Ho ho ho."

Savannah glowered at Maisy.

"Oh, you look so cute," Maisy cried. Joaquin turned around and took in the sight of Savannah. The grin beneath his bushy white beard was wide.

"Don't!" She pointed at him. "If anyone is laughing at anyone, I'm laughing at you because you're wearing a fake beard and a belly pillow."

"Better than fake ears," he said. He lifted a white-gloved finger and poked the pointy ear sewn into her hat. She smacked his hand away.

"Stop that," she said.

He snorted. She turned to Maisy. "You owe me so huge for this."

"No doubt," Maisy said. "This is definitely above and

beyond, especially for someone as ambivalent about the holidays as you. I really appreciate your digging deep and taking one for the team."

"Hmm." Savannah hummed, not feeling mollified in the least.

"Come on," Joaquin said. He grabbed Savy's hand and led her to the stairs. "Let's go out to the street and see if we can wave people in."

Maisy handed Savy a cloth sack full of candy canes. "Have fun!"

"What? No!" Savannah protested. It was bad enough people coming to the shop might see her, but if they stood on the street *everyone* would see her in this ridiculous getup.

"What's your elf name?" Quino asked. He was plowing down the walkway like he was on a mission.

"I don't have an elf name," she snapped.

"Then let's make one," he said. "How about Snicker-doodle Jingle Bells?"

"No."

"Ginger McSnowball."

"No." She gave him a grumpy look that she hoped masked the laugh that had almost escaped.

"I know." He snapped his gloved fingers but no sound came out. "Mistletoe Merrybottom."

"Shut up." This time a snort escaped and he grinned at her. She ignored him. "You can call me Elf. It's a nice gender-neutral name that's easy to remember."

"Boring." He rolled his eyes but he didn't argue. He turned around and continued down the walkway until they were out on the sidewalk. He checked the street in both directions but it was quiet. Maisy had put a sandwich board out on the sidewalk that read, **HAPPILY EVER AFTER BOOK-STORE BOGO TODAY ONLY!**

Joaquin hefted up the sign and began to walk down the sidewalk toward the center of town. Savy hurried to catch up to him.

"What are you doing?" she asked.

"Going where there's more foot traffic," he said. "This is a side street off the town green. We need to be on the corner to direct shoppers toward the bookstore."

He said this in a matter-of-fact way as if it was the most logical thing in the world to go stand on a corner dressed as Santa and an elf. Savy was not having it. She stopped walking. It took Joaquin a couple of paces to realize she wasn't behind him. He paused, putting the heavy wooden board down, and looked back at her.

"Problem?"

"I am not going to stand in the center of town dressed like an elf," she said. "I love Maisy and I love her bookstore but this is asking too much. Public humiliation was not a part of the bargain when I came to help her out."

He studied her for a moment. He looked as if he was undecided as to what to say. Savy almost told him not to bother since there was nothing he could say that would make her humiliate herself in front of the entire town of Fairdale.

Finally, he just sighed and hefted the sign up onto his shoulder. "Suit yourself," he said. "But since it's going to take a Christmas miracle to save Maisy's bookstore, I for one am willing to make an ass of myself if it helps her keep her shop."

With that he turned and walked away, striding up the sidewalk like the most badass Santa ever.

Save Maisy's bookstore? What was that supposed to mean? Savy ran after him.

"Hold up there, Kris Kringle," she said. She scooted around in front of him and planted herself so he was forced to stop. "What do you mean 'save Maisy's bookstore'?"

"I can't say," he said.

"Yes, you can."

"No, I can't," he said. "I was eavesdropping and I only heard part of the conversation."

"That's so rude," she said.

"I didn't mean to," he said. "I was dazed and confused and stumbled into the office—"

"Wait, why were you dazed and confused?" she asked.

"Because I had just finished kissing you, Red," he said.

Even behind the Santa beard the look he gave her was smokin' hot. Savy refused to get sidetracked even though her temperature had just spiked and she was sweating beneath the polyester fibers of her hideous outfit. She made a circular motion with her one free hand, signaling for him to continue.

"So, after you bolted upstairs, I went to the office to see what else needed to be done," he said. "The door was ajar and I heard Maisy talking to someone on the phone. I didn't want to interrupt so I figured I'd cool my heels until she was done. That's when I heard her say, 'So what you're saying is, we'll lose everything if we don't have the money by the end of the year.' She sounded upset, very upset. That's why I stepped up to be Santa when Ryder had to go. I'm worried that they might lose the bookstore, Red."

"Ah," Savannah gasped. "Do you know who was she talking to?"

"No, she never said their name, and after I heard that bit I ducked out of there because I knew I was out of line."

"Do you think Ryder knows?"

Quino shrugged, which looked silly in the Santa suit, but Savy didn't even smile. She was too consumed with worry over her friend's shop.

"He hasn't said anything to me."

"Maybe it's not that bad," Savy said. "Maybe you misunderstood."

"Maybe." He didn't sound like he believed that. "But like I said, she sounded . . . upset."

"Oh, man, how did I not notice we were in trouble? It had to have been Jeri she was talking to. Why didn't she tell me? I could help!"

"Breathe, Red," he said. "It sounds like she's got some time, but we have to make sure that the store does some killer business for the next month."

"Breathe? How can I breathe?" she demanded. "Did you know that thirty percent of small businesses fail in their first two years and fifty percent fail in the first five years? This is not good. Not good!"

"Yeah, I know," he said. "Which is why I'm dressed like Saint Nick and off to work the corner." He paused and grimaced slightly. "Oh, that sounded very wrong."

This time she did laugh, mostly because the image of him doing a pole dance in his Santa costume on the lamppost on the corner popped into her head and she couldn't shake it.

"Well, Mr. C., looks like it's time for you to go do the wild thing, because we are going to pimp the shizzle out of the Happily Ever After Bookstore," she said. She winked at him and then spread her arms wide and jiggled her front back and forth in a full-on shimmy shake. "Come on, work it, Santa, work it. Boom chica wah-wah."

"Stop," he said. He closed his eyes as if he couldn't bear to watch her and then he popped one open as if he couldn't bear not to. "I am dressed as an icon of all that is pure and good. I am not slutting up the Santa suit."

"Really?" she asked. She arched an eyebrow at him. "Then why do you keep a naughty list?"

"My God, it's hot out here, isn't it?" he asked. He tugged at the front of his velvet suit as if trying to find an opening for some air.

She laughed and then picked up one side of the heavy wooden sign. "Come on, if we're going to drive the people to Maisy's shop and save her from bankruptcy, we've got to get moving."

The center of town was in full holiday shopping mode. The foot traffic was thick and Santa and his reluctant elf worked the crowd, pointing them in the direction of the bookstore while handing out candy canes and posing for pictures.

Joaquin had the laugh down and Savy saw more than one child gaze at him in wonder with their eyes wide as they quivered with the hope that he was the real deal. One intrepid boy approached them, giving Quino a side-eye. He was clearly a doubter, which meant he was Savy's people, all right.

"He's a fake," the boy said to Savy.

She looked down at him, wondering what was the best

way to play this. She reached into her cloth sack and pulled out a candy cane. She held it out to him and he took it, turning it over in his hands.

"I've seen these candy canes at the store," he said. "They're not made by elves at the North Pole."

"That's because we're too busy making toys," she said.

"Toy companies make toys," he countered.

Savy blew one red curl off her forehead and fixed him with a hard stare. "Who do you think works at toy factories?" The boy was quiet. "That's right. Elves."

"No way," he said. He was short and skinny, with close-cropped hair and a missing front tooth.

"How old are you, kid?" she asked.

"Old enough not to believe that fat men in red suits can come down chimneys," he said. He crossed his arms over his chest and stared back at her.

Savy glanced over her shoulder, looking for backup, but Joaquin was taking pictures with an adorable set of twin girls, both of whom looked completely enamored with him. It seemed women of every age responded to the Solis charm. Every woman but her, she reminded herself.

"So, you're eight?" Savy guessed.

"Seven," the boy said.

Savy had her own issues with the holidays but she really hated that this kid was such a doubter. It seemed to her the magic of the holiday should last at least until a kid hit the double digits, like ten. Ten was a good age to move on from the folklore.

"Well, you know what they say," she said. "If you don't believe, you don't receive."

The boy pursed his lips, considering her words. It looked as if this possibility had never occurred to him. Savy kept her face blank and turned away to hand out candy canes to other children in the area. The boy remained watching Joaquin with a suspicious gaze.

Savy carefully sidled up to Santa. She jerked her head in the direction of the boy and whispered, "We have a doubter at two o'clock."

Joaquin glanced past her at the boy. He gave her a slow nod and said, "I've got this."

"Tyrese Walters," he said. "It's nice to see you. How have you been this year? Good?"

The boy's jaw dropped. Savy turned away so he couldn't see her smile.

"Uh, y-yes, sir," the boy stammered. He stared at Joaquin in shock.

"You did apologize to Mrs. Dwight for throwing sidewalk chalk into her swimming pool, didn't you?"

The boy's eyes went wide and he pressed his hands to the side of his face as if he couldn't believe the big guy knew what he'd done. Then he straightened up. "Yes, sir. I even jumped into her pool and got every bit of chalk out."

Joaquin stared down at the boy while stroking his beard as if considering Tyrese's answer. "I guess you get to stay on the good list, then. Ho ho ho."

"Phew." Tyrese sagged a bit in his shoes and Joaquin clapped him on the shoulder with one hand.

"You should probably go give your mom a hand," Joaquin said. He pointed to a woman who was struggling with a shopping bag as she came out of the shop behind them.

"Yes, sir." Tyrese hopped to it. Three paces away, he whipped around and said, "Since I'm on the good list, I just want to say that if it's not too much trouble, I'd love a new bike for Christmas, one with gears and a headlight. Please!"

The boy spun around and ran to help his mother before Joaquin could say a word. He turned to Savy with a rueful look. "Remind me to ask his parents if he's getting a new bike for Christmas. If not, I have some shopping to do."

"I take it you know them," she said.

"I went to high school with his dad, Carter," he said. "He's the football coach over at Fairdale U now. Thankfully, Tyrese didn't recognize me."

Savy nodded. That made sense. "Yeah, otherwise our doubter would have gone into full-on disbeliever."

"Not on my watch," he said. Savy smiled.

A couple walked by and she checked her bag to hand

them the last of the candy canes. The bag was empty. She took out her cell phone and glanced at the time. They'd been here for three hours. Huh, it hadn't felt that long. She glanced at the man beside her and he knelt down to hug a toddler. He was scary good at this; the kid didn't even cry.

"We're out of candy, should we head back?" she asked.

"Yes, please," he said. "These boots are a half size too small and my dogs are killing me."

He picked up the sign and led the way. Savy fell in behind him, waving to people as she went. It occurred to her that if anyone had ever told her that she would spend her morning dressed as an elf, passing out candy canes with a hot Santa by her side, she would have laughed in their face.

What was crazy was that the gig had actually been fun. She scrolled through the pictures on her cell phone. There were tons of adorable shots of Joaquin with kids, babies, and a few older ladies who'd enjoyed his attention. Then there was one of the two of them.

It was a posed shot in front of the Happily Ever After Bookstore sign. The woman taking the picture suggested that Savy kiss Joaquin's cheek and she had, kicking up one leg in a playful pose. Even with her critical publicist's eye, it was a great shot and she would absolutely use it to pimp the bookstore's holiday titles. After all, what was better to fight off the holiday blues than a holiday romantic comedy? Nothing, except perhaps some spiked eggnog on the side.

"Hey, that's a good one," Joaquin said. He had put the sign down on the sidewalk in front of the shop and was glancing over her shoulder at the pic.

Savy started feeling guilty for looking at the pic too long, which was totally ridiculous as it was just a work thing. She shrugged. "Yeah, it's okay."

Joaquin tugged on his beard until it was below his chin. Then he grinned at her. "Of course, mistletoe kisses are totally better."

He let go of his beard and it bounced back up to cover his face, but it didn't muffle his laugh as he strode up the walkway to the shop.

"That's not what I meant, and you know it," she said to his back. She hurried to follow in his wake but he didn't slow down and she felt as if she'd just lost a debate she didn't even know she was in. Darn that man! And how did he actually make that horrible Santa suit sexy? Because he did, he totally did. Argh!

Chapter Six

Quino could hear her behind him but he resisted the urge to look around just like he resisted the urge to stare at her whenever she was in his vicinity. There was something about Savannah Wilson that flipped his switch. Maybe it was her sassy personality, or that crazy mane of red hair, or maybe it was the vulnerability he saw in her pretty green eyes. Probably, it was a combination of all of the above. He didn't much care, except he wanted her to give them, him, a chance.

Now that they had a common purpose, saving Maisy's shop, maybe Red would actually take the time to get to know him. Up to now, she'd been civil but avoided being alone with him as though she thought he had a bad case of fleas. Today was the longest amount of time they'd ever spent on their own and he liked it—he liked it a lot. More accurately, he liked her. She talked to everyone and laughed with everyone and managed to charm people silly within minutes of meeting them. Is that what she'd done to him?

No. He thought back to the day he'd met her. He still remembered his first sight of her as she burst into the office of the bookstore, where he'd been talking to Ryder. She'd been wearing a slim skirt and a pretty blouse. Her long red hair had been an untamed mass of curls around her head and she had completely ignored him to give Ryder the business about how he was botching his courtship of Maisy. Within seconds, Quino had been 100 percent smitten.

When he'd asked her out, she had straight up refused him. That was the moment he fell in love with her and he'd been pining ever since. He supposed it was bad of him to use Maisy's financial troubles to get closer to Savannah, but if she was really planning to leave, he was running out of time. Also, if it helped Maisy keep her shop open, it was a good deed no matter the motivation, right? Yeah, he wasn't going to look at it too closely.

As he stepped up onto the front porch, he spun around and took Savy's hand in his, pulling her past the family of blow-up snowmen that Ryder had put up that morning, over to the side of the porch. Since they hadn't had any snow and the day was only in the midfifties, the snow family seemed a bit premature, but given that he was dressed as Santa, he couldn't really judge, now, could he?

"What are you doing?" she asked. She glanced up as if looking for mistletoe and Quino grinned. He did like his women smart.

"We need to talk," he said. He could hear the soft sound of Christmas music playing in the shop and a peek through the window showed that the place was rocking. King George, the gray bookstore tabby cat, was sitting on the counter swatting a tinsel garland as if it were a snake he had caught.

"What about?"

"Should we say anything to Maisy or Ryder about what I overheard?" he asked.

"No," she said. "We don't even know if Ryder knows that the bookstore is in trouble."

Quino made a face. He didn't like withholding information from his friend.

Savy met his gaze. "I know you think you should tell him," she said. "But Maisy was talking to someone in confidence.

Probably, she's going to tell him on her own, in her own way. We need to stay out of it."

He considered her words. "I suppose, but what if she needs help and she doesn't ask? She could be trying to shoulder all of this worry alone."

"Well, someone was on the other end of that call, so someone knows," she said. "Maybe it was Ryder and perhaps the chance to talk to them about it will come up, but in the meantime, I think we need to play it cool and just look for opportunities to help."

"Fair enough," he said. He looked down at her and was struck by the earnest expression on her face. She cared. A lot. And wasn't that a heartwarming thing to see, because he couldn't help but wonder what it would feel like to be on the receiving end of that sort of care and concern. "We need to make some plans, though. We have got to keep the foot traffic coming into this shop for the next month."

"I'm already way ahead of you," she said. "I have a calendar of events for the next few weeks that will blow your beard off. I just wish . . ."

Her voice trailed off and Quino found himself leaning in, eager to hear what it was she wished for. "What?"

She waved a dismissive hand. "Never mind, it's just a crazy idea."

"Maybe crazy is exactly what we need," he said.

She opened her mouth to answer him when the front door opened, and Maisy poked her head out. She had to hop up on her tiptoes to see them over the snowmen.

"Hey, you two, how did it go?"

"Great!" Savy said. "We ran out of candy canes, so we figured we'd come back and see how things are going here."

"The BOGO idea was genius," Maisy said. "We're clearing out some inventory and bringing in cash. Do you mind taking a turn at the register? Jeri's got to get home to her kids and I'm expecting an important phone call."

"Not at all," Savannah said. She glanced at Quino and muttered under her breath, "We'll talk later."

He watched as she bustled into the shop behind Maisy. *Yes!* They were going to talk later. He wanted to do a fist pump or a dab but he didn't think a Santa should be caught doing that when he was standing alone on the porch of a romance bookstore. Instead, he struck a pose, waving at people coming in and out and walking by on the street.

When the heat of the suit and the itching of the beard got to be too much, he decided to call it a day. He wondered if he should disregard what Savy had said and talk to Ryder about what he'd overheard. He rejected the idea. He didn't know if Ryder knew and if he didn't, Savannah was right, it was really up to Maisy to tell him. The best thing he could do for his friends would be to brainstorm with Savy about how to save the bookstore.

He glanced through the window into the shop and saw Savy chatting with a customer while ringing up her purchases. There wasn't a woman alive who could pull off wearing the elf suit as well as Savy did. As if drawn to her by a force he simply didn't have the strength to fight, he found himself pulling open the front door and entering the shop.

He had hours until Desi was due home from Asheville, and according to her last text, she was shopping like she had unlimited credit. It was just the neighborly thing to do to help Maisy out. And if it meant he had to be in close proximity to Savy all afternoon, well, he'd just have to suffer through it.

"Nice suit, bro," Ryder said from the doorway to the office. "Thanks for stepping in for me. We had an electrical problem at the house I'm working on."

"Nothing serious, I hope," Quino said.

"It didn't burn to the ground if that's what you mean," Ryder said. He looked stressed. "Come on, you look like you're going to suffocate in that thing."

He waved Quino into the office and Quino headed to the bathroom to peel off the heavy suit and change into jeans and his Christmas sweater. He made quick work of it, happy to lose the beard and the hat, which was making his head sweat. He ran his fingers through his hair, relieved to feel the air on his scalp. He hung up the suit and left it in the bathroom, joining Ryder, who was sitting at the drafting table he still maintained in Maisy's shop.

When Maisy had inherited the old Victorian and hired Ryder to renovate it, she'd set up a work area for him in the main office. Even though Ryder had started taking on new projects of his own, he still worked out of the bookstore.

Quino knew it was so he could spend his days near Maisy and he was surprised by the sudden spurt of envy he felt. Oh, he was happy for his friend. If anyone deserved a loving relationship, it was Ryder. But Quino keenly felt the lack of such a thing in his life, and he had no idea how he was going to get Savy, the only woman he'd ever imagined in that role, to give it a go. And after their kiss this morning, he was more determined than ever.

"Look at you," Ryder said as he glanced up from his desk. "You look like you just lost about forty pounds."

"It's called the pillow diet," Quino said. Ryder laughed, and Quino studied his friend, wondering if he knew how precarious the bookstore's finances were. Given that Ryder seemed relaxed and wasn't out front cajoling customers to buy books, he figured he didn't. Oh, boy. He had to play this smart. "So, how is Maisy liking the book business?"

Ryder got a warm look in his eyes and said, "She loves it. It suits her perfectly. Connecting readers to books, it's her passion and she's so good at it."

Quino glanced toward the door. Yeah, he'd seen Maisy in her element over the past few months. He couldn't imagine how devastated she'd be to lose this place.

"But I think the bigger question is how are you and Savy getting along?" Ryder asked. "I saw you two out on the street corner when I drove back to the shop. You looked to be working well together, and by working well, I mean she wasn't trying to bite you."

"Ha! Funny. Yeah, it's been an interesting day," Quino said. His mind went back to their kiss and suddenly he wondered where Savannah was in the bookstore, and was it too soon to try and kiss her again? Probably, but his feet were already moving in the direction of the door. "That reminds me. I have a thing . . ."

"Uh-huh," Ryder said, but Quino closed the door, not bothering to hear what else Ryder had to say.

Instead, he paused outside the door to get his bearings and scanned the area for Red. He didn't see his elf anywhere.

When he did spot her, he noticed she was talking to Hannah Phillips, the local veterinarian, who had an office down the street. He knew that the two women, along with Maisy, had all attended Fairdale University together and Hannah had helped them save King George, the sad little kitten they'd found abandoned on the bookstore porch six months ago. He felt a tug on his shoelace. Speaking of the devil.

He bent over and scooped up the gray tabby, who settled into his hands as if he'd just been waiting to be picked up. He rubbed the side of his face against Quino's sweater and made a sound that was more chatter than meow. Perry, chief cat wrangler, thought Little G believed he was a person and was trying to talk. Quino glanced around the bookstore. There were at least five different conversations going on, so the little guy certainly overheard enough chatter. Perhaps Perry was onto something.

He approached Red. He didn't really have an excuse to talk to her. Their gig as Santa and helper was done, but he figured he should update her with his theory that Ryder didn't know anything. They were in this saving-the-bookstore thing together, after all.

"Hi, Quino, how're things at Shadow Pine?" Hannah asked as he joined them. She paused to scratch King George under the chin.

"Good," he said. "We've had a nice run of good health out there, even Esther, who's getting up there in years, has been feeling her oats."

"Glad to hear it," she said. "Luke said as much when I saw him the other day."

Hannah glanced up from Little G, who swatted at her hand when she stopped petting him as if he thought he could antagonize some love from her. It worked. She immediately began to rub his head.

"Now you've done it," Quino said. "He'll never let you leave."

Hannah laughed. "All right, King George, that's all the love you get for now. I'm off to deliver a litter of puppies at the pound." She turned to Savannah. "We're overdue for a girls' night out, Savy."

"It would help if your patients would stop dropping litters every time we set one up," Savannah said.

"Agreed." Hannah made a phone gesture with her hand and said, "Call me."

She walked over to the counter where Maisy was ringing up sales, leaving Quino with Savy. Of course, King George decided to leap out of Quino's arms at that moment to chase a reflection on the floor made by something sparkly in the sunlight. Quino was left staring at Savy in her elf suit, not remembering why he'd needed to see her, because she laughed at Little G's antics and the sight of her smile made his brain fritz.

"George is such a scamp," she said. She shook her head. "The other day when I was bagging Mrs. Di Marco's books, he climbed in the bag. She almost walked out with him. If the bells on the doors hadn't scared him silly, she might have."

Quino forced his gaze away from her face and looked at George, whose head was whipping from side to side as he couldn't seem to figure out why the light he was so certain he'd caught between his paws kept escaping. Quino felt his own lips part in a smile.

He turned back to find Savy looking at him with the same sort of awareness he felt for her. Well, that was encouraging.

"So, Snowflake Sparklepants, here's the latest intel," he said.

She frowned at the elf name, the severity of which was ruined by the pointy ears sticking out of her hat. Then tipped her head to the side. "What do you know?"

"I talked to Ryder and it's more like what *he doesn't* know," he said. He lowered his voice and backed her up away from anyone who could overhear them. "I don't think he knows that the store is in trouble."

"I was afraid of that." Savy heaved a sigh and then asked, "Are you sure?"

"Not completely, but he was way too relaxed while talking about Maisy and the shop," he said. "I know him. Ryder would be freaking out if he thought she was going to lose the place she's worked so hard for."

Savy nodded. "I can see that. And I can see why she didn't tell him. They're still pretty new in their relationship and she might be thinking that dumping all of this on him will be the kiss of—"

"Kiss of what?" Maisy popped up beside them and Savy let out a little yelp. She looked at Quino in panic and he glanced up over her head. *Perfect.*

"Kiss of mistletoe," he said. He pointed up and both Savy and Maisy glanced at the bough of mistletoe hanging overhead. "You know. You're supposed to kiss if you get caught under it."

Savannah glared at him and he shrugged. She looked resigned, which was not exactly how he'd pictured their second kiss, but given that they had an audience he figured this one would be much more innocent anyway.

"May I, Ms. Holly Brightbuttons?"

If anything, Savy's glare got even more severe. With a put-upon sigh that he had a feeling was more for show, she said, "Fine."

Quino was certain that today was going to go down as one of his most favorite days ever. Not only had he gotten to kiss Savy once, and it had been even more amazing than he'd imagined, they had discovered a common purpose together, which he hoped would get her to see him in a new light. Preferably, the knight-in-shining-armor light as the man who helped her save her best friend's bookstore. And now he was going to kiss her again. Yes, this was definitely the best day ever.

Unlike last time, he took the initiative. He bent down and pressed his mouth against hers. He didn't touch her in any other way. He didn't have to. The magic that had been between them before flared up again and she kissed him back with just enough heat to make him more certain than ever that it would take him a lifetime to get his fill of this woman.

When he pulled back, he could see Maisy bouncing up and down on her toes as if she was giddy that she was witnessing what she thought was a first kiss. He grinned, especially when Savy had that dreamy glazed look in her eyes. He had done that. He had made her lose herself in their kiss even if it was just for a moment.

He leaned close and said, "Crazy hot, Red, admit this thing between us is crazy hot."

She lifted one eyebrow higher than the other and shrugged. Again, she said, "Meh."

Quino grinned. He leaned back. "Really?"

"I could kiss anyone under the mistletoe and it would be the same," she said.

"Is that so?" he asked. He crossed his arms over his chest.

"Now, you two, this is all in fun," Maisy said. Her expression was alarmed as if she thought they might square off in a full-on argument. Customers were beginning to stare. Quino didn't care.

"Yes, that's so," Savy said.

She looked away from him and scanned the room. It was bustling, thick with customers taking advantage of the buy-one, get-one sale. Quino didn't know what she was looking for until her gaze landed on John Michael, Hannah's brother, who owned and operated a local dairy farm. Savy snatched the pointy elf hat off her head and tossed it at Quino, pelting him in the face. Then she strode toward John Michael, who was holding a stack of books for his sister with the beleaguered look of a man waiting on a woman while she shopped.

Quino would have felt bad for the guy, but when he glanced up he noted that John Michael was standing under some mistletoe. Uh-oh. He had a feeling he didn't like where this was going. Savannah stalked the poor guy like she was King George and he was a light beam on the floor. When she stood right in front of him, she pointed up and then gave him a come-hither smile that made Quino's mouth go dry.

She'd never looked at him like that. He was torn between wanting to punch John Michael in the throat really hard, which made him feel awful because he'd always liked John Michael, or snatch Red up and toss her over his shoulder while he stormed out of the shop. Of course, he would never do either of those things because the alpha male thing was so not his jam, but the thoughts remained.

"It's okay," Maisy said. "She doesn't know what she's doing."

"Really?" Quino cut his glance to Maisy. "Because it sure looks like she knows what she's doing to me."

Maisy wrung her hands in front of her and stared at Quino through her rectangular-framed glasses. She looked stressed. She waved him down to her level, which was a considerable drop. He kept one eye on Savannah while lowering himself down to Maisy's height. Savy had just put her arms around John Michael's neck, and Quino felt a surge of dark emotion roil through him. It was an ugly feeling he couldn't identify. He'd never felt anything like it before. It took him a moment to name it. Jealousy. Oh, ick, he did not like this.

"The thing is"—Maisy cupped her mouth and whispered in his ear—"John Michael is gay."

"What?" Quino snapped his head in her direction. They were nose to nose. "What did you say?"

She looked at him and then glanced at Savy. Quino followed her gaze and watched as Savy rose up on her toes and pressed her mouth on John Michael's. It was clear to see from their posture that there was nothing crazy hot happening there. In fact, John Michael looked like a mannequin that Savy was practicing giving mouth-to-mouth to while his sister watched the goings-on, looking like she was trying not to laugh. She failed.

When Savy finally gave up kissing John Michael, he gave her a weak smile and then grabbed his sister by the hand and dragged her out the door. Hannah was full-on laughing now, waving at Savannah as she went.

"Savannah doesn't know?" Quino asked.

Maisy bit her lip and shook her head. "John Michael only came out a few years ago before Savannah moved back to town and we really haven't seen much of him."

Quino straightened up. The relief he felt was incredible. It made him laugh, a big deep belly laugh, because he no longer felt that unpleasant coiling feeling in his gut. Savannah looked at him and scowled. As she approached, her chin tipped up and a fire flared in her green gaze.

"Break it to her gently," Maisy said. Then she ran. Quino didn't blame her one bit.

He wasn't going to do it here in a roomful of people, however. Instead, he grabbed her hand and led her back to the office, where they could talk in peace. When they arrived Maisy and Ryder were draped around each other and Quino tipped his head toward the door.

"Isn't it time for lunch?" he asked.

"No—" Ryder began, but Maisy elbowed him hard and said, "Yes, in fact, we'll just be in the kitchen."

She took Ryder's hand in hers and led him out of the room. Quino shut the door behind them and turned to face Savannah. She was standing with her arms crossed, looking bored.

"So, Gingerbread Twinkle-Toes," he said.

"Stop. They're just getting worse and worse," she said. She narrowed her eyes. "What do you want?"

"How was that kiss with John Michael?" he asked. "Meh? Or crazy hot?"

Savannah glared at him. "I can't talk to you when I'm dressed like this."

She turned on her heel and walked to the staff bathroom. Much to Quino's shock and delight, she didn't close the door, opting to leave it open enough so that she could still talk to him while she changed out of the elf suit. He was kind of bummed about that. He dug those stripy tights, plus the nicknames.

"Well, what's your verdict?" he asked. "A mistletoe kiss is a mistletoe kiss? No big deal."

"I know what you're trying to get me to do," she said. He could hear the sound of clothes being removed and replaced. He tried to stop picturing the swish of fabric against her skin. He failed. "You want me to admit that our kiss was amazing and the one with John Michael wasn't. Well, I'm not going to."

"No?" he asked. He could hear her pant a bit as she struggled back into her clothes. The offer to help was right on the tip of his tongue but he wisely choked it down.

She stepped back into the office, back in her regular clothes. He acutely missed his elf.

"No," she said. "The kisses were exactly the same. If I was blindfolded, I wouldn't even be able to tell them apart."

Quino grinned. She was so full of it. "That's interesting."

She looked surprised. "Really?"

"Yes, especially since John Michael is gay and watching you kiss him was like watching a person in CPR class try to give mouth-to-mouth to a dummy."

"John Michael's gay?" she asked. Her eyes went wide. "Oh, thank God. I thought I was losing my skill set. I mean, I get that he might not want to have been kissed by his sister's friend but, jeez, he was so unresponsive I thought you had ruined me for . . ."

Chapter Seven

RED stopped talking. Quino rested his elbow on a book-case and planted his chin in his hand. He stared at her and said, "Oh, don't stop now. Go on. You're just getting to the good part."

Savannah's eyes narrowed into slits. "There are no good parts."

"Oh, sure there are, just back it up a little and tell me again how you thought I ruined you," he said.

"You're impossible."

"It's part of my charm."

"I'm not talking about this with you."

"Aw, come on," he said.

"No," she said. She crossed her arms over her chest. "I'm sure you think it's just hilarious that I made such an idiot of myself and poor John Michael. No wonder he looked like he'd turned to stone when I cornered him. I am completely not his type."

She put a hand over her face and Quino felt his amuse-ment vanish. Poor Red. He took his arm off the bookshelf and approached her cautiously, not sure if she was going to take a swing at him or not.

"Hey, it wasn't that bad," he said.

"You forget," she said. "I was on one end of it. It was that bad, and I owe him an apology."

"And now you're finally going to admit that our kiss was off the charts, yes?" he asked.

"Your ego is insufferable," she said. She glowered. He didn't care. He needed to get her to admit that what crackled between them was something special even if he had to drag every syllable out of her. "Okay, fine. Yes, our kiss was spectacular. There, I admit it. Happy?"

"Ecstatic," he said. "So much so that I may have to kiss you again just to prove to myself and you that it wasn't a fluke."

"No, no more kissing," she said. She glanced up and checked the ceiling for mistletoe. Quino made a mental note to hang some in the office at his first opportunity. "We have a situation and we need to make a plan."

"Situation?" he asked. Now that he was thinking about kissing her, he really couldn't think of anything else.

"Yes, remember, before Maisy appeared and we got sidetracked with the kissing talk, we were discussing what to do about the bookstore," she said.

"Oh, yeah," he agreed.

"So, we need a plan, a big one," she said. "I've been working on some angles but I'm not making any headway. We need to come up with more stuff. You're the lover of all things Christmas, and I'm not, so I think we should have a brainstorming sesh."

"Like a date?" he asked.

"No!" she scoffed. "Not like a date, like a meeting, a business meeting."

"Oh, well, that disappoints," he said.

She rolled her eyes, and he knew she was trying not to be charmed. At least, he thought she was trying not to be charmed. Red was tricky to read. Also, he'd never met a woman who was so resistant to dating him. If she hadn't responded to his kiss, he would have crawled off into some deep dark hole and licked his wounds, but Red was a mystery because she did respond more enthusiastically than any woman he'd ever known, which made this whole thing even more confusing for him.

He knew the only way he was going to figure out what was going on in that pretty head of hers was to spend more time with her. Until he figured out what exactly was between them, he was going all in.

"All right, what's your weekend look like?" he asked.

"I'm working in the shop today and tomorrow and then I have a thing on Sunday evening," she said.

She picked up a wooden box, about the size of a shoebox, painted gold with the word *Wishes* in black lettering. Quino could think of about a hundred wishes he could stuff into that box but they all involved Savy and were most definitely not PG-13.

"A thing?" he asked. He felt that weird roiling feeling in his chest again. He didn't like it. He forced his face to remain blank.

"A club meeting," she said.

Quino felt the jealousy inside stand down. He shook his head. He really needed to get a handle on this. "All right, I have a private riding lesson out of town tomorrow so I'm gone most of the day. That leaves tomorrow night, Saturday night—are you available then?"

Savy studied his face. "Do not get any funny ideas. Just because it's date night does not mean we're having a date. In fact, let's keep it on neutral territory. I'll meet you at Perk Up, the coffee shop in town."

"How romantic," he said. She ignored him.

"Seven o'clock work for you?"

Quino thought about the schedule at the stable. He should be done for the day by then. "Yeah, that works."

"Good. In the meantime, see if you can get anything out of Ryder," she said. "And I'll do the same with Maisy."

"Yes, ma'am," he said. He curbed the urge to salute, figuring it wouldn't be well received.

She sat down at her desk and Quino knew he was dismissed.

"So, tomorrow," he said. She nodded without looking at him. She had fired up her laptop and was already diving into her work. He couldn't resist adding, "I'll wear something pretty for you."

She didn't look up. He waited a moment for his words to sink in, in five, four, three . . .

She glanced up with a scowl and said, "Go."

He went.

With a hug for Maisy and knuckle bump for Ryder, Quino left the Happily Ever After Bookstore and headed for his pickup truck, which was parked on the street. He pulled out his cell phone and checked the app he had installed years ago that told him where his sister, Desi, was at all times and vice versa. It was getting late and she should be almost done with her shopping and about to head back home or already en route.

She didn't show up on the app. While he didn't like it, he knew that there were some dead spots on the route between Fairdale and Asheville, so he'd just head home and check again there. He drove through town, noting the decorations and the crowds of people shopping. He felt the crisp nip of late autumn in the air and felt renewed as if everything in life was suddenly possible.

Quino knew it was because after months of waiting, he had finally managed to slip beneath the polite facade with which Red had kept him at arm's length. Yes, it was mostly because Maisy's shop was in trouble and Savy would do anything to help her friend, but he also believed that their kiss had changed everything. She could deny it all she wanted but he had felt everything shift between them after that clinch under the mistletoe.

He turned onto the winding road that led to his stables. He hadn't planned to be away as long as he'd been. Lanie O'Brien was his right-hand woman and he knew if she'd needed him she would have sent word. She'd been with him ever since she'd arrived in Fairdale nine years ago. She was a specialist in equine therapy and had convinced him that the Shadow Pine Stables could be so much more than they were.

During his parents' time owning the stables, it had been a place for riding. Lessons in dressage, his mother's specialty, and trail rides, his father's portion of the business, were all the stable offered. When Lanie arrived, Quino had used her expertise to expand upon their standard offerings and now they were one of the premier places for equine therapy in the state. Luke Masters, his other key employee, had arrived about four years ago and had taken over the management of the stables. Luke now had a crew of stable hands that he employed year-round, leaving Quino to focus on the bigger picture of running a prosperous stable, and it gave him more time with Desi.

Upon her twentieth birthday, Quino had realized he needed to make sure that if anything happened to him, Desi would be able to take care of herself. He'd found her an occupational therapist and together they'd been working on her ability to navigate her social-emotional agnosia. Since her accident, Desi struggled with reading the expressions of others, which impaired her own ability to communicate effectively. She'd made tremendous progress, and she was good with people she was close to, otherwise he never would have let her go to Asheville by herself, but still he worried.

Quino parked his truck by the main house and strode over to the corral, seeing one of his favorite horses, an old nag named Esther, standing by the rail. At twenty-nine years old, Esther was too old to do anything at the stables, but she had been his mother's favorite horse and was a living connection to her that Quino cherished.

Esther recognized him and tossed her long gray mane. She bobbed her head and showed what remained of her big square teeth in what Quino supposed was a scowl. Esther was a notorious cranky pants, and the only person she had ever loved was his mom, Beatriz.

"Hey, Esther," he said. "Who's my pretty girl?" He patted her neck and she snuffled and lowered her head, nuzzling the front of his sweater, clearly looking for treats. "Sorry, love, I don't have anything on me right now."

Esther shook her head in disapproval and gave him the

side-eye in a look he and Desi called *a blast of stink eye*. Esther knew how to get her point across with that look. She backed away from him, pawed the ground, and then trotted off with her tail kinked up high. Quino grinned. She reminded him of Savannah in her own sassy way.

"You're being a bit of a diva, Esther," he cried after her.

She snorted and trotted to the other side of the corral where Lanie was standing with Luke. Quino walked around the fence to talk to his staff. He was also hoping one of them had a carrot or a slice of apple he could give to Esther. He shook his head. Man, he was whipped, horsewhipped. The play on words made him smile and he approached his crew with a grin.

Lanie was about his age. Of medium height and build, she lived in riding clothes and kept her thick black hair tied in one long braid that reached halfway down her back. She had a round face dusted with freckles, and bright-blue eyes that sparkled like sunlight on blue water. She was open and honest with her thoughts and feelings, and when she was in a temper, it was best to stay out of her way. Quino trusted her implicitly.

Luke was her complete and total opposite, and yet, like Lanie, Quino also trusted Luke absolutely. Luke was a big man with a thick head of dark red hair and a robust beard. He rarely spoke, but when he did it was worth listening to. He had an innate ability to understand the horses in his care. He knew before a mare when she was carrying and he could tell from a half mile away if one of the horses was coming up lame. Quino had never seen anyone, not even his father, so horse smart. About women, however, Luke was as dumb as the fencepost he was standing beside.

Everyone who worked at Shadow Pine knew that Lanie had been crushing on Luke since the day he arrived four years ago, everyone except Luke. Even now, Quino could see she was looking at Luke from beneath her thick dark lashes with a longing that made Quino's chest hurt with sympathy pangs. Luke, per usual, didn't seem to notice. What a dumbass.

"Lanie, Luke, how's it going?" he asked.

They exchanged a look that immediately put Quino on edge. It was the sort of look that told him they'd been preparing for him to come home so they could tell him something, and he was betting it wasn't something good.

"What is it? Are the horses okay?" he asked.

"Yeah," Luke said right away. "The horses are fine."

"Okay." Quino glanced between them. They said nothing. "Can you give me a hint?"

"It's Desi," Lanie said. She held up her phone and showed it to Quino. It was a text message from his sister to Lanie.

It read: Take care of Quino for me. I'll be in touch when I can.

Quino shook his head. What could that possibly mean? He glanced up and both Lanie and Luke were looking at him as if he knew what the hell his sister was talking about.

"What does she mean?" he asked.

Luke cursed. "We were hoping you knew."

"That's it?" Quino asked. "She didn't say anything else."

Lanie shrugged and took back her phone. "No. And when I texted her back, she didn't answer."

"What does that even mean?" he asked. "Take care of Quino? Like for dinner tonight? She knows I know how to cook. And what does she mean she'll be in touch?"

Quino pulled out his phone and checked his messages. There was nothing. Not a text. Not a voice mail. Nothing. He glanced up to find Lanie and Luke watching him—their expressions were grim.

"What do you think she meant?" he asked.

"I've got nothing," Luke said. "Sorry."

"I don't know, either," Lanie said. "Maybe she was just letting me know she was going to be late tonight."

"Why wouldn't she text me herself?" Quino asked.

"Maybe there's a dude involved," Luke said.

Quino thought he might have a heart attack. Not that his sister might be on a date. She'd been on dates before, but rather because if she was on a date and hadn't told him, it could be that she'd hooked up with a bad guy. This was the one thing he worried about above all others. After the accident that had left Desi in a coma, she'd had months of physical therapy to relearn how to walk and talk and write. Much of it came back to her very quickly but there were a few things, like her ability to accurately assess people, that had been lost for good.

Being so bighearted, she'd never been a great judge of character to begin with, but after the coma, the damage she had sustained to her right frontal lobe had made her even more vulnerable. She believed every sob story she heard and had once even tried to give her car to a man whose car had just been repossessed because she felt sorry for him. Quino felt a light sweat break out on his forehead. He could feel the panic coming but then he reminded himself that Desi had come a long way and it was still light out. Text messages were easily misinterpreted and he was not going to freak out. Not yet anyway.

"I'm sure she's fine," he said.

Both Lanie and Luke looked at him in surprise. In truth, he was surprised himself but he had agreed to let her drive to Asheville by herself. He wouldn't have if he didn't believe that she could handle it. She'd been in therapy for years just to get to this point and he wasn't going to doubt her until he had proof positive that bad decisions were being made.

He checked his phone again. Still nothing, because had he really expected to hear from her in the last five seconds? He sighed. He glanced up at Lanie and Luke and saw the same worry he was feeling etched in their faces. Desiree was very close to both of them and he knew they had to be feeling as worried as he was.

"I'm going to go visit Daisy," he said. "If you hear anything from her, call me."

"Will do," Luke said. His voice was low on a normal day; today it sounded as if it was coming from the bottom of a well. It did not make Quino feel any better.

"We promise," Lanie said. She gave a closed-lip smile, the sort of smile people used when the news was bad but they were trying to make it seem not so bad.

Quino walked around the corral, enjoying the crunch of the earth under his work books. The air smelled of fallen leaves and woodsmoke. He glanced up and noted the sky was a gray shade of blue that indicated the temperature was going to drop tonight. He tried not to worry. Desi never made him worry on purpose. She was always thoughtful, always kept in touch when she went places. Maybe the battery in her phone had died and her message to Lanie was a last-ditch message to keep him from stressing. Maybe she couldn't text him directly for some reason.

Yeah, and maybe she was lying dead in a ditch somewhere and her last text had been to Lanie because her name was listed higher up in her contacts than Quino's. He felt his heart rate increase and his palms were sweaty. He was light-headed and thought he might throw up. Maybe he should drive to Asheville and see if he could find her. No, that was crazy.

He'd likely just pass her on her way back home and then she'd dog him for getting worried and being overprotective. She'd gotten a lot pricklier lately about her privacy. Quino frowned. Oh, man, was Luke right? Was there a man involved? Had Desi gotten hooked up with some guy who was trying to convince her that he was the one? Who was just romancing her for her savings account?

Quino waved to a few of the stable hands who were cleaning the stalls and tending the horses as he made his way into the large stall in the back. Daisy was there. She would calm him down. She always did. He heard her whicker and he could see her toss her head, happy to see him.

Daisy had been a racehorse rescue that he'd found five years ago that he'd determined was being neglected by her owner. Quino had spotted her in a pasture in Kentucky. He'd been struck by how lonely she looked in the field all alone and then he'd noticed she was limping. On impulse he'd pulled over his pickup truck and approached the pasture where she stood in the snow. Her brown-and-white coat had been dull, her head hung low. The white spot on her forehead that was in the shape of a daisy caught his eye and he'd thought there was no way a horse with such a whimsical marking should be out in bad weather, looking half-starved and depressed.

He immediately tracked down her owner and bought her, bringing her home with the bay he had just bought at auction. Desi had laughed at him for being a marshmallow, but rehabilitating Daisy became a project for the entire stable and while Daisy loved everyone, it was clear that Quino was her special human.

Daisy's head appeared over the door of her stable. She eyed Quino with an intelligence he always found engaging as if she knew just by looking at him how he was feeling. He opened the door, swinging it out, and stepped inside, closing it after him. Daisy pressed her head against his shoulder. Unlike Esther, Daisy wasn't giving him cupboard love. She nuzzled him because they had a bond.

Despite growing up with horses his entire life, Daisy was the first horse he'd ever felt a spiritual connection with, and he genuinely believed that there had been some divine intervention at work the day he'd found her. To begin with, he'd gotten lost and wasn't supposed to be on that road. The odds of Daisy being by the fence rail where he'd see her were a thousand to one. But there she was and he did stop. People always said the horse needed him, but Quino had always felt that he needed Daisy.

"How're you doing, girl?" he asked.

He ran his hands along her neck, shoulders, and flank. She was so much stronger than the day he'd found her. He marveled at how she'd battled back from such brutal neglect. He remembered when he'd bought her, how hard it was not to put his fist in the face of the asshole who'd let her suffer. He'd happily called animal control on his way out of town just to be certain that the guy wasn't abusing any other animals on his farm but he still wished he could have punched him out just once.

Daisy moved her head toward the shelf where he kept her curry comb. His girl did like her special treatment and Quino chuckled as he patted her side. "All right, princess, I've got time."

He stepped around her to get to the shelf. When he went to grab the comb, he saw a folded piece of paper with his name scrawled in marker across the front. He recognized the handwriting as Desi's. He felt his heart sink as he reached for the note. Had she run away with a man?

He would kill him, Quino thought. If some guy had gotten it into her head that she needed to run away with him instead of coming to Quino to tell him she was in love, he would hunt the bastard down and choke the life out of him with his bare hands. His hand shook as he flipped the paper open and read the note penned in his sister's familiar loopy script.

Hey, Bro,

Don't get mad (too late, Quino thought)*, but I'm on my way to Kenya.*

(What?!)

> *I applied for and was accepted as an intern for the Kenya Elephant Rescue and Rehabilitation Institute. By the time you get this message, I will be halfway to my new home in Africa.*

(Quino felt his knees go weak. Africa? What the hell?)

> *Please know that I love you and that I would have told you, but I know you would have forbidden me to go and we would have had a big fight and I would have gone anyway because this is my dream and I am finally living it. Be happy for me. I will be in touch as soon as I land.*

> > *Love you forever, Desi*

Quino felt a hard shove to his back. It was Daisy. He spun around and hung on to her as if she was the only thing that made sense in his world right now. His sister was traveling to Africa! *Alone!*

Chapter Eight

HOW many miles away was Kenya from North Carolina? He didn't know. He couldn't remember from his high school geography class. Panic made his breath short and eyesight fuzzy. His little sister was out there, half a world away, on her own.

Daisy shook her head and he realized he was holding on too tight. "Sorry, girl."

He loosened his grip but threaded his fingers through her mane. He leaned hard against her while he read the note again and again. He took his phone out of his pocket and on the off chance Desi was still in the States waiting for her flight, he called her number. It went right to voice mail. He hung up before he started yelling.

What should he do? Charge to the airport? He didn't even know where she'd flown out from. How did she pay for a flight to Africa without him knowing? He took care of all of her expenses. Did she even have any money? His heart was thumping so hard in his chest, he thought he might have a stroke. Daisy nudged him with her nose.

He loosened his grip on her mane. "Sorry." He patted her neck. "I have to go."

He slipped out of her stall, latching the door as he strode back through the massive barn, which presently housed twenty horses but had room for up to thirty. He figured the best way to track his sister was to get online and check to see if there'd been any activity in her bank account.

"You all right, boss?" Luke called after him.

Quino nodded. He didn't have time to explain. Luke and Lanie were looking at him like he was nuts. He was sure he probably looked half-crazy with worry. He continued up to the house, where he kept an office. He jogged across the front porch and went inside. The house was dark and quiet, too quiet. Desi was a music lover and there was always music playing. As soon as Thanksgiving was over, she put on the Christmas tunes and cranked them all the way through to the New Year.

His office was the made-over front parlor. He turned right and approached his desk. There were no notes here from Desi. She had known to leave it with Daisy, as if she'd known that was the first place he'd go when he started to worry. He fired up his laptop and began checking their accounts. He monitored their joint account, then he checked her individual account. Neither of them had been touched. No withdrawals, no deposits, no transactions of any kind.

He opened up the browser and looked up the website for the Kenya elephant rescue and rehabilitation place she mentioned in her note. A baby elephant was the very first image that popped up. Quino closed his eyes. This was exactly the sort of thing that would hook his softhearted sister in: a baby elephant drinking from an enormous bottle of milk was stupid cute. He frowned. He looked at more pictures. It was a huge facility. There were loads of people working there, from caretakers to veterinarians to men with guns. Ack!

Quino looked for a phone number. He used his cell phone to call. After four rings, it switched over to voice mail. He glanced at the clock. Damn it. How many hours ahead was Kenya from North Carolina? Six? Seven? It would be late at night there. He slammed the lid of his laptop shut.

The only person who might know what the heck was going on was Desi's occupational therapist, Reyva Kumar. He left the house at a jog and barreled into his truck. He glanced at the corral but both Lanie and Luke were gone. He'd have to tell them what was going on later—right now he needed answers.

He tried not to speed. He really did, but he was in full-on crisis mode and he wasn't processing very well. The old Victorian building in the center of town that housed Reyva's practice was just a few streets over from the bookstore. For a nanosecond, Quino thought about stopping and sharing his freak-out with Ryder, but he didn't. Again, he was in too much of a hurry.

He parked in the one remaining spot by the big beige house with bright-blue trim. He took the steps two at a time and banged through the front door. The receptionist, Ann Ryan, glanced up at him in surprise and then smiled.

"Hi, Joaquin," she said. "What brings you by?"

"I need to talk to Reyva about Desi," he said. He didn't return her smile and he knew he sounded as upset as he felt.

"Oh, okay," she said. "Why don't you go ahead and sit down, hon? I'll get you some sweet tea and let Dr. Kumar know you're here."

Ann Ryan was a soft-spoken gray-haired woman with kind eyes and gentle Southern manners. Quino's upbringing made it impossible for him to completely lose his temper on her and demand to see Reyva right now. He sat.

Ann disappeared through a doorway that he knew led to the offices. He bounced his knee up and down in impatience. He just needed to ask her if she knew about this. If she'd encouraged this. And if so, why hadn't anyone told him?

Yeah, sure, he knew that Desi was right in her note that he would have discouraged this globe-trotting elephant-nanny nonsense. Desi was fragile. She was easily manipulated by strangers and she was now out there with a lot of them. He remembered the time she'd felt so bad for a kid selling magazines because he wasn't going to reach his goal that she bought subscriptions to all of his magazines, even one called *Potato Review* that, yes, reviewed potatoes.

"Here you go, Quino," Ann said. She handed him a glass of sweet tea. He took it, not feeling thirsty, but downed half of it in one gulp. Her eyes went wide. "Reyva is just finishing up with a patient and she'll be right with you."

"Thanks," Quino said.

He continued to jog his knee. He could hear the clock on the wall ticking. Ann resumed her seat behind her desk and put on her reading glasses as she went back to whatever work she'd been doing on her computer.

Quino forced himself to sit and not get up and pace. The waiting room featured a small bubbling fountain with a Buddha statue in the middle. The leather seats were comfortable but not so much that a guy would want to nap. Several magazines were scattered on the glass coffee table. He pulled out his phone, checking for any message or e-mail from Desi. Nothing. Radio silence was all he was getting.

A door behind Ann opened and a woman and her teenage son walked out of Reyva's office. The mother had her hand on her son's shoulder. They both wore a look of relief as if whatever was ailing him was on its way to being cured. Quino knew that look. He'd worn it the same day he and Desi had come for her first appointment with Reyva.

As the woman and son left, Reyva appeared in the doorway of her office. "Joaquin, it's good to see you. Come in."

He practically jumped out of his seat he was so eager to ask questions but he forced himself to slow his roll. Reyva was dressed in her usual office attire, tailored slacks, a blouse, and a long knit cardigan. Just the sight of her reminded him of her open-minded, encouraging presence. She was not a woman who got ruffled or hurried or impatient, which made her the perfect occupational therapist.

"It's good to see you, too, Reyva," he said.

"It's been too long," she agreed. She glanced at Ann. "Please see that we are not disturbed."

Ann nodded.

Reyva Kumar had streaks of gray in her long dark hair,

which she wore in a ponytail tied at the nape of her neck. Her dark brown skin was weathered by years passing, but both the hair and the wrinkles added to her grace as they were a testament to a life of acquired wisdom. Quino trusted her implicitly as he had watched the magic she had worked with Desi over the years, helping her get her speech, reading, and fine-motor skills back.

Reyva had a desk on one side of the large room. But it was to the leather couch and chairs in the corner that she led Quino. The room was full of plants of various sizes and had the faint scent of lavender and vanilla permeating the air. Quino felt his tension ease just by being in the room.

"I suspect I know why you are here," Reyva said. "But why don't you tell me?"

Quino put his sweet tea on a coaster on the glass coffee table as he sat in one chair and Reyva sat in the one beside him. He took Desi's note from his pocket and handed it to her. Reyva opened it and scanned the message.

"Did you know about this?" he asked. He tried to keep the hurt out of his voice. He wasn't sure he was successful. Reyva had been a part of their lives for so long, if she had advised Desi to keep something from him, the level of betrayal he was going to feel was going to be deep.

"No," she said. Her voice was gentle. When she glanced up at him, her face was wide with a big grin and her eyes were sparkling. Quino blinked. "Isn't it wonderful?"

"No!" Quino cried. He cleared his throat and said, "No, I don't think so."

"You're worried for her," Reyva said. Her tone was warm with understanding.

"Terrified would be closer to the mark," he said. "How can you be so calm?"

"Because she's been working for this for years," Reyva said. "And now she's done it. I'm very proud of her."

"But . . ." Quino protested.

"Don't mistake me." Reyva shook her head. "She should have told you she was going. She should have had the maturity to tell you her plan, but I believe she was afraid that you would talk her out of going."

"She would have been right," Quino said. "I'd have locked her up and . . ."

Reyva stared at him.

"Ah, hell," he said. He ran a hand over his face. "Excuse me."

"It's all right," she said. "I know how much you love her and how hard this must be."

"How do I get her to come home?" he asked.

"You don't," she said. "This is her journey. Not yours."

Quino reached for his tea. He took a long swallow. He wished it was something stronger than tea.

"She says she'll be in touch when she lands. Kenya is seven hours from North Carolina," Reyva said. "And if she's flying there, she'll likely have to stop somewhere along the way, like London. I'll bet she calls from there."

"Anything could happen to her," Quino muttered.

"Yes," Reyva said.

Quino looked at her like she was insane. Reyva didn't take offense but instead laughed and patted his hand where it rested on his knee.

"In all the years I've known her, your sister has dreamed of seeing the world and saving animals, big and small." Reyva paused and clasped her hands together over her chest. "I know this is terrifying for you, and I know what a good big brother you've been, stepping in to raise her when you lost your parents, putting aside your own grief to make sure she survived and thrived. But you have to remember, Quino, this is why you raised her . . . so that she could live her dreams."

"I just don't understand," Quino said. "Sure, she's talked about elephants and gorillas and tigers all the time. She belongs to all of the world rescue organizations and spends half her salary from the stable on animal causes, but I didn't think she was planning to enlist."

Reyva burst out laughing. "You make it sound like she joined the army."

"She'd be closer to home if she had," he groused.

"Quino, you heard what Desi was saying but you weren't

really listening," she said. "When she told you about these things, she was telling you her plans."

"But we have horses. Why does she need to go save animals on the other side of the planet?"

"You'll have to ask her that."

"What if she gets kidnapped? Or robbed? Or a poacher shoots her?" he asked.

"And what if she doesn't?"

"Argh, I thought you'd be on my side," he said. He knew he sounded like a big baby but he couldn't help it.

"There are no sides," Reyva said. "There is only a young woman, pursuing her dreams, hoping that the person she loves most in the world will support her."

"You're killing me here," he said. "I want to support her, I do, but . . ."

"No *buts*," she interrupted gently. "Desi has worked for this for years. She will call you and you can tell her that the way she left hurt you, but she will want your support."

"But—"

Reyva shook her head.

"What if she gets into trouble?" he asked.

"What if she doesn't?"

"Seriously, stop that," he said. She smiled so he knew he hadn't offended her. "All question of my supporting her aside, what if something happens to her?"

Reyva looked thoughtful for a moment. The look she turned on him was serious enough that he straightened up and met her dark gaze, trying not to be petrified by whatever she was about to say.

"A very large part of success is learning how to fail," she said. "Desi has to fail a little bit if she is going to learn how to succeed, and you have to let her. If she gets lost, she needs to figure out how to find her way. If she loses her passport, she needs to learn how to navigate getting a new one. If the internship is not what she hoped, she has to learn how to continue on or leave a bad situation. These are the skills we have been working on for years and this is her time to shine."

"I think I'm going to be sick," Quino said.

Reyva laughed. It was a light musical sound that actually made him feel a teeny bit better. If she could laugh at his worry and believe in Desi, her patient of so many years, then how could he, as Desi's big brother, do any less?

"When she calls, what should I say?" he asked. "Because I'm guessing *Get your behind home right now* would be wrong."

"Tell her you're proud of her, tell her that her exit left a lot to be desired," Reyva said. "And then ask her how she is doing, and when she tells you, listen."

"I'll try," he said.

"Good," she said. She smiled at him as if completely confident in his abilities and Quino had the feeling this was how she managed all of her patients. He didn't want to let her down.

"One thing is bothering me, however," he said. "How did she get the money to get to Africa and what will she be living on when she gets there? I looked at their website. They don't offer paid internships. The interns have to pay their own way, travel to and from Africa and living expenses. I checked the accounts and she hasn't taken out any money. How did she manage this?"

"I don't know," Reyva said. "She never told me about this internship, which proves to me that she was more than ready to do this all by herself. Have faith, Joaquin."

"I'll try," he said. He did feel a little bit better. Except he still wanted to know how she'd paid for the trip. If she'd taken out a credit card and was using that, they were going to have to have an entirely different conversation. He ran his hand over his face. He had a feeling he was in for a long night of worrying.

HIS phone rang at nine o'clock. Quino snatched it off the coffee table. It was Desi! He swiped the screen and barked, "Where the hell are you?"

Okay, that was wrong but *damn it*. He'd spent the past four hours in various states of excruciating worry.

"Hey, bro," Desi cried. "Or should I say *Cheerio*? I'm in London, eating a pasty and enjoying a pint before my flight to Nairobi."

"Desiree Maritza Solis," Quino said. It came out in his parent voice, the one he used when she was in big trouble, huge trouble, grounded-for-life trouble.

"That's my name," she said. Then she giggled. "Sorry, I'm not laughing at you, really—I think I might be a bit drunk. It was a super long flight and I'm only halfway there."

"Desi, you really need to turn around and hop on the next plane back to North Carolina," Quino said. He maintained his stern voice, fully aware that Reyva would not approve of this at all. In fact, if she heard him, she'd probably tackle him to the ground, rip the phone out of his hand, and tell Desi to go, go, go. He knew that and still he couldn't stop himself. This might be his last chance to get her to come home.

"Not gonna happen, big brother," Desi said. "I did it all by myself. I got the internship, got my physical and the required shots, I got my passport and a visa. I even got a grant, which is paying for the whole shebang. I worked so hard for this, and I'm not giving it up, not even for you."

"But . . . but Christmas," Quino said.

"I know you love the Christmas season and all of our traditions," Desi said. "It's probably weird for you to not have me there, but you'll be fine. Just throw yourself into the holiday like you always do. It'll be okay, big brother, I promise."

"Desi, this isn't about—"

"Oh, sorry, they're calling my flight. I have to go!" she cried. She sounded beyond excited and for a second Quino felt his heart lift at the pure joy in her voice. Then the fears kicked in.

"Don't talk to strangers," he said. "Don't let anyone buy you a drink, always go to the bathroom with a buddy, put your passport in a safe place, don't go out alone at night, don't—"

"Quino, breathe," she said. "I've got this, really, I do. I love you. I'll call you from Africa."

"I love you, too," he said. But she'd already hung up.

Quino dropped his phone onto the coffee table in the living room and collapsed back against the cushions. He'd blown it. She'd called from London and he'd blown it. He should have told her he was in the hospital for a mild stroke—then she would have come home.

The house was too quiet. He couldn't stand it. He shoved off the couch and grabbed his coat from the hook by the door. He had to be outside where it was cold and calm so he could clear his head. The corral was empty. The horses had been put in for the night.

He glanced above the detached garage at the small apartment he rented to Luke. The light was on, so Luke was home. Then his gaze cut across the front yard to the small cottage on a side lot by the main road. Lanie had moved into the guesthouse after Ryder and his daughter, Perry, had moved to their new house by the bookstore in town. Quino missed having Ryder and Perry underfoot, but he felt reassured seeing Lanie's and Luke's lights on, knowing he wasn't alone.

It wasn't that he couldn't be alone, he told himself. It was just that he hadn't had very much practice at it. He'd gone to school in Texas for a couple of years and worked construction around his classes, which was how he'd met Ryder. But he'd abandoned all that when he was called home to take care of Desi. He didn't think he'd been alone, truly alone, ever since.

As if she was the antidote to his loneliness a sudden image of Savannah hit him low and deep. He wondered what she was doing right now and how put off she would be if he showed up on her doorstep. He'd bet dollars to donuts she'd be furious. She'd made it pretty plain that she didn't want to go there with him and he knew he needed to respect her boundaries. He was holding out hope that in their quest to save Maisy's bookstore, she'd finally see him in a different, meaning datable, light.

It was that thought that made his anxiety ease. He shifted his brain from the panicked useless overload Desi had left it in to the much more manageable problem of Red.

A fantasy vision of Savannah talking with him, laughing with him, hanging on his arm as they walked through town, while melting under his kisses whenever they happened upon some mistletoe, filled his brain, pushing aside his frantic worry about his sister. There was nothing he could do there, but Savy was a different story.

No matter how much Red denied it, he knew—and he knew *she* knew—that there really was something crazy hot between them. He just had to figure out how to get her to admit it. And he sincerely hoped mistletoe was involved in the solution.

Chapter Nine

L ET'S review the schedule one more time," Savannah said.
 "No," Maisy argued. She flipped the **OPEN** sign to
CLOSED and glared at her friend. "I appreciate your enthusiasm, I do, but it's late and my feet are killing me and I want
to go home and soak in a tub full of bubbles until the jaun-
dice has left my skin and I resemble a human being and not
a waxy mannequin. I'm exhausted. Aren't you exhausted?"

"Yes, but it's only nine o'clock," Savy said. "During the
holidays, we should absolutely think about staying open
later, like eleven or midnight."

"Nine o'clock is late enough for holiday hours. Honestly,
I can't wait until we go back to closing at eight."

"M, I know you're all lovey-dovey with cowboy architect guy in your new house and you want to be home canoo-
dling with him, I do, but the first few months of opening a
new business are the most critical."

"When did you become so knowledgeable about small
businesses?" Maisy asked. She walked through the store,
straightening up the displays. Savy followed her, trying to
plead her case.

"I've been attending the small-business meetings held at the Fairdale Public Library," Savy said. "You should come with me. I'm trying to get us connected to other small businesses in the area, beyond the ones we already know."

"When are they?" Maisy asked.

"Tuesday evenings," Savy said.

"Can't. Ryder and I are taking dance lessons on Tuesdays," she said.

"Dancing?" Savy asked. "I've seen Ryder dance. It's terrifying."

Maisy laughed. "Thus, the dance lessons."

"Huh." Savy didn't know what to say.

She supposed if she was a better friend she'd be happy for Maisy, but there was a part of her that felt left out and she didn't like it. She didn't like that her friend was too busy for her and she didn't like it that her friend had a great guy and she was still flying solo. Yes, it was petty and ridiculous, and, sure, she'd decided not to date while in Fairdale because she knew she was leaving but that was before she'd kissed Quino and now she didn't know what to think.

"Do you want to come over for a while?" Maisy asked. "We're beginning the start of a month of Christmas movies. Perry is making popcorn as we speak."

Maisy shook a box of treats that she kept under the front counter and King George came trotting down the staircase from the second floor. Maisy opened the lid and gave him two treats while she slipped on his halter and leash. She'd been trying to leash-train him for months. It wasn't taking and she usually ended up tucking him under her arm like a football and carrying him home.

Holiday movies? Savy would rather watch live coverage of snails migrating. She supposed it was just as well. She knew she needed to stay in and strategize. Ryder clearly had Maisy so distracted, she wasn't showing the proper amount of concern about her own business endeavor. Savy had been blinded by new love-lust in her day, so she understood, really, she did, but if she left to go back to New York, who was going to make certain the bookstore succeeded? Quino could not possibly do it on his own.

"No, you go ahead," Savy said. "I have some things I want to get done."

"All right," Maisy said. She hugged her quick and then stepped back and studied her face. "But if you change your mind, you know where we are."

"Absolutely," she said. She waved Maisy and King George out of the shop and then locked the door. The bookstore seemed so empty without customers and coworkers. Savy almost ran after Maisy and joined her for the movie. No, she wasn't that desperate yet.

Instead, she took out her phone and called Archer Vossen. He answered on the fourth ring.

"Savannah, my favorite redhead, how are you?" He sounded upbeat and happy. Savannah could see him, martini in hand, wearing some ridiculously expensive designer ensemble, and staring out over the city from his Hell's Kitchen apartment that he shared with his surgeon lover, Gregory.

"Fine," she said.

"Which means you're not," he sighed. "I'm so sorry, Savy. New York is absolutely dismal without you."

"Such a liar," she accused. "I've been gone for months. You probably already have a new best friend."

"Hush your mouth," he said. "I could never replace you." She knew it was just lip service, but she did feel a bit better.

"So, is there any news?" she asked.

He sighed. "I was waiting for the right time to tell you."

Savy felt her heart sink. This couldn't be good. "What's happening?"

"Linda is doubling down," he said. "She's holding the line that you stole her work."

"But that's crazy!" Savannah said. "I mean, it's been months. She should have gone up in flames by now."

"Linda's been very cagey, but I'm trying to get a friend in IT to take a look at her hard drive and see if there are any clues there," Archer said. "She also hired your replacement. Sarah Cooper, a young dynamo in her twenties, who is very savvy about publicity. Sound familiar? Linda's been working her like a one-legged man in an ass-kicking contest.

Sarah has taken to crying in my office on a daily basis. Again, sound familiar?"

"Ugh," Savy said. "We have to stop her."

"I'm working on it," Archer said. "In fact, I'm taking Sarah out to dinner, and I'm going to see if I can get her to help spring a trap."

"Do you think that's wise?" Savy asked. "Her loyalties might lie with Linda."

"After the fifth crying jag, I decided I could turn her toward the light," he said. "This isn't just for you. It's for the company. We can't have someone this toxic in-house, but I have to catch her at her game first. She'll just victimize Sarah like she did you if I don't."

"Is there anything I can do to help?"

"Just be patient and trust me," he said.

"I do," Savy said. "Really, I do. It's just . . ."

"You want to come home," Archer said. "I get it. Hang tough, Savy. We'll get you home."

"Thanks, Archer."

"In the meantime, what are you doing to put your friend's bookstore on the map?" he asked. "It would help me prove your innocence if I could showcase some amazing publicity you've managed."

"I have all the usual stuff happening," Savannah said. "But my one *big* idea is not working."

"What's that?" he asked.

"I've been trying to convince Destiny Swann to come to the bookstore and do a signing," she said.

"Destiny Swann?" he asked. "*The* Destiny Swann?"

"Yes, she actually lives in this area," Savy said.

"But she hasn't gone out in public in over—"

"Ten years," Savannah said. "Yes, I know. Apparently, she retired from public life and I can't find out anything about why so I don't know how to coax her back into the world."

"How are you trying to draw her out?"

"So far? Not very successfully," she admitted. "I've tried flowers, chocolates, all the usual stuff, and the other day I sent a balloon-o-gram."

"You didn't."

"Did."

"You're crazy—in the most delightful way," he said. "Clearly, we have to move this thing along a lot faster before you lose your mind completely."

"I would appreciate that," she said. "The rejection is getting a bit depressing."

Archer promised to be in touch with any news and she ended the call. She stared out the window, feeling restless. If she was in New York, there'd be something to do. When she'd lived in the city her calendar had been jam-packed with book launches, power lunches, signings, restaurant openings, happy hours, gallery shows, concerts—ugh, she missed her life.

Oh, she loved having Maisy in her day-to-day life, but Maisy was with Ryder now and there was no room for Savy in their coupledom, which was how it was supposed to be. She stared out the window. It looked quiet out there, but what was the alternative? She didn't want to sit by herself in her apartment. Frankly, it was lonely.

She pulled on her coat and hat and decided to take a walk. Maybe she would get some promotion inspiration from all of the Christmas decorations in town. She strolled up the street until she reached the town center. The Fairdale green was massive and bordered by enormous maple trees, now barren of leaves but decked in colorful strings of lights. The gazebo that sat on one end of the square was dazzling, its posts done up in spirals of red and gold ribbon with white lights. The lampposts were festooned with garlands of red and green tinsel and with enormous gold bows on top.

Savy paused at the corner to take it all in. She remembered coming to the green with Maisy during their college years. Maisy would get excited, like a puppy wagging its tail off, about the holidays, but Savy would feel a cold hard knot form in her belly, knowing that she would be going home soon and dreading it.

She saw a few kids tearing around the open area. They had on coats and mittens and were running to the far end of the square, where she could see a crowd was gathered. She thought about turning around and heading back the way she had come, but curiosity propelled her forward. Well, that and the smell of cinnamon. She didn't know what was cooking but it had her salivary glands in overdrive.

When she approached, she noticed hip-high barricades had been erected in the shape of a large rectangle. Inside was a temporary ice skating rink. Christmas carols were playing, natch, and a large Christmas tree, decorated with ornaments of blue and silver, stood outside one end of the rink. Families were laughing and she watched a little girl, who looked to be about six years old, holding on to her father's hands while he skated backward and she tried to walk on her skates. She wore a pink hat with a pom-pom the size of her head and the sight of her and how she looked at her dad so adoringly made Savy smile even as it made her heart hurt.

"Almonds?" a voice asked.

Savy turned her head to see Joaquin, holding out a paper cone full of warm cinnamon-and-sugar-roasted almonds. "Is that what smells so good?"

"Yep, the food truck parks over there and sells roasted almonds of all flavors every night the rink is open," he said. He pointed and Savy glanced over at the truck. The side read **SACK O' NUTS**. Charming. The line was ten deep. She wasn't surprised. Despite the unfortunate name, it smelled like heaven.

He shook the bag, bringing her attention back to him. He held out the cone and she took a couple of almonds. "Thanks."

He looked at her with a frown, then he took her free hand and poured a fistful of almonds into her open hand.

"Whoa, no," she said. "I don't want to take all your nuts." She glanced up at him and he was laughing. "That sounded pervy, didn't it?"

"Only if you have a mind in the gutter," he said. "Which I totally do."

She laughed and tried to hand him back some of the almonds. He shook her off.

"Eat up," he said. "You're going to need your strength. We're going ice skating."

He dropped two pairs of skates at her feet. She looked from the skates to him and back at the skates. She didn't know what to say. She had loved ice skating for so long, but like so many losses in her life, she'd had to let it go.

"I haven't skated in years," she said. "This could be a catastrophe."

"It's like riding a bike," he said. He upended the paper cone and finished off his almonds. While he chewed he appeared to consider his statement. Then he swallowed and said, "Actually, it's nothing at all like riding a bike. What a horrible analogy."

"Did you rent those skates after you saw me?" she asked. "Or do you just carry around—" She paused to pick up one of the skates and check the size. "A pair of size-nine skates, hoping you'll get lucky?"

"That would be a helluva pickup line, wouldn't it?" he asked. He grinned and said in a smarmy voice, "Hey, baby, your rink or mine?"

Savy laughed and shoved him playfully. "Tell the truth."

"Okay, here is my tale of woe," he said. "It's a part of my family's holiday tradition to be here on the night the rink opens, but my family is off doing other things, so when I saw you standing here I thought maybe you'd want to skate with me."

Savy studied him. His expression was suddenly vulnerable and she wondered if he and Desi had had an argument. Given Joaquin's love of all things Christmas, she wasn't surprised that the deviation from the tradition was making him low. She surprised herself by using her free hand to grab the smaller pair of skates off the ground. Thankfully, nine was her size.

"Well, come on, then," she said.

She chomped on her almonds while she led the way to one of the park benches. He sat beside her as she kicked off her shoes and began to lace her skates. The muscle memory of exactly how many times she looped them around her ankles and the tightness she preferred in the laces came back to her as if she hadn't gone years without skates on her feet.

"Ready?" he asked. He tested the laces on his skates before standing.

"Yeah," she said. The almonds were suddenly sitting in her stomach like stones. What if this outing brought back all the grief? She hadn't allowed herself onto the ice in years because she was afraid the heartbreak would crush her.

But there was Joaquin, holding his hand out, and to her surprise she put her hand in his and let him pull her to her feet. Together they walked to the rink, getting in line to enter. Once on the rubber mat they took off their skate guards and Joaquin stuffed them into a cubbyhole to pick up later when they were done. The frigid air above the ice was so familiar. It made Savy's heart lift as it welcomed her back into its cold embrace.

Joaquin stepped onto the ice first. He glided a few feet out and turned to wait for her. Savy took a deep breath and stepped onto the ice. She glided to a stop right beside him. He held out his hand and it was the most natural thing in the world to take it. Together they pushed off and began to skate with the crowd, which moved in a staggered pace around the rink as the new skaters mixed in with the more experienced ones.

"You're pretty good," she said to him.

"I used to play hockey," he said. "I lack finesse but I get where I want to go. You're not so bad yourself."

He was making long passes, expertly riding on one blade and then the other with little to no effort. Since they were both tall, they were well matched and Savy was comfortable keeping up with him.

She wasn't sure what got into her. Maybe it was the way he looked with his dark hair and eyes gleaming under the overhead lights, or perhaps it was the *Nutcracker* music that was being piped in over the laughter and chatter of the crowd, but suddenly Savy wanted him to see her, really see her and who she once was. She broke away from him and skated into the center of the rink, which was reserved for the daredevils, the people who wanted to jump and spin and risk crashing onto the hard ice.

Savannah started to pump her legs in the old familiar rhythm. The crowd around her became a blur as she picked up speed and she spun so that she was skating backward. She heard a gasp as she began to build up more speed, feeling the euphoria she had only ever felt on the ice. It was the closest thing to flying she'd ever known and her heart felt as if it would lift right out of her chest with the joy of it.

She felt the crowd back up to get out of her way as she sped by. Feeling as if she were a tightly coiled spring, she waited until the ice and her skates felt just right and then she dug in her toe and kicked off the ice up into the air, twining her arms about herself for one spin and then a second before landing on her blade. She bobbled but caught herself without falling and glided right out of the spin and back to Joaquin's side.

His eyes were enormous, and he shouted, "That was amazing!"

He began to clap and the crowded rink began to clap as well. Savy felt her face get hot but she executed a small bow and then waved at everyone just as she had been trained to do during all her years of competition.

"Hey, lady, do it again," the little girl she'd seen earlier in the pink hat demanded.

Savy looked at Joaquin. He waved for her to go, so she did. She danced her way across the ice with some fancy footwork and then she did some jumps and twirls and ended with a spin that left her dizzy and out of breath. She was out of practice. She could feel the muscles she hadn't used in years begin to protest.

She gave another bow to the cheers and applause and then rejoined Joaquin, who was lounging on the side of the rink. He was looking at her with pride, as if he was delighted by her performance, and it was a balm to her injured soul.

"Sorry," she said. "I'm not trying to show off. It's been a long time since I've skated, and I think I got a little carried away."

"Don't say you're sorry," he said. He took her hand in his

and they joined the crowd as they moved around the ice. "That was the most incredible thing this sad little rink has ever seen. I am in awe."

"I've missed it," she said. She glanced around the rink. Why had she stayed away so long? "More than I realized."

"Red, if I could do that, I'd be out here every day. Hell, I'd charge people tickets to watch me," he said. "How did you learn to skate like that?"

"Nine years of lessons," she said. "I wanted to be an Olympic athlete, an ice skater, more than anything in the world."

He must have heard the note of heartbreak in her voice because he watched her face intently when he asked, "What happened?"

"When I was thirteen, my father decided it was time for me to quit. At my annual physical, the team doctor told him I was going to be too tall to continue in the sport with any more success than I'd already achieved, so that was it. My father had me take up volleyball instead."

"What?" Joaquin looked dumbstruck. Savannah imagined that was exactly how she'd looked when her father fired her coach.

"It sounds harsh, but he was right. The average height for figure skaters is five feet two inches," she said. "I'm five-ten. There was no way I was ever going to be able to compete on the national or global stage at this height. It would have been a waste of time and money for me to continue."

She tried to keep her tone light so as not to make a big deal out of something that had happened sixteen years ago, but Quino was not having it.

"That's total bullshit," he said. "So what if you were going to be too tall? You loved it and you have no idea what you might have achieved if you'd been allowed to keep pursuing your dream."

Savy shrugged. "It's not that big of a deal." Which was a lie, because to her thirteen-year-old self it had been a very big deal indeed.

"I disagree," he said. "A person should be allowed to pursue their dreams no matter—"

He stopped abruptly and Savannah looked at him. "You okay?"

"Yeah," he said. He shook his head as if shaking off his bad mood. He glanced at her and squeezed her fingers with his. "I'm sorry that happened to you."

"I got over it," she said. "Eventually."

He laughed. It hit her then that she liked this guy, genuinely liked him, even if he did love Christmas more than any other man she'd ever met. They skated in silence for a while, watching the other skaters as they glided by them. They even got fancy a time or two and Joaquin spun her under his arm and pulled her back, tucking her into his side. She tried not to focus on how safe she felt up against him, as if with him beside her, all of the wounds she'd accumulated over the years couldn't hurt her anymore. But, of course, that was ridiculous.

When a voice came over the public address that the rink would be closing, Savy realized with a sigh that she could have skated beside him all night. She felt as if he'd given something back to her, something she hadn't known was missing. They made for the exit of the rink, which was a garland-festooned archway. Savannah gasped when they moved directly underneath it. Joaquin glanced at her as if he thought she'd hurt herself.

"You all right?"

She nodded and pointed up. "Mistletoe."

He went to look up, but she grabbed him by the lapels of his coat and pulled him down. Then she kissed him. It was supposed to be a thank-you kiss. Swift and sweet, the soft press of her mouth against his, to let him know how grateful she was that tonight had happened, that she'd found a part of herself that she'd thought was lost forever. But the awareness that always snapped between them overrode her good intentions and she kissed him longer than she meant to.

A nudge to her back as someone tried to scoot around them made her break off the kiss. Joaquin stared at her as if she'd managed to rattle his brain loose with that lip-lock. Savy smiled. Then he looked up and her secret was out.

He grinned at her and said, "There's no mistletoe up there."

"Really?" she asked. She squinted up at the garland. "Huh, I could have sworn there was."

Then she turned and walked over to where they had stowed their skate guards. She grabbed hers and handed his to him. She tried to ignore the awareness of him when their hands brushed, but all she could see and feel was Quino.

"I'm onto you, Red," he said.

She bent over and put the guards on her skates. Then she walked over to the bench where they'd left their shoes. She sat down and began to work on the knots of her laces, trying to look casual. If he saw how her fingers were shaking, he'd clue in to how rattled she was. She decided she'd better walk back her impulsive gesture before it got her into more trouble than she wanted to handle right now.

"I was simply trying to say thank you," she said. "Don't read too much into it."

He studied her while working on his own laces. They were inches apart when he said, "Well, that's hard to do when my heart is racing in my chest like someone left the barn door open."

She laughed. She was relieved that her excess of emotion hadn't been misconstrued. She didn't want to make things awkward between them, especially since he was going to help her come up with ideas to promote the shop. She needed him more than ever, since her big idea, a visit from reclusive author Destiny Swann, was proving to be a bust.

"How about a cup of hot cider and I'll drive you home?" he asked.

Savy stood and her sore muscles protested. "I'd like that, thanks."

Together they walked their skates to the rental booth. A quick stop at the food truck for cider and he led her toward his pickup, which was parked in one of the spots beside the green. He opened the door for her and she climbed in, warming her hands with the thick paper cup of hot cider. It

had just the right amount of cinnamon and, unless she was
crazy, the faint flavor of vanilla. Yum.

Joaquin climbed into the driver's seat and they drove the
short distance back to the bookstore. As soon as he stopped,
Savy opened her door to hop out, thinking he would just
drop her off, but he got out on his side, too, and met her on
her side of the truck.

He walked her up to the front porch and Savy dug her
keys out of her jacket pocket. He held her cider while she
unlocked the door. When she turned back around, he
handed her what remained of her cider. It wasn't much and
it had cooled off. She finished it and crumpled the paper
cup in her fist.

"We have a problem, Red," he said.

"We do?" she asked. Oh, jeez, what if he thought she'd
made a pass at him and he'd decided he wasn't interested?
She was going to be so humiliated.

"Yup." He pointed up. "Mistletoe."

Savy glanced up. Sure enough, there it was. She smiled.

"Well, you know what to do," she teased.

And then he was kissing her. Cupping her face between
his two calloused hands, he kissed her softly as if checking
to make sure it was okay. Savy liked that about him. He
wasn't grabby. He always treated her as if she was something precious. As if he understood on an elemental level
that consent was sexy.

His mouth slid across hers in a sweet invitation. Savy
answered with a yes. She dropped the cup in her hand and
latched on to him, letting him know she was all in. She let
her fingers climb up his powerful arms and shoulders to the
nape of his neck, where they dug into his hair. It was just as
thick and soft as she remembered. If she were a cat, she was
pretty sure she'd purr.

He deepened the kiss and she met him with enthusiasm,
rolling up onto her toes to be closer to him. She inhaled the
particular scent of cedar and bergamot that was Joaquin
and it made her dizzy. She felt the rough burn of late-night
whiskers against her chin. She didn't care. When his mouth

left hers to trail across her jaw, she tipped her head to give him better access. She knew she was on shaky ground here but she didn't seem to have the fortitude to do anything to save herself. In fact, she wasn't sure that walking away from him was saving herself anymore.

Joaquin kissed her again on the mouth and then he released her. Savy rocked back onto her heels, feeling as if her legs were made of jelly. Had a man ever kissed her legless before? No, she was certain this was new.

He cleared his throat. "I'm thinking I should probably go home now. You're only supposed to kiss under mistletoe but you tempt me, Red. Oh, how you tempt me."

"Tempt you in what way?" she asked. The words flew out of her mouth before she had the good sense to stop them. She didn't mean to flirt with him, but it was as if she couldn't help it. The man brought out this sexy siren wannabe inside her that she hadn't known existed before.

Up to now, her dating life had consisted of corporate types from Wall Street and Madison Avenue, who expected her to be as much of a hard-ass as they were, but with Joaquin, she was a softer version of herself. She wasn't sure what to make of it. She wasn't sure she liked it. But she did like the way he was looking at her right now, as if she was his everything. She'd never had a man look at her like that before.

Joaquin's dark eyes met hers in a gaze that was so hot she was surprised sparks didn't shoot out of her fingertips. Then he said, in a voice that was little more than a growl, "I want you, Red. I want you naked beneath me, skin to skin, while I lick every delicious inch of you. I want to feel your legs wrapped around my waist as I slide into you. And I want to feel your nails dig into my back when you call out my name while you orgasm around me. That's how you tempt me."

"Oh . . . wow," she said. She felt her insides swirl down to one aching spot between her legs. She was about to grab him by the front of his jacket and haul him into the house with her, when he reached around her and opened the door.

With a kiss on her head, like she was five, he gently pushed her inside and closed the door. Through the thick frosted glass, he called, "See you tomorrow, Red."

Savannah wilted against the inside of the door. Damn, he was fine, and she knew if she got involved with him things could get ridiculously messy.

Which was exactly why she opened the door.

Chapter Ten

H E was halfway down the steps. She could have kept the
door closed. She could have locked the dead bolt, gone
upstairs, put on her comfy jammies, turned on a nonholiday movie, and popped some corn. She did none of those
things.

"Joaquin . . . Quino, wait!"

He stopped and turned around. The look on his face
mirrored how she felt. A deep hunger smoldered in his dark
eyes, reaching for her.

What she said in the next few seconds would change
everything between them. Either he would accept her invitation with no strings attached or he'd turn her down, leaving her feeling rejected, which was not her favorite feeling
in the world. But the truth was, she was lonely and Quino
was the first man who had interested her in forever.

She had lived long enough to know that the only things
people usually regretted were the chances they didn't take.
Would she regret not taking a chance on this man in this
moment? Yes, she would. Decision made.

"What is it, Red?" he asked. He hadn't moved from the steps.

Savy swallowed hard and then met his bold stare with one of her own. "I didn't get a chance to tell you that you tempt me, too."

He didn't move a muscle, except for one eyebrow that quirked up higher than the other as he considered her words. He was probably trying to figure out if she was inviting him in or just flirting some more. She felt the need to make her signal clear enough to be seen in a blackout.

"In other words"—she paused to clear her throat and then continued—"I want you in my bed tonight. I want to kiss every inch of your skin and sink my nails into your back when I feel you come inside of me."

Quino staggered a bit and steadied himself by grabbing the handrail.

"Way to turn the sexy talk around on a guy," he said. He fanned himself with one hand. "Everything went gray and I'm seeing spots. I'm gonna need a second here."

She laughed and watched as he shook himself from head to toe, like a dog shaking water off its coat after a swim.

"Are you inviting me in?" he asked. His glance was pure heat with a sliver of hope.

"Yes," she said.

Still he didn't move. He licked his lips. It was a ridiculously sexy gesture.

"And if I come in, are we going to . . . ?" He trailed off as if he wasn't sure how to fill in the blank.

Savy didn't want to offend his delicate sensibilities, if he had any, so she said, "Fornicate?"

"Yeah, that," he said. He looked a bit breathless.

She felt her grin spread across her lips. She knew without the aid of a mirror that it was undiluted wickedness and she didn't try to tone it down one bit.

"Yes," she said. That was all she got out before he came barreling at her like a bear.

She stepped back into the bookstore but he scooped her up into his arms, kissing her once, before plopping her onto the counter while he turned and locked the door. He leaned back against it with his arms crossed over his chest as if to prevent himself from touching her again. Savy smiled. It was nice to see he felt the same desire that she did. The difference was that she wasn't going to hold back.

She crooked her finger at him and said, "Come here."

He pushed off the door and stepped closer. He stopped just in front of her and she spread her legs wide, hooked him around the behind with her feet, and pulled him close so he was flush up against her. Ah, that was better. Then she put her arms around his neck and leaned forward, pressing her mouth against his.

"At the risk of ruining the moment with a bit of intro-spection," he said as she trailed kisses along his jaw. "I have to ask why now? You've held me at arm's length all these months. What changed?"

Savy didn't want to talk. She didn't want to get into feel-ings or motivations. They only made things messy and complicated. Still, she sensed her answer was important to him. She wondered if she told him the truth, that she just didn't want to be alone tonight, if he'd be okay with that. She had no interest in a relationship but she was so tired of being alone. She knew honesty was her only option.

"I just want some company tonight," she said.

He pulled back and looked at her. "Some company? You could get a goldfish. They're not even a huge commitment given their short life span."

She laughed. "Yes, but a goldfish didn't take me ice skat-ing for the first time in years. A goldfish didn't give me back a piece of myself I hadn't known I'd lost."

He nodded. He kept running his hands up and down her back as if to reassure himself that she was actually here in his arms. "Well, shoot, if I'd known a spin around the ice rink would convince you to give us a shot, I would have taken you skating months ago."

"I'm not giving us a shot," she said. "I'm giving us to-night."

He stiffened as her meaning became clear. "Ah."

Savy didn't want to pressure him but she didn't want him to have a false expectation of what this was, either. She didn't say anything but let him process it. His hands continued moving across her back, up and down, until one slid into her hair at the nape of her neck and the other gripped her hip.

"What if you wake up tomorrow and decide one night isn't enough?" he asked. This time he moved his mouth along her jaw, pausing at the sensitive spot just below her ear.

"Unh," Savy grunted. He'd asked a question. What was it? She racked her brain. Oh, yeah! "That won't happen."

"But what if it does?" he persisted.

"I'll just have to get over it," she said.

"Hmm," he hummed against the skin of her throat, and Savy felt her own vision blur.

With practiced ease, he unfastened her jacket and pushed it aside. Now his hands slid up underneath her sweater and the feel of his calloused fingers against her skin filled Savy with a restless ache. She had to get him to see the rightness of taking tonight.

She pushed his jacket off his shoulders and it dropped to the floor. She dug one hand into the hair at the nape of his neck and lifted his face so she could kiss him full on the mouth. Her kiss was thorough and deep, luring him in and holding him captive.

"What do you think?" she whispered. "Will you stay?"

"If I'm choosing between being with you now or never being with you at all," he said, "I think my choice is obvious." He pressed his forehead to hers and in a quiet voice said, "I choose you."

Then he kissed her and it was everything. He lifted her up in his arms and Savy instinctively wrapped her legs around his waist. He turned and carried her to the stairs. Savy began to protest but he stopped whatever she was about to say by kissing her again. In fact, he kissed her as he strode up both flights of stairs to the third floor. He pressed her up against the wall beside her door and she was impressed to find he wasn't even breathing heavy. She was not a petite woman.

"Are you sure?" he asked her.

With his body pressed the length of hers there was no other answer for her.

"Yes," she said.

He released her, letting her slide down his body. To Savy it felt as if he was the match to her fuse. She took his hand in hers and pushed open her door, pulling him in after her. Mercifully, her apartment wasn't too messy. She'd taken to picking up every evening when she didn't have anything better to do. How sad was that?

She would have plowed straight through to her bedroom, but he stopped her. He tugged her around so she was facing him. She glanced at his face, which was inscrutable. Oh, no, had he changed his mind? Maybe this was too much for him. Maybe she was too much for him. She braced for him to kiss her head again like he had downstairs and depart.

Instead, he reached into his pocket and pulled out his phone. Had he gotten a message? She stood wondering what to do. Was the guy really going to phub her *now*? She started to get miffed but then music started to play out of his phone. Softly, it filled the silence and she looked at him in confusion.

"If this night is all I get," he said, "I'm going to do everything I've ever thought of doing with you." He put his phone on the coffee table and pulled her into his arms. "Dance with me."

He'd fantasized about dancing with her? Savy thought for one second she might weep. But she took his hand and let him pull her in close while the upbeat number began to play out of his phone. He moved her around the floor in a snappy two-step, guiding her perfectly with his hand on her hip. It took a moment for the words to sink in.

"Kissin' by the mistletoe."

She glanced up at him in surprise. Then the singer's voice registered and she asked, "Aretha?"

"Of course," he said. He twirled her out and then spun her back into his arms. It was silly and romantic and Savy would have had to be made of stone not to respond to him. She wasn't stone; more like putty, she thought. Putty in his hands, or at least she wanted to be.

She was aware of everything: the rise and fall of his chest, the warmth of his hand at the small of her back, and the cheek he rested on her hair. Her self-imposed fortress of solitude, the icy barrier she kept between herself and others, began to melt and there was nothing she could do to stop it. Not that she even tried.

The first song rolled into a second, a slower number, and this time the crooner was a man. "Baby, It's Cold Outside," sung by Johnny Mercer and Margaret Whiting. Savy grinned at him.

Over the music, she said, "You know, this song is considered really inappropriate these days. The man coercing the woman to stay when she says she needs to go."

"Fair enough. Let's flip the script. You be Johnny and I'll be Margaret," he said.

"I don't think that's any better," she said.

But since it was her apartment and she wanted him to stay, it did fit. She lowered her voice and started to sing the Johnny Mercer part, and he laughed and then sang in a terrible falsetto with Margaret Whiting. By the time the song finished they were both laughing and any attempt to sing was lost as they struggled to breathe. Savy collapsed onto her couch, dragging him down with her in a tangle of arms and legs.

"Well, hello there," he said, landing on top of her.

"Hi," she breathed. When he would have moved off, she looped her arms around his neck and pulled him down. "Stay."

He reached up with one hand and brushed a hank of hair out of her eyes. His touch was gentle, as if he was trying not to frighten her away. Savy leaned into his hand and kissed his palm. She didn't scare that easily.

She could tell by the light in his eyes that he understood. He smiled and caught her chin in his hand. His thumb ran over her lower lip, and he seemed fascinated by the softness he found there. Then he lowered his head and kissed her. His mouth fit hers perfectly, two complimentary forces combining in a surge of energy, creating something new and magical between them. Was this what finding a soul mate felt like?

She shook the thought off. She didn't believe in Christmas, she didn't believe in soul mates, and she didn't believe in happily ever afters. She believed in herself and her ability to make things happen, and right now what she wanted to happen was some spectacular sex with Joaquin. She shifted so that he was under her, then she kissed him with every bit of the desire that was coursing through her.

Thankfully, he responded by letting her have her way. She kissed him long and deep and short and sweet and then sat up while straddling him, so that she could toss off the sweater that now felt like it was suffocating her. She had a tank top on under it and he murmured his appreciation for the display of skin. But Savannah wasn't satisfied on her end and she tugged at his ugly Christmas sweater until it went the way of hers and he was in just a T-shirt.

In a bold maneuver, he sat up and turned so that they were face-to-face and she was pressed up against him in the most intimate sense. That was not what he was after, however, as he lowered his head and let his mouth move over her exposed skin. He began at her collarbone and moved lower. He hooked a finger in her tank top and pulled it down until the swell of her breasts was revealed.

It felt as if he was drawing a line of heat across her skin. A moan slipped out of her mouth and she felt him smile against her. When he snagged one cup of her bra and lowered it so he had full access, Savy thought she might pass out. Had it been that long since she'd been with anyone? She tried to do the mental math but she couldn't think with his mouth on her, and then his hands cupped her bottom and he rolled to his feet.

Savy grabbed his shoulders and locked her legs around his waist, gasping when she felt the hard length of him against her. Pure undiluted lust shot through her and she met his gaze and said, "Now."

"I'm right there with you, Red," he said. Then he slid her up and down along the length of him, and Savy's head tipped back. She seriously might orgasm right here right now. His chuckle was low and deep as if he could read her that well. The thought would have been alarming if she wasn't lost in a deep fog of want that was making all brain function short out.

He strode toward her bedroom, which was just off the living room. She wondered how he knew which one was hers but then realized it was the one with the door open and the bed visible. He might have just been homing in on the bed. Fine with her.

He carried her all the way into the room but instead of tossing her onto the bed, he let her slide down the front of him until her feet touched the ground. Then he studied her as if trying to memorize every detail. It was sexy but also too intimate. Savy decided to distract him. She slid her hands beneath his shirt. He was all warm skin and hard muscle. She was fascinated and pushed his shirt out of the way. He helped by hauling it over his head.

One glance and she caught her breath. He was sculpted to perfection and she couldn't resist running her fingers up his defined abs to his pecs and across his broad shoulders. No wonder he hadn't been winded while carrying her. The man was ripped. She felt a feminine sigh of appreciation slip out of her and she tried to take it all in so she would remember him during the cold, lonely nights to come.

She leaned in and put her mouth gently on the base of his throat. Then she slid her lips up the side of his neck, where she paused to bite his earlobe. He shivered.

"You're killing me, Red," he said.

She laughed. It felt wonderfully empowering to make this man respond to her touch. That was as far as she got before he tugged off her tank top, leaving her in nothing but her bra and pants. He whistled low when he took in the sight of her and Savy had to force herself to keep her hands to her sides and not cover up. He hadn't and she wouldn't, either.

His calloused hands ran up her sides, pausing to cup her breasts. "Do you have any idea how beautiful you are?"

Savy smiled. She knew exactly what she looked like and

beautiful was not it. It wasn't that she thought she was hideous. Quite the contrary. She knew she was striking with her height and hair, but her features were plain and her overabundance of freckles kept her from ever being what anyone would consider beautiful. Except this guy, apparently.

His fingers traced patterns with her freckles along her arms and across her chest. "I feel as if you are this gorgeous woman that someone has dipped in cinnamon sugar just for me." He kissed her shoulder. "You're definitely as spicy as cinnamon and as sweet as sugar."

Savy snorted. "I am not sweet."

He raised his eyebrows as if he heard a challenge. "I'll bet you are."

Then he gave her a wicked look and lowered his mouth to hers, kissed her deeply, before moving his lips to her jaw and along her throat. He nuzzled the curve between her shoulder and her neck and then he slowly kissed his way down her body until he sank to his knees in front of her. His mouth moved across her belly, pausing at the place her pants began. Before Savy could register his movements, he had her shoes off and her pants followed, leaving her in just her underwear.

Praise all the gods in the heavens, she had chosen to wear a cute little matching set of pale purple underwear. Not that it mattered because she felt his hands slide up her back and he had her bra unclasped in a matter of seconds. One finger hooked into her bottoms and he pulled them down with a gentle tug. Savy was naked. It was thrilling and terrifying and she braced herself with her hands on his shoulders as he freed her feet. Then he sat back on his heels and took her in.

A slow smile curved his lips and he said, "Definitely the most beautiful woman I've ever seen."

Then he pressed his mouth right above the vee between her legs and Savy felt as if she'd been waiting her entire life to feel the white-hot surge of desire that flooded her. When he lifted one leg and put it over his shoulder, she had nothing to grasp and feared she'd fall. She threaded her fingers through his hair and held on. When he kissed her low and deep, she was certain she could hear color and see sound, so deliciously talented was the man kneeling before her.

He was insistent and his mouth and tongue were relentless as he drove her deeper and deeper into a state of bliss that made her insides spasm with an early warning sign of what was to come. Her head fell back. She was close. So close.

He moved his mouth to her hip and then up her side. Savy wanted to protest but she knew exactly what he was doing. He was going to draw this out until they were both at the point of desperation so that when they did finally reach release it was going to be excruciatingly exquisite. Fine. Two could play that game.

When he would have pulled her in for round two, she stepped away. She slid backward up onto her bed and crooked her finger at him, signaling for him to join her. He rose to standing. He reached for her but she slipped out of reach.

"Lose the clothes first," she said.

The look he gave her smoldered, but he did as he was told. He sat on the edge of the bed and ditched his shoes. He was just unfastening his jeans when she pressed against him from behind and he hissed at the contact. Savy whispered in his ear, "It's my turn."

She felt great satisfaction when she saw the hair on his arms rise. She pushed him to standing and then she stood behind him and reached around to unfasten his pants and push them and his boxers down his muscle-hardened thighs. *Have mercy.* He stepped out of the puddle of clothes and turned to face her. *Well, hello.*

Savy took in the sight of his cock, which like the rest of him was large and hard. She reached out a hand to touch him but he caught her fingers in his and pushed her back on the bed instead.

"Not sure I'm going to have much staying power if we start with a handshake," he said. "I've wanted you for too long."

Well, if that didn't go to a girl's head, Savy didn't know what would. The idea that this dark-haired, dark-eyed god of a man had wanted her for months made her tremble. She reclined on the bed and opened her arms. Quino slid in beside her so that they were facing each other.

"I want you, too," she said. Maybe his honesty was contagious but she felt as if she owed him the truth. "I have for quite a while now. Make love to me, Quino."

It was like she'd flipped a switch. An intense look passed over his face and he began to kiss and caress every part of her. It was exactly as he'd described before. He was attempting to taste every inch of her. It was wild and erotic and when his mouth moved from her ankle, up her leg, planting a soft kiss behind her knee, before moving along her inner thigh, Savy thought she might actually combust from the heat throbbing inside of her.

She tried to touch him, but he stayed just out of reach. She tried to kiss him but his mouth was too busy making a mockery of any sanity she had once possessed. She was utterly at his mercy, and when she started to feel as if she might actually die if he didn't join her, she wrenched herself out from under him and reached for the drawer of her nightstand, grabbing a condom out of it and flipping back around to find him watching her with one eyebrow raised.

"What if I wasn't done there?" he asked.

"You're done," she said. She tore the foil with her teeth and spat the piece across the bed. He looked duly impressed. She ripped open the packaging and in one deft motion slid the condom onto him, marveling at the heat and strength beneath her fingers.

"Red, I don't think—" he began but she interrupted.

"By all that's holy, do not think right now," she said.

Then she clambered up onto her knees and gave him a hearty shove, sending him sprawling. Before he could redirect her, she was straddling him. He opened his mouth but she put her lips over his, stopping whatever he was about to say, and she slid onto him in one clenching tight thrust that felt like the greatest thing Savy had ever felt in her life. She pushed off his chest and arched her back, trying to pull him in as deeply as she could.

She didn't move. She just let him fill her and stretch her

and make the desperate aching go away. It didn't, but having him inside of her helped. When she lifted her head and looked at him, he was staring at her as if she had just fulfilled every sexual fantasy he had ever had in his life. And then while his gaze held hers captive, he bucked underneath her, pushing himself up deeper inside of her, and Savannah lost it completely. One thrust and she came apart around him, clenching him so tight as she spasmed that she was afraid she'd hurt him.

Lost in throes of bliss, she couldn't do a thing about it, except say his name over and over, "Quino, Quino, oh, my God, Quino."

When the orgasm finally stopped and she could draw in a breath, she blinked her eyes open and found him staring at her in complete wonder. Then he rolled and she was under him. He thrust once, twice, three times and then clutched her close as he found his own release, with a deep grunt of satisfaction, within her. She felt his orgasm and it sent aftershocks of her own pleasure ricocheting within her.

When the sweet storm passed, Quino rolled to his side, pulling her with him, and they stayed that way, joined, while their heartbeats slowed and their skin cooled. Savy knew it was ridiculous but a part of her wished she could stay joined to him in this afterglow forever. It was the first time she could ever remember not feeling lonely and it was lovely.

QUINO felt her soft red curls under his chin. He wanted to kiss her. He wanted to hold her. He wanted to tell her that he loved her. That she was it for him and there would never be another like her. He did none of those things. Instead, he held her close and savored the feeling of being with her, of having her in his arms at last.

Making love to Savannah had been more life-altering than he had imagined and he had imagined it pretty much daily from the first time he'd laid eyes upon her. She was a goddess. She was his soul mate. He knew it. He just didn't know how to get her to believe it.

He ran his fingers up and down the curve of her back. He had tonight. He wouldn't fret about tomorrow. When he'd spied her across the park earlier, he'd been fighting off the blues. As he watched her, he'd sensed Savy was suffering the same sort of loneliness he was. She'd had the slumped shoulders and shuffling walk of a person who wondered if they even mattered, and he'd felt a connection so deep in his soul, that he'd rented the skates and hoped for the best. He'd never expected it to turn out like this. He had no idea what tomorrow would bring, so he decided to turn it over to the universe. If Red was meant to be his, he'd let the powers that be handle the long game while he enjoyed every single second of right now.

"Come on," he said. He shifted her off him and pulled her up into a sitting position. She blinked at him as if she'd been ready for a postcoital doze.

"What?" she asked. She looked confused and little taken aback. "Are you leaving?"

"Hell no," he said. "But you've only given me one night. So we have a lot of ground to cover, Red."

"Ground to cover?" She watched him as he carefully disengaged the condom and tied it off, tossing it into the wastebasket by the bed.

"I have at least one hundred fantasies in which you are the feature, and I'm willing to narrow it down to my top five, but we've got to get cracking. Morning will be here soon and I am not missing a second of my night with you."

She laughed and it sounded like music. "You're crazy."

"I prefer determined," he said. "Come on, it's shower time."

"Shower?" Judging by the size of her eyes, she was awake now.

Quino took her hand and led her toward the bathroom, pausing to kiss her once in the bedroom, once in the main room, and one more time in the bathroom. He cranked on the shower and when the temperature was right, he said, "Oh, what I am going to do to you."

Her pale-green eyes dilated and a pink flush filled her cheeks, and she sighed, "I can't wait."

Chapter Eleven

QUINO spent the day in the stables. He was exhausted in the best possible way and his mind was so full of Red, he was pretty much useless for anything other than assisting his team. A million times he wanted to text her or call her, but he didn't.

Quino had spent the early-morning hours watching Savy sleep. She slept on her stomach, her fiery hair in a tousled curtain around her, with one hand flung out and resting on his chest, reassuring herself that he was still there. At least, he liked to think that's what she was doing. It could be she was trying to push him off the bed, but her hand was resting gently like a caress so he chose to believe the former.

Last night had been the most singular experience of his sexual life. Savy was sweet and sassy. She'd let him lather her from head to toe and then make love to her up against the tile of the shower. The sight of the water running down her skin would be forever seared into his brain. He felt himself stiffen and was shocked that his cock could even get hard given that he'd made love to her two more times after the shower.

Once in the kitchen while their ice cream melted because her wet hair had smelled so good fresh from the shower and the other had been an accident. They'd been lying on the couch watching a movie, nonholiday, with her on top of him, and the next thing he knew his boxers had been down around his ankles and she'd awakened the dragon with her lips and tongue. For as long as he lived he'd never forget the sight of her sliding her beautiful mouth along the length of him.

When she stirred, he'd found himself hoping she'd fall back to sleep. He just wanted to have a few more minutes to watch her, to pretend she was his. She'd settled back down and he felt his heart rate slow. Time. He just needed a little more time. She'd given him this one amazing night but it wasn't enough; it was never going to be enough. He just didn't know how to get her to see that. But he had to try because the one thing he knew for sure was he was madly in love with this girl and letting her go was going to crush him.

Savy had been very clear that one night meant one night, and that morning when she'd woken up, she had all but shoved him out of her apartment, terrified that someone would find him and figure out what had happened between them. Not that she cared what anyone thought, she assured him, she just didn't want to hear their opinions. He understood that.

He'd had to play it at optimum cool to get her to still agree to meet him for coffee for their brainstorming session that night. When it looked like she'd balk, he'd used the old *I understand you might have gotten attached after last night* nonsense just so her pride would force her to show up to prove she wasn't emotionally invested. He of course pretended that the downshift to friends was perfectly fine with him. He had no idea how he was going to keep it up.

Thankfully, Saturday was the busiest day of the week at Shadow Pine, and he took two trail rides up into the hills with Luke, arriving back in time to assist Lanie with the autistic kids in her equine therapy group. Today's group had five children in it. Using hippotherapy, Lanie helped them to develop their motor skills, as well as make emotional connections to the horses while learning how to ride and groom them.

It was Quino's task to be an extra pair of hands and eyes in case any of the children got into trouble. He'd been working with Lanie and her kids for years and he always came out of the class with a renewed sense of purpose. The memory of the day that Sammy Jenkins hugged his horse, the first being he'd ever hugged in all of his eight years, still made Quino's throat get tight. Sam's mother had broken down and sobbed when she saw him, and she doubled down when young Sam then turned to hug her.

They were just finishing the class and releasing the kids to their parents, when Quino felt his phone buzz in his pocket. He snatched it out and checked the display. He was hoping it was Savannah but it wasn't. It was Desi! Relief hit him hard in the chest.

"Desi, how are you? Where are you? Are you all right?"

"I'm in Kenya!" Desi cried. She sounded giddy. "You should see it here. It's beautiful. Well, I think it's beautiful. It's very late at night but still so lovely. I'm in my own room and everyone is so nice."

"And you have your bags, and your wallet, what about your passport? Do you still have all of your belongings?"

"Yes, I kept track of everything," she said. "And I have a locker in my room, so I can put it all away until I return. I've even made a friend."

"Really? What's her name?"

"His name is Erick Mwangi," she said. "He met me and the other interns in London and flew to Kenya with us. I thought I would sleep on the plane but I had so many questions and Erick answered them all. He was very patient."

"Is he there now?"

"No, he is getting dinner for all of us. It's very late, but we're all hungry."

"Do you have a roommate?" he asked.

"No," she said. "But don't worry. There's a girl from Australia here named Poppy and she's right next door. Honestly, bro, I'm twenty-five. I think I can handle having my own room."

"Clearly, since you managed to get a grant to go there by yourself," he said. "Remind me again, how did you say you got that grant?"

"I didn't," she said. "But I simply—Oh, Poppy just knocked and said the food is ready. I have to go. I'm starving. Listen, check my Instagram. I'm going to be posting every second of my adventure and you'll see how great it is. I want you to be proud of me, Quino."

"I am—" he began, but she interrupted.

"Love you. Bye," she said, and then added, "Don't worry!"

The call ended and Quino swore a blue streak. "Don't worry? Don't worry?! Is she freaking kidding me?"

"You all right, boss?" Luke approached the corral from the stables.

"No." Quino hadn't told anyone about Desi's departure, because he supposed he felt that if he said it out loud then it was real and he didn't want it to be real. He hated that she wasn't here. She was supposed to be here with him on Christmas. Tomorrow was the night they decorated their tree during their annual viewing of *It's a Wonderful Life*. Who was going to verbally abuse Mr. Potter when he came on the screen with him if not Desi?

"Care to elaborate?" Luke asked.

"Desi's gone," he said.

Luke raised one eyebrow. "When you say 'gone,' you mean what exactly?"

"She took off for an internship *in Africa*."

"No way," Luke said.

"No way what?" Lanie asked. She joined them by the railing, waving to the last of her kids as the final minivan pulled out of the drive.

"Desi is in Africa," Luke said.

"What are you talking about?" She looked at Quino. "What is he talking about?"

"It's true. Desi is off rescuing baby elephants in Kenya," he said. "She told me to check her social media pages to-morrow because she plans to put up pictures of everything."

"Wait, how did she get to Africa without you knowing?" Lanie asked.

"Apparently she applied for a grant and managed to get all of her paperwork in order on her own—shots, visa, passport, plane tickets, all of it," he said. "And she said she didn't tell me because she knew I would say no."

"Well, she was right about that," Luke said. "So, when do we leave to go get her?"

"What?!" Lanie cried. "You can't go get her. Look at all that she did to go live her dream, and we all know this is her dream. She gives every cent of her discretionary income to animal charities."

"But she's Desi," Luke protested. "She's"—he glanced quickly at Quino before continuing—"fragile. She's very fragile. She could get hurt out there."

"The fact that she managed to get there is what I'm focused on," Lanie said. She shook her head in wonder. "I mean wow, just wow. Our little Desi is all grown up."

"No, she isn't," Luke argued. "She's on an adventure and, sure, she's okay now, but what if something goes wrong? What if she gets hurt or lost or is homesick?"

"And what if she doesn't?" Lanie countered.

Quino felt as if he were watching the two sides of him battling it out. On the one hand, he was so proud of Desi and all that she had managed on her own, but on the other hand, he was terrified. Maybe Reyva and Lanie were right and nothing would happen, and he hoped that was the case, but the fact that she was so far away from him when she might need him and there'd be no way for him to get there quickly—it gutted him.

"Grant writing is pretty advanced stuff," Luke said. "How did she manage that?"

"She didn't say, but I'm assuming she had someone write it for her," Quino said. He frowned at them. "I wish I knew who it was because I'd like to have a word with them."

Both Lanie and Luke raised their hands in innocence.

"Not a writer," Luke said.

"Me, either," Lanie agreed. "But I'd love to know who she used because we could sure use some grant money to expand the hippotherapy program."

Quino gave her a pointed look.

"Sorry," she said. "Not the right time, I get it. But seriously, if she mentions who helped her—"

Quino heaved a big sigh. "Yeah, I got it. I'll hook you up. If she ever says more than three words to me while she's running around Kenya, I'll be sure to ask."

"Thanks," Lanie said. She reached out her hand and squeezed his forearm. "She's going to be fine. You'll see."

"I don't even know how long she's going to be gone," he said. Ack! There it was, the pouty note he'd been trying to keep out of his voice. He felt the need to explain. "I mean, it's Christmas."

Lanie and Luke exchanged an amused glance.

"We know, boss," Luke said. "No one loves Christmas like you love Christmas."

"It has a lot of significance for me," Quino said. "And with Desi not here, well, it's just wrong."

Esther moseyed over to where the three of them stood. She methodically checked all of their pockets, hitting pay dirt with Luke, who had a carrot in his jacket pocket. He held it on the flat of his palm.

"That was for someone else," he scolded her. Esther did not care. She chewed the carrot and tossed her head, obviously disappointed that there wasn't more for her. Luke gave in and patted her neck. She nudged him playfully with her nose and Quino looked at the horse that used to be his mother's and felt his heart squeeze tight in his chest. He was having a hard time breathing.

"You okay, Quino?" Lanie asked. "You look pale."

"Yeah, I'm fine," he said. He glanced at them both and hoped he sounded more certain than he felt. "I'm sure Desi is going to do great things in Kenya. She's always wanted this and I should support her. And if things do go to hell, I'll get her out. One way or another, I'll make sure she comes home safely."

"Of course you will," Luke said.

The absolute faith in his voice was just what Quino needed to hear. His panic ebbed a bit. He reached over and rubbed Esther on the forehead the way she liked. She whinnied and twitched her tail in appreciation of the affection. He glanced at his staff, who were also his friends, and said, "I'll put her in for the night."

They watched him go with varying levels of worry in their eyes. Esther trotted beside him, knowing the routine and that a bucket of feed awaited her.

"I promise she'll come home," he said to the horse as they walked. He knew full well that he was really making a promise to his mom. The same one he made when he sat by Desi's hospital bed as she lay in a coma. He'd promised his parents then just like he did now. "I'll make sure nothing happens to her. I swear it."

Esther trotted ahead, clearly impatient with him. Quino followed, wondering if Desi was really okay and resisting the urge to call her again. Had she gotten enough to eat? Was her room secure? Did wild animals roam the grounds? What if a lion got into her room and made a midnight snack of her? Ugh. He hated this feeling of helplessness.

He glanced at his phone and noted there was a text message he had missed. It was a picture of Desi, sitting in a room with a group of people at a large table that was covered in food. She was making a kissy face at him and he knew that she had known he'd been worried about her and she had sent him this to ease his fear. He chuckled. Little sister knew him very well. He zoomed in on the people in the photo. It looked like a melting pot of every gender, age, and ethnicity, and they all seemed to have kind faces, or maybe he was projecting his hopes. He didn't know. All he knew for sure was that there was Desi right in the middle of it. A surge of pride swelled beneath his rib cage.

He texted back how proud he was of her and then stopped typing before his fingers feverishly released all of his fears in a text message overload. He didn't want his worry to dampen her adventure even though it about killed him not to badger her about safety. He glanced at the time on his phone. Six o'clock? Oh, man, he was supposed to meet Savy at seven at Perk Up. He hustled Esther into her stall and made quick work of feeding her and settling her for the night.

He had a date, or rather, not a date. But after last night, it sort of felt like a date even though he knew she had expressly said it wasn't. But was it? He had no idea, but one whiff of his horsey exterior and he knew, date or not, he had to shower and change clothes or there'd never be a *date* date.

S AVY put on leggings and a tunic top. She looked like she was going to the gym. She yanked them off and put on jeans and a flannel shirt. No, no, no! What was she dressing for? An evening of chopping wood? She grabbed a clingy knit dress and a pair of boots. Too sexy! Damn it!

She didn't know how to navigate this no-man's-land of not-dating after spending the night completely naked together. And what if there was mistletoe? That stuff was clearly her kryptonite. She needed to nip that. In fact, tomorrow, she was going to remove all of the mistletoe from the shop. No mistletoe, no smooches. Simple.

She decided on a pair of black velvet jeans—for warmth! And a heather-green cashmere top that accentuated her curves and the long line of her neck but was also totally for warmth. It was! The temperature had dropped today and a gal had to be prepared.

Lastly, she went with a pair of black suede ankle boots because the heels would make her almost eye to eye with Quino and she felt the need to be on level footing with the man who had ruined her for any other man. Honestly, if she'd known he was that good with his hands, his lips, his tongue—

She shook her head. Nope, no, nuh-uh. She wasn't going to keep thinking about last night. Clearly, she needed to reestablish some boundary lines with this man.

She ran a brush through her hair, checked that her makeup was light but accentuated her pale eyelashes and brows—seriously, thanks to the cosmetological advances in eyebrow pencils she no longer had eyebrows that rubbed off. She put on her favorite lipstick in a deep-lilac shade that didn't clash with her hair, always a concern, grabbed her coat, and headed for the door.

She jogged down the two flights of stairs, crossing through the shop on her way out. Maisy was working the front counter, dressed up in the elf suit Savy had worn the other day. If it was too short for Savannah it was too long for Maisy, and she looked like an elf playing dress-up in mother elf's clothes.

"Okay, so I'm headed out," Savy said. "See you later. Bye."

She thought if she didn't break stride, Maisy wouldn't question her. She had her hand on the door and was just opening it, when a foil-wrapped gold coin pinged her on the head.

"Not so fast," Maisy said. She had a bowl of the coins on the counter beside her.

"Ouch!" Savy let go of the door to rub her head. She glanced down. It was one of the big coins, the dollar ones. She glanced at her friend. "What'd you do that for?"

"I haven't seen you all day," Maisy said. "And when you finally appear, you're scuttling out the door like you've just robbed the joint."

"Sorry, but I'm in a hurry."

"For . . . ?" Maisy asked. She was watching Savy through her rectangular-framed glasses as if in anticipation of some great news.

"Nothing that exciting," Savy said. "It's merely a brainstorming session about the bookstore with a local business owner, you know, to see if there are ways to promote it that I haven't thought of." Oh, the lies! She was being vague on purpose, and if she got caught it was not going to go well.

She watched Maisy's face to see if she looked relieved by Savy's words as if she really was sweating the financial straits the shop was in and Savy's resourcefulness was a load off her mind. Maisy just smiled at her.

"Then why are you wearing your date lipstick?" she asked.

"What? No I'm not," Savy denied. She felt her face get hot, which was stupid because she was not going on a date even if she had, oh, damn, put on the lipstick she wore for dates.

"Yeah, you are," Maisy said. A customer approached the counter and she quickly asked, "Who are you meeting? Is it Quino? Because I heard from Jeri, who heard from Susan at the library, who heard from Kelly at the post office that you were ice-skating with Quino last night, and I thought to myself that can't possibly be because I worked with her all day and she didn't say a word to me. Not to mention the fact that, apparently, you're quite the accomplished skater and how is it that after eleven years of this friendship, I don't know this about you?"

"Uh . . . it's complicated," Savy said. She moved aside so the customers could put their books on the counter. "We'll talk later, okay?"

She dashed out the door with a wave. She didn't glance back, knowing Maisy's brow would be furrowed with concern.

It was cold tonight and she hurried down the walkway to the street, hoping the movement would warm her up. Perk Up was located on the town green and it would take her only a few minutes to get there. She saw the ice rink on the end of the square and smiled when she remembered the night before. Her leg muscles had been sore today but it was a good sore. Of course they might also be sore from the sex marathon she'd shared with Quino, but she preferred to think it was the skating.

She hurried into the coffeehouse, looking for a tall man with dark hair. There was no sign of him. She hated that. She'd been hoping he'd be there first so she didn't look so eager. It was seven o'clock on the dot. Savy had an inability to be late, drilled into her by her upbringing but also a part of her corporate life. She loathed waiting for people and tended to judge them harshly if they made her wait more than five minutes. She hoped Quino didn't keep her waiting or this meeting would be off to a rocky start. Then again it might help temper the fuzzy glow that seemed to appear around her every memory of him from last night. Yes, if he was late that would be a good start to breaking the spell he'd put her under.

She got in line at the counter and glanced at the board. A voice from behind her said, "I already ordered you a flat white. I hope that's okay?"

She turned around and there he was. His hair was fresh-from-a-shower damp, and his smile was wide and warm. She blinked. He was mouthwateringly handsome. Had he always been this good-looking? She couldn't remember. Then she glanced down and noted he was wearing the most obnoxious Christmas sweater she had ever seen. It had a giant reindeer head on it with the requisite red nose where his belly button would be and antlers that started at the shoulders and went all the way down his sleeves.

"Tell me that doesn't—" She pointed at the nose. It blinked red before she finished her sentence. "Never mind."

He grinned at her. "Festive? Am I right?"

"Oh, it's something, all right," she said. And then she grinned. She couldn't help it. Here was this big manly man, horse-wrangling dude, wearing a reindeer sweater. It was too much. She laughed.

He grinned and gestured to a booth in the corner. It had high sides, which explained why she hadn't seen him.

"How did you know I like flat whites?" she asked. If he had asked Maisy, she had no idea how she was going to explain this.

"Because that's what you're always drinking in the bookstore when I see you," he said.

Okay, paying attention to what she liked was major points, or at least it would be if they were becoming involved, which they weren't. She forced herself to remember this as she slid into the booth on the opposite side of him.

Her flat white was sitting there waiting for her with two macarons, a chocolate and a vanilla, on a plate next to it. Savy tried to remember the last time a guy had bought her coffee and dessert or a drink or dinner, for that matter. It had been so long she had no recall. Macarons—that was dirty pool if Quino was trying to get her to see him as more than a pal. Then she thought about how it had felt to be naked in his arms and she knew she was kidding herself if she thought she could walk back their relationship without a blunt conversation. She just didn't know how to begin even with that ridiculous reindeer nose blinking at her.

"How were things at the bookstore today?" he asked.

"Good," she said. "Busy. I tried a couple of times to get some details out of Maisy, you know, to learn how much financial trouble the place is in, but she's so besotted with Ryder that she's useless."

"What about Jeri Lancaster?" he asked. "She's the book-keeper, do you think she knows what's happening? And if she does, should we ask her? Saving the bookstore would be a lot easier if we knew what sort of cash amount we needed to keep it afloat."

"I haven't seen Jeri—her kids have a million holiday activities happening," Savy said. "But I plan to ask her directly the next time I do."

"Good," Quino said. "Maybe she can work some math magic and help us."

"In the meantime, I think I need to play to my strengths," Savy said. She pulled a small notebook and a pen out of her purse. "Which is publicity and promotion. We need something *big* to happen at the bookstore that will bring readers, *buying* readers, into the place."

"Okay, hit me," he said. "What have you thought of so far?"

"Well, I have one angle that I'm working on, but it's not promising so we can table that for now," she said. "Other ideas I've had that you can help me with, Mr. Christmas, are holiday-themed stuff."

"Such as?"

"Decorating gingerbread cookies, a family thing, so moms can show up with their kids, and have the kids decorate cookies while they shop for books."

"I like it," he said. "How about Christmas movie night? You can have big-screen showings of all the classics and provide popcorn. Everyone could show up in their holiday pajamas."

"Who owns holiday pajamas?" Savy made a face and he laughed.

"I do," he said. "You don't?"

"No."

"How is that even possible? And you really don't like the holiday movies? I can't believe that."

"Believe it. As for the movies, they're all so . . ." Words failed her.

"So . . . ?"

"Ridiculously optimistic," she said. "My holidays have never lived up to the expectation of those movies, and I am just . . . a bitter, bitter woman, apparently."

Quino laughed and Savy felt as if she had scored a major victory, which was ridiculous because she wasn't trying to charm him. She was just being herself.

"Watch *It's a Wonderful Life* with me tomorrow," he said. "It's a tradition for me and Desi to put up our tree and decorate while watching. She's not going to be able to join me tomorrow, so why don't you?"

"That sounds suspiciously like a date," Savy said. It was the date lipstick; she was sure of it. She was sending the wrong signal. She should have stuck to lip gloss. She blotted her lips with her napkin.

"No," he said. "Just friends hanging out, doing the Christmas thing that you don't like."

"It's not that I don't like the holiday," she said. "Okay, I don't like my version of the holiday. But I do like the idea of what it could be, you know, Christmas miracles and loving families coming together, but that's just never been my experience."

"Then come over tomorrow night and make new holiday memories," he said. "Better ones."

His dark gaze was earnest and Savy got the feeling that this wasn't about them dating or not dating; there was something more going on. There was a vulnerability in his gaze that made her pause. She got the feeling he needed her. Huh.

"All right, I can do it. But only if it's just friends hanging out," she said. "Last night was fun but we're done with that now."

He met her gaze and gave a slow nod. "Absolutely. One and done—well, more than one, but who's counting? It was more like four or was it five? Oh, apparently, I'm counting."

She glared at him. "Did you want me to come over or not?"

"Most definitely," he said.

"Okay, I have a thing in the evening, and I can't come over until after that, but I can swing by around eight thirty."

He grinned. "That would be great."

Savy pursed her lips. He looked like a kid relieved not to be picked last for the team. This made no sense. What was going on with him? She thought about pressing him but remembered that she was trying to maintain some boundaries.

"I really appreciate your help with ideas for the bookstore," she said. "And I know after last night, there might be some confusion that we are moving in a certain direction, but I just want to be clear that we're not."

He propped his chin on his hand and watched her.

"Ryder is your best friend and Maisy is mine," she said. "Things could get awfully complicated if we . . ."

"Got into a relationship?" he asked.

"Yeah, that." She pulled at the neck of her sweater, trying to let in some cool air.

"Then we won't," he said with a shrug. He looked very blasé about the whole thing.

Savy looked at him in confusion. Last night this man had been so smokin' hot, he'd practically imprinted on her and now he was *meh*. What was his damage? Was he really just over it now that they'd slept together? She knew she should be relieved, because men could be so darn clingy after a night of good sex, but still it seemed out of character for him.

And she wanted no surprises from him, like he was all cool now that he was sated but then turned on her later, wanting more sex or a relationship. That was never going to fly because she was leaving Fairdale for New York as soon as she got the high sign and she did not want any drama when she left. She hated drama.

"What are you thinking?" he asked. "I'm looking at your face and it's like watching a kaleidoscope, you have so many thoughts swirling in there."

Savy thought this was an opportune time to spell it out for him.

"Do you know why I need the bookstore to be a huge success?" she asked.

"Because you don't want to see Maisy lose everything?"

"Partly that," she said. She picked up a macaron. She broke off a small piece and dipped it in the froth of her flat white. She popped the macaron in her mouth and temporarily lost her train of thought as the sweet goodness filled her mouth.

"And the other part?" he prodded. He shifted in his seat and glanced away from her.

"I want to go home," she said. "I want to go back to New York. I want my career back. I miss the energy I feel when I walk those streets. Being in New York is like being plugged into an outlet. There is no other feeling like it in the world. Have you ever been to New York?"

"No," he said. "You make it sound electrifying."

She laughed. "I suppose in some ways it is. It's where I belong. And the reason I'm working so hard to get Maisy's bookstore launched is because if I can put her on the map, maybe I can make my way back home."

Quino tipped his head to the side. "What happened to make you leave?"

Savy shook her head. She didn't want to talk about it. She didn't want to show her vulnerability. Heck, she hadn't even told Maisy what had happened, letting her think it had been a corporate downsize that had pushed her out.

"Come on," he cajoled. "After last night, there are no secrets between us. You clearly didn't leave of your own volition. What happened?"

"I haven't talked about it with anyone here," she said.

He gave her a look of understanding and put his free hand over his heart. "I promise to keep it in the vault."

"I was fired," she said. Even now, the words made her choke. She had to take a calming breath and a long sip of her coffee. She continued, "My boss, Linda Briggs, started a campaign against me. I know I sound paranoid, but I swear I'm not. She somehow managed to co-opt all of my work, making it look like it was originally hers. Then she went to management, accused me of stealing her work, and had me sacked."

"That evil witch!" Quino said. He was frowning, making deep WTF lines between his eyebrows, and Savannah felt as if he understood exactly how upsetting it had been. Weirdly, his outrage on her behalf made her feel much better. She warmed to the subject.

"It gets worse," she said. "She managed to have my hard drive wiped out so any proof that I had that I'd been the one coordinating the publicity for a new author we were promoting was gone. Meanwhile, my original work mysteriously appeared on her computer time-stamped as hers."

"That's evil," he said.

"Diabolical," she agreed. "I have one ally at the office, Archer, and he keeps me apprised of what's going on. I'm just waiting for her to slip up, so I can prove what she did to me."

"How's that looking?" he asked.

"Well, she may have hacked into my work hard drive but she didn't have what was on my personal laptop, so a lot of what she took was only half-finished. According to Archer, she is flailing," Savy said. She tried to keep the satisfaction out of her voice. She failed.

"And you think if you hit it out of the park with Maisy's shop, you'll get your cred back with your old employers," he said. "Is that the plan?"

"Mostly," she said. "But it's more than that. Publishing is a very small community and she destroyed my reputation. When I was fired I couldn't get another job anywhere. I want my reputation back and then I want a job with a publisher that values me."

"I can understand that," he said. "So that's why you're so fired up to go back to New York."

"Not just that," she said. "New York is my home. I love it there. I *like* that crosswalk lights are mere suggestions, that the best concerts in town are on subway platforms, where good manners are considered folding your pizza slice before biting into it, and . . . egg creams."

"Wait. What? You fold your pizza slice before you eat it?" he asked. He shook his head. "Bunch of savages."

Savannah saw the teasing gleam in his eye and she laughed. "Don't be judgy. I miss it. It's lovely here, don't get me wrong, but I want to go home."

"All right," he said. "Then let's figure out how you do that."

Chapter Twelve

SAVANNAH hurried into the secret room that was not so secret. A hideaway room, the entrance of which was built into a bench seat on the second floor of the bookstore. Savannah popped the lid and climbed over the side, stepping onto the narrow staircase that led to the hidden room below. Maisy and Ryder had discovered it when they were remodeling the place and it had become a meeting place for the Royal Order of George, a secret society the women had formed over the summer.

When Perry and Savannah had found King George, the bookstore cat, abandoned on the front porch of the shop when he was just a teeny tiny kitten, they decided to rescue him. It had been no small feat since their veterinarian friend Hannah advised that they not get attached, as he was only a few days old and not likely to thrive. Perry had been determined, however, and saving King George was the mission that launched the Royal Order of George, which was essentially a good deed club which met every Sunday night in the secret room.

"You're late, Savy," Maisy called from below. "We were about to start without you."

"But I brought pumpkin spice donuts," Savy said.

"She's forgiven," Jeri Lancaster declared. She turned to Savy and took the box. "You're forgiven."

"Donuts make everything better, don't they?" Savy asked.

"Especially when I brought hot cocoa," Jeri said.

She was a lovely woman, tall and lithe with dark skin and hair and a smile as wide as the sky. She had been Maisy's babysitter when they were kids but the two had remained close, and now that Jeri was an accountant, Maisy had tapped her to help keep the books. Savy wondered if she should just ask outright how the bookstore was doing.

"Savy, have you seen what Little G can do?" Perry called.

The moment was lost and Savy turned to see Perry holding a ball of yarn. Perry tossed the yarn across the room and King George pounced after it. At a little over five months old, he hadn't quite grown into his feet or his ears yet. He managed to retrieve the yarn ball with his mouth and he trotted back to Perry, dropping it at her feet.

Savy's jaw dropped. "Is he playing fetch?"

Perry nodded and grinned. "Isn't that the best?"

Savy looked at Maisy. "Did you know this about him?"

Maisy shook her head. "He's clearly special."

"Yes, he is," Jeri agreed. She kneeled next to Perry and scratched George under the chin just the way he liked it. "Who's my pretty kitty? Is it Georgie? Yes, it is."

Maisy smiled at Savy. "So, how was your meeting last night?"

"Good," Savy said. "Very productive."

"Really?" Maisy asked. "Because I heard that you were having coffee with Quino, and I'm not sure how that translates into promoting the bookstore, so do enlighten me."

"Who told you I was having coffee with Quino?" she asked. "Oh, wait, let me guess. Mary told Ellen who told Stan who told Ryder who told you, or some variation on that telephone game, am I right?"

Maisy laughed. "Pretty close. It was Travis Wainwright,

chief of police, actually. He saw you through the window and wondered if there was something happening there. There isn't, is there?"

"Stop fishing," Savy said. "Quino and I are just friends."

She didn't choke on the words, for which she was ever grateful. One slipup and Maisy would pounce like George on that ball of yarn. Maybe for one night they had been a rumpled-sheet, sweaty version of friends. But that was a onetime deal and now that she knew things—intimate things such as how he looked when he was on the brink of—well, it didn't change what they were, what they had always been. Just friends.

"If you say so," Maisy said.

"I do."

"All right, ladies, we need to get this meeting started," Jeri said. "I have to get back to my boys before Davis decides that a wrestling match is a great way to wind the boys down before bed."

"Okay, I call the Royal Order of George to order," Maisy said. "Any personal items to share?"

"Drink the cocoa before it gets cold," Jeri said.

"I'll pour," Perry offered. She approached their spread set up on a small table and poured the cocoa Jeri had brought into mugs, putting a big marshmallow or two into each before passing them out.

Savy clutched her mug, appreciating the warmth in her hands. She sipped the velvety concoction—it was rich and chocolaty with just a hint of cinnamon—and toasted Jeri with her mug.

"Delicious."

"Thank you."

"All right," Maisy said. "Who wants to share first?"

Jeri raised her hand. "I'll go."

Savy listened with half an ear. This was the part of the meeting where they shared whatever anonymous good deeds they had managed during the week. Sometimes it was simple stuff like buying coffee for the person behind them in line, and other times it was a bigger deed like sending a ticket for a loved one to come and visit an aging parent.

Jeri was talking about how she had started a reverse advent calendar with her boys. Instead of opening a window for every day of December on a paper calendar with chocolates tucked inside, she had given each of her boys a box and every day they put one nonperishable item for the food bank in the box. The week before Christmas they would donate their boxes full of food to a shelter.

Maisy's eyes went wide. "We could do donations here. Only we can make it books. We can collect the very best in romance books about women who are learning to stand on their own two feet, like *The Duchess War* by Courtney Milan or *Not Quite a Husband* by Sherry Thomas." She looked at Savy. "What do you think?"

"That is definitely something we can promote on social media," she said. She glanced at Jeri. How could she ask her about the financial situation of the shop without it coming out weird? Maybe she could work it in sideways here. "Unless giving away books would hurt the shop's bottom line?"

Jeri looked at her and shook her head. "We could have people buy them and donate them. Spread that good karma around. Or we could match their donation by donating another book. Also, it's a tax write-off, so it's a loss now but a possible gain later."

"I love this idea," Perry said. "I wonder if I could start something like this at my school."

"Brilliant," Maisy said. "Maybe the front office would be willing to help with a canned food drive, too."

"I'll ask," Perry said.

"Who's next?" Maisy asked.

Perry jumped in and talked about what she and her boyfriend, Cooper, had done that week. Although he didn't attend the meetings, Cooper Wainwright, yep, the police chief's son, was never far from Perry's side. If she was doing a good deed, he was usually with her.

Maisy went next. She and Ryder were bringing King George to the senior center to visit the cat-loving old folks. King George had taken to the role like a champ and Maisy insisted that he was getting better about his leash, but Savy had yet to see any evidence of that.

Then it was Savy's turn. She had no idea what to say. She'd been so consumed with Quino and their night together, she hadn't really thought about her quota of good deeds this week. She supposed she could say that she had relieved the sexual frustration of a poor man, but she suspected this would be called into question since she'd relieved her own pent-up hormones as well. Plus, it really wasn't rated PG and Perry was only fourteen.

"I didn't manage anything this week," she said. "But I did find a note in the wish box, thanking me for the grant-writing help I gave a few months ago, so can I cash in that chip?"

"What grant writing?" Maisy asked.

"In August, I found a note in the wish box from someone wishing for a grant to help pay for them to go work with elephants in Africa. So I did some searching and found a list of grants available, then I wrote up what I would submit if I were applying and left instructions for them to tailor it to their own needs. I left it beside the wish box and in a few days—poof!—it was gone. Well, this week a note appeared thanking me, so I'm thinking maybe it helped."

"The wish box," Maisy said. "Well, that was clever. I thought we were just keeping that as a place for people to store wishes, not to raid for our own good deeds."

"It had an elephant drawn on it," Savy said. "I got sucked in and I'm glad I did."

She glanced at her phone to check the time.

"Have someplace you need to be?" Jeri asked.

"No, not me," Savy said. "Just tired."

"Uh-huh," Maisy said. "And why would that be?"

"Insomnia," Savy said. "I hardly slept at all last night." At least half of that statement was true.

"I hear that," Jeri said. "It's been go, go, go ever since Thanksgiving. In fact, I have to get on home because I have to work on the boys' costumes for the Christmas pageant. I have one wise man, a Joseph, and a lamb to create out of old bedsheets and the insides of a pillow."

"And I have finals to study for," Perry said with a sigh.

Maisy glanced around the room. "All right, then, I move to adjourn the Royal Order of George until next Sunday. Agreed?"

"Aye," Jeri, Savy, and Perry all answered.

They all helped clean up, bringing the leftovers to the kitchen to save for work the next day. Pumpkin spice donuts would definitely make Monday morning more palatable. Jeri hugged everyone and scooted out the front door. Perry was right behind her with King George in his harness, refusing to walk on his leash, leaving her no choice but to carry him. Shocker.

Maisy was about to follow them and Savy supposed she should let her go since it was almost eight thirty. If she loitered, she'd be late getting to Quino's, which was a fifteen-minute drive to the outskirts of town. But if she engaged Maisy in conversation, she might learn what sort of financial straits the bookstore was in. Decision made. Quino would have to wait.

"Maisy, can I ask you something?" she said as Maisy shrugged into her coat.

"Sure." Maisy pulled a knit beanie over her curls. "What's up?"

"Are you enjoying owning the bookstore?" Savy asked. "Is it everything you hoped it would be?"

Maisy's eyes went wide behind her glasses. "Oh, hell, yeah. I mean, I figured I'd enjoy it, but I had no idea I would love it so much. Connecting readers with books, meeting authors, running my own business. I love, love, love it. I wish I was better at the business side of things, but I'm hoping that will come with time."

"Are you worried about the business?" Savy asked. There, she said it. Now would be a great time for Maisy to share if there was a problem.

"Oh, shoot, does it show?" Maisy asked. "I try so hard to pretend I know what I'm doing, but I have to tell you, I don't have a clue. I am seriously doing the *fake it till you make it* thing. Do you think anyone else knows? Do you think they suspect? I'll just die if someone calls me out."

Unprepared for this gush of honesty, Savy blinked.
What to do? Tell her friend that she knew she was in financial trouble or blindly reassure her? She glanced at Maisy
and saw tears in her friend's eyes. Oh, no. She did not want
to be the one to pull Maisy under the water when she was
already drowning.

"No!" Savy said. "You are doing a phenomenal job. I
mean, look at this place. Not right now because it's empty
but day to day, we are rocking some serious foot traffic."

"You think so?" Maisy bit her thumbnail in a nervous
habit Savy recognized. She took her friend's hand and
pulled it away from her mouth.

"I know so," Savy said. She tried to infuse her words
with all of the confidence she could muster. "You've got
this. Now go be with your man. I'll lock up."

"Okay." Maisy flashed her a bright smile. Then she hugged
Savy hard. "I'm so glad you're here to help me. Love you."

"Love you, too." Savy hugged her back.

She watched from the porch as Maisy dashed across the
side yard to the house next door. Ryder had bought it as a
surprise for her and they were in the midst of refurbishing
it for their spring wedding. Unless the bookstore collapsed
around them and Maisy lost everything, including her new
home. *Ack!*

Savy dashed back into the bookstore, grabbed her purse,
set the alarm, and headed for her car, which was parked on
the street. The night air was cold with a bite to it and she
glanced up to see if the stars were shining. They weren't.
She wondered if that meant they were in for some snow.
While it would be lovely and festive, it would also mean
people would stay home instead of coming out to the store
and shopping. That settled it. She hoped there was no snow.

Her car was an old clunker she'd bought just to get
around Fairdale. Its heater didn't work, which she considered more incentive to get out of Fairdale and back to the
land of pedestrianism where she didn't need a car.

She drove out of town and down the winding roads toward Shadow Pine Stables. Maisy had dragged her on a trail
ride back in October when the leaves had been changing and

everything was gloriously colorful. It was quite the spread with several corrals, a huge barn, a guest cottage, and a big old farmhouse, with a full-on wraparound porch and everything. She turned a long corner and came over a small rise and there it was. Normally, on a dark night like tonight, on a road that had no streetlights, she would have barely been able to make out the place, but at the moment it was lit up like it had been hit with napalm.

Savy's foot slipped off the gas and her car began to slow as her eyes got wider and wider. The man was crackers. Completely, utterly bonkers.

She turned into the driveway, passing the cottage, which sported festive strings of white lights, and then followed the drive up to the house. The big white two-story house was presently covered in so many strands of lights that it was a beacon in the darkness to passing aircraft. Some of the lights twinkled, some flashed, and some played carols while the lights changed. An enormous blow-up Santa was on the roof, looking like he was about to jump down the chimney. The railings of the front porch were swathed in pine boughs and an enormous wreath hung on the front door. In every window of the house a single white candle glowed. Savy parked her car and stared and stared. She couldn't take it all in. It was too much.

She got out of her car and stood in the cold night air, staring at the house. She had heard stories of people who embraced the holiday with this much fervor but she'd never actually met one. She had way more than met Quino. Who would have thought that under his rugged cowboy exterior there lurked a Christmas sadist?

"Whatcha doin'?" a voice called from the porch.

Savy's gaze bounced around until she saw him, standing on the side of the porch, fussing with a strand of lights that was twined about the railing. He was wearing another Christmas sweater—this one was blue and had a present on it but did not appear to light up. Amen.

"I'm just taking it all in," she said.

He grinned and she could see a slash of white teeth in the face that was backlit by the display behind him. She walked over to where he stood and repeated his question to him. "Whatcha doin'?"

"Waiting for a friend," he said. He dropped the lights and looked at her with his dark gaze, and Savy felt the blast of affection warm her all the way to her toes. "Come on. Let's get inside out of the cold."

She followed him up the steps and into the house. There was an old-fashioned coatrack to one side of the front door and Savy hung up her purse and her jacket on one of the hooks. Following Quino's lead, she kicked off her shoes and moved them to the side. A large living room was off to the left while a staircase and a hallway offered two other exits off the foyer. Quino headed to the left into the large living room.

A fire was hissing and spitting in a large stone fireplace on the far side of the room. Two brown leather couches dominated most of the space, centered around a big flat-screen television that was on the wall between two large windows. Savy assumed from their location that they overlooked the side pasture and the barn, but it was dark and she couldn't be sure.

A bare Christmas tree was set up against the wall opposite from the fireplace and stacks of boxes surrounded it. Good grief. If they put all of these ornaments on the tree, they were going to be here all night. She wondered why that didn't immediately strike her as a bad thing.

"All right," he said. He put his hands together and said. "Eggnog?"

"Really?" she asked. "You actually drink that stuff?"

"Aw, come on, you don't like eggnog?" he asked. "It's homemade."

"Like with raw eggs?"

"No, with cooked egg yolks and more important, rum," he said. "Trust me."

Savy shook her head. "I've only had the stuff out of a carton at the grocery store."

"Yeah, that's like drinking cinnamon-laced half-and-half," he said. "Bleck."

"All right," she said. "But if I don't like it, I don't want you to get all pitiful."

"You'll like it," he said. "I'll be right back. Make yourself at home."

Savannah moved to stand by the fire. She did a quick glance up at the ceiling. No mistletoe. Huh. She was surprised she didn't feel more relieved.

She shook her head. Clearly, she was still under Quino's spell from last night. It would just take them a little while to find their friendship footing. But if they focused on the need to save the bookstore, that would keep their priorities in order. She was sure of it.

She noted the mantel had several framed photographs amidst all of the pine boughs. The pictures were older but she could see Quino as a young teen with a girl she recognized as his sister, Desi. The couple with them must be their parents. She noticed that Quino had his mother's smile and his father's eyes. They looked like a happy family and she wondered what growing up here with these parents must have been like.

There were several more photographs, some with all four of them and some just of Desi and Quino. None of the pictures were recent, as if that sort of thing had stopped with the passing of their parents. Savy knew that Quino had stepped up to raise his sister after their parents were killed. She wondered if living here and running the stables had been Quino's dream or if he had planned something else but life got in the way. She wondered how she could ask him without it being too intrusive.

"Here you go," he said. He was carrying two mugs, both filled to the brim with a dusting of cinnamon on top.

Savannah turned away from the photos and took the mug he held out to her. The fire at her back felt warm and she sipped the cold beverage, bracing herself for the slimy thick taste of eggnog. This had none of that. It was light and fluffy with a zip of alcohol. It was delicious.

"Okay, you win," she said. "That's amazing."

He grinned at her. It was a slow, lazy grin that reminded her of how he'd looked at her during their lone night of debauchery. Savy sighed. If only she wanted to stay here. She could see herself dating this man. But really, any relationship was doomed from the start because they wanted different things. It was best that she not forget this.

"So, how does this work?" she asked. "Do you watch the movie while you decorate the tree or do you decorate and then watch the movie?"

"Little bit of both," he said. "It doesn't take the whole length of the movie to decorate, so we usually start at the same time and then sit to watch the end."

"All right," Savy said. She took a big glug of eggnog. The rum was a bit stronger than she'd anticipated. "Let's get this party started."

Quino took the mug out of her hand and set it on the coffee table. Then he picked up a box of ornaments and handed them to her. She gave him a sassy salute but turned to the tree and set to work while Quino started the movie. The box he had given her was full of vintage glass ornaments that looked like they were from the '50s.

"What's the story behind these ornaments?" she asked.

He glanced up from the remote as the opening credits started to roll. He put the controller on the coffee table and joined her by the tree.

"Those were my grandparents'," he said. "When they were first married. See? All twelve are the symbols for a happy marriage."

He lifted an ornament out of the box. It was shaped like a heart. The date, hand painted on it, read *December 15, 1955.* "That's the date they were married." He hung it high on the tree. "The rest of these are symbolic."

Savy lifted out a pretty glass pinecone. "Explain."

His grin was wicked and his chuckle low and deep, making her shiver in a delicious way. She shook it off.

"Really?" she asked. "What does it represent, a naughty game of hide the pinecone?"

"Close, actually," he said. "It stands for fertility, fruitfulness, and motherhood."

Savy dropped it gently back into the box. She pointed at the teapot. "And that one?"

"Hospitality," he said as he picked it up and put it on the tree. Then he put on the pinecone.

"And the rabbit?" she asked. "Call me crazy but that seems off-season."

"It stands for nature and hope," he said. He picked it up and handed it to her. "Here."

Savy put the box down and took the ornament. She'd never put up a tree of her own. She didn't even own any Christmas decorations. Her mother's tree was always done by her interior decorator and had a different color scheme every year. As far as Savy knew, they didn't have any family ornaments. She gingerly put the rabbit on the front of the tree, below the heart but with enough space between so it wasn't crowded.

They continued decorating. Some boxes were just regulation ornaments but some were obviously treasures. There was a child's handprint in clay, painted green and glitter-bombed. She looked at the back and saw the name *Desi* written with the date '98. It was such a tiny handprint. It made her throat tighten, thinking about the little girl who made it.

"Where is Desi?" she asked. "I haven't seen her lately."

Quino turned away from adjusting a string of lights on the tree to face her. He looked resigned when he said, "She's traveling."

Savy could tell he missed his sister. She knew Quino and Desi well enough to know they were close. It was clear Quino felt the absence of his sister and she was glad she could be here to fill the void in a friendly capacity.

"Uh-oh, there he is!" Quino cried. "Ten points if you hit him on the nose, five points on the face, one point for body shots!"

"What? Who?" Savy glanced around the room.

"Mr. Potter!" Quino said. He pointed at the screen. He snatched a bowl of popcorn up off the table, snagged a kernel, and hit Potter right on the beak. He gave Savy a triumphant look. "Ten points."

She frowned at him and then at the bowl. She grabbed a fistful of kernels and chucked the whole handful at the television screen. "Fifty points!"

"It's supposed to be one kernel at a time," Quino protested, but he was laughing. "But I like your style."

He was so sexy when he laughed. His thick dark hair fell back from his face in waves and his chiseled features softened with youthful exuberance. Savy got a sense of what he had looked like when he was young and she knew that if they had met when they were teens, she would have been crushing so hard on him.

"Sorry, I got carried away," she said.

She turned away from him, afraid she was going to reveal too much, and instead she began to pick up the popcorn she had thrown. Quino knelt down beside her and helped.

"No harm in that," he said.

She glanced up and met his gaze. She wondered if he was referring to popcorn tossing or their night where they had both been spectacularly carried away. She swallowed hard and then reached for her eggnog, downing the frothy goodness in one long chug.

"Easy there," he said. "That nog's got some kick."

"Pfff." She waved a dismissive hand. Then she took her mug and her fistful of throwaway popcorn and headed to the kitchen. "I'm having more. How about you?"

"Right behind you," he said.

She glanced at him to see if he'd meant that in a pervy way but he just smiled at her. The picture of innocence. Huh.

"So, I meant to ask you," he said. "Did you find out anything from Jeri about the shop?"

"No," she said. She navigated the hallway that opened into a large dining room, with a lovely antique table and chairs and a matching hutch, and continued on to the kitchen beyond. It was a beautiful space with white cabinets and concrete counters done in the palest shade of blue. The garbage was exactly where she would put it, under the kitchen sink, and she dumped her kernels there and then headed for the refrigerator. A big glass pitcher full of frothy yumminess was sitting there and she grabbed it and put it on the counter.

When she would have started pouring, Quino stopped her and said, "Wait, it's important to do this right."

She relinquished her mug and watched as he refreshed both of their beverages and then proceeded to sprinkle cinnamon and grate fresh nutmeg on top of the nog. The man was a marvel.

"Quino," she said. "This might be the rum talking, but you are going to make someone a fabulous wife someday."

He grinned as he put the pitcher back. "Yeah, it's the rum talking, but I'll take it."

He led the way back to the living room. They resumed decorating the tree while watching the movie and Savy killed off another mug of eggnog and then another. When the tree was done, Quino snapped off the living room lights so they could enjoy the glow of the tree and the sparkle of ornaments. Savy felt a warmth inside of her that she knew was most likely the rum, but she was too self-aware and honest to deny that there was a tiny jingle bell of Christmas spirit, ring-a-ling-a-linging down deep inside of her.

Is this what people felt during the holidays? This glowing warmth from within, where everything seemed as precious and pure as a new snowfall? Well, no wonder people got all giddy about the holidays. This felt really . . . nice.

They sat on the couch to watch the end of the movie. Savy had seen bits of the movie before but never in a farmhouse, with a cozy fire, a bellyful of eggnog and popcorn, and a hot cowboy beside her, having just decorated a Christmas tree.

When the joyous moment came in the movie, she felt her throat close up and her eyes were watery. She tried to push it down, but she couldn't. A tear slipped out and she tried to covertly wipe it away. Quino saw her, however. He lifted his arm in silent invitation, and she scooted across the couch and slipped underneath it, letting him pull her close.

It felt right. She tried not to dwell on it. As the credits rolled, she felt her eyes begin to droop. It had been a full day and she was beat, plus, he smelled so good and he was so warm and solid. In a life that had been full of defeat lately, this felt like a win.

She battled to stay awake to see the bell ring on the Christmas tree, but she had one foot in the here and now and one foot in the dreamy place where kisses were exchanged under the mistletoe with a guy who made her heart beat fast.

"It's too bad," she said.

"What's too bad?" His voice was a soft low growl in her ear.

"That you don't have any mistletoe hanging. This place could use some mistletoe."

"Excuse me?" he asked. He was watching her with a small smile and Savy felt compelled to tell him the truth.

"I have to tell you, stable boy," she said. His eyebrows went up but he didn't interrupt. "That night with you was the best I've ever had. I mean, off the charts, it's never ever going to be that *Please, sir, may I have some more?* wowsie wow wow again." She leaned close, making sure she looked him in the eye when she whispered, "I had no idea sex could be that, you know—sexy."

Chapter Thirteen

QUINO didn't move. Savy slumped in his arms and he just sat there. Did she just say . . . ? A soft snore interrupted his train of thought. He glanced down at the woman in his arms. Her eyes were shut, her mouth was slightly parted, her breathing was long and deep. Red was down for the count.

He lifted the remote from the cushion beside him and muted the television. In the glow of the tree's lights he could see the colors in her hair. It wasn't just red; it was shot with individual strands of gold and copper. He was fascinated. She fit perfectly against him and he rested his cheek on her soft curls. He pulled the pretty blue afghan his mother had knit when he was a boy over them and held her close while she slept. Probably, he should wake her, but she'd had a lot of eggnog and he didn't think she should drive. He was really just being responsible.

He wondered about her comment on the lack of mistletoe and their previous night together. Had she been hoping he'd kiss her tonight? He had promised not to push and he wouldn't. Not unless she gave him a clear signal that she wanted more. He felt like it was a victory just getting her here in his house.

He glanced around the room full of so many memories of his parents and Desi. He remembered his dad kissing his mom under the mistletoe in the doorway over there and by the window and in the kitchen. He smiled. His dad had known how to work the mistletoe, but he also remembered that his mother had always been the one to buy the mistletoe, so clearly, she encouraged him.

Quino had always hoped to have what his parents had had. They were best friends, devoted to each other and their kids. He wanted that. And he wanted it with this crazy redhead in his arms. He knew that Savy had to figure it out for herself. What they had was more than just a combustible attraction, which she had just so helpfully acknowledged. Over the past few months, he had discovered that they had the same sense of humor, the same set of values, and the same pigheadedness. Which unfortunately meant that as much as he believed they should be together, she believed they shouldn't. All of which made him certain they had the potential to be something really great together.

The question was, How did he get her to see that? They had a mission now. Saving Maisy's bookstore. It would give them a chance to work together for a common goal. Maybe if they were successful, Savy would see what they could have together and give a relationship between them a real chance instead of one night, which was never ever going to be enough for him.

SAVY awoke with her head feeling fuzzy and her mouth dry. She was snuggly warm with a thick afghan over her and a pillow . . . wait. She didn't own a pillow with a heartbeat. She opened her eyes. Gray early-morning light peeked in through the window as if trying not to disturb her. It took a moment to register the ugly Christmas sweater beneath her cheek as belonging to Quino.

She glanced down. All her clothes were on. All his clothes were on. The fire was dead. The Christmas tree lights and the television were off. The world was so quiet all she could hear were the sounds of Quino's heartbeat and the steady inhale and exhale of his breath. She didn't want to move. She just wanted to lie half on top of him on the sofa, where they'd clearly fallen asleep last night.

She vaguely remembered conking out during the end of the movie. Oh, man, had she been snoring? Had she been so out of it that he couldn't wake her and send her on her way? Is that why they were curled up together like two teenagers breaking curfew? How embarrassing. Then again, it could be worse. If they'd slept together, it'd be all sorts of awkward. She'd be doing the *shove the bra in a pocket and scuttle out the door* walk of shame, so thank heavens she had nothing to be embarrassed about.

It came then. A memory crystalizing from the ether of her mind. She'd been looking up at him and she had—*oh, God*—told him he was the best she'd ever had. And she'd asked why he didn't have any mistletoe up. Aw, man, it was the mixed-signal thing. This was what guys rightly complained about, and she had just done it. Savy always prided herself on being very clear with her wants and needs. She tried not to give anyone the wrong idea. And here she was blowing hot and cold with Quino. Argh!

This was mortifying. What was she supposed to say to him? *Sorry I got plastered on eggnog. I didn't mean anything in that truth bomb I lobbed at you.* She wanted to do a facepalm. But she didn't want to wake him. In fact, she wanted to scuttle out of here under the cold light of day and avoid him altogether. Maybe he'd had too much nog, too, and wouldn't remember her careless words. She certainly hoped so.

She pushed herself up, painfully slowly, and moved off him. She froze once when his hand moved. He ran it across her back as if to reassure himself of her and then it fell back to his side. She slid over him, hoping he didn't wake up, and then slowly rose to her feet, making sure he was covered by the afghan so he wouldn't get cold. She tiptoed out of the room. With one last look at the handsome man asleep on the couch and the pretty tree they'd decorated together, she slid on her shoes, grabbed her coat and purse, and slipped from the house.

S AVY spent the morning loaded up on pain reliever for her headache and consuming copious amounts of water and caffeine. She had a crick in her neck from sleeping in a weird position on Quino's couch, or more accurately, on Quino. And she vowed to herself that she was never going to drink eggnog again. Ever.

The other day, she had launched her latest campaign to get Destiny Swann to come to the bookstore for a signing, and by noon, she had her answer. Destiny's assistant, Genevieve Spencer, with whom Savy felt she was now on a first-name basis, sent a pointed e-mail that while Destiny appreciated the balloon-o-gram very much, she was still not interested in a signing at the Happily Ever After Bookshop.

Savy put her head down on her desk. She needed soup. She needed some retail therapy. She needed Destiny to change her mind but it didn't look like that was going to happen, and so she was down to cookie-decorating parties and holiday-movie gatherings and whatever else she and Quino could come up with in the next few weeks to keep the foot traffic coming through the door.

For a moment she felt less lonely for having Quino with her on this mission, but then she remembered last night and how she didn't think she could ever face him again and she sank back into the depths of despair. There was no help for it. On this miserable Monday, retail therapy was the only thing that was going to pull her through.

Savannah put on her coat and her hat and grabbed her handbag out of her desk drawer. Maisy was working out front in the empty shop. Savy scanned the room. There were literally no customers and they'd been open for hours.

She felt the panic bubble in her belly and she called to Maisy, "I'll be right back. Just stepping out for a bit."

"Take your time," Maisy called. She spread her arms wide. "I think I can manage the hordes by myself."

Savy flashed a smile even though she felt like crying.

Her job was publicity and marketing. With the store empty, the feeling of failure was a crushing weight on her chest.

The day was brisk and she opted to walk to Main Street, hoping it would clear her head. She kicked over some new ideas for the store. So what if she couldn't get Destiny to come to the bookstore? There had to be some other authors in the area who would be willing to help promote the shop with a signing.

She paused at a psychic's shop, wondering if she should get her fortune read. Nah, she didn't want to get the news that the shop was going to fail and they were all doomed. She figured her aura was pretty black right now and would likely send the psychic into a full-on panic attack and she'd be smudging her shop with burning sage for days after a visit from Savy.

She continued down the street, ducking a mom with a stroller, two older ladies, and a pack of teens that she was quite certain should be in school. She could smell the faint scent of cinnamon in the air. The bakery on the corner was baking their chewy gooey cinnamon rolls and she had to stop herself from buying a couple and comfort-eating them right there on the spot.

She didn't know what she was going to do. It felt like everything she touched was a mess. She couldn't get her old job back. Maisy's bookstore was on the brink of ruin. And she'd slept with a guy she clearly should have kept in the friend zone. She couldn't seem to do anything right. How was this her life? She didn't know. She couldn't weigh this hot disaster against the successful career she'd once enjoyed.

Savy paused to take in the decorations on the town green. Garlands and holiday banners decorated every lamppost. It was homey and lovely. She started humming. It took her a few bars to realize she was humming a Christmas tune. *What?* As far as she knew, she had never sung a Christmas carol in her life. She was not a singer or a hummer. Oh, man, what was happening to her? Savy didn't even recognize herself anymore and she had no idea what to do about it.

She glanced down the street, thinking she'd buy some

gifts to send home to her family. Her father was a tie, always a tie. Her mother was perfume, always the same brand. About five years ago, she'd tried to break out and buy them something unexpected. She'd gotten her father a golf shirt and her mother a pretty bathrobe. She'd found both items in the annual pile of donations to charity that her mother had their housekeeper gather every year around New Year's. Lesson learned.

With a sigh, she headed toward Perryman's, the only large department store in town. She had no desire to drive all the way to Greenville just to hit the mall there. She'd just stepped through the revolving door when she saw a man out of the corner of her eye. He was wearing a denim shearling jacket and a black cowboy hat. He had on jeans and boots and he was standing by the jewelry counter.

Savy would know the backside, sideside, or frontside of that man anywhere. It was Joaquin! What the heck was he doing in Perryman's? As if he felt the heat of her laserlike stare upon him, he looked up from the counter and their eyes met.

He raised a hand in greeting but Savy was too mortified to speak to him. She pretended she didn't see him and made a big show of looking all around at the enormous glitter-covered snowflakes that were suspended from the ceiling. Then she all but ran into the women's department to hide.

She should have known it wouldn't be that easy. She was dodging behind a rack of dresses when she heard him call, "Hey, Red!"

She picked up her speed. She knew she was being an immature idiot but it was too much. He was too much. She didn't know what to say to him after last night, which weirdly had felt even more intimate than the night they'd had sex. Savy wasn't good with intimacy. It made her feel vulnerable and she hated that.

She glanced behind her to see if she'd lost him. He wasn't there. Phew. She turned around and sprinted into the women's undergarment department. Surely, that would curb his enthusiasm. What man wanted to talk amidst racks of bras and undies? Confident, Savy circled a tall rack of holiday bras and slammed right into a broad chest. She glanced up. Quino. Damn it!

"If I didn't know better, I'd say you were ducking me," he said.

"I am ducking you," she retorted.

He looked confused. "Why?"

"Because of last night," she said.

"But nothing happened last night," he said.

A female employee, working on sorting a rack of underwear sets, stopped what she was doing to listen to their conversation. Savy stared at her and the woman glanced away, pretending to be straightening all the straps while moving closer to them, all the better to hear.

Savy spun on her heel and approached the shelf of packaged cotton undergarments. She intentionally picked the least sexy, most boring, white cotton bundle. There. Nothing to see here. That should put him off.

Nope.

"Red, I could understand if you'd ditched me after the night we—"

"Don't," Savy cut him off.

"But last night, we just fell asleep," he said. "Really, not a big deal."

Savy clutched the package to her chest. Maybe he didn't remember her declaration that he was the best sex she'd ever had. Maybe he'd been eggnog-impaired as well. She sent a silent hopeful prayer up into the glittery snowflakes.

"So, we're cool?" she asked.

His grin when it came was smokin' hot. It made Savy's heart rate kick up into the danger zone and she felt a little dizzy.

"Well, judging by what you said last night, I'd say we're more *hot* than cool," he said. There was a teasing glint in his eyes but Savy wasn't having it.

"Ugh," she grunted. She could feel her face get fiery and she thumped him on the chest with the package of underwear. "So you do remember what I said."

"Red, when a woman says you're the best she's ever had, you're not likely to forget it," he said.

"Making this whole thing"—she paused to point between them—"a bust. We can't possibly work together now."

"What?" he asked. "Why not?"

"Because you don't really care about any of this," she said. "You don't care about the bookstore or whether I get back to New York. You're in this for all the wrong reasons."

He straightened up and glowered at her, pushing his hat back on his head. "And what reasons would those be?"

"Sex," she snapped. "You're just being helpful to see if we'll hook up again. Well, we won't. So, now you're free to go. So git."

"You could not be more wrong," he said. "I do care about the bookstore and about you getting back to New York."

"Well, it doesn't even matter because I can't save the bookstore and I can't get my reputation back and I hate Christmas," Savy said. She glared at a mannequin dressed up in a slinky elf costume, turned, and left.

Quino sprinted in front of her, walking backward as he faced her, slowing her progress. "Whoa, whoa, whoa, slow your roll there, Red."

She scowled at him. "Stop calling me Red. And I am not one of your horses. Do not 'whoa' me."

He raised his hands in the air as if she were waving a gun at him and not a package of underwear.

"Tell me what's going on," he said. His voice was soft, gentle, and a part of Savy suspected it was the same tone he used on his horses when they were acting up. She felt like she should be outraged and kick him, but she just didn't have the energy.

"Stop being nice when I'm trying to be mad at you," she said.

He smiled as if he found her adorable. It was the tipping point. Much to Savy's mortification, she burst into tears right there in the undergarment section of Perryman's while holding a package of white cotton underpants.

"Uh-oh," Quino said. "Okay, I didn't see that coming. Let's get out of here before someone gets the wrong idea."

He took the package of underpants and put them on the base of a display, then took her arm and steered her out of the shop. A few heads swiveled in their direction, and the security guard by the door looked at them as if he was trying to decide whether he needed to get involved or not.

Quino patted her back and said, loudly, "There, there, we'll find your missing puppy. No worries."

Savy's head snapped up, but Quino pushed her into the revolving door and out onto the street.

Her tears vanished and she looked at him in confusion.

"I don't have a puppy." she said.

"I know. It was the first excuse I could come up with for the waterworks," he said. He gave her side-eye. "Are you okay?"

At the concern in his voice, Savy felt her lower lip quiver. She tried to stop it, but from the way he was looking at her, she knew she failed. A strangled sob came out of her and she sighed.

"Aw, come here, Red," he said. He took her hand and led her across the street to the town green. Given the chilly temperatures, the square was empty and he found a bench for them to share. He sat and pulled her down beside him. "Tell me what's wrong."

"Everything," she said. "The night we went ice-skating, I talked to my friend Archer in New York and he hasn't had any luck proving that my old boss made fast and loose with my work. I've tried so hard to do something big for the bookstore, and this morning I was soundly rejected—again. I just keep failing. I'm not used to failure. I don't like it."

He watched her with a sympathetic gaze and it hooked her in. She kept talking, sharing a lot more than she normally would have. It hit her then that she trusted him.

"If I could just get Destiny Swann to agree to visit the bookstore," she said. "It would be the hugest event in the romance novel industry, and it would secure Maisy's success and prove that I am the single greatest publicist ever—not that this is about me."

Quino's eyes went wide. Then he chuckled. It was a deep sound that barreled out of his chest and at any other time it would have made Savy laugh in return. But at the moment, he was laughing at her and it cut so deep and made her so mad, it took all the dignity she possessed not to slug him. Instead, she rose to her feet, planning to softly glide away. She absolutely would not flounce even though she really wanted to.

"Wait!" Quino reached out and grabbed her hand.

"No," she said. "You can laugh at me all by yourself. You don't need me for an audience."

"I'm not laughing at you," he said, still laughing.

"Really?" she asked. She waved her free hand to encompass all of him. "'Cause you look like you're laughing to me."

"Okay, I am laughing," he said, still chuckling.

Savy growled low in her throat and tried to yank her hand out of his.

"But it's not at you," he insisted. "Rather, it's because of the situation."

"Because my pain is hilarious?" she asked.

"No, it's not."

"Whatever," she said. "Let go. I'm leaving."

He let her go, but leaned back on the bench, watching her as she stomped away.

"Are you sure you want to leave when you have full access to Destiny Swann's riding coach?"

"Yes!" she snarled. She took two steps and then spun back around. "What did you say?"

"Let me introduce myself," he said. "I am Joaquin Solis. I own the Shadow Pine Stables, and also give private lessons to Destiny Swann at her home, Windemere Manor."

"Are you messing with me?" she asked. She could hardly breathe. "Because the hurt I will put on you if you are pranking me will be legendary."

Quino stood up and raised his hands in the air. "I swear."

"You know Destiny Swann?" Savy asked. Now her heart was racing for completely different reasons.

"Yeah, she's actually become a good friend over the years," he said.

Savy didn't pause to think it through. She got a running start and threw herself into his arms, planting a kiss on him that would have wrecked a lesser man.

Chapter Fourteen

QUINO had his arms full of Savannah, an event he hadn't anticipated but was happy to enjoy to the fullest. When her mouth landed on his, he felt that same surge of feeling he always felt when she was near. The feeling that she was *the one*. It was heady stuff and he couldn't help it if the kiss turned into a more passionate undertaking than she'd likely been planning.

As she slid down the front of him, he released his arms from around her waist and cupped her face. Kissing her just a little bit longer, savoring the taste and touch of the woman he was madly in love with. It had hit him this morning when he woke up without her. He'd felt bereft as if something integral to his very existence had vanished and all he could think about was getting it back. When he'd seen her walk into Perryman's today, it was as if the universe understood his plight and was giving him a hand.

When the kiss ended, his ears were ringing and it took him a moment to register her words.

"You are my hero!" she cried. "Do you have any idea how hard I have tried to get her to talk to me? Just talk to me?"

"Oh." He made a cringe face. "I can't imagine Genevieve was very receptive."

"Her assistant," Savy said. "You know Genevieve Spencer?"

"She sets up the lessons," he said. "Nice girl, Genevieve."

"Nice?" Savy asked. "I've tried to go around her, through her, over her. It's like trying to bypass Cerberus."

"She's not a three-headed dog," he said. "I promise."

"A dragon, then."

"That, either."

"I'll take your word for it," Savy said. She sat back down on the bench and he sat beside her. She looked at him in panic. "Wait. I'm assuming you're going to help me. Are you going to help me? Please help me."

"Of course," he said. As if he could deny this woman anything. "In fact, I have a lesson scheduled with Destiny on Thursday. Want to come with me?"

"Yes!" she shouted. He flinched. "Sorry. Was that too eager?"

"A bit," he said. "Listen, she might still say no. She and I are friends but she's been a recluse for a very long time."

"Over ten years," Savy said. "Do you know why?"

"I've never asked." Quino shook his head. He knew that Destiny was an author so he'd just assumed that it was a part of her creative process, to shut out the world. Now he wondered if it was something more.

They sat silently for a while, pondering the best way to approach Destiny.

"I hesitate to say this," Quino said. "But it might be best if she thinks you're my . . . special lady friend."

"You mean your girlfriend?" Savy asked.

"In a manner of speaking." He watched her face to see what she thought of this.

"Any reason why?" she asked.

"Well, it explains your presence at the lesson without making it look like I brought you there to ambush her," he said. "Genevieve is not an ogre, really, but she is very protective of Destiny, and if she thinks you're there for any other reason than to watch your man give riding lessons,

I'm pretty sure she'll have us both hauled off the premises without hesitation."

"All right," Savy said. "I'll be your GINO."

"Huh?" he asked. "That doesn't sound like something I am even remotely interested in having."

She laughed. The sunlight highlighted the gold in her reddish curls and her light-green eyes turned up in the corners with her smile. "GINO. 'Girlfriend in name only.'"

So, he'd been right. He had no interest in that acronym whatsoever. But he did have an interest in her. Winning over Savy was a marathon, not a sprint, and getting her to Destiny was one more step closer to the finish line, or so he hoped.

They strategized over coffee and bagels at the Perk Up and agreed that Savy would meet him at his house since he had to load up his horse and Destiny's favorite ride, a pretty bay named Cocoa. When Savy hugged him good-bye, Quino forced himself not to hold on too tight or too long but let her slide out of his arms with a spring in her step that he felt very pleased to have put there even if it was due to a happenstance.

He then went back to Perryman's to finish the shopping he'd been doing when he caught sight of Savy. At the fine-jewelry counter, he'd found a pendant for Desi. It was a delicate gold elephant, a baby elephant, that he knew she would love. True to her word, she'd sent him some pictures and a short video of her working with the elephants.

To him, the animals looked enormous, like they could drop and roll on his sister and she'd be crushed to death and he wouldn't be there to help her or save her. He'd had to put his head down between his knees and breathe through his first viewing of the images.

The time change made calling difficult, but when he couldn't take it anymore, he called her, waking her up. She sounded groggy but happy and exhausted. She had fallen asleep while describing one of her charges, a young bull elephant named Maktao. She said he was quite the handful, trying to steal the milk bottles, which, judging by the pictures she'd sent, were the size of water cooler bottles. He could hear how happy she was. It was the only thing that kept him from boarding the first plane out of North Carolina and jetting to Kenya as fast as he could.

Quino paid for the gift, and the woman behind the counter wrapped the velvet box the pendant was in with pretty silver paper with a bright-blue bow. Quino pocketed the gift, wondering when he would even see Desi for the holiday—she hadn't said how long her internship lasted—and if not, how could he get the present to her in Africa in time?

His heart sank a bit at the thought of not having his sister with him. It would be the first Christmas they hadn't spent together. He didn't know how to process that, and he wondered if maybe he had locked in on Savy as *the one* because she was a delightful redheaded distraction. No, he knew that wasn't it. He'd fallen hard for Red the first time he saw her when she'd freshly arrived in town and was so full of sass and attitude that he had boasted to Ryder that he'd marry her by Christmas. What an idiot.

Sensing he was full of himself, Savy hadn't given him the time of day. Good thing, too. If he'd known then how it would be between them when he finally did get her in his arms, he'd have trailed after her like a lovesick puppy. He wasn't sure how he was managing enough restraint not to do so now. It was going to take forever for Thursday to get here.

He wondered how the day would go, bringing her to meet Destiny. Should he call Genevieve and give her a heads-up or let it play out as it would? He liked Destiny. Oh, she was a character, of that there was no question, but she had a big heart and afternoons spent with her were always entertaining. He decided to stay out of it. He didn't want to pressure his friend to do his girlfriend, rather GINO, a favor. And he didn't want to take charge of something Savy needed to do for herself. He could set up the meeting but he had a feeling if Savy's idea was going to fly, she would only be happy if it came from her. She was trying to prove herself and he wasn't going to mess that up for her.

Quino stepped back outside. The temperature had dropped

and he glanced up at the sky. He'd really thought they'd have gotten some snow the night before. The air had held the promise of cold damp flakes dusting the evergreen trees and the dry lawns and leaf-bare trees in a coat of white, but so far nothing. He tried not to be disappointed, as he really loved the first snow of the season. But then he remembered that he wanted this season to go by as slowly as possible, because if Savy got her way, and he had no reason to think she wouldn't, then she'd get Destiny to do her book signing at the shop and then she'd be gone for good.

THE morning of the visit to Windemere, Savannah had a complete and total meltdown. Having been raised by a socialite mother, she usually knew exactly what to wear and how to dress. Today, all of those miserable lessons in deportment had completely abandoned her.

She'd put on jeans, traded them for slacks, then tried a skirt with tights, and, finally, went for a knit dress. Nothing felt right. She didn't know what to wear to throw herself on the mercy of the grande dame of romance novels. She was completely freaking out. She grabbed up all the choices in her arms and hurried out of her apartment, through the bookstore, heading to her car.

Maisy was with Sawyer Copeland, Ryder's brother, who was standing on a ladder, fixing the overhead light fixture in the main part of the bookstore.

Savy slowed down with her armful of clothes just enough to ask, "Is everything all right?"

Maisy smiled up at her. "Yes, Sawyer's just doing some handyman work for us."

Savy glanced up. The broad-shouldered, dark-haired man, wearing a formfitting T-shirt with his jeans riding low on his hips, was straight-up poster-worthy.

"Hi, Sawyer," she said.

"Hi, Savy." He smiled down at her. It was the sort of smile that made a woman catch her breath. Savy would have fanned her face but her arms were full.

"Where are you going?" Maisy asked.

"Errand," Savy said. "I'll be back later."

The ladder rocked and Maisy quickly grabbed it as if her petite self could keep it from toppling. Sawyer grinned down at her. "Nice, but if I fall, stand clear. I don't want to explain to my brother how I flattened the love of his life."

At his words, Maisy's face went scarlet and Sawyer laughed before he returned his attention to the light fixture.

Jeri was working the front desk and was watching him work with the same appreciation as Savy.

"If we could just position that ladder in the front window, under a spotlight and visible from the street, we'd have more customers than books," Savy said.

"Mercy, I hear that," Jeri said. She fanned herself with a paperback. "It's warm in here, isn't it?"

Savannah laughed and banged out the door calling, "Back later."

She tossed her clothes into her car and sped over to Quino's. When she arrived, she found him just finishing hooking up the horse trailer to a large pickup truck. He straightened up as she hopped out of her car, grabbed all of her clothes, and came rushing at him.

She recognized Luke Masters, whom she'd met when he led her and Maisy on a trail ride through the Smoky Mountains. He glanced from her to Quino and back as if expecting a scene. Well, there was going to be one, just not like he expected.

"Hi, Luke," she said.

"Ma'am." He tipped his hat at her. Okay, Southern men could charm a girl stupid with a gesture as simple as a hat tip. Of that, there was no question.

Quino eyed the clothes in her arms. "Running away, Red?"

"No, I'm having a fashion crisis," she said. She shook the clothes at him. "You have to help me."

"Boss, I had no idea you were a fashionista," Luke said. He pushed the cowboy hat back on his head and with amused interest studied Quino.

Quino gave him a superior look and said, "Don't be jealous just because I have fabulous taste and you don't."

"Yeah, that's the first thing that comes to mind when I look at you. Your couture collection." Luke looked Quino up and down in his jeans and ridiculous Christmas sweater, this one with an enormous embroidered Santa riding a unicorn on it.

Quino laughed and Savy stomped her foot in exasperation. "I'm sorry, is my crisis intruding on you two insulting each other? Should I come back later?"

"No, no," Quino said. "Here, let's go up to the house and you can tell me what's wrong."

He gave a Luke a wide-eyed look that Savy chose to ignore. Instead, she bundled her clothes close to her chest and trudged ahead of him. He slid around her to open the door and she charged into the living room, where they'd slept a few nights before. She tried not to think about it, even as the memory of his arms around her came back to her in a rush. She dumped her clothes on the couch and turned to face him.

With her arms stretched wide, she said, "I have no idea what to wear today."

Quino took his hat off and tossed it onto a nearby chair. "That's the crisis?"

"Yes!" she cried. "This is quite possibly the single most important meeting of my life. I have to have the perfect outfit to meet Destiny."

"You do remember it's a riding lesson, right?" he asked.

"Yes, but I figured I need to present myself in the best possible light," she said. She snatched up a dress. "Too much?"

Quino stared at the dress and then her.

"It is, isn't it?" she asked. She dropped the dress and held up a skirt and tights. "Okay, how about this?"

"We're going to be outside," he said. "You want to dress warm."

"Warm?" she asked. She looked at the pile. She was wearing jeans and a purple sweater and she had a coat. But these weren't power clothes like the ones she'd wear in a boardroom in New York. "I can't impress her with warm."

Quino reached out and put his hands on her shoulders.

He looked her in the eyes and said, "You're freaking out, Red."

"I know, and you're not helping."

"Come here," he said. He opened his arms and Savy shook her head and crossed her arms over her chest. She was not going to be placated with a hug. He looked at her from beneath his lashes, a dimple winking in his cheek, and said, "Aw, come on. Let's hug it out."

She stared at him. He looked at her with infinite patience. It shouldn't have moved her, but it did. She uncrossed her arms. She dragged her feet until she was standing in front of him and then he hugged her.

He felt solid against her, and as his hand swept up and down her back and he rested his cheek against her hair, she felt her tension ease. She lifted her arms and hugged him around the middle. The scent that was uniquely his, bergamot and cedar, enveloped her and she felt all of her anxiety melt away.

"It's going to be okay," he said. "You're not going there as a bookstore publicist. You're going as my special lady friend. Destiny is a romance writer. The thought that I've brought someone special to meet her will win her over more than anything else."

"But what if she doesn't believe we're a couple?" she said into his sweater front. "What if she thinks I'm just some flighty girl you picked up?"

Quino stepped back and studied her. "Well, there is one way we could convince her."

He looked her over, his gaze lingering on her sweater, and Savy started to shake her head. "No, I know what you're thinking and that is a hard no."

"You don't know what I'm thinking," he said.

"Oh, yes, I do," she said. "You think you're going to get me to wear one of your horrible Christmas sweaters because only a woman in love would wear something that hideous by choice."

He laughed. "Just wait. Desi has as many sweaters as I do. You're about the same size."

"No, I won't do it," she said. "You can't make me."

It was too late. He was already climbing the stairs two at a time. He was back in moments and Savy cringed at the amount of sparkle in his arms.

"What?" he asked. "Stop looking at me like I'm trying to get you to wear a live snake."

She took the sweater he handed her. It had big sparkly ornaments all over it. She shook her head. He handed her another one. It had a big fruitcake on it. She shook her head even more vigorously. He sighed and handed her the last one. It had an embroidered gingerbread man twirling a candy cane on it.

"I'm in hell," she said.

Quino laughed. "I'm telling you this will work. She'll absolutely be taken with you if you wear a sweater like mine."

"Well, I'd have to be madly in love with you to wear this," she said. There was an awkward silence between them. And she quickly added, "You know, if we weren't setting this whole thing up just to get me to meet her."

He was grinning at her as if he thought there was more meaning behind her words than there was. She tried to ignore him. Flustered, she went to pull her boring purple sweater over her head but stopped. His eyes went wide as he realized she was about to change in front of him. She made a gesture for him to turn around.

"Just because you've played with them before doesn't mean you get to ogle," she said.

"Right, sorry, right, and I'm turning around . . . now."

He looked flustered and Savy smiled, feeling a surge of feminine power. That would help when she put this hideous sweater on. She yanked it over her head and arms, pulled her long red hair free of the collar, and tugged down on the hem. It fit well but when she looked down and saw the gingerbread man grinning up at her, she almost lost her nerve. There could never be any photographic evidence of this ever.

"Decent yet?" Quino asked.

"I think that's a matter of opinion," she said. "I feel like an abomination."

He turned around and took in the sight of her. "Aw, I think you look cute."

"Cute?" she asked. "Kill me now."

"Cute is perfect," he said. "It's nonthreatening."

"It's puppies and kittens and cinnamon rolls," she said. "I am not a cinnamon roll."

"But I like cinnamon rolls," he said.

"You also like eggnog and Christmas sweaters, so your taste is questionable at best."

He grinned. "I also like redheads, so I have that going for me."

She grunted, refusing to debate him on this.

He took her hand and said, "Come on, if we don't leave now, we'll be late. You don't keep Destiny Swann waiting."

And just like that Savy was racked with nerves. Quino must have sensed it because he put his hands on her shoulders and gave them a quick squeeze.

"Don't worry. Just be you. You're beautiful and funny and charming and Destiny will adore you. Trust me. It'll go just fine."

Savy looked up at him. Their faces were just inches apart and the desire to kiss him hit her low and deep, but she didn't want to be the sort of woman who played with a man's emotions in an effort to make herself feel better.

She swiftly stepped away from him. She tucked her hair behind her ears in a nervous gesture she'd had since she was a kid. It was a habit that drove her mother crazy and her mother used to slap Savy's hands when she did it and hiss at her to leave her hair alone. Her mother was a blonde. Her sisters were blondes. No one knew where Savy's red curls came from but it was quite clear that no one approved. Savy dropped her hands to her sides.

Looking at Quino, she wished she could be the petite blonde for him. Like her mother or her sisters, all three of whom she knew would be enamored with this hot cowboy. She remembered from the author picture on the book jacket of *Her One and Only* that Destiny, too, was a petite blonde. Oh, no, what if Destiny had a thing for Quino? If Savy showed up as his girlfriend, it could ruin everything.

"Um, is there any chance that Destiny is interested in you as more than her riding buddy?" Savy asked as they walked back outside.

Quino looked at her. He slapped his hat on his head and gave her side-eye as if she was a few sandwiches shy of a picnic. "She's old enough to be my mom."

"So what? A lot of older women fancy having a younger man," she said. "I mean, she's Destiny Swann—why would she settle for some shriveled-up prune of a man with no stamina when she could have you?"

He pushed his hat back and grinned at her. "So, you think I have stamina, huh?"

Savy felt her cheeks get warm but she refused to engage in fluffing his ego. "Well, duh. But more important, Destiny probably thinks you're her young stud and she won't appreciate having me show up. Maybe we should say I'm your cousin."

Quino shook his head. "No, you're my special lady friend, and I'll tell you why. Destiny has been trying to set me up with every young woman she thinks is worthy of me for the past three years. It would do me a great service to have her think I've finally met someone special so she can stand down with the matchmaking."

"So, you have an ulterior motive for having me come with you," she said. She nodded. "Now it's all coming into focus."

"Is it?" he asked. They were stalled on his front porch while they hashed this out. He tilted his head back and looked up. There above them was a small bough of mistletoe.

Savy narrowed her eyes. "Was that here the other day?"

He shrugged. "I don't remember."

"Uh-huh."

"Aw, come here, Red," he said. "How about a quick smooch for good luck?"

"Incorrigible," she said. "That's how I would describe you if anyone asked."

He put his hands on her hips and pulled her in close but not so close as to be touching. Savy acknowledged her disappointment but didn't press to be closer.

"I would prefer irresistible," he said. And then he kissed her.

It was swift and sweet, over before she even registered his mouth on hers. And then he was letting her go. He plucked a berry and handed it to her and then turned and walked down the steps toward the waiting horse trailer.

Savy scrambled after him, wondering how he could be so casual. Did he not feel the pull between them that she felt? Yeah, sure, she had slammed on the brakes, but that didn't mean she didn't feel the longing. Maybe Joaquin Solis was more of a player than she was prepared to handle. She supposed she should consider it lucky that she'd put a stop to their shenanigans when she did. Weirdly, she didn't feel lucky. She felt gypped.

She hurried after him, feeling as if she was leaving her wits behind her along with her outfits in the house. When they arrived at the truck, Luke was just loading a pretty bay horse into the trailer. She was dainty and she tossed her head, but he patted her neck and soothed her. Another horse was already in the trailer and together Quino and Luke closed the back and secured it.

"Thanks, Luke. I'll be back at the usual time," Quino said.

Luke glanced up at the sky. "Looks like snow might be coming in later."

"I'll keep an eye," Quino said.

"Bye, Luke," Savy said.

"See ya, Savannah," he said. He got a funny look on his face and Savy followed the direction of his gaze, which was riveted on her gingerbread man sweater. "He's corrupted you, hasn't he?" He shook his head as if this were a tragedy of epic proportions.

"Do me a solid, and do not tell a soul that you ever saw me in anything like this," she said. "My reputation would be shredded."

"Which is what should be done with that sweater," Luke said. Savy laughed and held up a hand for a high five.

"Hey, I like the gingerbread man sweater," Quino said. "It's cute."

Savy and Luke exchanged a look. Clearly Quino was beyond help.

"Fear not, your secret is safe with me," Luke said. He tipped his hat at Savy and turned and headed for the barn.

"I do not understand why everyone disses my sweaters," Quino said. He shouted after Luke, "Have you people no holiday cheer?"

Luke ignored him and Quino shook his head. He opened the passenger door for Savy and when she climbed in, he shut it and circled around the truck to slide into the driver's seat.

He fired up the truck and tapped on the CD player. Savy was not the least bit surprised when Christmas music flooded the cab of the truck. It was a Harry Connick Jr. compilation that Quino sang along with, and as they rolled through the tall trees even she started to hum some of the standards. She could almost feel a happiness fill her as she listened to his deep voice croon the words, but she shut it down. She was not going to get swept up in holiday silliness. She was on a mission. She needed to focus.

When there was a pause between songs, she lowered the volume and said, "Okay, tell me everything you know about Destiny, so I can figure out how to play this today."

"No," he said.

"What?"

"She's my friend," he said. "If she likes you, she'll do what you ask, and if she doesn't she won't, but I'm not going to reveal all of her personal stuff so you can bend her to your will."

"But . . ." she protested.

"Nope."

Savy gave him a disgusted look as he turned up the music and began to sing. This was not at all how she'd expected this to go. He was supposed to be helping her plot and plan. Sheesh, if she had to rely on her personality, this whole thing could blow up in her face. She frowned. Well, she'd show him. She'd charm the pants off Destiny and there'd be a signing at the bookstore and it would be amazing.

They drove in silence the rest of the way with Quino

singing and Savy fuming. When he turned off the main road and onto a long winding drive on the outskirts of Asheville, Savy sat up. She had heard that Destiny Swann's home, Windemere Manor, was something right out of a Gothic novel and she was eager to see it.

The trees lining the drive were bare of leaves, the day was still overcast, and it took them a while before the drive turned around a thick row of poplars and gave way to one of the most breathtaking buildings Savy had ever seen.

Windemere Manor was a Federal-style mansion, with massive columns supporting the roof, that perched above the two stories that each boasted floor-to-ceiling windows and French doors and wraparound porches. With a cupola and dormer windows popping out of the roof, it looked like a massive wedding cake perched in front of a large pond that had a spout of water shooting up out of the middle of it.

Savy could picture dark storm clouds looming above and a heroine in a gossamer dress, running from the manor as if in flight for her life. It was beautiful and stately, but also cold and severe. A perfect home for a romance novelist.

"Whoa," she breathed, wondering not for the first time if maybe she was in over her head.

Chapter Fifteen

A S they drove between the pond and the house, Savy
gawked out the window. Blue smoke wafted from one
of the mansion's chimneys and scented the air with the fra-
grance of burning wood. Lights were on in the downstairs
windows but the upstairs remained dark.

"Does she live here alone?" Savy asked.

"No, she has a cook, a housekeeper, and a grounds-
keeper who also works as her handyman. They've all been
with her for years and they live in the manor, too. On the
third floor, I think," he said.

Savy glanced up at the row of dormer windows. The
place was big enough that they all probably had a suite to
themselves. Amazing. It was like falling back in time. She
glanced at the mountains surrounding them. She was certain she'd go crazy being this cut off from the world.

Quino drove the truck around the house and down a narrow road until they reached a big gray barn and paddock in
the back. Savy glanced back to see an immaculate lawn
with an in-ground swimming pool and a massive terrace
between them and the house. This property was immense.

She could see empty garden beds encircling the enormous yard and she wondered what this place looked like in the spring. She was betting it was beautiful.

Quino parked and hopped out of the truck. Savy popped out on her side and asked, "Can I help you?"

He pointed to the paddock and said, "If you could open the gate, that'd be great."

She hurried to unlatch the gate and then swung it wide, holding it open as he led first one horse, which she recognized as his horse, Daisy, and then Cocoa, who was to be Destiny's ride. Quino let the horses run into the paddock and then signaled for Savy to close the gate. While she did, he took his phone out.

He held it to his ear and Savy listened when he spoke, hoping she'd get something to work with when she met Destiny.

"Hi, Genevieve," he said.

Darn it, that was Destiny's dragon of an assistant. Savy hadn't really thought about encountering her. What would she say?

"The horses are just stretching," he said. "I'll get them saddled and set to go if Destiny's about ready." There was a pause as he listened. Then he said, "Perfect."

He ended the call and put his phone back. He looked at Savy and said, "She'll be here in fifteen minutes. Want to help me saddle up?"

"Sure," she said.

She followed him to the trailer and helped him carry the tack to the paddock rails. She watched as he saddled and bridled the pretty bay.

"Good girl, Cocoa, there's a pretty girl," he said.

Savy was not as versed in horse expressions as she'd like to be, but she was certain she wasn't imagining the flirtatious eye Cocoa was giving Joaquin. In fact, when she nudged him with her nose and he chuckled, Savy knew it for sure.

"Did you always want to work with horses?" she asked.

"No," he said. "I wanted to be an engineer. I was enrolled part-time at the University of Texas for engineering, which is where I met Ryder."

"Hook 'em horns," she said. He grinned.

"I was working construction to pay my tuition and we were on the same crew," he continued. "But then my parents were killed, and I came back to take care of Desi."

"And when she was better, you never went back to school?" she asked.

His voice when he spoke was hesitant. "Desi needed a lot of care in the beginning. There just wasn't time and then, well, life moves on, doesn't it?"

Savy didn't know what to say. She realized that standing in front of her was likely one of the best men she'd ever met. An older brother who gave up his life so that his sister could have a better shot at hers.

He glanced over her shoulder and said, "Get ready. Here they come."

Savy started. She turned and glanced at the house. A jaunty little golf cart was zipping across the lawn, coming at them at a clip. Inside the covered cart, Savy could just make out a woman in an English-style riding outfit and beside her was a dark-haired woman in a tweed suit. Given that the rider had to be Destiny, that meant the suit was Genevieve. Great.

The cart stopped beside Quino's truck and Savy expected a woman of an advanced age to gingerly climb out of the cart. Instead, Destiny sprang out of her side while the dark-haired woman switched off the engine and stepped out as well. Genevieve was wearing a darling pair of dark brown boots that went well with the tweed skirt, which matched her jacket. She had a beautiful beige cashmere scarf around her neck and dark-brown leather gloves.

"Quino, darling, so good to see you," Destiny cried. She rolled up on her toes and kissed his cheek.

"You, too, Destiny, and as usual, you look stunning," he said.

Destiny waved a dismissive hand, but Savy could tell she was pleased by the compliment. She looked Quino over and said, "I would say the same about you but that sweater is an absolute horror."

Genevieve laughed and said, "I like it. It suits him."

"Thank you," he said. She kissed his cheek, too, and Savy felt an inexplicable twisting feeling in her gut that she feared was jealousy. Which was ridiculous because number one, she didn't get jealous and number two, well, there was no number two. She didn't get jealous. Period. So what the heck was this? Indigestion, she decided.

"Well, today I have company in my love of holiday sweater cheer," Quino said. He held out a hand to Savy and she stepped forward. "I'd like you both to meet my friend Savannah Wilson. Savy, this is Destiny Swann and Genevieve Spencer."

Destiny clapped her gloved hands together. "Does this mean what I think it means?"

Quino grinned and asked, "That Savy and I are a couple? Yes, it does."

"Oh, my dear." Destiny grabbed Savy's hands in hers and squeezed them tight. "I am delighted to meet you."

"Thank you, but it's me who is delighted to meet you," Savy said. "I am a huge fan of your work."

She could feel Genevieve staring at her, and when she glanced her way the woman had one eyebrow up as if assessing Savy's sincerity. Destiny continued to hold her hands and Savy wasn't sure what to do, so she decided to pour it on thick.

"I just finished reading *Her One and Only* and, oh, wow, it was so perfect. I just loved it," she gushed. "Although, I did tell my friend that you really set the bar pretty high with Tag McAllister. I mean, what man could live up to that guy? He is completely swoon-worthy."

"Ahem." Quino cleared his throat and Savy turned to look at him. He had his eyebrows raised and she laughed.

"Sorry," she said. "But Tag is . . ."

"Uh-huh," he said. He looked at Destiny and said, "Tell her you modeled him after me."

Destiny glanced between them and laughed. She looked delighted. She let go of Savy and clasped her hands in front of her. "You two have such spark. This is simply delightful."

Upon closer inspection, Destiny looked more like she was fifty instead of seventy, which, according to her biography, was her actual age. Her hair was a glorious shade of platinum blond. Her face was slightly lined but not tight. She still had a fluidity of expression and she was tall and thin, although not as tall as Savy. When she smiled at them, she positively beamed, and it occurred to Savy that the thing that made her appear more youthful than her age was that she just seemed happy.

"The horses are ready when you are, Destiny," Quino said.

Destiny looked at him and said, "Of course, poor dears, mustn't keep them waiting."

Quino escorted Destiny into the paddock and Savy turned to Genevieve. "It's a pleasure to meet you, too."

"Likewise," Genevieve said. "It's nice to put a face to all the flowers, chocolates, and the amazing balloon-o-gram."

The woman turned and walked back to her golf cart. Savy felt her heart sink. She had a feeling everything was about to explode on her. Genevieve fired up the cart and drove back to the manor, leaving Savy to watch as Quino gave Destiny a leg up onto her saddle.

She leaned against the rail and watched as he swung up into the saddle with ease. He rode Western style, all loose-legged and stirrups long, while Destiny was English style with stirrups high and knees in tight. Before they rode off, Quino rode over to her and leaned low in his saddle and planted a kiss on Savy that was swift but no less intense for its brevity.

He winked at her and said, "I would never ride off without kissing my girl."

It was ridiculous, but Savy felt her heart flutter in her chest. What would it be like to be his girl for real? She knew better than to dwell on what couldn't be. She was leaving. His life was here. This was why she'd allowed herself that one night with him so that she didn't have to wonder what it would be like. But now, unfortunately, she knew, and when he kissed her, it all came back and she felt a longing for this man that hit her low and deep.

"Don't stay out here in the cold," he said. He fished out his keys and handed them to her. "There's a fleece blanket in the truck if you get cold, or you can wait for us up at the house."

"Thanks," she said. "I'm not cold. The humiliation of wearing this sweater is keeping me plenty warm."

He laughed and Savy smiled. It felt good to make him laugh. He wheeled Daisy around and they trotted across the paddock to meet up with Destiny. She seemed to handle Cocoa just fine, and Savy watched as they looped the corral a few times before Quino dismounted and opened the far gate. The two of them set off across the fields and Savy climbed into the truck and wrapped herself up in the big red fleece while she awaited their return.

She took out her phone and checked her messages. There was nothing urgent. She decided to tease Archer and texted a picture of herself in the hideous sweater. His response was immediate.

What is that?

My Christmas sweater, she texted back.

That's it! You have to come back to NY. You've clearly lost your mind. She could hear the hysteria even in his text.

What if I told you I was at Destiny Swann's house right now?

Shut up!

I am! Calling you right now.

Savy closed her text window and opened her contacts. Archer popped up first and she pressed his number and waited for him to pick up.

"Are you bullshitting me?" he asked.

"No." She laughed. "I am at Windemere Manor right now."

"Pics or it didn't happen," he said.

"Fine," Savy agreed. "Hang on."

She opened her camera and snapped a few pictures of the house, one of her with the house behind her, and then some more of Quino and Destiny riding across the field. It was a very poetic shot and she wondered again if Destiny was attached to Quino—but that was ridiculous; she had seemed so happy that Quino had brought Savy to meet her. She opened her text app and sent the pictures.

"Okay, there's your proof," she said.

"Opening the text," Archer said. There was a pause. "Oh, my God, that is you, in that hideous sweater, at Windemere Manor! What the hell were you thinking? Are you trying to terrorize her into a book signing?"

There was some heavy breathing and she was afraid Archer might pass out.

"Breathe, Archer," she said.

"I'm trying but, holy reclusive writers, you have gained access to the most hermetic author in the literary world second only to J. D. Salinger when he was alive. How? And who is the hot cowboy riding horseback with her? These are the things I need to know *right now*!"

"Interestingly enough, the hot cowboy is a friend of a friend." Savy paused. That didn't sound right. "Who has become a good friend of mine." That sounded better.

"How good of a friend?" Archer asked. "I mean *meow*. He's yummy." He never did pull any punches.

"Close friend," Savy said.

"You slept with him," Archer declared.

"How can you say that?" she asked. "You don't know that."

"You didn't deny it," he said. "So, now I know it for sure."

"None of that is the point. The point is that Quino is Destiny's riding coach and he is the one who got me here."

"Quino?"

"Short for Joaquin," Savy said. She could feel her face getting hot, which was ridiculous because she was a grown-ass woman who could do whatever she liked with her personal life. "Listen, the reason I am calling is to ask how great for my career would it be to be the one who engineered Destiny Swann coming out of seclusion to do a book signing at Maisy's store?"

"How great?" Archer asked. "Like *they'll give you a float in the Macy's Thanksgiving Day Parade* great. Seriously, she is the hottest romance author in the business and ten years ago, she stopped touring, doing publicity, or having any interactions with her fans. If you could bring her out of hiding, it would be the coup of the year, possibly the decade."

"That's what I thought, too," she said. "All right, I'm going all in. I'll keep you posted."

"Try to get a peek into her closet for me," Archer said.

"Because that wouldn't be weird."

"I hear she has a couture collection to die for," he said. "You have to get a picture of it for me."

"No."

"Oh, come on," he wheedled.

"No. Also, you have to keep this on the down-low," she said. "I don't want anyone to know what I'm doing."

"Well, duh," he said. "That diva Linda has already stolen every bit of your glory she could get her sticky fingers on. I'm certainly not going to let her try to swipe this."

"Thank you," Savy said. And she meant it. Archer had been steadfast in his support of her since the dark day she'd been let go. "I'll let you know what happens."

"Pictures," he said. "I must have pictures of the interior."

"I'll do my best," Savy said.

After several back-and-forths of *I love you*, she ended the call.

She hunkered into the fleece and turned to lean against the passenger door, where she had the best view of Quino riding. The sunlight shone down upon him and Daisy. He galloped across the field and Destiny followed. They looked like they were having a great time. Savy was surprised that she didn't feel the old spurt of jealousy she might have felt for one of her faithless boyfriends from New York. Instead, she felt alarmingly sure of Quino. She just knew he was a man of his word and even if what they were doing was a sham, she still trusted him not to do her wrong. So that was a novel feeling.

She liked watching him ride. Aside from the alluring sight of his hips moving in the saddle, he rode with confidence. He knew his horse, he knew what she could do, and he communicated with her in silent understanding. Watching Quino and Daisy, Savy realized if there was any female who would be a rival for Quino's affection, it was Daisy. She smiled. The big brown-and-white horse was beautiful, and Savy was A-OK with that sort of competition.

She supposed she should use her phone to check her e-mail or craft some ads for the bookstore, but she didn't. Instead, she just watched Quino, thrilled to be able to watch him undisturbed and unquestioned, because, after all, she was his girlfriend today and wouldn't a girlfriend watch her man while he went riding, especially when the man was Quino? Of course she would.

She didn't bother to pretend she wasn't staring. Quino's cowboy hat shielded his eyes from the sun while he and Daisy rode together in perfect sync. Watching how he guided his horse with just a squeeze from his powerful legs made Savannah break into a light sweat and she shoved the blanket off even as she didn't look away. As if aware of her scrutiny, Quino turned toward her and gave her a slow smile and a wicked wink. Savannah's brain turned to mush and all good intentions aside, she had no idea how she was going to keep her hands off him during the ride home.

After exactly one hour, Genevieve reappeared in the golf cart. She parked beside the corral and Quino and Destiny rode in. Quino dismounted first and tied Cocoa, holding up his arms to catch Destiny as she swung her leg over the back of the horse. He put her gently on the ground and she smiled up at him in affection. Savy felt something in her chest tighten. Who was this man who was great with horses, looked after his sister, loved Christmas, and was kind to older ladies? He was just so elementally good, it made her want to hug him hard and never let go.

She hopped out of the truck and joined them at the corral. This might be her only chance to talk to Destiny about the bookstore. She couldn't let it slip by, but Destiny was half in the golf cart before she got there. The author waved at Savy.

"Meet us up at the house for tea, dear?" Destiny asked.

Savy glanced at Quino and he nodded. She turned back to Destiny with a grin. "That would be lovely, thank you."

Genevieve glanced at her with one eyebrow raised. She didn't say anything before she started the cart and drove back to the house.

Savy joined Quino by the horses. He was removing their

saddles and bridles and Savy hefted them up and carried them back to the truck. While he groomed Daisy she grabbed a currycomb and groomed Cocoa. When they were finished, Quino fetched two horse blankets out of the trailer and they put one on each horse, as the temperature had dropped. Quino fastened the gate to the corral, where the horses would wait, and turned to Savy.

"Ready for tea?"

"One question," she said. "Do you have tea with her after every ride or is this because I'm here and she wants to know more about your girlfriend?"

"I have tea with her after every ride," he said. "At first, I was mortified. Drinking Earl Grey out of these paper-thin china cups. I was sure I was going to smash something. But then she brought out the tiny sandwiches. Ermagawd. Nom nom nom."

Savy stared at him. "Cucumber sandwiches? You like cucumber sandwiches?"

"Yeah, because they have cream cheese and dill. I love dill. But there's also a curry egg salad and chicken almond something or other. The cucumber is where it's at, though."

Savannah started to laugh.

"What?" he asked.

"The big rough-and-tumble cowboy loves high tea," she said. She chuckled. "It's too much."

"Did I mention the blueberry macarons, the mini coconut cupcake, or the raspberry white chocolate petit fours? Hmm, did I?"

"Why are we standing here?" Savy asked. "Move it!"

Now Quino laughed, and as if it was the most natural thing in the world, he draped his arm over her shoulders, pulled her close, and planted a kiss on her hair.

"That's what I'm talking about, Red. Petit fours to die for."

They strolled across the lawn and Savy flirted with a ridiculous fantasy that this was their house and they were coming in from a day's ride. They'd clean up together and then light a fire and enjoy high tea in their parlor while reading books or listening to music or watching their children romp around. Wait . . . what?

She shook her head. Clearly Windemere was the sort of place that gave a girl ideas. Maybe this was why Destiny was so successful. All she had to do was look at the lush landscape, the Smoky Mountain vista, and the big white house with columns and she was brimming with characters and plots and the stories just wrote themselves.

Quino led Savy up the steps to the wide terrace. He paused to knock on the back door. A woman in an apron over jeans and a flannel shirt answered. She was young with long dark hair that she wore in a braid that hung down her back. Her face was pretty with high cheekbones and round eyes, and her smile warm and friendly as she gestured for them to come in.

They stepped into a massive kitchen, with copper appliances and quartz counters, three ovens, and two dishwashers. It was a beautiful workspace and it smelled heavenly, of fresh-baked bread and some sort of savory meat dish that almost caused Savy to drool.

"Quino, how are you?" the woman asked.

"Good, Maddie, how are you, Doug, the kids?"

"Doug and I are fine, but the kids are bonkers," she said. She looked at Savy and explained. "They're three and five so Christmas is all they can talk about, think about, and dream about."

Savy smiled. She may not be a fan of Christmas but she loved seeing kids excited about the holiday. Maybe it was because she loved that they got to believe when she hadn't been allowed. She didn't know. She just knew that she found their excitement charming.

"Savannah, this is Maddie—Destiny's personal chef."

"Nice to meet you," Maddie said. She held out her hand but Savy said, "I'm covered in horse. Would you be offended if I washed up in the sink first?"

"Not at all," she said. "The powder room is right there." She glanced at Quino. "You can use the kitchen sink."

"Look at you," Quino said to Savy. "Getting the special privileges."

"She's a guest, you're family," Maddie said.

"Thank you," Savy said.

She left them to go wash up. In the bathroom, she noted that her hair was an unruly mess. Her cheeks were pink from the cold outside and the gingerbread man on her sweater was looking back at her with a smirk as if he knew the impure thoughts she'd had about Quino. When she returned to the kitchen, he was seated at the counter, talking to Maddie. Savannah slipped onto the seat beside him.

Maddie was rolling out pastry dough, and as they watched she whipped together an apple pie, crimping the edges with the tines of a fork and perfuming the air with nutmeg, apples, and cinnamon sugar that made Savy almost dizzy with want. They talked about when the first snowfall would be, what Maddie's kids wanted for Christmas, and whose sweater was more obnoxious—Quino's or Savy's. Maddie said Quino's but Savy had a feeling she was trying to spare her feelings. When Maddie popped the pie into the oven, Genevieve appeared in the doorway.

"If you two are ready, Destiny will join you for tea now," she said.

They rose from their counter seats and stretched.

"Always a pleasure," Quino said. "Especially when I know you made extra cucumber sandwiches?"

Maddie smiled. "Just for you."

"Yes!" Quino pumped his fist and Maddie laughed.

"It was lovely to meet you, Maddie," Savy said.

"Please come back again," Maddie said. "You can wait in the kitchen with me while he rides."

"I'd like that," Savy said. "Maybe you could teach me to bake a pie."

Maddie grinned. "And I'd like that."

They followed Genevieve from the kitchen and down a short hallway. They turned left and went down a longer hallway with doors on each side—some were open and some were closed. Large portraits in gilded frames hung on the walls. It took Savy a second to realize they were all the original artwork from Destiny's book covers. She paused to study a cowboy in a pasture with a horse, looking at a house in the background that looked very much like Windemere. The artist had definitely captured a look of longing on the cowboy's face and Savy felt drawn to him, much as the artist had intended, she was sure.

She glanced up just in time to see Genevieve and Quino disappear around the corner. She hurried after them. They were crossing the enormous entryway, under a sparkling chandelier and over an exquisite Oriental carpet, straight into a large parlor that overlooked the pond they had passed on the drive to the manor.

A fire was lit in the large fireplace, which crackled and hissed invitingly. A comfortable dark-blue love seat and two wing chairs were arranged in front of the fire. The house was a bit on the chilly side so Savy was happy to stand in front of the fireplace while they waited for Destiny, who hadn't arrived yet.

"Can I ask what you plan to say to Destiny to convince her to sign at your bookstore?" Genevieve asked.

Quino's eyes went wide.

"Genevieve recognized my name," Savy said. "I did mention to you that I reached out to her before."

"You did. But now I'm wondering. 'Reached out' means what exactly?" he asked.

"The usual," Savy said. "Phone call, e-mail, letter of inquiry, you know."

Quino looked at Genevieve and she smiled and added, "As well as the unusual: flowers, cookie bouquet, and a balloon-o-gram."

"Genius!" Quino said with a laugh.

"Yes, except it didn't work, did it?" Savy asked.

"No," Genevieve said. "Destiny has been adamant that she will not do another book signing so long as she lives."

"Well, that's no good," Quino said.

"No, it isn't," Genevieve agreed, surprising Savy. "I'm worried about her. As she's become more and more reclusive, the writing has comparatively been more difficult. I think she needs to get back out there and get inspired, and I am really hoping you can convince her to do so."

"You are?" Savy asked. She felt a surge of optimism.

"Yes. Now, can I ask you two something?" Genevieve

said. They both nodded. "Are you really dating? Because if Destiny discovers you're not, it'll hurt her terribly."

"We are," Savy said. She'd noted that Quino said nothing, clearly letting her handle the big lie. "In fact, I didn't even know he knew Destiny until after we were together."

"That's true," he said, and smiled at her. She knew from the mischievous glint in his eye, he was thinking about their first night together, which actually was before she knew of his connection to Destiny. She would have shaken her head at his wayward thoughts, but she didn't want Genevieve to guess that things weren't as they seemed between them.

"Excellent." Genevieve beamed. "I am really hoping you can get Destiny to consider doing a signing."

"I'll do my best," Savy said. She felt her palms get sweaty. No pressure.

Quino sat down on the love seat, and Savy took the seat beside him. In a few moments, Genevieve, who had taken one of the wing chairs, popped to her feet. Quino glanced over his shoulder and did the same, so Savy did, too.

It didn't take her long to realize why Genevieve and Quino had stood. She may not be a queen in the royal sense, but when Destiny entered a room it was as if royalty had arrived. Of course, it could also have been the diaphanous dress she was wearing. Tea length in a gorgeous blue organza, it had a flared skirt, nipped waist, and wide neckline that showed off Destiny's collarbones and fantastic figure. Savy glanced down at her sweater with the glittery gingerbread man and felt like she'd dressed for a costume party only to show up and find out it was actually a formal.

Chapter Sixteen

"DOES she always dress up for tea?" she whispered to Quino.

"Yes."

"You might have warned me," she said.

"Why? You look cute."

Savy growled low in her throat.

"Darlings, do sit down," Destiny said. "Please forgive me for keeping you waiting. I just couldn't decide what to wear. I don't get visitors very often and I'm not one for going out, so I like to dress up when I can."

Genevieve shot Savy a pointed look as if to say, *See? She's lonely.* Oh, boy, the pressure to get Destiny to the bookstore was mounting. Savy felt a trickle of sweat roll down her back, or maybe that was just a reaction to the synthetic fibers of the sweater she was wearing.

Maddie came in behind Destiny, pushing a rolling cart that was loaded with two three-tiered curate stands of food and two teapots, as well as separate servers for clotted cream, a variety of jams and lemon curd, sugar cubes, milk, and honey. Savy felt her stomach growl. She hoped this wasn't like tea with the queen of England. She had heard that guests were allowed to eat only what the queen ate, so if she chose a solitary inedible melba toast, that's all anyone else got to eat. Savy was pretty sure she'd die.

As soon as they resumed their seats, Genevieve poured their tea and Quino dug into the tower of food, going for the second tier, where the sandwiches were. The upper tier was scones and breads, and the bottom, sweets. Savy couldn't wait to get there. There was a mini coconut cake with her name on it. Using the silver tongs to choose the sandwiches, Quino loaded a plate and then handed it to Savy.

"Try the cucumber," he said.

"Thank you, I will," she said. Having him serve her tea was too much. She was positively dying inside.

Destiny smiled fondly at them and Savy bit into the tiny sandwich, hoping to calm her nerves. Freshly baked bread, thinly sliced, with slivers of cucumber swabbed with cream cheese infused with dill—it was perfection. Quino's love of the tiny sandwiches was understandable to her.

"Amazing," she said.

He nodded and grinned. "Told you so."

Genevieve handed her a cup of black tea, so Savy put her sandwiches on the coffee table so she could add a little cream and sugar. Destiny seemed happy to bask in the glow of watching her guests enjoy their food, but Savy was very aware that this was her one shot to get her to come to the bookstore.

She decided the direct approach was too blunt, so she went for the soft sell instead.

"You are a wonderful rider, Destiny," she said. "How long have you been taking lessons with Quino?"

"Oh, I don't know," Destiny said. She looked at Quino. "Several years now, yes?"

"He tells me you're his favorite student," Savy said.

Destiny looked pleased but she waved a dismissive hand and said, "That's just because he loves high tea."

Quino laughed. He was devouring his sandwiches with gusto. "But I never would have learned to love high tea if I hadn't met you."

"There is that," Destiny agreed. She took her tea from Genevieve. She didn't drink right away. Instead, she asked, "So, how did you two become a couple? You must tell the story and inspire another novel in me."

"We—" Savy paused. Having Destiny look at her with her pretty blue eyes and wide smile, she was suddenly racked with guilt. She didn't want to lie to her. As if sensing her quandary, Quino took over.

"It was fate," he said. He gave Savy a meaningful look and she resisted the urge to roll her eyes. Fine. She wouldn't go for full disclosure but she wasn't going to pretend it was something it wasn't. She decided to talk it down.

"It was through friends," she said. "My best friend is engaged to his best friend, so we met through them."

"Which was fate. Right, Red?" Quino asked. Savy felt her face get hot at the nickname, but she refused to look at him because he'd probably wink at her and she'd combust on the spot.

"How wonderful," Destiny cried. "Quino, I think this lady is going to keep you on your toes."

"She has from the moment I first laid on eyes on her," he said. "I was talking to my friend Ryder, and this sassy redhead walked into the room, ignoring me as she reamed my buddy out for how he'd treated his girl."

"He deserved it," Savy said

"Of course he did, dear." Destiny smiled. She turned to Quino and said, "Go on."

Savy turned to Quino to get him to stop but he ignored her pointed look.

"And as I watched this feisty woman stand up for her friend, I was completely captivated by her. Her red hair crackled with sparks and her green eyes flashed with fire, and when I butted in to ask her out, because it felt imperative that I get this woman to go out with me, she put me soundly in my place."

"You deserved it, too," Savy said.

"Of course he did, dear, go on," Destiny said.

"Yes, tell us what she said," Genevieve chimed in. She was sitting on the edge of her seat, completely enthralled.

Savy tried not to roll her eyes and reached for a tiny blueberry macaron instead. Mostly, to keep herself from talking.

"I took one look at her in her spiky heels and pencil skirt and I knew she wasn't from around here, so I said, 'You're a city girl, aren't you?' And what do you think she said?"

"No idea," Destiny said. She leaned her chin in her hand and her eyes twinkled as if she couldn't wait to hear it.

"She said, 'Woman. I am a woman, not a girl. And, yes, I'm from Manhattan, or as we like to call it, *civilization.*'"

Destiny whooped with laughter and Genevieve hooted, too. Savy felt her face get warm. She had said that.

"What did you say?" Genevieve asked him.

"I said, 'Well, *woman*, since we've established that I lack manners, I'm going to say exactly what I'm thinking,'" he said. "And then she said, 'That should be a short sentence.'"

Destiny and Genevieve both laughed even harder and glanced at Savy as if to verify if this was true. It was. Savy nodded and they laughed louder.

"Then I said, 'I think you should go on a date with me,'" he continued. "And she said, 'That is never going to happen, but thanks for the offer.' It then took me exactly one hundred and twenty-three days to get her to go on a date with me, but she was worth every second of the wait."

The warm smile he sent her way made Savy's heart hammer hard in her chest. Had he really waited for her for all of those days?

"Yes, I waited," he said. "I've never felt about anyone the way that I feel about you."

Oh, wow. She couldn't believe he had remembered their first conversation verbatim, and she really couldn't believe that he'd stayed interested in her after that. But he was, and the tender way he was looking at her right now told her he was still interested. Oh, man, after that speech, she was more than half in love with him. Any more speeches like that and she was done for.

"So, you've only recently gotten together?" Destiny asked.

"Yes," Savy said. "But we don't get to go out much with work and all."

She could feel Quino watching her and she was suddenly overly self-conscious. She put down her tea in case she spilled.

"That's a shame. What is it that you do, Savannah?" Destiny asked.

From her tone, Savy could tell she was asking out of genuine interest and not to ascertain whether Savy was good enough for Quino or not. Although, even Savy would argue that he was definitely a better person than she was. This was not something she wanted to think too much about right now. In fact, she really had to stop thinking about him at all. She needed to focus. This was her chance to segue into the entire point of this visit.

"I'm in publicity," Savy said. "In fact, I am working for my best friend right now."

"What do you publicize?" Destiny was so polite, Savy felt as if she'd sprung a trap for the woman. Still, she answered.

"A romance bookstore in Fairdale," she said. "It's called the Happily Ever After Bookshop."

Destiny's eyes widened. "I'm sorry, what?"

"A romance bookstore," Genevieve repeated. "Doesn't that sound nice?"

"I wasn't aware that there was a bookstore in Fairdale," Destiny said. She frowned and glared at Savy. "Wait, are you the one who's been asking me to come for a signing?"

Savannah glanced at Genevieve, who nodded her head almost imperceptibly. Savannah met Destiny's gaze and said, "Yes."

She didn't say anything else. She didn't take the opportunity to try to convince Destiny to come to the bookstore. Honestly, she didn't know what to say. She liked Destiny and she didn't want to damage the fragile connection they seemed to have made.

"I see," Destiny said. She glanced from Savannah to Quino. "Forgive me, but it seems awfully convenient that you two are a couple." She looked hurt and distrustful, and Savannah felt her insides twist with guilt.

"I'd say it's more coincidental," Quino said.

"I don't trust coincidences," Destiny said. Her face was set in hard lines and she smoothed her skirts as if trying to smooth her own turbulent emotions. "I also don't do book signings—ever."

"So, this is going to go well," Savy said as an aside to Quino.

He snorted. Good man.

"Destiny, I've been your friend for years," he said. He waited for her to look up at him and acknowledge the truth of his statement with a nod. "I'm going to ask you as a friend, why don't you do book signings? Why have you made yourself inaccessible to your readers?"

Destiny didn't answer but lifted her teacup with shaking fingers and sipped her tea. She looked rattled and Savy felt sorry for her. They were intruding on Destiny's private life. It was crossing a line.

"We don't have to talk about it," Savy said. "This tea is delicious; what kind is it?"

Several seconds ticked by where no one spoke.

"I'm sorry," Destiny said. "You must think I'm horribly rude, because I was. Of course you're my friend, one of my dearest, and I shouldn't doubt you."

Savy couldn't look at Quino. They'd made a tactical mistake by letting Destiny think they were together. Now she felt like a bottom-feeding, manipulative liar. And telling herself it was for the greater good, saving Maisy's bookstore, didn't really help at the moment.

"Actually—" Savy began, but Quino interrupted her.

"What happened, Destiny?" he asked. His voice was gentle. "Talk to us."

Destiny gave a heartfelt sigh. "I don't like to think about that time."

"So, don't think, just talk," he said. She raised one eyebrow in a look that was meant to quell, but Quino wasn't having it. "Maybe you'll feel better if you do."

"I think you should talk about it," Genevieve said. "I've never asked, but I do wonder. Why have you chosen to live such a solitary life?"

Destiny studied them. She glanced at her tea. She took

a petit four off the sweet tier and nibbled the corner. Savy thought this was her way of saying no without actually saying no, and she was disappointed because she found she really wanted to know what had driven Destiny into seclusion.

"I'm sorry," Destiny said. "It's so much easier to lose myself in the trials and tribulations of my characters than to look too closely at my own."

"I know," Genevieve said. Her voice was full of sympathy.

Destiny sighed. She finished her petit four. "I don't want you to think I'm being ridiculous."

"I've been with you for five years," Genevieve said. "I see you work from sunup to sundown, I watch you personally answer every letter from your readers, and I know you help those less fortunate than you as much as you can. I would never think you're being ridiculous."

Destiny reached across their seats and patted Genevieve's knee. "Thank you, my dear."

Then she took a sip of tea. Savy looked at Quino and he shrugged. Would Destiny share? There was simply no way to tell. It was maddening!

Savy nibbled her own tiny sandwich, the cucumber really was delicious, and watched as Quino and Genevieve did the same. No one spoke until Destiny put her plate back on the tray and dabbed the corners of her mouth with her napkin.

"It was ten years ago," she said. "I was doing a book tour, something like twenty-one cities in fourteen days. It was grueling. I had one book due, copyedits on another book that were late, and page proofs for yet another book coming up fast. I was wrung out, dead tired, and fighting off a case of walking pneumonia. My agent and publisher wanted to cancel the tour, but I refused. I felt I owed it to my readers to be there, be present, and thank them—you can never thank your readers enough for their support—and so I pushed myself to the absolute limit. Why? Because I was addicted to the limelight. I soaked up the love from my readers as if it could fix me. When I landed in the hospital, a shallow breath from death, I realized it couldn't.

"The truth was, I was addicted to the adulation I got from my readers and I knew if I started back on the circuit of signings and appearances, I'd fall into the same trap again. Like a junkie giving up their drug of choice, I had to walk away from the limelight—for good."

"Destiny, this is simply unacceptable," Quino said.

"What do you mean?" she asked.

"Ten years have passed," he said. "You're not the same person you were then."

"Maybe, but now I'm afraid," Destiny said. "I'm afraid of getting hooked again and it's made me paranoid about getting back out there." She looked at Genevieve. "Tell them about the time I tried to do a TV interview last year."

"She threw up for three days beforehand," Genevieve said. "We had to cancel."

"And the time I tried to do a live reading online," Destiny said.

"A rash," Genevieve said. "She was covered head to toe."

"I simply can't put myself out there," Destiny said. "I can't shake the feeling that I'll lose control and get swept up in the fandom and something bad will happen. It's like a full-on phobia now."

"But your fans would be so happy to see you again," Savy said. "And you have Genevieve, who I can attest from personal experience is one heck of a gatekeeper."

"I know," Destiny said. "My readers are wonderful, and I read every letter and e-mail I receive and I write back, but I just can't manage to get myself back out there."

"Isn't there any way we can help you?" Savy asked.

"No, I'm sorry," Destiny said. "And I apologize for not being able to do a signing at your friend's bookstore."

"I'll only forgive you if you promise to just consider it," Savy teased.

Destiny looked at her with wide eyes and then she looked at Quino. "She's a bold one. Are you sure you can handle her?"

Quino grinned. "Yeah, I've got that down."

Savy felt her face get hot and she glowered at him, which only made him deepen his grin.

He turned back to Destiny and said, "Here's the thing, Destiny. If you come to the Happily Ever After Bookstore—"

"Oh, I do like that name," she said.

Savy smiled. Wouldn't Maisy flip her lid if she knew Destiny Swann liked the name of her bookstore?

"Yeah, it's a good one and the place is spectacular," Quino said. "It's an old Victorian in the middle of Fairdale that's been converted to a romance-specific bookstore. Maisy Kelly, the owner, is one of your biggest fans."

Destiny perked up at that and Savy nodded in agreement. "She really is. In fact, the architect she hired to redo the house to make it into a bookstore is a ringer for your hero Jake Sinclair on the cover of *One Last Chance*. I'm pretty sure that's why they're a couple now."

"Well, that and he built her a turret," Quino said.

"Wait, are you telling me that the owner found a man who looks like one of my heroes?" Destiny asked.

"It's uncanny," Savy said.

"And the store's new?" Destiny asked.

"Brand-new," Quino said. "In fact, we're concerned that it's in trouble."

"Oh, no," Destiny said. "I hate it when bookstores close. It always feels like having a friend move out of town."

"But just think what a famous author coming out of seclusion could do for the place," Savy said. "Why, I bet she could single-handedly save the joint."

"You do, huh?" Destiny asked. Savy could tell by the arch in her eyebrows, she was onto her. Savy didn't care. This was hugely important for Maisy's success and her own. She had to go for it.

"I do," Savy said.

"I wish I had your confidence," Destiny said. She glanced past them out the window. "Writing isn't the simple act of putting words on paper. It's so much more. It's taking your own life experience and putting it in a blender with your observations about the world and then spitting them out into a new format that you then share so that your readers can use your story as a compass point to navigate their own lives.

"Frankly, it feels more like slitting open a vein and bleeding onto the page. It's one thing to put your work out there, that's hard enough, but to do publicity for your work is a whole new level of vulnerability, and a person can get swept up and lose their way." She smiled. "Maybe that's just me. I just don't know if I can risk putting myself out there again."

"But what about the readers who adore you?" Quino asked. "You know, the ones who get you? Surely, you want to meet them."

"I do," Destiny said. "But what if I start to overcommit myself again? I don't mean to be a wimp, but after that bout with pneumonia, I couldn't write for months. I can't risk that happening again." She looked at Savy. "I'm sorry."

"It's all right. I understand," Savy said. She was disappointed, no doubt, but she couldn't fault Destiny for not wanting to risk her health again.

"Destiny, do you remember the very first time I came here for your riding lesson?" Quino asked.

"Of course," she said. She smiled at him. "It was a lovely day in May, and the horses were frisky and I was so nervous."

"Yes, you were," he agreed. "You were scared because you hadn't ridden in years."

Destiny turned her head and gave him side-eye. It was pretty clear what he was doing. "But I did it."

"Yes, you did," he said. "And the very first time your horse started to gallop, you bounced right off its rump into the dirt."

This surprised a laugh out of Destiny. "I did!"

Quino smiled. "I thought for sure I was fired and you'd never ride again, but you brushed yourself off and climbed right back up in the saddle. I was so proud of you."

They were all quiet as Destiny processed Quino's words. Then Genevieve chimed in. Her voice was soft, as if she didn't want to heap more reasons to do the signing on Destiny but felt compelled to say what she had to say.

"Destiny, your readers need you," she said. "The world can be a powerfully sad place, and just like your readers need your stories, they need you, too. They need to meet you and tell you how much they value the stories you give them. And not to put too fine a point on it, but you need them, too."

Destiny studied her assistant as if surprised that Genevieve was so adamant. "I'm not . . . I can't . . ."

"Yes, you can," Genevieve said. "You've been saying for months that you've lost your spark."

Destiny gave her a wide-eyed look and glanced at Quino and Savy to see what they thought of this. Savy kept her face very still and noted that Quino did the same. Destiny glanced back at Genevieve.

"And you think getting back out there and meeting my readers will help?" Destiny asked.

"I know it will, and I'll be with you every step of the way," Genevieve said. "I won't let you get swept up. You need to do this. Not just to help the bookstore but to help yourself as well."

"But what if there are mean readers out there just waiting to pounce?" Destiny asked. "I mean, when you get back out there in the world, you get the lovers and the haters."

"There won't be," Quino said. "And if there are, I'll escort them from the premises myself."

"You'll be there?" Destiny asked in surprise.

"Are you kidding?" he asked. "I wouldn't miss it. I'll be your escort or your bodyguard or both."

"All right," Destiny said. Savy felt her hopes soar. "I'll consider it." And then they fell.

She glanced at Quino and he gave her a wink, letting her know he thought they'd be able to convince Destiny to do the signing. Savy felt her hopes lift again, not exactly at soaring range, but she was at least hopeful.

They finished tea and talked about other things. Savy learned that Quino was an accomplished guitar player, which did not surprise her since she had heard him belting out Christmas carols and knew he could sing.

When Destiny asked about his sister, Desi, his face got tight but he said she was fine. Savy wondered if he and Desi were having a tiff, because she hadn't been there to help with the tree and his face had taken on the same lockdown expression then, too.

When it was time to leave, Quino and Destiny led the way and Savy and Genevieve fell into step behind them.

"I'll do what I can to talk her into the signing," Genevieve said so just Savy could hear her. "She doesn't even realize how badly she needs this."

"Thanks, that would be a huge help."

Genevieve squeezed her arm in a gesture of understanding. Savy turned to Destiny to say good-bye, but Destiny looked past her at Genevieve.

"Did you find a copy?"

"I did," Genevieve said. With a smile she turned and picked up a book that was sitting on the table by the door. She handed it to Destiny.

"I thought you might like a signed book," Destiny said to Savy. She took the pen Genevieve held out to her and signed the title page. "I think you'll like this one especially well. I know it has a special place in my heart."

"Thank you, that's so nice of you." Savy took the book entitled *The Keeper* and glanced at the cover. She looked up and then back down in a double take. Was it? Could it be? Her jaw dropped and she held up the cover of the book next to the man. "This is extraordinary!"

"Aw, Destiny, you didn't," he said. He gave her an annoyed look that lacked any real heat.

"Of course I did," she said. "You and Daisy were my cover models for that book. It's one of my very favorites."

"It *is* you!" Savy said. She kept looking from the book to him. "And Daisy. She looks amazing! Destiny, I had no idea! This is the best thing anyone has ever given me."

"You need to set your standards a little higher," Quino said. Destiny gave him a look and he added, "Not the story but the cover."

"It's the greatest cover I've ever seen," Savy said, and she clutched it to her chest. Impulsively she leaned forward and kissed Destiny's cheek. "Thank you so much, I'll cherish it."

They left the house with a wave and headed across the enormous lawn to the corral, where the horses waited. Savy kept looking at the book and then at the man.

"Stop it, Red," he said.

"I can't," she said. "You are a cover model. I mean, I always knew you were gorgeous, but seeing you like this kind of brings it home, you know?"

He snorted. "I am not gorgeous."

"No?" she asked. "Then why are you on the cover?"

"Because they needed a dude and his horse, and Daisy and I were available."

They arrived at the corral and he swung the gate open. Cocoa was ready to go and he clipped her harness with a lead and led her to the waiting trailer.

"That is not it," she said. "They wouldn't put any old guy on a Destiny Swann novel. He had to be hot. Readers want hot guys. Too bad they let you keep your shirt on."

"Oh, my God, are you objectifying me, Red?"

"Totally."

"Well, quit it."

He loaded Cocoa and went back for Daisy. Daisy was ready to go, too, and climbed in beside Cocoa without a fuss. Quino closed the trailer and double-checked the latches before signaling for Savy to follow him. He opened the passenger door to his truck and she stepped up beside him.

"You are gorgeous," she said. "I'm not even saying that as a woman with privileged information. I'm saying that as a completely objective observer of a book cover with a total hottie on the front. A hottie who is standing right in front of me. A hottie who is also one of the nicest people I've ever met."

He shook his head at her. "You can't talk to me like that."

"Why not?"

"Because it makes me want to kiss you and I'm trying to respect your boundaries," he said.

"What boundaries are those?" she asked. At the moment, she was so smitten she couldn't remember why she had ever thought that keeping him at arm's length was a good idea. So what if he loved Christmas? Who cared if she would, hopefully, be leaving soon? Suddenly, her entire world had been whittled down to the next few moments. Moments in which all she could think about was his mouth on hers.

"Aw, hell, Red," he said. "You know you shouldn't look at me like that."

"Like what?" she breathed.

"Like you want me to kiss you."

"But I do."

And just like that, he did. With one hand on her hip and one hand buried in her hair, he kissed her long and deep.

Savy dropped the book onto the seat behind her and latched on to him. She kissed him back with all of the desire she'd felt over the past few days. She'd missed him. She'd missed this. She didn't know what to do about it but she knew that doing nothing was not working for her.

She slid her mouth along his and opened her lips to draw him in. Quino answered by deepening the kiss until the only sensation Savy could grasp was the feel of his mouth against hers as he wooed her with kisses that let her know he hadn't forgotten the other night, either. Not one little bit of it.

Something sharp and wet hit Savy's cheek. She ignored it but then felt it again. Reluctantly, she pulled back to discover that she and Quino were both covered in big fat snowflakes that clung to their clothes and hair. He even had a few on his long thick eyelashes.

"Oh, wow," she said. "The first snow of the season."

Quino looked up at the falling snow and then back down at her. He grinned. "See what happens when I kiss you?"

"Snow? Really?" she asked. "You're saying our kiss made it snow?"

"Being with you always seems to change my world," he said. He tucked a long strand of her hair behind her ear and kissed her quick. "So it seems perfectly reasonable to me."

He leaned close and kissed her again as if he just couldn't help himself.

A horse whinnied and a loud stomp sounded from the trailer. It interrupted the sultry haze they were wrapped in and Quino stepped back. He sucked in a breath and said, "Sorry."

"Don't be," she said. She sounded breathless, because she was, and she smiled. "I'm not."

With that she turned and climbed into her seat, afraid that if she didn't she'd grab him by the front of his hideous sweater and kiss him again. Quino closed the door after her and she heard him whistling as he walked around the front of the truck. It took her a moment to identify the tune and when she did, she smiled. "All I Want for Christmas Is You." Well, the feeling was mutual.

Chapter Seventeen

"FROSTING and books don't mix," Maisy said. She was wiping down a paperback book that had just been shellacked with dark green frosting by a toddler with a wild aim.

"Sorry about that," Savy said. She helped Maisy unload the book cart onto the shelves in their office. Most of the books looked fine. There was a stack of cookies and several bowls of frosting that needed to be thrown out since the germ factor with toddlers was high. "I didn't really think it through with the cookie decorating. Who knew two-year-olds had so much range with flinging the frosting?"

Maisy laughed. "It's fine. We can always charge extra for the added buttercream smell."

Savy grinned. She studied her friend. Maisy had hit the ground running every day for the past week. In fact, they all had. Cookie decorating, carol singing, holiday movies, even a Debbie Macomber—inspired knitting class where they learned to knit mittens while listening to the audio edition of one of her books.

Every day there was something new and wonderful to do. Was it helping? Savy had no idea. It seemed like people were buying, but when she'd walked into the office two days ago, she'd overheard Maisy on the phone saying she didn't know if she could gather that much money by the end of the year. Savy tried not to panic. She failed. It took everything she had not to call Quino and beg him to ask Destiny to please do the bookstore signing.

She hadn't seen Quino since Destiny's riding lesson last week. When they'd arrived back at Shadow Pine, a class was under way and Quino was needed to assist Lanie with the students receiving equine therapy.

Savy supposed it was for the best, since his kiss at Windemere Manor had reduced her resistance to rubble, but she missed him. She learned from Sawyer, who was helping out at Shadow Pine with odd jobs as much as he was at the bookstore, that Quino was juggling a packed schedule at the stables with holiday work parties that included snowy trail rides up into the mountains, as well as sleigh rides in and around Fairdale. Now that the snow had arrived it seemed determined to stay, and they'd had several snowfalls, adding to the holiday spirit as it dipped the area in a thick coating of winter.

Even Savy with her usual dour sense of the holidays had to admit that she felt a little more bounce in her step than usual. Maybe it was her evenings spent at the ice rink. She'd taken to going once a day and had started to give impromptu lessons to a pack of kids who flocked to her when she arrived. It felt so good to have this part of herself back. She owed Quino for that. She even felt optimistic that Destiny would come around. She suspected this new level of happiness had to do with Quino, too. Every day she debated whether or not to call him and see if he had heard from Destiny, but she knew it was a lame excuse at best and obvious at worst.

If Quino had heard from Destiny, she knew he would have told her. Maybe he was over their flirtation. After all, they had slept together. It could be that there was no mystery left for him in regard to her. Perhaps he'd even found someone else at one of those office-party-horseback-riding things.

Savy frowned.

"Did the cookie do something to offend you?" Maisy asked.

Savannah looked down. She'd been picking up the extra unused sugar cookies and one in the shape of a snowman was crumbled in her fist. She opened her fingers and let it spill into the garbage bin.

"Faulty cookie construction," she said.

"Uh-huh," Maisy said.

A screech of car tires and a shout came from outside. Both women glanced at the windows.

"What is he doing?" A shout came from the front of the bookstore. "He is going to get himself killed!"

Savy and Maisy exchanged a glance and darted to the front of the bookstore. Jeri was standing at the front window along with three customers, one of whom was Hannah Phillips, the veterinarian, and they were watching something out on the street.

Savy glanced over the heads of the others while Maisy stepped onto a step stool for a better view. A man was running back and forth across the busy street, ducking through cars, with his arms outstretched as if trying to catch something.

"Is that Sawyer?" Maisy asked.

"Yes," Jeri answered. "He was in here a minute ago, fixing the radiator that keeps whistling, and then he just dropped his tools and ran outside."

They all watched as the handsome dark-haired man ran across the street again. He'd just stepped onto the curb when something flew up at him and he jumped backward.

"Oh, no," Hannah said. "Franklin." The note of dread in her voice was unmistakable. She stepped back from the window and shoved her armful of books at Jeri. "Hold these for me. I'll be right back."

Hannah ran outside, yelling, "Stop! Wait!"

Jeri dropped the books on the counter and charged to the door. "I am not missing a second of this. Maybe Sawyer will have to take his shirt off."

"Right behind you!" Savy said.

Maisy shook her head, sending her short curls bouncing, but she followed them out, as did every customer in the shop. When they reached the porch, they heard Hannah yelling, "Don't hurt him! He doesn't know any better."

She was standing on the sidewalk, wearing a long cardigan over her veterinarian scrubs. Her thick blond hair was in a fat braid that ran halfway down her back and she was holding her arms outstretched with her hands up in the universal sign for *stop*.

"Hurt him?" Sawyer shouted. He moved his arms over his head just as a big, rough-looking rooster flew up at him. He ducked and the rooster went right over him. "I'm trying to keep the stupid bird out of the road!"

"He's not stupid!" Hannah said. She crouched low, pulled off her sweater, and started to make kissy noises. "Franklin, come here, boy."

"Franklin? That creature of darkness is named Franklin?" Sawyer cried. The rooster, as if understanding he'd been insulted, began to strut toward Sawyer. "Don't even think it, you shifty-eyed, limp-feathered ground pecker. If it weren't for me, you'd be roadkill."

"Franklin," Hannah called. "Franklin, come."

Sawyer loomed and Franklin turned and scuttled toward Hannah. She held out her arm and when he drew close she swiftly wrapped him up in her sweater and tucked him under her arm. The ladies on the porch burst into spontaneous applause.

"Is that the rooster she saved a few years ago?" Savy asked.

"Yup, that's Franklin. She found him half-dead as a baby chick and nursed him back to life," Maisy said. "He loves Hannah and only Hannah. She swears he's better than having a watchdog."

"Well, it could have been worse," Jeri said. "With that menagerie she's got, it could have been Matilda the goat who got loose. She butts first and asks questions later."

They watched as Sawyer stepped around Hannah and strode up the sidewalk to the bookstore.

"Nice work, Sawyer," Jeri called out. As an aside to

those on the porch, she added, "Still, it's too bad he didn't have to take his shirt off."

"Yeah," Mrs. La Costa, a gray-haired octogenarian and one of their regulars, agreed. "Total bummer."

Savy watched as Sawyer and Hannah bickered on their way up to the porch.

"Well, he wouldn't have flown at you, if you hadn't frightened him," she said.

"Frightened him?" Sawyer stopped and turned to stare at her. "When I saw him from the window, he was trying to shank a passing car with those heel spurs of his. He's damn lucky he didn't get run over."

"Thank you for saving him," Hannah said. She rested her cheek on Franklin's crest and he nuzzled her back. "I do appreciate it, and I'm sorry he behaved badly. He's very sensitive."

"Sensitive?" Sawyer gaped at her. "That bird is a menace." He pointed at Franklin, who poked his head forward and tried to peck his finger. "See?"

"He's not," Hannah insisted. "He's just misunderstood."

Sawyer clapped his palm to his forehead. He shook his head at Hannah and said, "Lady, the only thing that bird is good for is stuffing with corn bread."

"Ah!" Hannah gasped and clutched Franklin closer. She glanced up at the porch and said, "Jeri, hold my books for me, please. I'm taking Franklin home."

"Will do," Jeri said. "Bye, Franklin."

The rooster didn't respond.

Sawyer watched Hannah stomp away. He turned around and ran a hand through his hair. As he passed Savy and Maisy on his way into the bookstore, he said, "I don't know who's crazier, her or her damn bird."

The door banged shut behind him, and the women all burst into chuckles. They reentered the store and resumed what they'd been doing before the incident. Savannah wandered from the office to the store and back to the office. She couldn't seem to get settled. The scene between Hannah and Sawyer had been a nice diversion, but now that they were back inside, the bookstore was quiet. Too quiet.

"That was the most exciting thing to happen all week," Savy said to Maisy as she made her second pass through the office. "The drama of living in Fairdale. How have I existed without this?"

"Search me," Maisy said. She studied Savy's face and frowned. "Listen, I've got things here. You've worked open to close for the past three days. Go take a break, walk around downtown, soak in the holiday spirit."

"Yeah, because I'm all about that holiday spirit," Savy said.

"Go." Maisy made a shooing motion with her hands and Savy knew she would just keep badgering her until she went.

"Fine, but I refuse to get swept up in the holiday nonsense," she said. "I'm going to get my eyebrows threaded and possibly a manicure, and then I'll be back."

Maisy rolled her eyes. "Just so long as I don't see you until tomorrow. Take the rest of the day off. That's an order."

Savy frowned as she grabbed her coat and hat and mittens and suited up for the chilly temperatures outside. She hefted her purse onto her shoulder and said, "I'm going but I'm not going to have any fun."

Maisy threw a popcorn ball at her, but Savy was too quick for her. She caught it in one hand and took a big bite out of it on her way out the door. She heard Maisy laughing as the door swung shut behind her.

Savy walked to town, not wanting to drive in the snow. Her errands didn't require a car and it was easy to trudge through the small drifts in her thick rubber-soled boots. In fact, it almost felt therapeutic. She bought a cup of cocoa at the deli on the corner and sipped while browsing the window displays, unsure of whether she could manage to sit still for a manicure. She thought about calling Genevieve to see if there'd been any progress with Destiny. She resisted. She debated calling Archer to see if there was any news about how her old boss was doing without her. She didn't feel like doing that, either. She cut across the street to the big town square.

There was an empty bench that was free of snow so she

sat, deciding that people-watching without having to inter-
act with them was preferable. She drank her rapidly cooling
cocoa while she watched a pack of kids have a snowball
fight in the middle of the green.

They ran, they yelled, they hid behind trees. Snowballs
were lobbed, some with accuracy but most without. The
war lasted until one boy got a face full of snow that sent his
glasses flying. A harried mother came out of a nearby store
and began yelling at all the kids.

"Do you have any idea how much glasses cost?" she
cried. The kid with the snow in his face cried even harder.

The mom put her packages down on another bench and
inspected the glasses. They weren't damaged, which was
lucky, the mom informed the child, because Santa didn't
bring presents to boys who broke their glasses in silly
snowball fights. The boy looked duly horrified at this possibility.

Savy watched as the mom herded her boy away. Peace
reigned over the town green as most people were too busy
rushing here and there, getting all of the holiday chores
done. She heard a faint jingling and wondered which store
had hired a guy to stand outside and ring bells. She wondered what the job paid and if she'd be doing that next
Christmas if she couldn't save Maisy's bookstore or get her
old job back. The thought did not lift her spirits.

As the jingling became louder, people stopped and
stared. Savy glanced in the direction of the noise and her
eyes went wide as she took in the sight of an old-fashioned
wagon being pulled by a team of horses, coasting onto the
town green from a snowy path in the trees. Was that . . . ?
She squinted. Yes, of course, it was.

Quino was leading the team while wearing a ridiculously loud green-and-red plaid sweater and a Santa hat.
The wagon was full of kids, a few grown-ups who looked
like caregivers, and they were laughing and singing as
Lanie, the equine therapist, sat with them in the back. Except for one little boy, who was on the bench seat beside
Quino. Savy felt her heart hitch as she watched him hand
the boy the reins. The boy's eyes were huge and his grin

wide as he commanded the team, looking as if his chest had just expanded about six inches. The sight of the man and the boy turned Savy's poor heart to mush.

The kids waved to the pedestrians, who waved back with big smiles. Quino helped the boy bring the team to a halt and then he climbed down, opening the back of the wagon and helping everyone down. Lanie ushered them all into an ice cream shop on the corner while Quino waited with the horses.

Savy supposed she could have left without him seeing her. He was across the park and busy. But she found she'd missed the big Christmas-loving cowboy and she wanted to say hello. She crossed the town green, feeling unusually self-conscious. She wished she had her date lipstick on or a better outfit, but there was no help for it now.

"Hey, Kris Kringle," she said as she approached. "Aren't you supposed to be driving reindeer?"

Quino spun around at the sound of her voice and his smile was quick as if he was delighted to see her and not bothering to pretend he wasn't. He was such a better person than she was. She sighed.

"I'm no Kringle," he said. "Just a poor relation, so I have to make do with these slackers who don't fly."

Savy laughed. She approached the horse closest to her and rubbed its nose. "You shouldn't let him talk about you that way."

"Meh, I'm sure they say worse about me," Quino said. "To begin with I'm lacking in the beard department."

"And you're woefully underweight," she said. "You need to carb-load on some cookies or something."

He grinned. Then his brown eyes turned warm. "I've missed you."

Inexplicably, this brought a bout of honesty out of Savy. "I've missed you, too."

"So, you should spend some time with me to help you get over that," he said. "Which should take at least a day, right?"

"More like a half hour," she said drily. He laughed, as she'd intended.

He sobered quickly and she noted there was a shadow in his eyes she hadn't seen before. "Is everything all right?"

"Yeah, just family stuff, you know, the holidays make everything . . ." His voice trailed off.

"Hard? Sad? Lonely?" Savy supplied. It occurred to her she may have just overshared as Quino didn't answer but instead pulled her close and hugged her tight.

"Lanie and the kids will be back from their ice cream party soon. Join us on the ride back to Shadow Pine," he said. "It's a beautiful ride through the snow-covered trees. You'll love it."

"Oh, I don't want to impose . . ." she said.

"You won't be," he said. "So, it's settled?"

Savy tried to find a reason not to go, but she couldn't. The fact was she wanted to be with him and she'd spend time with him however she could, even with a pack of kids on a wagon in the snow.

"All right," she said. "Can I get you a coffee while you wait?"

"Thanks, but I have a thermos in the wagon," he said. "Want to meet the team?"

"Yes, please," she said.

As if it was the most natural thing in the world, Quino took her hand in his as they stood in front of the horses. "This is Justice," he said. "He's cranky and can only pull the wagon with Belvedere."

"Belvedere?" She laughed.

"What?" Quino asked. "He is a Belvedere, very gentle-manly and a little uptight."

"And Justice isn't?"

"No, he's more of a get-off-my-lawn old man," Quino said. "He's been known to nip people he doesn't like. He loves the kids, though, so there's hope for the old cur-mudgeon."

Savy patted Belvedere's neck and then Justice's. They were both big and brown, but where Belvedere had a blond mane and tail, Justice's were black. Savy could feel their muscles ripple beneath her fingers as she patted their shoulders. To her they were simply magnificent.

"You know, it would be great to get some pictures of the horses and the kids for your website," she said.

He tipped his head to the side and studied her. "You're always working, aren't you?"

"Nature of the publicist," she said. Then she pulled out her phone and took a picture of him between Belvedere and Justice. The camera loved the sharp angles of his face and she knew it was no coincidence that he'd been used as a cover model for one of Destiny's books.

"Question," she said.

"Yes?"

"Are you only on one cover of Destiny's books or did she use you for more?"

Quino smiled. "One. Which was more than enough."

"Was it hard work to stand there and look pretty?" she asked. Teasing him, getting a smile out of him, was more alluring than Savy could resist. To her delight a faint pink stained his cheeks and he smiled at her. It was just the slight curve of his lips, a shy smile, and it charmed her all the way to her cold toes.

"Are you laughing at me?" he asked. "I'll have you know that one photo took hours. It was the most boring afternoon of my life."

"Did they do your hair and makeup?" she asked. The pink in his cheeks deepened and she knew it wasn't from the cold. She gasped. "They did!"

"I am not talking about this anymore," he said. He turned away and she was afraid she'd offended him. Some men were like that when it came to teasing about girly stuff, although Quino hadn't struck her as one of those guys. He was rummaging through a knapsack he had in the wagon and she stepped up behind him so she didn't have to shout her apology.

"Oh, hey," she said. "I'm sorry. I didn't mean to make you feel—"

He turned around, replacing his Santa hat with a bright red-and-green baseball hat that had a bough of mistletoe hanging off the brim. She frowned at it but the expectant look on his face made her laugh.

"Did you rig that up yourself?" she asked.

"Yes," he said. "I was hoping I'd see you at some point." He wagged his eyebrows at her and she shook her head. Had any man ever tried to charm her so ham-fistedly? No. Why was it working? She looked into his dark-brown gaze. Because she'd have to be made of stone not to respond to the warmth she found there.

"Fine," she said. She heaved a put-upon sigh and rolled up on her toes to kiss him.

It started as a chaste kiss, the sort appropriate for public displays of affection, but it didn't stay that way for long. As if they felt compelled to make up for every moment they'd been apart over the past few days, they lingered with their mouths pressed together, until she gave in and looped her arms about his neck, pulling him in close and tight.

He grunted in approval and slid his hands around her waist, anchoring her to him. Then the kiss changed. In the relative cover of the wagon, he kissed her deeply as if trying to take in the essence of her, and Savy did the same. She wanted more and more and more of him. He drove out the cold and brought the warmth, but it wasn't just the physical sensation of closeness or the desire that flared between them. Somehow, he managed to drive out the loneliness that Savy always felt during the holidays. The constant feeling of being an outsider looking in vanished when she was with him.

One giggle and then another interrupted their smooch. Savy eased back from Quino and peered over his shoulder at a group of kids, parents, and Lanie O'Brien, the pretty brunette who worked at Shadow Pine.

"We have company," Savy said to Quino.

"Is that right?" he asked. "Sorry, I'm trying to remember why I care."

She laughed. "Because you need to drive them home."

"Oh, right, that's it," he said. He stared at her hard. "Join us?"

After the slightest hesitation, Savy nodded. She couldn't think of a better way to spend her day and maybe, just maybe, she'd get inspired with a new publicity angle for the bookstore.

The kids and their caregivers were loaded up into the wagon with Lanie. The boy who had ridden in front with Quino on the way to town insisted on riding with him on the way back but was happy to make room for Savy to join them. Quino replaced his mistletoe cap with his Santa hat but not before he took off a berry and handed it to her. She wondered how many berries she'd find in her pockets after the holidays.

"Savannah, this is Jake," Quino introduced the boy as the three of them took their seats on the bench with Quino and Savy on the ends and Jake in the middle. "Jake, this is Savannah."

Jake studied Savannah and then turned back to Quino. "Is she your girlfriend?"

Savannah looked at Quino and found him looking back at her with an amused smile. Then he looked at Jake. "What makes you ask that?"

"You were kissing her," Jake said. He didn't add *duh* but it was clearly implied.

Savy felt her face get hot. Great, so it was her turn to be embarrassed. She supposed that was only fair. Still, she didn't want Jake, who looked to be about ten, to get the wrong idea. She opened her mouth to answer but Quino beat her to it.

"I think she might be," he said. "Assuming I can convince her that it's a good idea. Can you vouch for me?"

"What's *vouch* mean?" Jake asked.

"Tell her I'm a good guy," Quino said. "That's what a wingman does for his pals—he vouches for them."

Jake nodded. He turned to Savy and with the most earnest expression she'd ever seen, he said, "You should be Quino's girlfriend. He's the best. He's kind and patient, and when I can't remember things or I do something wrong, he never gets mad. When I grow up, I want to be just like him."

Savy's heart turned over in her chest. It wasn't fair. Jake was telling her everything she knew to be true about Quino, but having it stated by this boy made it so much harder to ignore. She decided not to, not today.

"I think you have a solid argument there," she said. "I

saw you handle the horses earlier. You are well on your way to being as good a horseman as Quino."

Jake laughed and then he winked at her. "Maybe you should date me instead."

A surprised laugh burst out of Savy and she glanced past Jake at Quino. "He really is quite a lot like you, isn't he?"

Quino gave Jake a considering look. "Sorry, kid, you can handle the horses but the girl is mine."

Jake shrugged. "I can live with that."

Savy and Quino exchanged amused smiles over his head. It hit Savy again how much she liked, genuinely liked, this man. He was thoughtful, generous, and had such a natural way with kids and animals. She didn't think she'd ever met anyone quite like him before.

"Well, that's settled, then," Quino said. Before Savy could respond, he glanced back to see that everyone was seated in the wagon bed, and then, with a snap of the reins and a "Hyah!," they were off.

Once they cleared the town green and were back in the wide path amongst the tall trees dusted with snow, Quino handed the reins to Jake. The boy looked so serious, Savy wanted to hug him and tell him it would be all right, but she didn't. Instead, she watched as he held the reins in his gloved hands in a perfect imitation of how Quino had done it. He even curved his mouth up on one side just like his idol.

Was this what a child of Quino's would look like? Boy or girl, would they have the same facial expressions, the same way with animals, the same heart? She imagined that they would. She felt something stir inside of her. She wasn't sure what it was because Savy had never, not once, in her entire life longed for a husband or children. Oh, she enjoyed visiting her nieces and nephews, but she enjoyed leaving just a little bit more.

But watching Joaquin with Jake was punching her in all the feels. She could imagine how he would be with a wife, tender and caring, and she could see him as a father, patient, kind, and concerned but with a sparkle of mischief just to keep things interesting. Whoever ended up with Quino as a partner was going to be a lucky woman.

What if it was her? The thought flitted through her mind, but she shook it off. It wasn't going to be her. She was headed back to New York to the first job that would have her, and that was no place for a man like Quino. The concrete and steel would choke the life out of him. She glanced at him as they whipped through the trees with the horses moving at a clip. His cheeks were ruddy, his eyes sparkled, and his teeth were a slash of white as he smiled. She pulled out her phone and began to snap pictures of the horses, the wagon, the woods, the kids, and then, just for posterity, she took a few close-ups of Quino, just for her, while he was looking at Jake.

The air was clear and cold with a faint scent of woodsmoke. The woods were quiet except for the sound of the children laughing and chatting and the jingle of the bells on the horses' bridles. The methodic clop of the horses' feet in the light snow kept time with their occasional snorts and snuffles.

Savy lost her sense of time and place. The deeper into the woods they went, the more magical the ride became as brown leaves danced in the air, trees dusted with snow bent their limbs to the ground, and a flock of wild turkeys scrambled through the undergrowth, sounding very much like goblins or boggarts. Savy was half-convinced they were going to end up in some other fairy world instead of their actual destination, but no.

All too soon, the big barn of the Shadow Pine Stables appeared through the trees. Luke Masters and two of the stable hands were putting away a string of horses left over from what Savy assumed had been a trial ride.

Quino took the reins from Jake, who looked equal parts disappointed and relieved. Quino guided the horses to a stop right in front of the barn, and one of the stable hands held them steady while the kids scrambled out of the wagon to dash to their parents, who were waiting by the small parking lot on the other side of the corral.

Lanie hopped down and said, "That was a perfect outing." She lifted a gloved hand and she and Quino exchanged a muffled high five. "I'll make sure each kid gets to their parents."

"Thanks," Quino said.

"Savy, can you send me some of those pictures?" Lanie asked. "I'd like to use them on our social media."

"Finally," Savy said. "Someone who cares about the publicity. I'll text them to you."

"Thanks," Lanie said. She and the other caregivers dashed after the kids. Savy noticed that Luke watched her go with a look of yearning. She wondered what the story was there, knowing full well it was none of her business.

"Thanks, Quino," Jake said as he hopped off the wagon. He hugged Quino tight around the waist and then ran off, yelling, "Mom, did you see? Did you see what I did? I drove the wagon!"

A woman was laughing and she raised her hand in the air and waved at Quino. He waved back. She opened her arms and Jake gave his mom a huge hug.

"You've just given that boy the best day of his life," Savy said.

"He's a natural," Quino said. "He's got a real gift for animals. Even Esther likes him and she hates everyone."

He pointed and, sure enough, a gray horse was making her way across the corral to greet the boy. Jake let go of his mom and climbed up on the rail to pat the horse. Once he was finished, she reared around and set her sights on Quino.

"Uh-oh," Quino said. "I'm about to get shaken down."

Savy glanced from him to the horse. She was a compact gray mare with a lighter gray mane and tail. She approached the rail where they stood and gave Quino a look that was full of censure.

He laughed at her as he reached over the rail and patted her neck. "Stop giving me stink eye, Esther. I just came in from a wagon ride. That's why I don't have anything for you."

Esther tossed her head in obvious pique, and Savy laughed. "She has a lot of personality."

Quino shook his head. "You have no idea. Still, I love her."

Esther was not satisfied and pressed her nose to all of Quino's pockets. When she determined he really didn't have any treats, she stomped off in a huff. Savy had never seen a horse have a hissy fit. It was, in its own way, charming.

"Quino, why don't you call it a day?" Luke said. "We'll take care of the team for you. We have to take care of our horses anyway."

He was about as subtle as a hammer as he glanced between Quino and Savy. She smiled. She wondered how Quino would finesse the situation.

"Well," he said. He pushed back his Santa hat and studied her face. "Are you interested in having dinner with me tonight?"

"Hmm," Savy said. "I might be. What are we having?"

"How do green corn tamales grab you?" he asked.

Savy realized right then that she was starving. "Sounds amazing."

His grin was slow and he took her hand, and with a wave to Luke, they set off for the house. The lights weren't on, but she could see that he had added even more to the exterior. She shook her head. She had seriously never met anyone who loved Christmas as much as he did.

The inside of the house was cozy warm and the tree they had decorated shimmered even in the dim light. Savy felt her heart swell just a little as she recognized some of the sentimental ornaments she'd put on it. The house smelled of evergreen and cinnamon and it filled her senses, reminding her of the night she'd spent here in his arms.

Quino took her coat and they both toed off their boots, walking in socks to the living room, where he flipped a switch that illuminated the tree and then hunkered down in front of the fireplace to light the fire. If there was ever a moment in her life that sparkled with perfection, Savy was pretty sure this was it. The tree shimmered, the man shined, and her heart felt full for the first time she could ever remember.

Once the fire was crackling, Quino took her hand and led her back to the kitchen. It was a small space, the appliances were new but the counters and cupboards were older. She suspected not much had been changed since he was a teenager. She wondered if that was intentional.

There was a picture on a shelf above the sink. It was a black-and-white of a beautiful couple on their wedding day.

She knew without asking that these were Quino's parents. He had his father's hair and eyes, but the lips were his mother's. She could tell because the woman smiling out at her had the same curve to her lips that Quino had when he smiled.

"My parents," he said. She looked to see what emotion came with this announcement but there was none. It was just a fact. "Beatriz Munoz and Victor Solis. Happiest couple I have ever seen in my life."

Savy glanced from him back to the picture. It was easy to believe that they'd been happy. The way they looked at each other in the picture made Savy think, *That, I want that.* Mercifully, she didn't say it out loud.

"Did your mother teach you to make tamales?" she asked.

"No, these were sent to us by Tía Carmen, my mother's sister. Every year since my mom died, she sends the tamales from Texas so that we aren't missing out," he said.

"If you're saving them for Christmas, please don't use them on my account," Savy said. "I can treat us to a pizza."

"Oh, no, trust me," he said. "My aunt sends enough to feed twelve people, never mind two. Plus they take no time to heat up. Have a seat and I'll cook up some tamales with extra red sauce and frijoles. Wine?"

"Actually, beer, if you have it," she said. She slid onto a seat at the counter.

He blinked at her. "Excellent choice, madam."

He said it like a wine steward at a trending restaurant and Savy laughed. He grabbed two bottles of Green Man Brewery IPA out of his refrigerator and poured them into glasses. He lifted his in a toast and Savy clinked her glass with his.

Before he took a sip, Quino lowered his glass and said, "So, about what Jake said."

"What about it?"

"For clarity's sake I have to ask, *are* you my girlfriend?"

Chapter Eighteen

D O you want me to be?" she countered. "Knowing that I'm likely leaving soon."

He sipped his beer, considering her over the rim of the glass. "What if I say yes?"

Time stopped. Savy felt as if she were standing on the edge of a precipice, looking down into an abyss. She supposed it was an overly dramatic image, but she felt things with Quino she'd never felt before and she wanted to tread carefully on the off chance that the loose gravel beneath her feet sent her spiraling into the void.

The truth was a week had gone by and Destiny hadn't called. It was early December and the author wasn't likely to do a signing at the bookstore, and Savy wouldn't be going back to New York because she felt compelled to stay with Maisy until the bitter end when the bookstore failed completely and had to be dismantled and sold. Gah, that was a depressing thought. She sipped her beer. But what if in all this failure, she could find one spark of happiness? Was she willing to take it?

She studied the dark-haired man across the counter.

Wasn't it best to make the most out of the access she had to him now?

"If you say yes, then I say yes," she said.

He straightened up. The surprise on his face was almost comical but she didn't laugh because the intensity with which he was staring at her made her mouth dry. He glanced up at the ceiling, then back at her with a fierce light in his eyes.

"So, I'm thinking if you're my girlfriend, I don't have to look for mistletoe to kiss you," he said.

"Sounds about right," she agreed.

He was around the island in three strides, snatched her up in two more, planted his mouth on hers while depositing her onto the counter so he could move in close, hang on tight, and make her moan with his mouth.

Savy was all in. She pushed their beer bottles and glasses out of the way. Then she dug her fingers into his hair while wrapping her legs around his waist. She hauled him in close, feeling the spark between them ignite into a desire so fierce it bordered on painful.

Quino slid his lips down the side of her neck and Savy let her head fall back, enjoying the feel of his soft mouth on her skin. She wanted more and more. She reached for the front of his sweater and began to tug at it. She wanted to be skin-to-skin with this man and she wanted it now.

"Dinner can wait?" he asked.

"Yes," she breathed.

She barely got the words out when he hauled her up into his arms and carried her through the house and up the stairs to his bedroom. He was halfway up the stairs when he paused to kiss her. Savy was a bit afraid he'd lose his footing and they'd tumble to the bottom in a pile of broken bones, but he wasn't even breathing heavy. The man was as steady as a rock.

Instead, once he'd finished kissing her, he pulled back and said, "We might have to skip breakfast, too. I don't think I'm going to be done with you for a long, long while."

Dizzy. The man made her positively dizzy. She had never felt as connected to anyone as she did to him. He was warm and kind, funny and considerate, with broad shoulders, chiseled features, and a deep laugh that reverberated down her spine in the most delicious way. If things were different . . . but she wasn't going to think about that now.

Instead, she tightened her arms about his neck, pressing herself against him. She kissed his jawline all the way to his ear, where she gently bit down and whispered, "Make me yours, Quino."

SO hot. With her mass of tumbled red curls, green cat's eyes, and siren's smile, he was toast. Burnt toast. He hauled her up close and finished the walk toward the bedroom.

He was actually a bit stunned by his good fortune. Savy had been insistent that there would be no repeats but his patience had been rewarded and now here they were, and he'd gotten her to level up on this relationship. From the moment he'd first seen her, he'd known she was it for him. And now she was his girlfriend. Quino wasn't sure what had made her change her mind about him, about them. He didn't much care. He just knew that he was here with her and suddenly his world seemed infinitely brighter.

Everything melted away when he was with her. His worry about his sister, his melancholy about the holiday, his dislike of change, all of it was pushed back by the force of nature that was Savannah Wilson. She filled his senses and he couldn't see or feel anything else.

He was consumed by her. The sound of her laugh, the feel of her fingers as they skimmed his skin, the way her hair caught the light as if it actually trapped and held sunshine in its depths. He strode into his bedroom. It was at the back of the house and offered a view of the mountains. At the moment he didn't care other than to be relieved that it was clean. That was one perk of his nervous energy. The house was the cleanest it had been in months.

He slowly released Savy, letting her slide down his body until her feet touched the floor. He kept one hand on her waist while he flipped on the lights. He used the dimmer to set them to low. He didn't want to ruin the mood with harsh lighting, although he was pretty sure he'd be able to make love to Savy anytime, anywhere, even with his boots on. Of course, he knew better than to say that to her.

Instead he cupped her jaw, stared into her eyes, and kissed her long and slow. He let his hands roam over her curves, memorizing the soft feel of her in his hands, from the flare of her hips to the nip of her waist and up along her sides to the generous curve of her breasts. She was perfection.

"Now can we lose the sweater?" she asked. Her voice was low and it rubbed across his senses with just the right friction. She tugged at the hem and he obliged her by pulling it over his head. Then he reached for hers. She lifted her arms and he tossed aside the pretty pink sweater and pulled her close.

He wanted to hiss at the contact, the sizzle of skin to skin, as he inhaled the delicious scent of her, which reminded him of cinnamon sugar. He lowered his mouth to the exposed skin of her throat and it was her turn to hiss. He smiled against her skin.

This. He wanted this. Her coming apart in his arms while he loved every single inch of her. He moved his lips across her collarbone, nuzzling the vee between her breasts until she arched back with a low groan, buried her fingers in his hair, and whispered, "More."

He nipped her gently on the peak of one breast through the sheer lace of her bra. She gasped. He kneeled before her and kissed his way down, over her taut abdomen, to pause at her waist, while he unfastened her waistband and slid her pants down the long, shapely lengths of her legs.

He helped her to step out of her pants and then tossed them the way of her sweater. He ran his hands up the backs of her legs until he had one hand on each thigh. She was looking down at him, with kiss-swollen lips and eyes that were half-closed with desire. Her hair was wild around her face, which was flushed with want. He was quite certain that in his last moments on this earth, just before he punched his ticket for good, this would be the last image he would see in his mind's eye. This gloriously beautiful woman looking at him just like this.

As much as he had wanted to draw out every second of this celebration of their new status, he found that the need to have her beneath him, calling out his name in that way only she could, was overriding any other thought in his head. He simply needed to make her his. Now.

He stood up, hauling her into his arms as he carried her across the room. He put her gently on the bed. Against the dark-blue comforter, she looked like a vibrant flame with her faintly freckled peachy skin and red curls.

"You have a wicked look in your eye, Joaquin Solis," she said. Her voice was husky. It made him sweat. In seconds, he had shucked off his own jeans and was climbing up onto the bed. She greeted him by opening her legs and pulling him down on top of her.

Quino couldn't help but feel as if he was coming home. He kissed her long and deep, ran his fingers through her hair, and when he couldn't stand the barrier of their underclothes between them anymore, he unfastened her bra and slid her undies down her legs. By the time he slipped off his own boxers, he was on the razor edge of pleasure and pain. On the one hand he wanted the torment to go on forever but the idea of slipping inside her welcoming warmth was almost more than he could stand.

Savy was in the same fevered state. She kissed him, ran her fingers through his hair. She tugged him close and pressed up against him in a blatant invitation. Quino wasn't answering it, however, not yet. Instead, he kissed his way down her body, determined that she know that she wasn't just his girlfriend but she was his for all time. He was going to absolutely ruin her for any other man. It seemed only fair since she'd ruined him for any other woman.

He settled himself between her legs and lowered his mouth to her most sensitive flesh. She shot upright at the first shock of contact. She was shaking and panting and she looked a little crazed. It was a good look on her.

"Shh," he said. Then he tugged the backs of her knees, which flattened her before him, and he said, "Behave."

"I don't think I can—" Whatever she was going to say got lost in a garble of "oh, my," "yes, please," and "there, right there." At least those were the words that were intelligible. When her back arched and she ground her hips into the mattress, her words turned into a series of moans that he was pretty sure would ring in his ears for days to come.

He reached for a condom in his nightstand and made quick work of sliding it on. He wanted this woman more than he had ever wanted any woman ever. Savy reached for him, pulling him into her as if what she needed wasn't just the release he had given her but the connection she found when they were joined—at least that's what he told himself he saw in her. He didn't want to be the only one caught up in the magic that was the two of them. He wanted her to feel it, too.

He tried to keep it slow, let it build, make it last, but the momentum between them was too great. She fit him perfectly, clenching around him in a tight, hot grip that had him seeing stars. He pulled out a bit, trying to maintain his cool. He should have known better. Savy hooked her legs around his waist and pulled him in. She arched her back, drawing him in even deeper, and Quino lost it. The need to thrust into her was too much. He couldn't fight it.

He planted one hand by her head, and used the other to lift her hips up into the perfect angle, and then he drilled into her again and again until he felt her go rigid as another orgasm rocketed through her, making it impossible to resist his own. He felt the fire shoot down his spine, tighten his balls, and surge out of him. He pulled her in close and tight, while his release throbbed out of him and into her, connecting them on the most elemental level.

The force of it left him dizzy and he was almost afraid he was going to pass out. He collapsed onto the bed, rolling so that they were on their sides, still joined and pressed together while their hearts beat crazy messages to each other as if trying to tell each other what they felt without having to use words.

Savy tucked her head beneath his chin, and Quino reached over her to pull the edges of the thick comforter over their rapidly cooling skin. He wished he could stay in this cocoon with her forever. Was it possible to be more than in love with another person? He didn't know. He just knew that Savy was becoming his everything, and when she left, he wasn't certain he'd survive.

S O, since you're my boyfriend, I feel I have to ask you, Why are you such a nut about Christmas?" Savy asked.

Quino had rolled back the comforter, cleaned up, and then tucked them into his supersoft flannel sheets. Of course these were his Christmas ones that had snowmen exchanging presents on them. He supposed it could be worse. He also had a set that had reindeer flying with Santa in his sleigh.

He glanced down at her nestled in the crook of his arm. He didn't particularly want to talk about this, so he let his hand roam. When she let out a gasp and then a sigh, he thought he had successfully diverted her. No such luck.

She captured his hand in hers and laced their fingers together. "You can't distract me."

He sighed. He pulled her close and kissed her. She kissed him back and he almost got her off the topic, but after several long kisses, she put her hand on his chest and said, "Stop it. It won't work. I am a woman on a quest."

Quino slid his free hand down her spine and cupped her behind, bringing her up close and personal. "So many quests to take here, are you sure you want that one?"

Her green eyes grew dark and her breath was short when she said, "To start with."

There would be no distracting her. Quino didn't really mind, he just didn't enjoy talking about the past. He'd always been a glass-half-full sort of guy and remembering a time when the glass had not only been empty but smashed to bits by the fates wasn't his idea of a good time.

"Christmas was never a big holiday for me," he said. He sifted his fingers through her hair. "I mean, as a kid I loved it, of course, because presents."

Savy smiled. He got the feeling she was picturing him as a boy. Oh, brother.

"But I didn't really get into it," he said. "My parents both loved it, you know, with the mistletoe and decking the halls and all." He heard the wistful note in his voice but it couldn't be helped. He'd missed his parents for ten years and he knew he would until the day he died. Savy put her arm around him and squeezed him tight.

"They were killed in a freak car crash two weeks before Christmas," he said. "One of the tires blew out right as my dad hit a patch of ice. The car spun out of control and slammed into a tree head-on. My sister, Desi, was with them. They had all just gotten the Christmas tree."

He paused. His voice was softer and even lower when he spoke. The words were still hard for him even after all these years. "I remember getting the call in Texas that there'd been an accident. I caught the next flight out of Austin, but I was too late. Both of my parents were dead on arrival at the hospital, and Desi was clinging to life."

"Oh, Quino," Savy said. Her voice was tender. It felt like a balm on his jagged memories.

"I spent the next two weeks by her bed," he said. "I talked, I sang, I threatened, I cajoled. I did everything I could to try and get my baby sister to come back to me. She was in a coma. The doctors weren't optimistic. They said even if she did come back, she'd likely be brain-damaged. With every day that passed her odds of getting better, of recovery, became exponentially worse."

He paused. He could still feel the desperation he'd felt. He would have done anything to bring Desi back.

"I spent Christmas Eve in the hospital chapel. I lit candles, I prayed to my parents, I made deals with God, I cried. It was a rough evening.

"On my way back from the chapel, I stopped by the hospital gift shop. I bought a Santa hat and a gift for Desi. Obviously, I hadn't prepped for the holiday up to this point, but I was determined that if it was going to be her last Christmas, she was going to get a visit from Santa and a present.

"There wasn't a great selection, so I settled on a stuffed bear, holding a heart. I brought it up to her room, and I sat on the side of her bed and I sang, 'Santa Claus Is Coming to Town.' I'm sure the hospital staff thought I was cracked. I didn't care. I told Desi that she had to wake up, that it was Christmas, and that there was a present for her but only if she woke up. I then told her that we were going to have the biggest, brightest, best Christmases ever but only if she came back to me.

"She didn't wake up," he said. "I fell asleep in the chair beside her bed." He glanced down at Savy and saw a tear slide down her cheek. He wiped it away with his thumb. "And then a miracle happened. On Christmas morning, Desi woke up and asked why I was holding a bear and wearing a Santa hat."

He grinned and Savy chuckled. Then he said softly, "Desi coming back to me was the greatest Christmas gift ever, and I promised from that day forward, I would always celebrate Christmas with my whole heart, and so I do."

More tears slipped down Savy's cheeks, and she pulled him close and kissed him until his ears rang. It was the most natural thing in the world to make love to her again. And this time it was slow and sweet, wicked and wanton, and he knew, just like the Christmas miracle that had brought Desi back to him, he needed to find the miracle that would make the woman he loved stay.

I T was late by the time hunger forced them down to the kitchen. Thankfully, tamales really were the fastest reheat food in the world. Wrapped in a corn husk, the masa harina was stuffed with spicy shredded pork, giving the tamales a little bit of heat that was welcome on this cold December night. They sat at the counter, side by side, with Quino's bare feet hooked into the rungs of her stool, as if he didn't want her to get away.

Savy glanced at the man beside her. She was glad she understood his obsession with Christmas now. It made her overlook the hideous sweater he had on. In fact, she even wanted to celebrate with him. How awful to have lost his parents just weeks before the holiday and then to wonder if he was going to lose his sister, too. It had clearly marked him.

Since she had no reason to leave Fairdale for the holiday, she wondered if she should stay and celebrate with her boyfriend. *Whoosh!* Even the word *boyfriend* made the blood rush to her head and she felt a bit dizzy. This was going to take some getting used to.

"Are you all right, Red?" he asked. He looked at her in concern. "Tamales too spicy?"

"No, they're perfect," she said. In a gush of girliness she didn't recognize in herself, she said, "You're perfect."

His grin was a slow slide into a sensual invitation that made Savy break out in a light sweat. He leaned close and kissed the sweet spot right below her ear. "Tell me more."

When he leaned back expectantly, her breathing was erratic and so was her heartbeat. For the first time, she wondered if this man might be more than she could handle.

"Well, you're very nice," she said. He made a face like she'd said something bad. She fought her laugh and continued. "You're kind and considerate, and you have excellent manners."

He made a retching noise.

"Let's see, what else." She tapped her chin with her finger. "You're good with animals, kids, and ladies of a certain age. You're loyal and trustworthy—"

"Okay, stop," he said. "Before my manliness shrinks in on itself and starts to weep and wail."

"Huh?" she asked, feigning confusion. "Aren't those all the qualities of a perfect man?"

"I suppose." He sounded disgruntled.

"Would you have preferred a different description?"

"Yes," he said. He looked at her with a wicked glint in his eye. "I would have preferred you focus on my sexual prowess, you know, my ability to make you moan and cry out my name, repeatedly, and orgasm so hard you almost black out."

Savy felt her temperature rise and it wasn't the tamales. Oh, this boy knew how to play. She took a long, slow sip of her beer. Then she turned to him with an innocent look.

"Well, duh, but that doesn't fall under the *perfect* category," she said.

"It doesn't?" he looked confused.

"No, that's the *How did I get so lucky that this guy is my boyfriend?* category," she said.

One second she was in her seat and the next she was lifted up into his arms and being carried toward the stairs. She laughed as she clung to his shoulders and wrapped her legs around his waist. The desire between them was so raw that the only salve was to make love until the ache diminished. She wondered if that would ever be possible or would she always long for this man as she did right now? The thought was too frightening to contemplate so she shoved it aside.

Halfway up the stairs, a chime sounded and it took her a moment to recognize the ringtone from her phone. She thought about ignoring it, but the publicist in her couldn't do it. She pulled the phone from the back pocket of her jeans and glanced at the display while she held on to him with one arm. She gasped.

"What is it?" he asked. He stopped halfway up the stairs, looking at her face as if he expected catastrophic news.

"It's Genevieve," she said.

Quino plopped her on her feet and said, "Answer it. At least, one way or another, you'll know for sure."

Savy nodded quickly and swiped her thumb across the phone. "Hello?"

"Savannah, it's Genevieve. I hope I'm not catching you at a bad time."

Savy glanced at Quino. He raised his eyebrows as if in question and she knew he'd heard Genevieve. She smiled. No, it hadn't been a bad time—quite the opposite.

"No, not at all," she said. "Nothing happening here."

Quino looked outraged. Then he pinched her bottom and she swatted his hand away, turning her yelp into a cough. He chuckled.

"Yes, well, I have some news," Genevieve said.

Savy froze. She looked at Quino and knew her nerves were on full display when he abruptly sobered and looked intently at her phone.

"Oh, okay," Savy said. She decided to go for optimism. "What's the good word?"

"After much consideration and discussion, Destiny has decided to do a book signing at the Happily Ever After Bookstore on the Saturday before Christmas," she said. "Congratulations."

Chapter Nineteen

"YES!" Savy pumped her fist. Quino let out a whoop of triumph, grinned, and held up his hand. Savy hit him with a hard high five.

"Oh, man, this is so great!" Savy said. "It's going to be fantastic—epic even! She won't regret it. You won't regret it. I promise."

"We can discuss the details—there are many—tomorrow," Genevieve said. "For now, go celebrate. Oh, and if that's Quino I hear whooping in the background, tell him I said hi."

"I will, and thank you, Genevieve, thank you so much," she said.

"There's no need," Genevieve said. "Destiny ultimately chose to do the signing because she trusts you and Quino. Don't let her down."

"We won't. I swear."

Genevieve ended the call and Savy jumped into Quino's arms, kissing his face wherever her lips could reach. "We did it! We did it! Destiny is coming to Happily Ever After!"

He laughed and hugged her tight, planting one sweetly extended kiss on her lips.

"Now, Ms. Wilson, what's the next step?" he asked.

She blinked at him. Destiny was coming to the bookstore on the Saturday before Christmas, which—she did a quick glance at the calendar on her phone—fell on a Friday this year. Oh, man, she only had two weeks to promote the signing of the decade.

She had to get going. She had calls to make and press releases to issue. But first, she had to tell Maisy. She opened her phone. She was about to call but then she stopped. No, this was too big.

"I have to go see Maisy," she said. "I have to tell her the news in person."

"Of course you do," he said. He grabbed her hand and pulled her down the stairs. "Come on, I'll drive you over."

"Are you sure?" she asked. She hiked her thumb toward the stairs. "You're not disappointed about . . . ?"

He gave her a look so hot she half expected flames to appear on her clothes. "There's always later."

She grinned. Yes, there was, because he was her boyfriend. Man, a gal could get used to this.

They pulled on jackets, boots, scarves, and mittens and headed out into the cold, clear night. Quino's house was lit up with decorations and Savy felt like it was a celebration just for her and the miracle she had just achieved. She realized she could really get into this Christmas thing after all.

THE drive over to Maisy and Ryder's was short. Savy threw out ideas for the signing, and Quino nodded. He loved how her mind worked. She was on fire with ideas for promotion. Every few seconds she made notes on her phone to call this person, that person, or the other person. He couldn't even keep up. When he pulled up in front of Ryder and Maisy's house, she jumped out of the truck before he'd even come to a full stop. Lord-a-mercy, the woman was a force of nature. Then he remembered their evening together and realized she was in more ways than one.

She knocked on the door and Ryder answered. His hair was mussed, his flannel shirt was hanging off one shoulder, and Quino was pretty sure their timing could not have been worse. He grinned, happy to know he wasn't the only man suffering. Because he knew once Savy unloaded her news on Maisy, the two women were going to spend the rest of the evening plotting and planning.

"Um . . . hello," Ryder said. He shoved a hand through his hair as Savy pushed past him into the house.

"Hi," she said. "Where's Maisy?" She continued into the house until she was next to the staircase, then she bellowed, "Maisy!"

Ryder looked at Quino. "Most people call before they pop in at ten o'clock at night."

"Sorry, but it's like trying to contain a tsunami in a fishbowl."

"I'm coming!" Maisy called from somewhere upstairs.

"Is something wrong?" Ryder asked Quino. "Do I need to grab a box of tissue or something?"

"No, something is definitely right."

"Oh, cool. Beer?"

"Always."

Ryder led the way to the kitchen. The open floor plan of the house allowed the men to see what was happening. When Maisy appeared at the top of the stairs, looking just as disheveled as Ryder, Savy started to bounce on her feet.

Ryder handed Quino a beer. He twisted off the top and watched the woman he loved lose her mind.

"You are never ever ever ever going to guess what I'm about to tell you!" Savy said. She was jumping and clapping now.

"You and Quino are a couple," Maisy said.

Savy stopped jumping. She blinked. "How did you know?"

"You are?!" Maisy asked. "I mean, I hoped, but you've been so adamant you weren't going to get involved. This is wonderful!"

She stepped off the stairs and hugged her friend tight. Savy hugged her back, and Quino felt Ryder watching him. He turned to look at his friend.

"What?" he asked.

"You two?" Ryder asked. "For real?"

Quino grinned. "I told you she was the one."

Ryder took a sip of his beer and held his fist up. Quino bumped knuckles with him and it occurred to him that he was now in the club of guys with a serious girlfriend. He liked it. He wanted to stay. He tried not to dwell on the fact that Destiny's signing might change all of that.

"Thank you," Savy said. "But that's not my news."

"It isn't?" Maisy asked. She came into the kitchen and leaned against Ryder as if she couldn't stand to be apart from him. Much to Quino's delight, Savy did the same to him. It made something inside his chest bloom; he thought it might be hope.

Savy clasped his free hand in hers and asked her friend, "Are you ready for this?"

"Yes, what is it that has you so crazy?"

Savy drew in a deep breath and said, "Destiny Swann is coming to the Happily Ever After Bookstore to do a signing on the Saturday before Christmas." Then she let out a tiny yelp of joy and clapped a hand over her mouth.

Maisy's eyes went huge. Her mouth dropped open. She stared at Savy. She looked at Ryder. She looked back at Savy. Then she asked, "Are you pranking me?"

"No!" Savy said. "Why would you think that?"

"To get even for the time I told you that the guy at the bar who asked for your phone number was actually Adam Levine from Maroon 5," Maisy said. Savy cringed. Maisy looked at Ryder and Quino and explained, "I didn't think she'd really believe me."

"Oh, my God, I was so excited I almost passed out. I forgot about that," Savy said. "I still owe you payback on that one."

Quino made a bad face. "He's a bit pointy-faced, isn't he?"

"Like a ferret," Ryder added.

The men clinked beers and Savy waved her hand in the air. "Not the point! Maisy, I swear, this is not a drill. Destiny Swann, after being in seclusion for a decade, is coming to the Happily Ever After Bookstore! Your bookstore! To do a signing!" At this point, she let go of Quino's hand and began to jump up and down.

Maisy stared at her, blinked twice, and then her eyes rolled back into her head and she went limp.

"Whoa!" Ryder cried out. He caught Maisy in one arm as he let go of his beer, which Quino caught, and used the other to scoop up her limp form before she hit the floor. "Maisy!"

"Oh, crap!" Savy spun away to the sink. She grabbed a cloth and soaked it in cold water. She wrung it out and followed Ryder to the couch in the adjacent living room, where he gently set Maisy down. Savy dabbed the cloth on Maisy's forehead while Ryder squeezed her hands.

Quino leaned over the back of the couch. He studied Maisy's face and said, "She'll be all right. Look, her color is already coming back. I imagine it was just a bit of a shock."

Sure enough, Maisy blinked and stared up at Savy. She had tears in her eyes and her lower lip quivered when she said, "Savy, thank you. This means everything to me. You have no idea."

"Well, I had a little bit of help from a certain cover model I know," Savy said.

She leaned against Quino and grinned up at him, and he felt as if they'd made a Christmas miracle together. The feeling was everything. Then she kissed him right in front of their best friends, giving him hope that he might just be able to corral this girl into staying in his life somehow.

Maisy sat up. Her eyes were wide. Her cheeks flushed. "We have to plan. There's so much to do."

"I know," Savy agreed. "We have a million details to nail down."

"Are you sure you're up to it?" Ryder asked. He looked at his fiancée in concern.

"Yes, it was just the shock. I mean, Destiny Swann— this is incredible. She's been a recluse for over ten years!" Maisy said. "You can't buy publicity like this."

"Come on, let's sketch out a few ideas," Savy said. She led the way to the front parlor, which Ryder and Maisy had made into a home office.

"Wait!" Maisy dashed into the kitchen and grabbed a chilled bottle of Riesling and two glasses. "Let's celebrate while we work."

"Good idea," Savy said. "I always think better with a beverage."

The two women disappeared and Ryder gestured for Quino to have a seat on the big couch Maisy had just vacated while he clicked on the TV so they could watch a basketball game. He kept the volume on low and retrieved their beers from the kitchen. He handed Quino his and joined him on the couch.

"Destiny Swann is that big of a deal?" Ryder asked.

"Apparently." Quino shrugged. He'd known Destiny as a friend for so long it was hard to wrap his head around her being the key to the bookstore's success. "Not only will the signing help the bookstore, but it will help Destiny, too. She's been out of the public eye for a long time."

"Seems like it's all fated, doesn't it?" Ryder asked.

"Maybe," Quino said. He didn't want to jinx it.

"Well, I can't thank you enough," Ryder said. "The bookstore means everything to Maisy and if she's this excited then I know this is a huge deal. So, thanks."

"Don't mention it," Quino said. "I did have some ulterior motives in play."

Ryder followed his gaze through the doorway to where the two women sat. He grinned.

"Understood," Ryder said. They watched the game in silence for a bit but during the commercial, Ryder asked, "So, what's the word from Desi? Perry's been following her posts from Kenya. She's put up some amazing stuff. I'm so proud of her. Will she be home for Christmas?"

"I don't know," Quino said. "She's so busy, our talks have been short, and with the time change, it's been hard for us to catch each other. Lots of phone tag."

Ryder studied his friend's face. "You're not happy about her internship, are you?"

"Happy?" Quino asked. "Hell no. I can't believe she was so sneaky and underhanded and slipped out of the country without even discussing it. She could get crushed in a stampede, shot by a poacher—hell, have you seen some of those baby elephants? They could flatten her if they wanted to."

Ryder looked him over. "Yeah, I can't imagine why she didn't tell you she was leaving."

Quino shot him a hot glare. "It's dangerous. And you know Desi, she has no sense when it comes to people. She could be taken advantage of so easily. How am I supposed to protect her from here?"

"Quino, I know how much you love Desi, I do, but you can't deny her dreams. If working in an elephant orphanage is how she wants to spend her life, you can't keep her from that," Ryder said.

"We'll see. She's only been over there for a few weeks. By now, she's got to be getting homesick. When she returns, I'm sure she'll reconsider leaving Fairdale. I've already got my passport and visa and I'm going in for my shots. If I get even a hint that things are not going well, I'm going to get her."

Ryder studied him. "What did Reyva say?"

"Phff," Quino huffed out a breath. "She was impressed with Desi's ability to manage all of this. She got all of her paperwork—she even managed to get a grant to pay for whatever the internship didn't cover."

"That *is* impressive," Ryder said. Quino frowned. "It is! You can't deny that it was very resourceful of her to navigate this all by herself."

"But she didn't," Quino said. "Someone helped her. Reyva swears it wasn't her but someone had to have helped her to apply for that grant."

"You don't think she could have done it on her own?"

"She could have, but I doubt she would have been successful without someone's guidance," Quino said. "She has trouble with writing. The letters get jumbled and she sometimes uses the wrong words in certain places. No, I know someone must have helped her, but who? Who would send a girl halfway around the world from everyone and everything she's ever known?"

"Someone who believed the young woman could do it,"

Ryder said. "Quino, have you considered the possibility that it was time for Desi to go?"

Quino looked at his friend as if he'd suggested Desi become a tightrope walker for the circus. "No."

"Listen, I think you can stand down. Desi can handle this."

Quino ignored him. He didn't want to hear what his friend had to say about Desi. He didn't understand. How could he? He and his brother, Sawyer, weren't close like Desi and Quino. Quino had raised her since their parents had died and he had promised he would take care of her. How could he do that when she was on another continent? No, she needed to come home, and the sooner the better.

"Okay, then," Ryder said. He had clearly caught on that the subject of Desi was closed. "How about you and Savy?"

"What about us?" Quino asked. He took a long swig of his beer.

"Savy said you're a couple. I have to hand it to you, I didn't really think you'd be able to pull it off."

"Well, I've only gotten her to agree to the girlfriend-boyfriend thing, but I still have time before Christmas to put a lock on it," Quino said.

Ryder laughed and shook his head. "Your optimism is astounding."

Quino lifted his beer. "I know. I just have to believe that she'll realize that what we have doesn't come along every day. You know what I mean."

Ryder glanced at the door that led to the office, and Quino followed his glance. The two women were sitting side by side with a laptop open between them. There was a low murmur coming from the room and every now and then there was a laugh or a clap. They were in their element. The sight of them made him smile and he noted Ryder had the same goofy look on his face.

"Yeah, I know what you mean," Ryder said. "I think I was half-dead before I met Maisy."

Quino nodded. He'd felt exactly the same. The only trouble was with Destiny coming to the bookstore, it was likely that Red would ride this success back to New York, leaving him here in Fairdale, a heartbroken lump of a man. He refused to accept that. No, he had time. He just had to romance the woman silly, until she couldn't imagine her life without him.

"Uh-oh," Ryder said. He was watching Quino's face. "You're formulating a plan, aren't you?"

"Yup."

"Care to share?"

"Nope."

"Should I be concerned?"

"Not yet."

"Why am I not reassured?" Ryder asked. "Your plan doesn't involve anything illegal, does it?"

"What?" Quino was offended. "No. I am merely going to play to my strengths."

"Movie star good looks and a buttload of charisma?" Ryder asked. "No offense, but those qualities didn't seem to get you too far with her over the past few months."

"Don't I know it," Quino said. "Red is one tough cookie but I can offer her something she's never had before."

"Are we entering TMI territory? Because I really am not into hearing about your sex life."

Quino rolled his eyes. "No. Red is completely *meh* about Christmas, but I think it's just because her family is lousy at it. I, however, am not. So, I'm going to use the holiday spirit to woo that woman until she can't live without me."

Ryder looked at him with an expression that appeared impressed. "I think you might have a worthy plan there."

"Here's hoping." Quino held up his beer and they clinked bottles. As far as he was concerned, failure was not an option.

Chapter Twenty

SAVANNAH woke up with a weight across her middle and warmth along her back. The December nights had gotten cold, the temperatures dropping below freezing, and the top floor of the old house turned bookstore was the draftiest part. She snuggled into the heat at her back and then stilled when a soft snore sounded in her ear. A slow smile spread across her lips.

Joaquin. He had one arm draped over her, locking her in against his chest as his body curved around hers. It was a delicious feeling to be entwined with him.

After they had left Maisy and Ryder's last night, it had been late and they'd come back to her place. She'd made them hot cocoa while Quino assessed her zero-decoration apartment and found it wanting. Savy pointed out that his house had enough decorations for ten homes, so he wasn't one to judge. He argued that was precisely why he could judge. Then he had carted her off to her bedroom, where they had made love until late in the night. She wondered if she'd ever get enough of this man. She couldn't imagine it.

Savy knew she should be exhausted but instead she felt

fabulously energized. There was so much to do before Destiny's signing. She couldn't wait to get started even if it was the darker side of dawn. Coffee. She'd make coffee while her man slumbered. Her man.

A smile tipped her lips as she glanced over her shoulder at her gentle giant. With his dark hair falling over his forehead, and his chiseled features slack with sleep, he looked more beautiful than any man should and, yet, he had a rough-hewn sensuality about him that gave him a certain knuckle-dragger appeal that she couldn't resist. She wanted to kiss him awake, but he looked so utterly exhausted, so completely deep in his dreams, that she didn't.

Instead, she decided to go work on her to-do list while the coffee brewed. She'd just work for a little while and then sneak back in before he noticed she was gone. She slipped out from under his arm. He didn't move. He really was done in. The cold air made her shiver and she missed his warmth immediately. She snatched up her pajamas and her robe and quietly slipped them on. Then she crept to the bedroom door and let herself out.

She stopped in the doorway. Her jaw dropped. Her living room was positively aglow. In the corner was an enormous white Christmas tree with white lights, and it was covered in glittering pink and aqua ornaments all in an atomic '50s style, mid-century modern, that she loved. Garlands of wide ribbons in aqua and pink looped the tree and sitting on the very top was a silver retro star with enormous pearls on its ends. It was the most beautiful Christmas tree Savy had ever seen. She put her hand over her mouth. How? When?

She glanced back over her shoulder at the man who was still dead asleep. He must have left her last night, gone out, gotten all of this, and put it up while she slept. She stepped further into the main room and glanced around the rest of the apartment. She noted the pink and aqua garlands hanging over the window frames and the single white lights in the shape of candles perched on every sill. And there, hanging on the mantel of the small fireplace, beneath more candle lights and garlands, were two stockings. They were hand-knit and didn't have names but one was pink and one was aqua and she knew they were meant for him and her.

She'd never had a Christmas stocking. She crossed the room and gently ran her fingers over the pink one. It was soft to the touch and she wondered what it would be like to wake up on Christmas morning with this man in this place. Her heart felt the pull, the longing, to have this and to have him. This wonderful, generous, loving man.

She glanced back at the bedroom and saw him, standing there, framed in the doorway, watching her. He looked at her from beneath his lashes as if afraid of what her response might be. She didn't have the heart to tease him, not when she could barely breathe because her throat was so tight with emotion.

"Oh, Quino," she said. And then to her complete mortification, she burst into tears.

"Oh, hey," he whispered. "It's all right, Red. If you really hate it, I can take it all down. Heck, I'll just open a window and throw it all out on the lawn." He crossed the room and pulled her into his arms. "Seriously, don't cry."

"I can't . . . it's just . . . no one has ever . . ." She buried her face in his T-shirt and sobbed. "In all the time I've been on my own, I've never had a tree and it's b . . . beau . . . beautiful."

She felt his shoulders relax. Had he really been worried that she wouldn't like it? It was . . . how could she put it? Extraordinary? Amazing? Magical? This man, her boyfriend, truly was a keeper, just like the title of the book Destiny had given her on which he'd been the model. He was a keeper, a Christmas keeper, and she was so in love with him it made her breathless. The realization hit her right between the eyes. She was in love with Joaquin Solis. Oh, no, this was bad. So bad.

She stepped away and wiped off her face with the backs of her hands. Then she blinked at him, trying to pretend that everything was okay. It wasn't and it probably never would be again. He cupped her face in his hands and stared into her eyes.

"What is it, Red? You look like you're freaking out on me," he said.

"No, it's just." She paused. She could tell him the truth without telling him the truth. He deserved that. "This is the nicest thing that anyone has ever done for me, and I am overcome."

His grin was brighter than the tree. "Yeah?"

"Yeah," she said. She turned and glanced back at her living room, which looked so festive and she felt the stirring of something. Could it be? She looked at him in mock alarm. "I have this sudden urge to bake cookies. What is wrong with me?"

He laughed and hugged her tight. "Red, I'm afraid you're coming down with something very serious."

She hugged him back and then looked at his face to see if he'd figured it out. That the feelings consuming her were her love and affection for him. "And what would that be?"

"Well, let's check your symptoms to be sure," he said. "Do you feel like doing nice things for people just because?"

She nodded.

"Buying presents just to see people happy?"

"Yup."

"Singing Christmas carols?"

"Fa la la la."

"Watching Christmas movies while snuggled with your sweetie by the fire?"

"Definitely."

He put his hand on her forehead and made a *tsk*ing sound. "Darlin', I'm afraid you have an advanced case of Christmas spirit."

She laughed. Relieved that he hadn't discovered her Christmas spirit was really the realization that she was ass over teakettle in love with him, but also a little disappointed that he didn't know it was him, just him, that made her feel this way.

"What should I do?" she asked.

"There's no known cure," he said. "I think you're just going to have to go all in with full immersion and hope you come out the other side. Maybe we could watch *A Christ-*

mas Carol, the good one with Alastair Sim, tonight while we bake cookies and sing carols and make love beside the Christmas tree."

Her pupils dilated at that last suggestion and she was a bit dizzy when she answered, "Sounds like a date."

He kissed her then. It was a slow, lingering kiss that led them back to the bedroom, where all thoughts of making a to-do list fled from her mind as she wrapped herself around her man and loved on him until the sun came up.

THE days leading up to Destiny's signing passed in a blur of activity. On top of their original holiday events they now had this massive feature. Using every available room, the bookstore had a capacity of two hundred. The only fair way to accommodate guests was to sell tickets. The price of the ticket included listening to Destiny talk, a copy of her latest book, and a spot in line for her signing.

Savy sent the press releases out a week before the event. She was nervous that they didn't have enough lead time to promote the day properly, but what could she do? Hope for the best. That was it.

Her phone began to ring shortly after the releases went out.

"Savannah Wilson, Happily Ever After Bookstore. Can I help you?" she answered.

"Hi, this is Simone Chester from Channel Twelve in Raleigh. Is this press release you sent . . . um . . . accurate?"

"Channel Twelve, did you say?" Savy grinned. She saw Maisy's eyes go wide from her seat at her desk across from Savy's.

"Yes," Simone answered. "Is Destiny Swann really coming out of seclusion to sign at your store?"

"Why, yes, she is," Savy said. "We're very excited to host her first appearance in over ten years."

"I'll bet you are," Simone said. "Any chance we could get an interview with the owner of the bookstore?"

"Let me see," Savy said. "Ms. Kelly's schedule is pretty packed with requests, but, oh, wait, I have an opening tomorrow. Say, ten o'clock?"

"We'll be there with a news van," Simone said. "Of course, we'll want to film Ms. Swann's arrival for her signing, too."

"And we'll be happy to discuss that with you tomorrow," Savy said.

"Thank you, Ms. Wilson."

"My pleasure," Savy said. She ended the call. She glanced at Maisy. "Channel Twelve interview tomorrow morning. Ten o'clock."

"Oh, my God," Maisy said. She looked panicked.

"Don't." Savannah shook her head. "This is exactly what you need to get this bookstore on solid ground. We'll go through your closet tonight and find the perfect outfit. You've got this. Do not panic."

"I'm not panicking," Maisy said. Her voice was high and tight and she bit the side of her thumb. "Why do you think I'm panicking?"

The door to the office burst open. It was Jeri. Her eyes were huge and her long black braids flew about her head, making a sweet jingling sound as she'd weaved some bells in for the holidays.

"What is it?" Maisy asked.

"We sold out," Jeri said. She looked at them in disbelief. "In a half hour. We are out of tickets for Destiny Swann."

"All two hundred?" Maisy asked. Jeri nodded. "Holy wow!"

"We need to open up the front lawn," Savy said. "We won't sell tickets, but we can rig up a large screen out there so people can watch Destiny, and if they want to get in line for the signing we'll let them. I need to call Genevieve and see how many books Destiny is willing to sign in total." She glanced at the two women both staring at her in awe. "I don't want to alarm you, but this event is conceivably even bigger than we imagined."

"Oh. My. God." Maisy said.

QUINO was barely awake when his phone chimed. It was Desi's designated ringtone and he sat bolt upright and grabbed his phone. It was still dark. He glanced at the display. In fact, it was the middle of the night.

"Desi, are you all right? Is everything okay? Where are you?" he asked.

"I'm fine!" Desi yelled into the phone. "Quino, I did it!"

"Did what?"

"I rescued an orphan out in the wild," she said. "It was amazing!"

Quino ran a hand over his face. His heart was racing and his vision was fuzzy. He thought he might be having a heart attack.

"I'm sorry to call so late, but I didn't want you to freak out when you saw the video," she said.

"What video?" he asked. His throat was dry and he coughed.

"The one I posted on my Instagram," she said. "It looks much more frightening than it actually was. The poachers shot at us, but I think they were just trying to scare us."

"Poachers?" he asked. "Shot at you?!"

"Yeah, there was some rich guy from the States who paid the poachers to bring him onto the preserve so he could bag an elephant," Desi said. Her voice was filled with disgust. "Honestly, what's wrong with these people?"

Quino felt his chest get tight. "Desi, I want you on the first plane out of there. It's too dangerous. You could have been killed."

His voice sounded strangled and he knew he was entering a state of full-on panic.

"See, this is why I called," she said. "I was in the truck the whole time. I didn't get out until the poachers had been run off. Quino, they were going to kill the mama elephant for her tusks but we got there in time. She has superficial wounds but we'll be able to treat her and her calf is safe. I know this is hard for you, but this is what I was born to do. You have to believe in me."

Quino couldn't hear her. Her words had stopped for him the second he heard she'd been shot at.

"No, Desi, enough. This is too dangerous. I've been trying to be patient but you're asking too much of me to know you're in danger and do nothing about it. I'm coming to Kenya to collect you."

"You'll be wasting your time," Desi said. "Because I'm not leaving."

"How did you even get there?" he asked. His teeth were gritted with frustration and the words were coming out in more of a growl.

"I told you," she said. "I found a person to help me write a grant for my living and travel expenses."

"How? How did you find them?"

"The wish box. I put a wish in the wish box at the Happily Ever After Bookstore and then a few days later, someone had left a packet of information and a rough outline for a grant."

"When did you do this?"

"Over the summer. Why does it matter?"

"It matters." A fury filled Quino. Someone who clearly didn't know Desi or her struggles had meddled in her life, facilitated this crazy idea, and in doing so put her in grave danger. He wanted to know who, and he wanted to shut them down. He needed to ask Maisy about this damn wish box pronto.

"Quino, why can't you just believe in me?" Desi asked. "Why can't you support my dream?"

"I do," he said. Even as the words left his mouth, he knew it was a lie. He would support her dream if it happened here in Fairdale where he could swoop in and rescue her as needed. He did not support her dream to be half a world away, taking crazy risks. She was asking too much of him.

"Then let me go," she said. "Let me be what I have to be."

"I can't."

"You have to. Don't ask me to be less than who I am. I'll call you soon."

"No, don't hang up. We need to talk about your coming home."

"I'm not coming home," she said decisively. "I love you."

She ended the call and Quino felt bereft and frustrated and bewildered. He glanced at the empty bed beside him and wished that Red was here. She would understand. She would back him up on this. But she wasn't here. She and

Maisy had pulled a late night last night plotting every moment of Destiny's signing, and he had promised to help. Damn it!

If he left now for Africa, he'd be abandoning Destiny, who'd said she'd do this only with him as her escort and bodyguard, and Savy. He did not want to let Savy down. She was so certain this publicity coup was going to relaunch her career and she wanted that so desperately.

The irony that the very thing he was helping Savy achieve was the same thing that was going to expedite her departure was not lost on him. At the moment, he was hoping that the success she was enjoying, the triumph of bringing Destiny out of seclusion, would make her reconsider her plan and stay in Fairdale. He knew it had a snowball's chance in Florida of working out that way but still he hoped.

Realizing he wasn't going back to sleep, he opened up the app on his phone that let him look at Desi's social media. He watched in horror as a large mama elephant was on her side on the ground, her baby bleating in a panic beside her. A large cargo truck pulled up in between the poachers and the elephant. The footage was being shot from a smaller vehicle, following the truck. Several gunshots were heard and then the person shooting the footage—Desi, presumably—was jumping to the ground and running toward the injured elephant. It looked like a war zone. Quino thought he might throw up.

The next segment in Desi's feed showed the mama and the baby elephant being tended to. Even though he already knew the outcome thanks to Desi's call, he was weak with relief to see both the animals and his sister, as she flipped her phone around and smiled and waved for the camera, were safe. She could have been killed. A stray bullet, a charging elephant, the vehicle tipping over as they raced through the bush. He knew he should be proud of her commitment and courage, and he was, but his fear was pushing all of those feelings aside and all he could feel was panic, the helplessness of which made him furious.

He replayed the videos. The sound of gunfire and the

idea that his sister was out there in the thick of it made him woozy. He made coffee, showered, and roamed around his house. He thought about heading down to the stable but it was too early even for that. He wondered who had found Desi's request in the wish box and helped her write her grant. It was like a niggling worm in his brain. He couldn't let it go.

The what-ifs of Desi's situation kept replaying in his head. What if she got hurt? Who would take care of her? How could he get to her? And the worst of them all—what if she got killed? His blood ran cold. He couldn't even think it.

He pushed the thought away. When he glanced out the window he saw the sun was just beginning to lighten the sky. He'd take Daisy out for an early-morning ride. He'd neglected her lately with the holidays and with his preoccupation with Red, and he and Daisy could both use this time together.

He shrugged on his coat, hat, and gloves, and left the house. His boots crunched in the new-fallen snow. He took a second to marvel at the beauty of the night's pristine snowfall. Everything was blanketed in a bright brilliant white and it was quiet, so quiet. Not even the birds were up yet. He found himself walking slowly toward the barn, more quietly than usual as if he was trying to not to wake the wildlife. Desi would have laughed at him. The thought made his heart hurt.

When he arrived at the barn, it was to find the horses were distressed. He could hear nervous pacing and whinnying. For a second he wondered if a bear had gotten into the barn. He snapped on the overhead lights and heard a loud thump sound from the back of the barn. He knew that noise. He'd heard it before. A horse had collapsed.

He ran. The horses heard him coming and most poked their heads out of their stalls. He scanned, wondering which of his herd had gone down. He saw Daisy poking her head out of her stall and he calmed down but then he passed Esther's stall. His cranky old girl wasn't looking for him to give her a carrot or an apple slice.

"No, no, no," he hissed the words. He fumbled with the latch until the door swung wide. There she was, collapsed on the ground. Her head poked up to look at him, she blinked as if recognizing his face. He would have sworn she gave him her usual stink eye, and then her lips pulled back in a smile.

Quino dropped to his knees beside her head and put his hand on her cheek. "Come on, Esther, old gal. Don't you die on me. Whatever's wrong we'll fix it. You'll be okay. Come on, girl, I need you."

She let out a soft whicker, her lips nuzzling his coat sleeve as if looking for one last treat or gently trying to say good-bye.

"Oh, Esther, no, don't go," he said through the lump in his throat.

An enormous shudder rippled through her body and her eyes rolled back into her head. With one last rattling breath, Esther was gone.

Chapter Twenty-One

QUINO didn't know how long he sat there. He'd been around horses all his life, and he knew a cardiac arrest when he saw one. After a while, he called Hannah to come out and check Esther over one last time. She didn't answer so he pressed the option to leave an urgent message and then, as simply as he could, told her what had happened. There were decisions to be made, but he knew he was going to have the old girl cremated. Then he'd bury her ashes by his mother's grave. That's where Esther would want to be, beside her favorite person.

He ran his hand down her smooth gray coat. It was hard to imagine that he wouldn't see her in her pasture anymore. Esther with her sassy tail, knowing eyes, and insistent nudges. Oh, he was going to miss the old girl. His throat was tight and his eyes felt damp. He pushed the feelings down. He'd grieve later.

"Quino! You in there?"

He recognized Hannah's voice and he rolled to his feet. He stepped out of the stall and into the brighter light of the barn. He glanced up and saw Hannah jogging toward him, with her medical backpack slung over her shoulder, and on her heels was Red. She looked frantic.

"I brought someone to give you moral support," Hannah said. She patted his arm before she slid into the stall like a pro, dropping to the ground right next to Esther. She began to pull out her equipment. Savannah paused, looking at Quino. It was then that he noticed her green cat's eyes were red-rimmed.

"Is she really . . . ?" she asked. Her voice was barely above a whisper.

"Yeah," he said. He opened his arms and she stepped into them, hugging him tight as if she could squeeze the grief out of him. He pressed his cheek against her soft curls and sighed. "She had a great life here."

"The best," Savannah said fiercely. "No horse could ask for a better home, but oh, I'm going to miss her grumpy face." Then she sobbed. It loosened something in Quino's chest and he felt a few of his own tears spill out.

He wasn't a crier, not since his parents had died. Something in him had hardened that day. But as they stood, standing in the circle of each other's arms, trying to find solace in each other, he felt the tears slide down his face and he knew it was because with Red he was safe.

"I'm so sorry, Quino," Hannah said as she joined them. They broke apart and turned to face her. Her nose was running and her eyes were puffy. She gestured to her face. "Sorry. No matter how many times I lose an animal in my care, I never get used to it." She sniffed a couple of times and rubbed her eyes with her hand. "It looks like it was cardiac arrest. She went very fast."

Quino nodded and wiped his own damp face with the back of his hand. "When I came into the barn, I heard her collapse. She was gone just a few minutes after that."

Hannah nodded. Quietly, she said, "Would you like me to arrange for pickup?"

Quino nodded. "Thanks. I want her cremated."

Hannah reached out a hand and squeezed his arm. "Of course." She took her phone out and wandered away to place the call, obviously not wanting to distress them any more than she had to.

"I want to say good-bye," Savy said.

Quino nodded. She slipped into the stall and he watched as she knelt beside Esther. It almost broke him. To see the woman he loved grieve the passing of one of his favorite horses. She patted Esther's neck and whispered so softly he couldn't hear her words into the horse's still ear. Savy patted her shoulder one last time and came out of the stall, her face crumpled with grief.

She slid right into his side as if that was where she belonged and together they greeted Lanie and Luke, who arrived shortly after, breaking the bad news to them as gently as possible. Lanie cried. Luke took the news more stoically but there was a telltale sheen to his eyes as well. This wasn't just losing a horse. Esther had been family.

HANNAH had to go back to her clinic, but Savy decided to stay with Joaquin and make certain he was all right. Yes, Esther had been old and, sure, they knew she'd been on borrowed time. Still, it was a huge shock to lose her so suddenly.

Savannah forced Quino to go back to the house and eat something. She wasn't much of a chef but she could fry bacon and scramble eggs. He sat at the counter sipping coffee while she puttered around his kitchen. She had a post–crying jag headache and a heavy heart but when she looked at him, none of it mattered. All she wanted to do was ease his pain.

They pushed their eggs around their plates. Their coffee grew cold. Every time Savy glanced out the kitchen window toward the corral where Esther used to watch the comings and goings of the stables she felt the sadness rush up over her like an ocean wave.

"Does Desi know?" she asked. She knew that Desi loved the horses of Shadow Pine and she imagined she was going to take it very hard.

"No, I have to call her," he said. He glanced at the clock. "It's getting late there."

"Where?" Savy asked. "You said she was traveling but

you've never mentioned where she went. Is she visiting your mother's family in Texas?"

"I wish," he said. His features settled into a scowl. "She's on some cockamamie internship in Kenya."

"Kenya?" Savy's eyes went wide. "As in Africa, Kenya?"

"Well, there's no Kenya in Georgia," he said. He pushed his plate away and ran a hand through his hair. "Sorry, I don't mean to be snarky. I had a rough night and now Esther." He sighed. "Desi left the day after Thanksgiving, without telling me, and I've only managed a handful of calls to her since. The time change makes it impossible to catch her."

"What's she doing in Kenya?" Savy asked. Desi had been a regular at the bookshop and Savy had missed seeing her. When Quino had said she was traveling she'd assumed it was to visit relatives. But Africa? Wow.

"Risking her life and making me crazy," he said. At Savy's alarmed look, he toned it down. "Somehow she managed to get an internship and some do-gooder helped her get a grant, so she's working with the Kenya Elephant Rescue and Rehabilitation Institute."

Savy felt her stomach drop. Oh, no. Then she shook her head. No, it couldn't be. What were the odds? She refused to believe the grant she had helped with was Desi's, but how could it possibly be anyone else?

"That's fantastic," she said. Quino glowered. "Or not." She studied his face. "Why is it not?"

"Because she's out there all alone," he said. "She actually posted footage last night of being in a shoot-out with poachers. She could have been killed."

A cold sweat covered Savy's body. There was no helping it. She had to come clean, or maybe not. Maybe it was just a crazy coincidence. "I don't suppose she mentioned who helped her?" she asked. She was hoping with everything she had that it was an answer they could live with.

"No," he said. "She said something about a wish box in the bookstore. I have to talk to Maisy about that. She said someone left her all the particulars for grant writing and she used it to get the funding because she knew I would never approve of her wiping out her savings account. If I ever find out who—"

"It was me," Savannah said. The words came out in a rush. "But I didn't know it was Desi. I saw a note with an elephant on it in the wish box we keep for customers to write random wishes on and I was intrigued. When I saw it was a wish for money to go help orphaned elephants, I made a packet of materials of possible grants and a rough draft of how I would write the grant, thinking it would give them a running start. I'm sorry, Quino, I di—"

"Didn't know, yeah, I got that part," he said. He leaned back in his chair as if trying to put distance between them while, frowning, he studied her. "Do you have any idea of what you've done?"

Savannah didn't know what to say. She hated the thought of Desi being in peril because of her. She felt sick to her stomach and wanted to throw up her eggs.

Quino took his phone out of his pocket. He opened Instagram and then went to Desi's story. He handed the phone to Savy. She glanced down. There she was, just as he'd said. Desi in Africa. It was . . . incredible.

The newest post was from a few hours ago. She was sitting cross-legged on the ground when a baby elephant, called Maktao in the caption, ran at her. Savy felt her breath catch, thinking she'd be squashed, but the baby elephant slowed down, lowered its head, and bumped Desi on the shoulder. She laughed and opened her arms and the baby flopped into her lap just like a big dog. Desi was scratching the big-eared baby all over its gray body. The elephant looked delighted.

Desi's eyes were sparkling and she was laughing while she hugged the big baby, who used its trunk to snatch her hat. She tried to get it back but the elephant held it out of reach while bumping against her, demanding to be petted. The other caregivers standing nearby were laughing, too, and it hit Savy that Desi looked like she belonged. As if she'd found her place in the world and like a seed taken on the wind to a point unknown, she had started to bloom where she was planted.

"She looks happy," Savy said.

"Happy?" he asked. "She's going to get squashed flat by one of those behemoths."

Savy glanced at the phone and then back up at Quino. She turned it in his direction so he could see the post. "Is it possible to be snuggled to death?"

"I'm sure there are statistics," he snapped. He took his phone back and dropped it onto the counter. He stared at her. "You probably think this is great."

Savy wasn't sure what to say. She could tell he was upset, and given the passing of Esther and having his sister so far away, she understood why, but it didn't change the fact that Desi's life was her own, to live her way. Savy needed to stand up for her even if it meant saying things Quino didn't want to hear.

"I do think it's great," she said. "I'm proud of her and I'm pleased to have helped her."

He gaped at her. "Do you understand what you're saying? You've put her at risk. She could die over there!"

Savy frowned at him. "That facility looks perfectly safe. If they offer internships, I'm certain they are prepared to take care of the people who intern there. It won't do their rescue organization any good to have people die on their watch, will it?"

"You don't get it!" he said. He rose to his feet. "You can't just meddle in people's lives like this. If anything happens to her, I'll never forg—"

He stopped himself before he said the words, but Savy knew what he'd been about to say, and she had no doubt it was the truth.

"I didn't meddle," she said. "I answered a request for help."

"Which enabled her to do this trek into danger," he said. "Do you really think she would have pulled this off without you?"

"If she wanted to go badly enough, she would have. What if it wasn't going to Africa that she wanted?" she asked.

"What do you mean?"

"What if she had wanted to study art in Paris?"

"Pff." He made a noise that Savy interpreted to mean that idea wouldn't fly, either.

"All right, what if she wanted to learn winemaking in California?"

He made an impatient gesture with his hand. "What's your point?"

"My point is that no matter where Desi wanted to go, you wouldn't be happy about her leaving home," she said.

"Of course not," he agreed. He looked exasperated. "She can't take care of herself. She's fragile and vulnerable."

Savy shook her head. "No, she isn't." She picked up his phone. "Look at her."

"You have no say," he said. He ignored the phone. "You don't know her like I do, and if you hadn't interfered, she'd be here—"

Savy blinked at him. There it was. "You blame me."

"No . . . yes . . . no," he said. "You had no right, Red."

They stared at each other. Savy wasn't sure how they went from grieving over the loss of Esther to yelling at each other about a grant for Desi, but here they were. Quino was never going to forgive her for helping his sister. It didn't matter that she hadn't known it was Desi and that her intentions had been good. He didn't want his world to change and Savy had been the agent of change, something he clearly couldn't bear.

"I think we're done here," she said.

He didn't say a word. He just nodded, looking hurt and lost and angry. Savy wanted to turn back and hug him, but she didn't. She grabbed her hat and coat and bolted from the house. She'd catch a ride back to town with Hannah or maybe she could get Luke or Lanie to give her a lift. Either way, as she shut the door behind her, she had no doubt that whatever coupledom she and Quino had shared, it was over.

H E should have gone after her. He knew it the minute the door slammed behind her, but he didn't. Stupid pride. He just couldn't believe that after all these weeks of trying to figure out how Desi had managed to get a grant, the person responsible for helping his sister turned out to be the woman he was crazy in love with.

He didn't know what to do with all of his feelings right now. Maybe he and Savy just needed some space, a little time apart. He had to deal with Esther, which made his heart feel as if it were being squeezed by a giant fist. He needed to call Desi and tell her. And then, maybe he could talk to Savannah more calmly. He cleaned up the kitchen before he went upstairs to his bedroom.

The wall along the staircase had always been a rogues' gallery of their family. His mother had put up all of the pictures. Quino had never taken any of them down or changed them. In fact, he hadn't changed anything in the house since his parents had passed. He paused by his favorite picture of Desi, taken shortly before the accident. It was a close-up of her face and she looked so happy and carefree with her dark eyes sparkling as she grinned with deep dimples bracketing her mouth. After the accident, her eyes had stopped sparkling like that and her grin had become small.

The accident that had stolen their parents' lives had changed Desi for good. She was never the same no matter how hard he'd tried to fix her world. And now she was a world away, and if she got into trouble, he wouldn't be there to help her. The helpless feeling terrified him. No, he couldn't forgive Red for helping her with that grant. Because even though he hadn't said the words aloud, the truth was, if anything happened to Desi, not only would he not be able to forgive Savannah, he wouldn't be able to forgive himself.

Quino waited until Esther's body had been taken away before he called Desi. Much as he'd suspected, his sweet, sensitive sister fell apart at the news. She cried for a while, asked him for details, and cried some more.

"I should have been there. I should have been with her," she sobbed. "Was she scared?"

"No," Quino said. "I was with her the whole time and"—he paused to clear his throat before he could continue—"she looked at me in her particular Esther way right before she passed."

"She gave you stink eye," Desi said. The words came out as half a laugh and half a sob.

"She was the master," he said. They were both quiet. "You okay, Des?"

"Yeah," she sniffed. "I'm sorry you had to deal with it alone. I know it must be hard, given that she's mom's horse and all."

Quino was surprised by the maturity in her voice. "It's okay."

"It has to be tough, though," she said.

"Yeah," he said.

"Is Savannah there?"

"Why do you ask?"

"Because Lanie told me you two are dating," she said.

"When did you talk to Lanie?"

"I talk to her and Luke all the time, you know, to check on you," she said.

"I don't need you to check on me," he said.

She snorted.

"I don't!"

"Bro, I love you dearly, but you have a pathological fear of change and my being all the way in Africa has probably sent you into a tailspin," she said. "Which is why I was thrilled to hear about you and Savy."

"I don't have a fear of change," he insisted. It occurred to him that it sounded as if their roles were reversed, as if she were the wiser older sibling and he were the younger, more immature one. He wasn't sure what to make of that.

"Yeah, you do," she said. "You have not changed one thing in that house since Mom and Dad passed."

"That was for you," he said. He refused to acknowledge that he'd just had the same thought when he was walking upstairs. "So you wouldn't feel their loss so much. I thought if I kept it all the same, you would feel as if they were still here."

"Oh, Quino, I feel them with me every day," she said. Her voice was so sincere and sweet, it almost made him weep. "They're always with me just like they're always with you. You know, I think they'd like Savy. She's good for you. She doesn't fall at your feet like the rest of the ladies do."

"Yeah, well," he said. He was not going to mention their tiff.

"Oh, no, please tell me you didn't mess it up already," she said.

"I didn't mess it up," he lied. He didn't want to get his ass chewed by Desi because while she was the sweetest person he'd ever known, she could also be very biting in her criticism if she felt he was being a dumbass, and he was pretty sure that in Desi's opinion his dustup with Red would more than qualify.

"Good," she said. "Then I don't have to worry about you. Hey, I have to go feed the babies. I'll call you tomorrow?"

"Yeah, okay," he said. He tried to be cool. He failed. "Be careful, Desi. Please."

"Always," she said. "Don't you worry about me. I've got this. Love you."

"Love you, too."

Quino ended the call. He'd paced the house while they talked and he was standing in the large living room in front of the cold fireplace. He'd put up the decorations just as his mother always had. He glanced at the photographs of their family. They were all from before. There wasn't one that had been put up after his parents had died. Desi was right. He hadn't made any changes to the house since his parents had passed. How had he not noticed this?

He thought about calling Red to tell her he was sorry, but he knew the only way to truly apologize was to look her in the eye and confess that he was wrong and then beg for forgiveness and hope she granted it.

He put on his coat and hat and drove his pickup truck to the bookstore. He spent the drive over practicing his speech. He wanted to have the right amount of grovel in it, sincerity without being pathetic. It was a fine line.

When he pulled up, he found the place overrun with reporters. No less than three news vans were parked out front. He elbowed his way into the gathered crowd to see what was happening. His heart beat hard in his chest. Had they been robbed? He scanned the crowd for Red but there was no sign of her. A nervous sweat broke out across his back and he strode into the shop.

The place was packed. People were in line buying every Destiny Swann book they could get their hands on. It was then that he remembered tomorrow was the signing. He'd agreed to escort Destiny; now he wondered if Red still wanted him to.

"Hi, Quino," Maisy greeted him with a big smile from behind the register. "She's in the office."

"Thanks." Two things hit him at once. One, Red hadn't told Maisy about their tiff or she wouldn't have beamed at him, and, two, they no longer needed to worry about the solvency of the bookstore. It was quite plain from the crowd that the Happily Ever After Bookstore was going to be just fine.

He made his way to the office and opened the door. Savannah was inside. She had her back to him and was on the phone. He settled against the door to wait, but her words. Her words hit him like stones to the chest.

"Archer, are you serious?" she asked. "They want me back? With a promotion and a raise? When?"

There was a pause.

"No, I can't come back until after the signing," she said. "That is my big moment, after all." She laughed but it faded quickly and she paused as if listening. When she spoke again, her voice sounded sad when she added, "No, in a few days is fine—there's nothing keeping me here."

Chapter Twenty-Two

SAVANNAH could have sworn she heard a noise behind her, but when she turned around no one was there. She frowned. This drafty old building made so many creaks and shudders. If Jeri was here with her, she'd insist it was the ghost of Maisy's auntie El. They'd been collectively trying to talk Jeri out of that notion for months.

She checked her phone. There was no message from Quino. No text, no phone call, no nothing. She thought about calling him but what could she say? She still believed that Desi had a right to live her own life. She also realized that Quino, being completely entrenched in the past, refusing to make any changes in their life, their house, even the way he celebrated the holiday, meant there was no room for her in his life.

Given that she was now leaving after Destiny's signing, perhaps it was for the best that they parted ways now. She refused to acknowledge how much the thought of not seeing him again, not being with him, crushed her. She'd gotten attached. Damn it. She felt as if she were Aline Marsden in Lisa Kleypas's *Again the Magic*. She knew better than to have fallen for the stable boy, but she'd done it anyway.

The fact that he'd been so furious that she'd helped Desi might be a good thing. It would make their breakup more bearable. Even as she thought this, she knew it was a lie. The past few days had been crazy busy but when Hannah called this morning and said that Quino needed her, Savy hadn't even hesitated but had run to Quino's side to help him in any way she could.

She thought of Esther and she sighed. She really was going to miss that old gal, but now the words she'd whispered to the old horse seemed like a lie. She'd promised to look after Quino for Esther. How was she going to do that all the way from New York?

Her heart hurt. New York seemed so far away, an impossible distance to keep her eye on him. While his loud Christmas sweaters made him easy to spot in Fairdale, they weren't quite loud enough to be seen from Manhattan. Ridiculously, she hated the thought of never seeing one of his hideous sweaters again. It was then that she knew for certain, she was never ever going to get over Joaquin Solis.

"Hey, everything all right?" Maisy poked her head around the door.

"Huh?" Savy turned to face her. "Yeah, I'm good. How's the horde out there?"

"Crazy!" Maisy said. "Do you mind jumping in?"

"Not at all," Savy said. She knew the best thing she could do to keep the heartache at bay was to stay busy. It's what she'd always done and when she headed home to New York, it was what she'd do again. She debated telling Maisy about her impending departure but she didn't want to dim Maisy's joy at Destiny's signing. She'd wait until after the big day.

They spent the afternoon in a state of chaotic preparation. The decorations in the shop were ramped up. Two massive tents with heaters were put out on the front lawn. Guide ropes to keep the crowds back were installed, along with a red carpet that led from the curb to the front door.

Savy had found an event planner who was happy to tap

their resources to set up a camera crew to film Destiny's talk, not only for the screens stationed throughout the bookstore and the front yard, but also as a live feed on the bookstore's social media platforms, as well as their webpage.

Because of the nature of online trolls, Savy had Perry and her crew of technology-smart teens on board to shut down, block, or mute any mean commenters who might pop up in the live feed just to harass Destiny, since she was out of seclusion for the first time in years.

They finished all the prep work by midnight that night and Savy gratefully climbed up to her apartment to get ready for bed. She checked her phone one last time by the light of the Christmas tree in her living room. She'd sent a text to Quino earlier asking if he was still able to escort Destiny. A curt *Yes* had been his only response, so they were clearly still at odds.

Once she was in her pajamas, she curled up on her couch and stared at the twinkling tree. It was the first time she'd felt this lonely since the night she'd met up with Quino in the park and gone ice-skating. It was an old familiar feeling but the familiarity didn't comfort her, rather it just made her feel the loneliness more acutely. She missed him. She missed them. She missed the infusion of Christmas spirit she'd been enjoying with him, but now she knew it for what it was.

She hadn't been feeling the Christmas spirit as much as she'd been falling in love. Well, that was over now, obvy. Quino was furious with her for helping Desi and there wasn't anything Savy could do to make it right. She was torn between groveling for his forgiveness because she hated that she'd caused him distress and being furious that he wasn't embracing how amazing a thing it was that Desi was doing. Honestly, the girl had gotten herself all the way to Africa and was coddling orphaned baby elephants. What was not to love about that?

She stared at the tree, her beautiful tree, until the lights became blurry and she fell asleep.

Bang. Bang. Bang.

A fist pounding on her door woke Savy up. She shoved

off the blanket and blinked. It was still dark but her tree glowed, showing her the way to the door.

Bang. Bang. Bang.

"I'm coming! Keep your shirt on!" she called.

She staggered, her muscles tight from the bunched-up position she'd slept in on the couch. She crossed the room, not bothering to ask who was at the door, unlocked it, and yanked it open.

Maisy was standing there with two industrial coffees. "Good morning! Are you ready for the most exciting day ever?"

Savy squinted at her. She took the coffee held out to her and took a huge swallow. Then she took a deep breath and shook herself from head to toe. "I'm getting there."

"Good," Maisy said. "Come here."

She took Savy's hand and led her to the window that overlooked the front of the property, where the tents had been set up. She pointed and Savy looked out. She didn't see anything.

"What?" she asked.

"Look at the curb," Maisy said.

Savy's jaw dropped. "No way."

"They've been camped out for hours," Maisy said.

Savy pressed her face up against the glass, trying to get a better look. The line of people went as far as she could see all the way down the street. While she sipped her coffee and watched the growing crowd, news vans began to arrive. She glanced at the clock. The signing wasn't for another five hours. This was madness and she really hoped Destiny was up to it because there was no turning back now.

QUINO was driving Destiny's classic Bentley while she and Genevieve sat in back. He glanced in the rearview mirror every now and again to see how Destiny was doing. When they had started out, she looked excited and a little nervous, but the closer they got, the paler she grew, and he caught Genevieve looking at her with concern.

When they were fifteen minutes out from the bookstore

and stopped at a red light, he called Savy to let her know. He tried not to dwell on the fact that he was eager to hear her voice. This phone call was what they'd agreed upon via text this morning, nothing more.

"Hi, Quino," she answered. "Is everything all right?"

"We're fifteen minutes out," he said. He winced at how cold he sounded. This wasn't how he wanted things to be between them, but he couldn't shake off the words he'd overheard, "there's nothing keeping me here," no matter how hard he tried.

"Great," she said. She sounded nervous. That made him pause.

"Is everything ready on your end?" he asked.

"Oh, it's ready," she said. She sounded breathless. "It's possible I might have underestimated the interest in Destiny's return, however."

"What's going on, Red?" he asked. The nickname slipped out before he could catch it.

"We anticipated a few hundred attendees," she said. "But I think we're looking more at thousands."

"What?" he asked. He glanced in the mirror to see if Destiny had heard him, but she had her eyes closed and Genevieve was leading her through a softly spoken visualization. He lowered his voice. "Are you serious?"

"I'm afraid so," Savy said. She sounded worried. "You'll help her, won't you? I'm afraid she'll be overwhelmed. Don't leave her side for a second."

"I won't," he said. "Don't worry. *I'm* not going anywhere."

He left the words hanging out there but either she didn't catch his not-so-subtle jab or she chose to ignore him. He wondered if she even planned to tell him before she left or if she'd just leave.

"Thank you, Quino." She ended the call.

He put his phone down and resumed driving just as the light turned green. He drove through town and his first inkling that Savannah hadn't been exaggerating was when he turned onto Willow Lane, only to find crowds of people going in both directions down the walkway. He glanced at

Destiny, who looked perfectly composed, and then at Genevieve, whose eyebrows were up to her hairline.

"Looks like it's going to be quite the turnout," he said. Genevieve's eyes got wider, but Destiny looked completely serene.

He pulled up to the curb, since the driveway was full of people, and parked. Stanchions had been set up, roping off the area so that Destiny could make her way to the bookstore unimpeded. Camera crews were just past the ropes and Quino felt a small flutter of nerves in his own belly. Dang, Savy was right. They had underestimated the impact of Destiny's return by a lot.

He glanced over the seat back. "Are you ready?"

Destiny nodded once. "Yes."

Quino climbed out of the driver's seat and tugged his suit into place. He hadn't planned to dress the part of professional bodyguard but knowing how Destiny liked to doll herself up, he'd figured he'd better raise his game if he was to be her escort.

He was glad he did, because Destiny had pulled out all the stops in a designer gown, a deep-red sheath that hugged her slender form and accentuated her arms with angel sleeves that reached almost to the ground. Her blond hair was styled in a soft cloud about her head and her makeup was light but accentuated her best features, her pale-blue eyes and generous lips. When she'd walked down the central staircase at Windemere, he'd stared at her in awe. She looked like a movie star.

He opened the back door of the Bentley and extended his hand to Destiny. She executed a smooth step out of the car in her silver pumps and used his hand to steady herself. An explosion of flashing bulbs went off as everyone started to scream her name. The diamonds at her throat and ears sparkled in the light, giving her celebrity polish. He had to give her credit. She didn't even blink. She tipped up her chin, gave the crowd a smile, and then lifted one gloved hand and executed the perfect royal wave. He grinned.

"Attagirl," he said so that only she could hear him. She gave him a side-eye and a small smile back.

He reached into the car and helped Genevieve out. Her hands were cold and she looked like a cat walking on tacks. She leaned close to him and said, "Thank goodness you're here. If I had to do this alone with her, I'd bolt."

Quino smiled. "Nah, look at her. She's a pro. She's got this."

They fell in behind Destiny, who walked slowly up to the bookstore, pausing every now and then to clasp the hands that were held out to her and to respond to the people who were yelling her name.

They were almost to the porch when Quino saw Red standing on the front steps beside Maisy. Savy was dressed in a deep-green velvet dress that hugged her curves and flared out at her knees. Her hair was done up in an elaborate pile of curls on her head and all he could think about was how much he wanted to undo it. When he glanced at her face, their eyes met and he discovered she was watching him with the same intensity.

He was so focused on Red that he didn't notice Destiny had stopped walking until he almost plowed into her. He stopped short just in time and looked to see what the holdup was. If someone crowded Destiny, he was ready to bodily lift them and carry them out. Fortunately, it was quite the opposite.

A woman wearing a beautifully knit aqua-colored scarf over her bald head, and with her coat zipped up to her throat to keep out the cold, was standing by the stanchion and sobbing. She had a tissue pressed to her face, trying to catch the tears that were running down her cheeks. With her other arm she cradled an armful of paperback books to her chest.

"I'm sorry, I'm sorry," she sobbed. "I didn't mean to get emotional. It's just that your books mean so much to me."

Destiny patted her arm and said, "Oh, no, that's fine. Don't apologize."

"I've been fighting stage-four breast cancer," the woman sobbed. "And the only thing that has gotten me through the chemo is your writing."

"Oh, you poor thing," Destiny said. She reached across

the rope and hugged the woman tight. The woman cried harder. Destiny didn't let go. She let the woman cry until her sobs softened into hiccups. Then she stepped back and cupped the woman's face in her hands and said, "You are a warrior, my dear—never forget that."

The words were said with genuine love and affection and the woman looked positively undone. Quino felt his throat get tight and his own eyes were damp. He glanced at the porch and saw that Maisy and Savy were surreptitiously wiping the tears from their faces, too. In fact, when he glanced at the crowd, he noted most of them were crying, about to cry, or trying not to cry.

"What's your name?" Destiny asked the woman.

"Allison," she said. Her voice quavered with emotion.

"Well, Allison, you are going to be my special guest today," Destiny said. She reached down and lifted the rope and gestured for the woman to come under. Quino reached out to help the woman duck under as Destiny took her books and handed them to Genevieve, then Destiny linked arms with Allison and together they walked to the bookstore.

"Pure of heart, she is," Genevieve said. She glanced at Quino. "And that's why we all love her."

"Agreed," he said. They fell in behind Destiny and her new friend and entered the house.

Maisy had arranged the turret room that Ryder had built for her to be the center of the day's activities. After Savy introduced Destiny and Maisy, who thankfully did not faint, Maisy led them upstairs to Destiny's base of operations. A plush thronelike chair was in front of a small writing desk, and a few chairs had been set up behind Destiny's where Quino assumed that he and Genevieve were to stay and keep watch.

Once Destiny was settled with Allison beside her in one of the extra chairs, Maisy gave them a five-minute warning until the event was to start. Genevieve huddled with Destiny to go over her talk and Maisy and the film crew did a last-minute check that every video screen inside and outside the building was functional. Maisy was in her element and it occurred to Quino that he was thrilled that he and Red had managed to save her bookstore, because she really was exceptionally good at this.

While the crew did a couple of sound and lighting checks, he moved to the back of the room, where he could see but also be out of the way. He leaned against the wall, marveling at how they had transformed the room into one of holiday cheer. Destiny sitting at the desk looked magnificent. When she glanced his way, he gave her a thumbs-up and she beamed. He knew she had to be nervous, but it didn't show at all. He was so proud of her.

He sensed Red before he felt her move to stand beside him. He glanced down and his heart hurt. She was so very lovely, with her sugar-and-cinnamon skin, her fiery hair, and her pale-green eyes. He wanted to pull her close and tell her he was sorry. He hadn't meant to say he'd never forgive her if something happened to Desi, but it was there between them. If words could make walls, he'd laid the foundation. And her declaration that there was nothing here for her had finished the wall off and now it stood between them as strong as any prison.

"Thank you for bringing her and for being here," she said. And then she slipped away, out of his grasp and out of his reach.

Chapter Twenty-Three

DESTINY signed her last book at half past ten that night. Maisy had sold every single copy of every Destiny Swann book in stock. Everyone was tired with a side of exhausted. Quino loaded Destiny and Genevieve into the Bentley and drove them home. Genevieve conked out halfway to Windemere, but Destiny didn't. She stared out the window, watching the big fat snowflakes illuminated by the car's headlights plop onto the hood or the windshield. She was so quiet Quino was worried that maybe today had been too much for her.

"You all right, Destiny?"

She glanced from the windshield to him. She met his gaze in the rearview mirror and gave him a small smile. "Never better," she said. "Except—"

He waited but she didn't continue. He nudged. "Except?"

She met his gaze again and looked rueful. "Why did I wait so long? I never should have let my fear get the best of me. How many Allisons are out there who just want to say hi, who need a good bracing hug, who I've let down because I was afraid? I was afraid of letting my own vanity take over, so I became a hermit and then I was afraid of change so I did nothing . . . for years." She shook her head. "Such a coward. Don't be like me, Quino. When something needs to be said, say it. When something needs to be changed, change it. Don't hide from life because you'll soon discover you have no life at all, and time wasted can never be returned."

She sank back into her seat and pondered the snowflakes again, while Quino drove through the darkness with only the large old headlights piercing through the whirling snow. He glanced at her face in the rearview mirror and wondered if she knew or was it just coincidence that her words so precisely suited the situation between him and Red?

He needed to tell Savannah how he felt about her. He needed her to hear the words. And he needed to make changes. He had been hiding from life at Shadow Pine, keeping everything exactly as it had always been. Oh, he'd told himself it was for Desi so that she didn't feel the lack of what they'd once had, but the truth was that it was for him, too. He'd thought if he held on to the memories as tightly as he could then they would never leave him, but the reality was, the memories would never leave him. As Desi had said, their parents were with her all the time in everything she did.

He thought about this morning when he'd left his house to go pick up Destiny. It had been foggy and the mist had swirled through the trees, and for one fanciful moment, he could have sworn he saw Esther trotting up the path into the woods. His parents had never left him, Esther would never leave him. They would carry on in his heart just as they were meant to, just like they did for Desi. He didn't have to hang on so tight.

When he pulled onto the long drive to Windemere, he knew what he had to do. Tomorrow, he would find Savannah and he would pour out his heart. If she still wanted to leave Fairdale, then so be it. At least he would have had his say—he would have tried to make a change—and she would know how he felt. He didn't want to go another day without Savannah knowing exactly how he felt about her.

By the time Quino parked the Bentley, escorted the ladies to the house, and got back into his own truck it was past midnight. He wished he could go straight to Red's and declare his feelings, but the woman had been running all day, finessing that signing like a champ. He was so proud of her, he could have burst with it, but he'd never even gotten the chance to tell her as she had been in a frenzy of motion all day.

By the time Destiny signed the last book, she'd looked ready to drop and Savy had asked Quino to take Destiny home. In front of everyone, he couldn't say anything except that he thought it had gone very well. She had nodded with a small smile and that was it. He'd been sure that was the end of them. But Destiny's words about not messing it up had struck true. Maybe, just maybe, he could turn this thing around.

He decided to catch a couple hours of sleep before going to Red's. She had to be dead tired and would probably be as thrilled about a declaration of feelings at this hour as she would a case of rickets. She had said on the phone that she had to get through the signing before she could go anywhere, so she likely planned to leave on Monday at the earliest. Christmas was on Friday, and since he knew her family wasn't big on the holiday, it could be that she planned to stay here. That would give him a few days to plead his case.

Feeling optimistic, Quino hit the gas and headed for home. It was late when he arrived and he was yawning as he parked in front of the garage. He didn't want to wake Luke by opening the garage door and the truck would be fine spending one night out in the cold.

He approached his house and noticed that all of the Christmas lights were on. The place glowed in the darkness and he realized he might have been going a little overboard all these years. But why were they on? He was sure he hadn't switched them on before he left that morning. And he didn't think burglars switched on your Christmas lights for you as it wasn't exactly stealth. He wondered if Luke or Lanie had done it when they realized he'd be home late. It was the only answer that made sense.

He climbed the steps, feeling weary all the way down to his feet. He stepped inside the house and began to toe off his boots when he heard his name right before he was grabbed in a crusher hug. He knew immediately from impact exactly who it was. Desi!

"What are you doing here?" he asked. He released her. He hugged her again. She was here. Desi was here!

"I came for Christmas, of course," she said. "You didn't think I was going to miss it, did you?"

"Well . . . yeah," he said. She turned and walked into the living room. The pretty blue afghan they kept draped over the back of the couch was wadded up on the cushions. It appeared Desi had been asleep when he came home.

"Bro, I could never miss Christmas in Fairdale," she said. She didn't meet his gaze.

"Who called you?" he asked.

"Lanie," she sighed. "She said that you were taking Esther's death pretty hard and she was concerned because she hadn't seen Savannah around lately and she suspected there'd been a breakup and you weren't talking about it."

Quino said nothing.

"So was there?" Desi asked. She plopped back down onto the sofa and pulled the blanket around her.

"None of your business," he said. "How did you get here so fast?"

"Charles, er, Mr. Kendrick flew me in on his private plane," she said.

"Charles Kendrick? The man who inherited the Kenya Elephant Rescue and Rehabilitation Institute from his grandmother?"

"Yep, that's the one," she said.

"How did you get to be pals with him?" he asked.

"I'm not," she insisted. "He was headed to the States and when he heard I needed to go home, he offered me a lift."

"A lift? In a private jet?"

Desi nodded. "Crazy, huh?"

"That's one word for it," Quino said. "So, do I need to track down this Charles guy and punch him in the mouth?"

"I hope not," she said. "He's asleep in the spare bedroom."

"What?"

"It was late when we arrived and he was exhausted," she said. "You don't mind, do you? I mean, he flew me all the way in from Kenya."

"No, I don't mind," he said. But he felt out of sorts as if everything was off. He didn't want to complain, but nothing felt right.

"Come on, sit down, and tell me how you messed up with Savy," she said.

"I didn't mess up," he protested. He sank onto the sofa beside her. "Why do you assume I messed up? Do you know who left you that packet of grant material?"

"Savy?"

"You knew?"

"Not until just now when you asked," she said. "I figured it was one of the Happily Ever After ladies, but it makes sense it was Savy. I can't think of any other reason why you'd muck up a new relationship with the woman who is perfect for you."

"Perfect, huh?"

"I've never seen a woman reject you before," Desi said. "I knew she was the one the minute she ignored you."

Quino laughed. "So did I."

"Then what's the problem?"

"She's going back to New York to her career," he said. "And my life is here."

"No, it isn't," Desi said. "It's wherever she is."

"But now that you're home, that changes everything," he said. "I can't leave you here by yourself."

"You won't be, because I'm heading back to Kenya right after the New Year. Charles has offered me a job, a permanent position at the institute, and I'm going to say yes."

"But you've only been there a few weeks—how can he offer you a permanent job?"

"One of the staff has left and everyone likes me and I'm a quick learner," she said. "I'll be on probation for a few months, but if we're both agreed at the end of it, then I'll get to stay."

Quino wanted to shout *No!* He didn't. Instead, he forced himself to breathe and then he said, "So, you're leaving Shadow Pine for good?"

"No, this will always be my home, and I'll come back— a lot," she said. "But there's a world of creatures that need saving. I'm going to start with elephants and see where I go from there. I'd like to help the orangutan next. Did you know the massive expansion of palm oil plantations in Borneo and Sumatra is decimating their habitat? And palm oil is in everything! People need to read the labels."

"Borneo and Sumatra?" he asked faintly.

"I have to help," Desi said with a shrug. "I know it's what I was born to do. I know it's why I survived that car crash, to make a difference, to help."

Quino felt his throat get tight. Now that Desi had spread her wings, there was no way he could stop her from flying. He swallowed the lump in his throat that was half pride in his baby sister and half mourning the girl he had raised to womanhood.

"I meant what I said before. I could not be more proud of you," he said.

She grinned at him and hugged him hard. "Hey, want to watch some home movies?"

"Sure."

She had the old family movies already loaded up on the big-screen television. "I was boring Charles with these earlier while we waited for you."

She pressed play and they both reclined on the couch with their feet on the coffee table. It was bittersweet to see his parents on the screen. This house, which looked exactly the same, was full of love and laughs frame by frame. The ache in his chest was like a bruise when he watched his dad kiss him mom under the mistletoe as ten-year-old him slapped a hand over his face in embarrassment. The films rolled through the years right to Desi's quinceañera, her fifteenth birthday. She was dancing in her beautiful gown with their dad, and she was laughing with her eyes bright and sparkling and the happiness bubbling up out of her like a fountain of joy.

Quino stilled. That was the last time she had looked like that until . . .

"Desi, can you show me the footage of you with the baby elephant?"

"That's a lot of footage," she said. "Can you be more specific?"

"The one where he was trying to climb into your lap," he said. "I think you called him Maktao."

"Oh, yeah," she said. She bounced up from the couch and crossed to the TV. Her phone was plugged into the television and she closed the app that held all of their family home movies and opened her videos. When she pressed play, there she was.

Quino studied her expression as Maktao, the scamp, tried to nudge his way into her lap and then stole her hat. There it was. What Savy had seen but he hadn't because he'd been too paralyzed by change and fear. The expression on Desi's face, the pure joy and the sparkle, was one she hadn't worn since their parents had died.

Desi had left Shadow Pine but somewhere out there she had found herself again. And with that realization, Quino felt himself let go. Oh, he'd always be her big brother and she'd always have a home with him, for sure, but she didn't need him anymore, and he didn't need to maintain the past anymore. She was free and so was he.

She glanced at him and asked, "Why did you want to see this again?"

"Because it's you, doing what you love, living your best life," he said. "Mom and Dad would be so proud."

Desi pressed her lips together and he noticed there were tears in her eyes. He held open his arms and gave her a hug. "And I'm proud of you, too."

At that she did cry, and she hugged him tight. "Thank you. That means everything to me." She released him and leaned back, wiping the tears off her face. "Now, what are we going to do to fix the mess you've made of things with Savy? Because now that I'm following my dream, you need to go follow yours."

* * *

THE plan started with Quino in a suit and was accompanied by flowers, a box of chocolates, and a carefully rehearsed speech on Quino's part where he groveled. He was completely fine with that if it would win Red over. When he arrived at the Happily Ever After Bookstore the next morning, he was as ready as he'd ever be.

Breakfast had been spent with Desi and Charles coaching him. Quino wasn't sure how he felt about Charles, especially when he caught him looking at Desi with a softness of expression that was *not* employer to employee. For her part Desi seemed completely unaware, so Quino resolved to talk to her about it at some point over her holiday. His priority right now had to be getting Savannah to accept his apology and listen to what he had to say.

His hands were slick with sweat when he approached the front door. Jeri was seated at the counter when he entered and she looked him over from head to toe.

"Joaquin Solis," she cried. "Are you wearing a suit two days in a row? Who died?"

"My relationship," he said. "I'm trying to bring it back."

"Oh." Jeri's eyes went wide as if she knew how unlikely this was going to be. He chose to remain undaunted.

Knowing Savannah was likely in the office, he made his way there. The door was ajar so he pushed it open with his heart pounding in his chest. No one was inside except for a forlorn-looking Maisy.

"Hey, Maisy, is Savy around?"

She glanced up from her desk and her shoulders slumped. "No, I'm sorry, but you've missed her."

"When will she be back?" He felt the prickles of alarm at the back of his neck. She couldn't have left already, could she?

"Oh, Quino, she's not coming back," Maisy said. She looked at him as if she hated being the one to tell him the bad news.

"What?" he asked.

"She left for New York early this morning," she said.

"But we saved the bookstore," he said. "Didn't she want to stay to celebrate through the holidays?"

"She couldn't," Maisy said. "The offer was too good and they needed her right away. Wait . . . what do you mean, you saved the bookstore?"

Quino sighed. He dropped the flowers and the box of candy on Savannah's old desk. It was then that he noticed her ever-present laptop was gone. He sank into her desk chair and leaned back in the seat, studying the ceiling.

He glanced at Maisy. "I'm sorry, but we knew."

"Knew what?" she asked.

"The day after Thanksgiving when we were decorating the bookstore, I overheard you on the phone. I didn't mean to, but I heard you say, 'We'll lose everything if we don't have the money by the end of the year' and I knew the bookstore was in trouble."

Maisy frowned at him. Quino felt horrible. She must feel so embarrassed to have her financial difficulties out in the open like this.

"Then I told Savannah and she overheard you in a similar conversation, so the two of us started coming up with ways to drive business to the bookstore, including having Destiny sign here."

"Oh, my God." Maisy put her hands over her eyes.

"I'm sorry," he said. "We never told anyone. It was just us. I didn't even mention it to Ryder."

"Well, it would have been news to him," Maisy said.

"I figured, that's why I didn't say anything," he said.

"No, not because it was true," she said. Her smile when she looked at him was lopsided as if she found him to be a charming doofus. "The conversations that you two overheard were me haggling with the venue for our wedding."

"What?" he asked.

"Yes," she said, laughing. "We'd lose everything, meaning our reservation, if I didn't put down a deposit by the end of the year, but I wasn't completely sold on the location, so I was trying to haggle them down in price."

"Oh," Quino said. "So, the bookstore?"

"Completely solvent," she said. "And after Destiny, we're beyond imagination into the black for a business less than a year old."

"I am an idiot."

"In the best possible way." She smiled at him. "So, what are you going to do about Savy?"

He looked down at her empty desk and blew out a breath. Then he met Maisy's gaze and asked, "What would the hero of Destiny's novel *The Keeper* do?"

Maisy put her hand over her heart as if it was beating too fast. Ever so softly, she said, "He'd go after her."

Quino nodded. "That seems reasonable."

Chapter Twenty-Four

SHE'D been back in the city that never sleeps for three days and it felt exactly as she remembered. The pulse of the city punched her in the chest like a zap with defibrillator pads the second she climbed out of Penn Station, off the train from her late-night flight into Newark, and the restless energy had carried her through an interview and two meetings and a substantial job offer from her former employer that she accepted.

It had been a whirlwind and she'd thought she'd be here for a couple of days before she went back to Fairdale to give her friends a proper good-bye and spend Christmas packing, but there was a hot debut author to promote and the department was in chaos. So here she was. She didn't think about Quino, or rather she tried not to. He was there, though, constantly in the back of her mind.

She missed him more than she could have imagined, and that was saying something given that she had already known she was in love with him and fully expected that leaving him was going to be brutal. It was worse. She wandered by the ice skaters at Rockefeller Center and longed for him to be there with her to skate. She passed shop windows, much like Perryman's, and wanted to have him chase her around the women's underwear department again. She saw Christmas window displays all over Midtown and all she could think was that Quino would have loved it.

The real kicker was when she woke up in her temporary lodgings at the Waldorf Astoria—her employer was putting her up until she found a place—and she stepped out onto her small patio and surveyed the city. The loneliness echoed low and deep. It should have felt normal, like coming home, but now that she'd known a life that wasn't lonely, the sad emotion cut her with its rusty jagged blade and left her to bleed.

She missed him, the bergamot and cedar scent of him, the feel of his arms around her, the smile that curved his lips when he glanced her way, the wicked thoughts in his black eyes when they were alone. How had she fallen so hard so fast for a man who could never fit into her life? It was a cosmic joke. A one-two punch of "screw you" from the fates. Here's the perfect man but you can't have him.

She'd picked up her phone a million times to call him, but what could she say? He was angry with her about Desi but she didn't think she'd been wrong to help. Her life was here and his was there. There was no way they were ever going to meet in the middle. What even was the middle now? Someplace in Virginia? They were seven hundred miles apart! The thought tanked her spirits even lower.

Tomorrow was Christmas Eve and she'd never felt less like celebrating, not even when she'd been forced to spend holidays with her parents. This year, she would be in her hotel, working. It seemed rather pathetic, but she reminded herself, this was what she'd wanted. Her reputation, her career, all of it, back—and she'd gotten it. She should have been all fist pumps, high kicks, and look out worlds, but instead, she was dragging around her stupid heartache like a cinder block and she didn't know how to let it go. She didn't know how to let him go.

As she walked the four blocks to work, she passed a Santa standing on the corner and dug a few bills out of her purse to shove in his metal bucket. He thanked her and she nodded. He wasn't as good a Santa as Quino. He didn't bring the over-the-top joy to the task that Quino had brought. The ache in her chest made her catch her breath but she soldiered on, pushing through the doors to her building to face another day in the job she had been so sure she couldn't live without.

I T was midafternoon. Savannah was overcaffeinated and hungry, never a good mix, and the update meeting that was mandatory for senior staff felt as if it were dragging on for eternity. Why couldn't they keep it short and sweet? It should be limited to everyone's best thing, worst thing, and next thing. Carl Heyer from accounting was the human equivalent of an algebra problem. He made no sense and had an inability to get to the freaking point.

She wanted to bang her head on the tabletop. She had a to-do list a mile long and it was not getting any shorter with her trapped in here. She glanced across the table at Archer and he pretended to shoot himself. She glanced away, turning her snort into a cough. She was happy to see Archer again. He and his partner had invited her over on Christmas, so there was that to look forward to.

Carl took a deep breath and she realized Carl was winding up, not down. She closed her eyes briefly and was transported back to Fairdale, to meetings of the Royal Order of George where Maisy, Perry, Jeri, and she talked about good deeds and gorged on donuts. There were carrot sticks and celery at this meeting. The inhumanity!

She pondered how the Royal Order was doing. She wondered if they'd replace her. She thought about playing yarnball fetch with George in the office and she was surprised by how much she missed the persistent little critter. She felt her throat get tight. Carl droned on.

When she thought she couldn't take it for one more nanosecond, the receptionist, Amy, from the main lobby, poked her head into the meeting.

"Excuse me, sorry to interrupt," she said. Carl shot her

a dark look and she ignored him. "There's someone here to see you, Savannah, and . . . well, I couldn't say no to him."

Savannah frowned. Then her eyes went wide. Standing in the hallway behind Amy was Quino. In his cowboy hat, boots, and shearling jacket he looked as out of place as Disney's Tinker Bell in a slasher movie.

"Quino," she whispered his name in surprise.

"You left *that*?" Archer hissed from across the table. She had told him very briefly about the breakup.

"Excuse me," she said to the room. She rose from her seat, left her things on the table, and hurried to the door. He was here! *Here!* Her heart was beating triple time, her ears were ringing, she wanted to run to him, but she forced herself to walk, mostly.

"Thank you, Amy," she said as she brushed past her through the door. When she stepped into the hallway, Quino removed his hat and ran a hand through his thick dark hair. Savy heard Amy heave a sigh behind her. She knew exactly how the other woman felt.

"Hey, Red," he said. His North Carolina drawl drizzled over her like the sweetest honey. It made her dizzy.

She clutched his elbow and dragged him toward her office. She could feel the office eyes upon them as she led him down the corridor and around the corner, past three offices, until they got to hers, which was bare except for her laptop and a landline. Her current decor could best be described as *barren*.

She pulled him into the room and shut the door behind them. Quino tossed his hat onto her desk and grinned at her in that way he had that made her knees weak. She leaned against her desk and crossed her arms over her chest. She would not jump on him no matter how much she wanted to.

"Nice office," he said. The tenth-story windows gave a lovely view of the surrounding skyscrapers, the building across the way, and the view of the street below.

"Thanks."

He glanced up. "No mistletoe."

"No."

"Pity."

"What brings you to New York, Quino?" she asked. She was pleased her voice was steady, if a little breathless, because her nerves were stretched to the breaking point.

"I came to apologize," he said. "You were right about Desi. She is doing amazing things in Africa and I should have thanked you for helping her instead of blaming you for her being gone."

Savy felt her insides sigh. A man who could own his bullshit. They were as rare as a yeti sighting, weren't they? Still, she kept her arms crossed.

"What brought you to this conclusion?"

"Desi," he said. "She came home for Christmas."

Savy dropped her arms. She knew how much having his sister there meant to him. "I'm really happy for you, Quino. So, she finished the internship that quickly?"

"No," he said. "She's going back after the holidays. They've offered her a permanent position and she's accepted."

"But . . . wow . . . that's incredible," she said. "Good for her."

He nodded.

"But if she's in Fairdale, what are you doing here?" she asked. "You could have just texted an apology. I would have accepted."

He started to walk toward her. His look was predatory and dead sexy. Savy felt a thrill flutter through her. "Desi told me that she was following her dream and that I should follow mine." He stopped right in front of her. He cupped her face with both hands as tenderly as if she were a buttercup. "You're my dream, Red."

Savy couldn't breathe. He kissed her softly and then said, "I'm done with clinging to the past and being afraid of change. I have Luke and Lanie to help me run Shadow Pine and I can literally oversee it from anywhere, even here. Wherever you are, that's where I want to be."

Then he kissed her. The feel of his mouth against hers was everything. Suddenly kissing him was more than the erotic press of lips, although it was that, too. It was the magic of first snowfalls, the warmth of hot cider, the flirt of mistletoe, and the joy of coming home.

Yes! Everything inside Savy cried her answer as she dug her fingers into his hair and kissed him back with every bit of longing she'd felt since they'd been apart.

"Say you forgive me for being an idiot," he whispered in her ear before kissing her again.

"I forgive you," she sighed as his lips moved to her throat.

"Say you'll give us another chance," he said.

The words snapped Savy out of the sensual fog that had descended over her like a cloud. She pushed away from him, sliding out of his embrace.

"No." She shook her head.

Quino looked taken aback as if he hadn't expected such a flat refusal. Savannah strode across the room and opened her office door. Archer, Amy, and Luce, another employee, all straightened up as if she hadn't just caught them listening at her door.

"Found it!" Archer declared, holding his index finger up. He looked past Savannah at Quino. "Contact lens. Pesky th—"

Savannah shut the door on him.

"Red, I don't think you understand," Quino said. "I'm trying to tell you I lo—"

"Don't!" she cried. She held up her hands in a stop gesture as if she could ward off the sentiment with her bare hands. "Don't say it."

"Why not?" he asked. "It's how I feel. I love you. I'm always going to love you and wherever you are, that's home for me."

"But it won't work," she said. "And I can't do this."

Quino didn't move. He watched her as if trying to read between her words. "What can't you do, Red? Love me?"

She didn't answer. She needed him to understand. She needed him to be even more flexible and she was afraid this might be the bend that broke him.

"Do you know why I had to come back?" she asked.

"Because this job is your dream."

She shook her head. "I thought it was. I thought getting my reputation back and proving myself indispensable was the only thing that mattered. Everything was driven by my ego and my need to be vindicated. And then I was—I pulled off the Destiny Swann signing and the truth came out about Linda—and it felt flat. None of it felt right. I had everything I thought I wanted, and it didn't fit any longer. New York, as much as I love it, and my career, aren't what I want anymore."

"What do you want?" Quino lifted one eyebrow in inquiry, but he didn't move. She wondered if he was even breathing and she knew exactly how he felt. She couldn't breathe without him, either.

"You have to stop looking at me like that," she said, teasing him.

His smile when it came was slow and it uncurled across his lips as if it were a bow being untied. "And how would that look be?" he asked.

"Like you want me to marry you," she said. Her heart skipped three beats and she thought she might pass out. "Because I love you, too."

He laughed and his jacket parted and Savy saw he was wearing yet another horrible Christmas sweater. This one had a chorus line of dancing reindeer on it, and, oh, it made her laugh.

"Well, when you put it like that," he said. He reached out and tugged her into his arms. "Yes, I'll marry you."

There was a ruckus outside the door, and Savy was vaguely aware that Archer was cheering and there was clapping, but she didn't really register the noise because Quino was kissing her and there was absolutely no place she'd rather be than in his arms, getting smooched within an inch of her life, mistletoe or no.

THE wedding took place six days later at Windemere Manor. Much to Quino and Savy's surprise, when they called to invite Destiny to their wedding, she insisted on hosting the wedding at her house. Given that it was to be a small affair, with just their closest family and friends, they agreed.

"I can't believe you're getting married," Maisy said as she helped Savannah into her dress.

"I know," Savy said. She fluffed her skirt. "A month ago, if anyone had told me I'd be here today, I wouldn't have believed them."

There was a knock on the door and Perry, holding Savy's bouquet, bustled into the room. Ruby-red roses decorated with sprigs of cedar, eucalyptus, and Queen Anne's lace, the stems of which were all wrapped together with white ribbon. Perry was staring at the bouquet as if trying to puzzle something out.

"What is it?" Maisy asked.

"Uncle Quino added something to your bouquet," Perry said. She handed the flowers to Savy.

Savannah glanced at her flowers. There in the center was a sprig of mistletoe with five berries. She laughed.

"It's perfect," she said.

Maisy and Perry exchanged a look but before they could ask, Destiny swept into the room. She was resplendent in a cocktail dress of ice blue. She took one look at Savy and clasped her hands over her heart. Her eyes filled and she blinked several times.

"You are stunning," she said.

"Thank you," Savannah said. The compliment meant a lot coming from a woman who always looked on point. Savannah glanced at her reflection in the mirror. Her hair was half up and half down with pearl-tipped hairpins woven into her hair instead of a veil. She wore a simple pearl necklace and earrings that her sisters had brought with them when they arrived with their families yesterday, much to Savy's surprise and delight. Her parents had declined to attend but she had expected as much.

Her dress was creamy white, off the shoulders, fitted her curves perfectly, and flared out with a tea-length skirt that had a delicate embroidered hem. She'd bought it off the sale rack at Perryman's, and it was perfect. Her shoes, also found at Perryman's, were white leather Mary Janes with bows on the toes, which made her smile.

"Your groom, who is positively swoon-worthy, is pacing a hole in my Aubusson rug in the parlor," Destiny said. "Are you ready to put him out of his misery?"

Savannah laughed. "Yes, I suppose so."

Destiny took her hands in hers and said, "I knew from the first moment I saw you two that you belonged together, and since romance is my business, I think I am an expert in these things."

Savy saw Maisy's eyes widen. She had still not quite gotten over her awe of the famous author, but at least she hadn't fainted.

"If I can give you one piece of advice, my dear?" Destiny asked.

"Yes, please," Savy said.

"As you start, so shall you go," she said. Then she smiled, leaned forward, and kissed Savy's cheek. She turned around and looked at Perry, who looked lovely in a dress of bright blue, which matched her eyes. "Let's go take our seats."

Perry nodded. She gave Savy a thumbs-up and a finger wave as she hurried out the door after Destiny.

"'As you start, so shall you go.' What does that even mean?" Savy asked Maisy. "You see? This is what happens when you let a writer into your life. And now I'm her publicist, running my own company out of the bookstore. Can you believe it?"

"No, I really can't. I'm trying not to be bitter that after all my months of trying to get you to stay in Fairdale, Destiny snaps her fingers and here you are." Maisy shook her head.

"Between you and me," Savy said, "it had more to do with Quino."

"I know," Maisy said, laughing. "He really is the perfect guy for you and I'm so happy you found each other."

In her ruby-red maid of honor dress, she sparkled like a gemstone. Savannah hugged her friend and felt her throat get tight. This, this was family, and she understood now why Quino had held on to the memories of his so tightly.

"Thanks for bringing me back to Fairdale, M," she said. Her voice wobbled a bit but she pushed on. "You realize none of this would be happening if you hadn't opened your bookstore."

Maisy tipped her head, considering. "Maybe. Or maybe you and Quino would have found each other somewhere else just like Ryder and I would have. I think people who are fated to be together find each other one way or another."

Savannah smiled. "I think that makes you an even bigger romantic than Destiny."

Maisy took Savy's hand in hers and they walked to the door of the bedroom where they'd been holed up all morning.

"I think there might be one person who is an even bigger romantic than me," Maisy said.

"Who's that?"

Maisy pointed at the mistletoe in Savy's bouquet. "Quino."

Savy studied the small sprigs in her bouquet. He was a romantic. He was her romantic. And he would be for the rest of their lives.

They stepped out into the hallway and music floated up from downstairs. Savy took a deep, steadying breath.

"Are you ready?" Maisy asked.

Savy nodded.

Maisy led the way down the sweeping staircase. Halfway down she paused and glanced back over her shoulder at Savy. From here she could see into the room where the guests were all in attendance. She lifted an eyebrow in inquiry and Savannah nodded. She was ready.

Maisy continued down the steps and Savy saw everyone stand when Maisy crossed the threshold into the room. This was it. She felt her hands tremble. She stepped off the stairs and crossed over the marble foyer. Destiny had pulled out all the stops and the room was decked out in flowers and pine boughs and swaths of cream-colored tulle. And there at the end of the aisle that ran between all of the rented folding chairs stood Quino.

Her heart practically stopped, so handsome was her

groom in his black suit with his bold ruby-red tie. Their gazes met and as he took her in, he visibly caught his breath. It was all the encouragement Savy needed. She didn't sashay or meander down the aisle. Heck no. She practically sprinted.

The faces she passed, Jeri and her family, Perry, Hannah and her brother, John Michael, Sawyer, Savy's two sisters and their families, Desi and her new boss, Archer and his partner, Destiny, Genevieve, and the household staff, were just a blur of smiles and tears in her peripheral vision. When she arrived at his side, Quino grabbed her free hand in his and twined his fingers with hers. Then he leaned close and whispered in her ear, "You are beautiful, Red."

She blushed and glanced down at her bouquet. The mistletoe caught her eye and she looked back up at him. With a quick side-eye at the pastor, who was smiling at them, Savy rose up on her toes and kissed him right on the mouth.

It was supposed to be just a peck, but of course with Quino, it never was. Suddenly he was cupping her face and kissing her deeply as if he'd die if he didn't. From far away, Savy heard the chuckles which rolled into laughter. She didn't care.

When they broke apart, the pastor cleared his throat and said, good-naturedly, "Ahem, we're not quite at that part yet."

Savy and Quino exchanged a glance of perfect understanding. They were at that part. They had been since the day they'd met—she'd just been slower to realize it.

As they turned to face the pastor, to pledge their lives together, Savy knew that she had found what she hadn't even known she was looking for: a best friend, a lover, a keeper. And she knew she would keep him, her Christmas-loving cowboy, for the rest of their lives. Ugly Christmas sweaters and all.

Turn the page to read an excerpt from
Jenn McKinlay's new novel

PARIS IS ALWAYS A GOOD IDEA

coming soon from Berkley.

I 'M getting married."

"Huh?"

"We've already picked our colors, pink and gray."

"Um . . . pink and what?"

"Gray. What do you think, Chelsea? I want your honest opinion. Is that too retro?"

I stared at my middle-aged widowed father. We were standing in a bridal store in central Boston on the corner of Boylston and Berkeley streets and he was talking to me about wedding colors. *His* wedding colors.

"I'm sorry, I need a sec," I said. I held up my hand and blinked hard while trying to figure out just what the hell was happening.

I had raced here from my apartment in Cambridge after a text from my dad had popped up on my phone, asking me to meet him at this address because it was an emergency. I was prepared for heart surgery, not wedding colors!

Suddenly, I couldn't breathe. I wrestled the constricting wool scarf from around my neck, yanked the beanie off my head, and stuffed them in my pockets. I scrubbed my scalp with my fingers in an attempt to make the blood flow to my brain. It didn't help. *Come on, Martin,* I coached myself, *pull it together.* Lastly, I unzipped my puffy winter jacket to let some air in, then I focused on my father.

"What did you say?" I asked.

"Pink and gray, too retro?" Glen Martin, aka Dad, asked. He pushed his wire frame glasses up on his nose and looked at me as if he was asking a perfectly reasonable question.

"No, before that." I waved my hand in a circular motion to indicate he needed to back it all the way up.

"I'm getting married!" His voice went up when he said it and I decided my normally staid fifty-five-year-old dad was somehow currently possessed by a twentysomething bridezilla.

"You okay, Dad?" I asked gently, not wanting to set him off. "Have you recently slipped on some ice and whacked your head? I ask because you don't seem to be yourself."

"Sorry," he said. He reached out and wrapped me in an impulsive hug, another indicator that he was not his usual buttoned-down mathematician self. "I'm just . . . I'm just so happy. What do you think about being a flower girl?"

"Um . . . I'm almost thirty." I tipped my head to the side and squinted at him.

"Yes, but we already have a full wedding party, and you and your sister would be really cute in matching dresses, maybe something sparkly."

"Matching dresses? Sparkly?" I repeated. I struggled for air. It was clear. My father had lost his ever-lovin' mind. I should probably call my sister. Dad needed medical attention, possibly an intervention. Oh, man, would we have to have him committed?

I studied his face, trying to determine just how crazy he was. The same brown-green hazel eyes I saw in my own mirror every morning held mine, but where my eyes frequently looked flat with a matte finish, his positively sparkled. He really looked happy.

"You're serious," I gasped. I glanced around the bridal store that was stuffed to the rafters with big white fluffy dresses. None of this made any sense and yet here I was. "You're not pranking me?"

"Nope." He grinned again. "Congratulate me, peanut, I'm getting married."

I felt as if my chest was collapsing into itself. Never, not once, in the past seven years had I ever considered the possibility that my father would remarry.

"To who?" I asked. It couldn't be . . . nah. That would be *insane*.

"Really, Chels?" Dad straightened up. The smile slid from his face and he cocked his head to the side, which was his go-to disappointed parent look.

I had not been on the receiving end of this look very often in life. Not like my younger sister, Annabelle, who seemed to thrive on "the look." Usually it made me fall right in line, but not today.

"Sheri. You're marrying Sheri." I tried to keep my voice neutral. Major failure, as I stepped backward, tripped on the trailing end of my scarf, and gracelessly sprawled onto one of the cream-colored velvet chairs that were scattered around the ultrafeminine store. From the look on my father's face, I thought it was a good thing I was sitting, because if he answered in the affirmative I might faint.

"Yes, I asked her to marry me and to my delight she accepted," he said. Another happy stupid grin spread across his lips as if he just couldn't help it.

"But . . . but . . . she won you in a bachelor auction two weeks ago!" I cried. "This is completely mental!"

The store seamstress, who was assisting a bride up on the dais in front of a huge trifold mirror, turned to look at us. Her dark hair was scraped up into a knot on top of her head and her face was contoured to perfection. She made me feel like a frump in my Sunday no-makeup face. Which, in my defense, was not my fault because when I'd left the house to meet Dad, I'd had no idea the address he'd sent was for Bella's Bridal. I'd been expecting an urgent care; in fact, I wasn't sure yet that we didn't need one.

Glen Martin, Harvard mathematician and all-around

nerd dad, had been coerced into participating in a silver fox bachelor auction for prominent Bostonians by my sister, Annabelle, to help raise funds for the Boston Children's Hospital. I had gone, of course, to support my sister and my dad, and it had mostly been a total snoozefest.

The highlight of the event had been when two socialites got into a bidding war over a surgeon, and the loser slapped the winner across the face with her cardboard paddle. Good thing the guy was a cosmetic surgeon, because there was most definitely some repair work needed on that paper cut.

But my father had not been anywhere near that popular with the ladies. No one wanted a mathematician. No one. After several minutes of excruciating silence, following the MC trying to sell the lonely gals on my dad's attempts to solve the Riemann hypothesis, I had been about to bid on him myself when Sheri, a petite brunette, had raised her paddle with an initial bid. The smile of gratitude Dad had sent Sheri had been blinding, and the next thing we knew, a flurry of bids happened, but Sheri stuck in there and landed the winning bid for four hundred-thirty-five dollars and fifty cents.

"Two weeks is all it took," Dad said. He shrugged and held out his hands like a blackjack dealer showing he had no hidden cards, chips, or cash.

I clapped a hand to my forehead. "It takes more time to get a first paycheck on a new job than you've spent in this relationship. Is it even considered a relationship at the two-week mark?"

"I know it's a surprise, Chels, but when—" he began, but I interrupted him.

"Dad, a bachelor auction is not the basis for a stable long-lasting relationship."

"You have to admit it makes a great story," he said.

"No, I don't! What do you even know about Sheri? What's her favorite color?"

"Pink, duh." He looked at me with a know-it-all expression more commonly seen on a teenager than a grown-ass man.

"Who are you and what have you done with my father?"

I wanted to check him for a fever; maybe he had the flu and he was hallucinating.

"I'm still me, Chels," he said. He gazed at me gently. "I'm just a happy me, for a change."

Was that it? Was that what was so different about him? He was happy? How could he be happy with a woman he hardly knew? Maybe . . . oh, dear. My dad hadn't circulated much after my mom's death. Maybe he was finally getting a little something something and he had it confused with love. Oh, god, how was I supposed to talk about this with him?

I closed my eyes. I took a deep breath. Parents did this all the time. Surely, I could manage it. Heck, it would be great practice if I ever popped out a kid. I opened my eyes. Three women were standing in the far corner in the ugliest chartreuse dresses I had ever seen. Clearly, they were the attendants of a bride who hated them. And that might be me in sparkly pink or gray if I didn't put a stop to this madness.

"Sit down, Dad," I said. "I think we need to have a talk."

He took the seat beside mine and looked at me with same patience he had when he'd taught me to tie my shoes. I looked away. Ugh, this was more awkward than when my gynecologist told me to scoot down, repeatedly. It's like they didn't know a woman's ass needs some purchase during an annual. *Focus, Martin!*

"I know that you've been living alone for several years." I cleared my throat. "And I imagine you've had some needs that have gone unmet."

"Chels, no," he said. "It isn't about that."

I ignored him, forging on while not making eye contact because, Lordy, if I had to have this conversation with him, I absolutely could not look at him.

"And I understand that after such a long dry spell, you might be confused about what you feel, and that's okay," I said. Jeebus, this sounded like a sex talk by Mr. Rogers. "The thing is, you don't have to marry the first person you sleep with after Mom."

There, I'd said it. And my wise advice and counsel was

met with complete silence. I waited for him to express relief that he didn't have to get married. And I waited. Finally, I glanced up at my father, who was looking at me with the same expression he'd worn when I found out that he was actually the tooth fairy. Chagrin.

"Sheri is not the first," he said.

"She's not?" I was shocked. Shocked, I tell you.

"No."

"But you never told me about anyone before," I said.

"You didn't need to know," he said. "They were companions, not relationships."

"They?!" I shouted. I didn't mean to. The seamstress sent me another critical look, and I coughed, trying to get it together.

Dad shifted in his seat, sending me a small smile of understanding. "Maybe meeting here wasn't the best idea. I thought you'd be excited to help plan the wedding, but perhaps you're not ready."

"Of course I'm not ready," I said. "But you're not, either."

"Yes, I am."

"Oh, really? Answer me this: Does Sheri prefer dogs or cats?"

"I don't—" He blinked.

"Yes, because it's only been two weeks," I said. "You remember that lump on your forehead? It took longer than two weeks to get that biopsied, but you're prepared to marry a woman you haven't even known long enough for a biopsy."

My voice was getting higher, and Dad put his hands out in an *inside voice, please* gesture. I would have tried, but I felt as if I was hitting my stride in making my point. I went for the crushing blow.

"Dad, do you even know whether she is a pie or cake sort of person?"

"I . . . um . . ."

"Do you realize you're contemplating spending the rest of your life with a person who might celebrate birthdays with pie?"

"Chels, I know this is coming at you pretty fast," he said. "I do, but I don't think Sheri liking pie or cake is really that big of a deal. Who knows, she might be an ice cream person and ice cream goes with everything."

"Mom was a cake person," I said. There. I'd done it. I'd brought in the biggest argument against this whole rushed matrimonial insanity. Mom.

My father's smile vanished as if I'd snuffed it out between my fingers like a match flame. I felt lousy about it, but not quite as lousy as I did at the thought of Sheri—oh, but no—becoming my stepmother.

"Your mother's been gone for seven years, Chels," he said. "That's a long time for a person to be alone."

"But you haven't been alone . . . apparently," I protested. "Besides, you have me and Annabelle, who is always in crisis, so I know she keeps you busy."

His smile flickered. "She does at that."

"So, why do you need to get married?" I pressed.

Dad sighed. "Because I love Sheri and I want to make her my wife."

I gasped. I felt as if he'd slapped me across the face. Yes, I knew I was reacting badly, but this was my father. The man who had sworn to love my mother until death did them part. But that was the problem, wasn't it? Mom had died seven years ago, and Dad had been alone ever since, right up until he met Sheri Armstrong two weeks ago when she just kept raising her auction paddle for the marginally hot mathematician.

I got it. Really, I did. I'd been known to have bidding fever when a mint pair of Jimmy Choos showed up on eBay. It was hard to let go of something when it was in your grasp, especially when another bidder kept raising the stakes. But this was my dad, not shoes.

One of the bridal salon employees came by with a tray of mimosas. I grabbed two, double-fisting the sparkling beverage. Sweet baby Jesus, I hoped there was more fizz than pulp in them. The fizzing bubbles hit the roof of my mouth, and I wished they could wash away the taste of my father's bad news, but they didn't.

"Listen, I know that being the object of desire by a crowd of single, horny women is heady stuff—"

"Really, you know this?" Dad propped his chin in his hand as he studied me with his eyebrows raised and a twinkle in his eye.

"Okay, not exactly, but my point—and I have one—is that you and Sheri aren't operating in the real world here," I said. "I understand that Sheri is feeling quite victorious having won you, but that doesn't mean she gets to wed you. I mean, why do you have to marry her? Why can't you just live in sin like other old people?"

"Because we love each other and we want to be married."

"You can't know this so soon," I argued. "It's not possible. Her representative hasn't even left yet."

Her father frowned, clearly not understanding.

"The first six months to a year, you're not really dating a person," I explained. "You're dating their representative. The real person, the one who leaves the seat up and can't find the ketchup in the fridge even when it's right in front of him, doesn't show up until months into the relationship. Trust me."

"What are you talking about? Of course I'm dating a person. I can assure you, Sheri is very much a woman," he said. "Boy howdy, is she." The tips of his ears turned red and I felt my gag reflex kick in.

"Dad, first *ew*," I said. "And second, a person's representative is their best self. After two weeks, you haven't seen the real Sheri yet. The real Sheri is hiding behind the twenty-four-seven perfect hair and makeup, the placid temper, the woman who thinks your dad jokes are funny. They're not."

"No, no, no." He shook his head. "I've seen her without makeup. She's still beautiful. And she does have a temper; just drive with her sometime. I've learned some new words. Very educational. And my dad jokes *are too* funny."

I rolled my eyes. I was going to have to give some tough love here. I was going to have to be blunt.

"Dad, I hate to be rude, but you're giving me no choice.

She's probably only marrying you for your money," I said. I felt like a horrible person for pointing it out, but he needed protection from gold diggers like Sheri. It was a kindness, really.

To my surprise, he actually laughed. "Sheri is more well off than I am by quite a lot. I'm the charity case in this relationship."

"Then why on earth does she want to marry *you*?" I asked.

The words flew out before I had the brains to stifle them. It was a nasty thing to say. I knew that, but I was freaked out and frantic and not processing very well.

"I didn't mean that the way it sounded," I began, but he cut me off.

"Yes, you did."

He stood, retrieving his coat from a nearby coatrack. As he shrugged into it, the look of hurt on his face made my stomach ache. I loved my father. I wouldn't inflict pain upon him for anything, and yet I had. I'd hurt him very much.

"You did mean it and, sadly, I'm not even surprised. I mistakenly hoped you could find it in your heart to be happy for me," he said. "I have mourned the loss of your mother every day since she passed and I will mourn her every day for the rest of my life, but I have found someone who makes me happy and I want to spend my life with her. That doesn't take away what I had with your mother."

"Doesn't it?" I argued. How could he not see that by replacing my mother he was absolutely diminishing what they'd had? "Sheri's going to take your name, isn't she? And she's going to move into our house, right? So, everything thing that was once Mom's—the title of Mrs. Glen Martin and the house where she loved and raised her family—you're just giving to another woman. How is that not erasing Mom?"

Dad stared down at me with his head to the side and his right eyebrow arched, a double whammy of parental disappointment. He wrapped his scarf about his neck and pulled on his gloves.

"I don't know if Sheri will take my name. We haven't talked about it," he said. "As for the house, I am planning to sell it so we can start our life together somewhere new."

I sucked in a breath. My childhood home. Gone? Sold? To strangers? I thought I might throw up. Instead, I polished off one of the mimosas.

"Sheri and I are getting married in three months," he said. "We're planning a nice June wedding, and we very much want you to be a part of it."

"As a flower girl?" I scoffed. "Whose crazy idea was that?"

"It was Sheri's," he said. His mouth tightened. "She's never been married before, and she's a little excited. It's actually quite lovely to see."

"A thirty-year-old flower girl," I repeated. I was like a dog with a bone. I just couldn't let it go.

"All right, I get it. Come as anything you want, then," he said. "You can give me away, be my best man, be a bridesmaid, or officiate the damn thing. I don't care. I just want you there. It would mean everything to Sheri and me to have your blessing."

I stared at him. The mild-mannered Harvard math professor who had taught me to throw a curveball, ride a bike, and knee a boy in the junk if he got too fresh had never looked so determined. He meant it. He was going to marry Sheri Armstrong, and there wasn't a damn thing I could do about it.

"I don't know, Dad," I said. "I don't think I can be a part of . . . this." I couldn't even make myself say the word *wedding*.

My father turned up his collar, bracing for the cold March air. He looked equal parts disappointed and frustrated. "Suit yourself."

He turned away, and I sat frozen. I hated this. I didn't want us to part company like this, but I couldn't change how I felt. I waited, feeling miserable, for him to walk away, but instead he turned back toward me. Rather than being furious with me, which would have allowed me to dig in my heels and push back, he looked sad.

"What happened to you?" he asked. "You used to be the girl with the big heart who was going to save the world."

I didn't say anything. His disappointment and confusion washed over me like a bath of rank sludge.

"I grew up," I said. But even in my own ears I sounded defensive.

He shook his head. "No, you didn't. Quite the opposite. You stopped growing at all."

"Are you kidding me? In the past seven years, I have raised millions to help the fight against cancer—how can you say I haven't grown?" I asked. I was working up a nice froth of indignation. "I'm trying to make a difference."

"That's your career," he said. "Being great at your profession doesn't mean you've grown personally. Chels, look at your life. You work seven days a week. You never take time off. You don't date. You have no friends. Heck, if we didn't have a standing brunch date, I doubt I'd ever see you except on holidays. What kind of life is that?"

I turned my head to stare out the window at Boylston Street. I couldn't believe my father was belittling how hard I worked for the American Cancer Coalition. I had busted my butt to become the top corporate fund-raiser in the organization, and with the exception of one pesky coworker, my status was unquestioned.

He sighed. I refused to look at him. "Chels, I'm not saying what you've accomplished isn't important. It's just that you've changed over the past few years. I can't remember the last time you brought someone special home for me to meet. It's as if you've sealed yourself off since your mother—"

I whipped my head in his direction, daring him to talk about my mother in the same conversation where he announced he was remarrying.

"Chels, you're here!" A voice cried from the fitting-room entrance on the opposite side of the store. I glanced away from my dad to see my younger sister, Annabelle, standing there in an explosion of hot-pink satin and tulle trimmed with a wide swath of sparkling crystals.

"What. Is. That?" I looked from Annabelle to our father

and back. The crystals reflected the fluorescent light over-head, making me see spots—or perhaps I was having a stroke. Hard to say.

"It's our dress!" Annabelle squealed. Then she twirled. The long tulle skirt fanned out from the formfitting satin bodice, and Annabelle's long dark curls streamed out around her. She looked like a demented fairy princess. "Do you love it or do you love it?"

"No, I don't love it. It's hideous!" I cried. The seamstress glared at me, looking as if she was going to take some of the pins out of the pincushion strapped to her wrist and come stab me a few hundred times. I lowered my voice, a little. "Have you both gone insane? Seriously, what the hell is happening?"

Annabelle staggered to a stop. She reeled a little bit as she walked toward us, looking more like a drunk princess than a fey one.

"How can you be happy about this?" I snapped at her. I gestured to the dress. "Have you not known me for all of your twenty-seven years? How could you possibly think I would be okay with this?"

Annabelle grabbed the back of a chair to steady herself. "By *this*, do you mean the dress or the whole wedding thing?"

"Of course, I mean the whole wedding thing," I growled. "Dad is clearly having some middle-aged crisis and there's you just going along with it for a sparkly dress. Damn it, Annabelle, couldn't you for once get your head out of your ass and think about someone other than yourself?"

"Chelsea." Dad's voice was low with warning. "Don't speak to your sister that way."

Annabelle blinked at me, looking surprised and a little hurt. "I am thinking about someone. I'm thinking about Dad. I kind of feel like I have a vested interest given that it was my auction that brought Dad and Sheri together."

"Because you, like Dad, have gone completely mental!" I snapped. "Two weeks is not long enough to determine whether you should marry someone or not. My god, it takes longer to get a passport. What are you thinking, supporting this insanity?"

"Chels, that's not fair and you know it," Dad said.

My expression must have been full-on angry bear, because he changed tack immediately, his expression softening.

"When did you stop letting love into your heart?" he asked. His voice was gentler, full of parental concern, which rolled off my back like water off a duck. He didn't get to judge me when he was remarrying a person he barely knew. "Is this really how you want to live your life, Chels, with no one special to share it with? Because I don't."

I turned back to the window, refusing to answer. With a sigh weighty with disappointment, he left. I watched his reflection in the glass grow smaller and smaller as he departed. I couldn't remember the last time we had argued, leaving harsh words between us festering like a canker sore. Ever since mom had died, the awareness of how precious life was remained ever present, and we always, always said *I love you* at the end of a conversation, even when we weren't getting along.

I thought about running after him and saying I was sorry, that I was happy for him and Sheri, but it would be a lie, and I knew I wasn't a good enough actress to pull it off. I just couldn't make myself do it. Instead, I tossed back my second mimosa, because mimosas, unlike family, were always reliable.